The

"Drink! To the old gods and an end to the cursed Well!"

The fighting men leaped to their feet and roared with brandished weapons, this time with Airar joining fully. Then around the hall the warriors pledged their cups of war to bloody victory

Though Airar had taken much less of these strong northern beers than the others, the excitement soon captured his mind . . . and there was no escape.

"I swear by this cup of war," he vowed, "that I will not leave this rebellion till my homeland is free—*and that I will love and wed no woman but Argyra of Stassia, and she shall escape never, though she flee across the world!*"

As the sound filled the hall like a tide, Airar of Trangsted began to wonder whether he had pledged his life to the triumph of his dreams . . . or had condemned himself to a violent folly that would doom them all!

*Published by Ballantine Books

The
Well
of the
Unicorn

by Fletcher Pratt

BALLANTINE BOOKS • NEW YORK

ISBN 0-345-25012-5-195

Manufactured in the United States of America

First Ballantine Books Edition: May, 1976

Cover art by The Brothers Hildebrandt

To Edith:
her idea

PUBLISHER'S FOREWORD

IT IS THE READER'S PRIVILEGE, AT LEAST in part, to lay out the geography of the world created in this novel as best suits the needs of his imagination. The author has mapped the areas principally concerned in the action of the narrative, but he has not drawn the whole of this world nor is there any guarantee that what he has done is correct. The geography of the world of The Well is necessarily subjective and is probably different for each reader.

The vague and yet extremely definite nature of the physical world in which this tale occurs is no mistake. A precise, dramatic and factual story is narrated here which is a distinguished piece of disciplined imagination on that level alone. But beyond that, on any one of half a dozen planes, what any reader feels is the meaning of this book is likely to be the map of his own conception of good and evil, of authority and voluntary agreement, of free will and foreordination, of original sin, confession, atonement and a state of grace.

The reader is not introduced to this world in easy stages; it is a going concern when the reader arrives on the scene and he is expected to find his way around in it by the same process of keeping his mouth shut and his eyes and ears open that he is frequently forced to use when he takes a new job or moves to a new community.

The political facts of the world of The Well can be described, however, and on their own authority the editors think it is a good idea to say a little about them. What follows can be thought of as the kind of portentous *mise en scène* that movie producers sometimes still use for the benefit of those who they think are historically illiterate. Condescension, however, is absent in this case since no one has had the chance to become historically literate. Also the editors make no assumption that either the author or the reader will agree with their description.

The reader enters the world of The Well through the county of Vastmanstad inhabited by the Dale-carles, a race of independent, self-reliant prosperous yeomen. As the story opens Vastmanstad has recently been overrun and conquered by the Vulkings, a stern and warlike people who have laid much of the civilized world under their power and who are proceeding ruthlessly and brutally to make over their conquests in accordance with their own rigid ethic. Young Airar Alvarson, the central character of the story, has just been dispossessed of his family property by the Vulkings and is confronted with the choice of submitting tamely to the kind of half-life he will be able to lead in the Vulking world or of joining one of the smoldering but scattered and poorly organized elements of revolt.

There are powers and nations at this time in this world, some like the pirate earl Mikalegon and the corrupt peoples of Salmonessa, still independent of the Vulkings, and some in either partial or complete subjection. There is one power, however, which even the Vulkings have not yet dared to challenge and which they treat with at least nominal respect, The Empire.

In the background, through all the stormy doings of this tale, are the power and influence of The Empire. The Empire is not only a great political and military force, it is also a spiritual one, the highest spiritual power of this turbulent civilization. Its hold over the conscience of the world comes from its possession of The Well of the Unicorn. The significance of the Well is perhaps best not discussed here except to say that the drinking of its waters brings peace.

Thus briefly are an important few of the basic facts of this strange and haunting world into which the reader must now step for himself.

Author's Note

BEFORE THE TALE BEGINS

THIS IS THE READER'S BOOK. ALL PROPER names are therefore to be pronounced in any way he chooses, except in conversation with another reader, in which case the two must settle their differences as best they can, for there is no rule.

It may be that one imagines he has caught a warcry or a movement that reminds him of something he has known in another world than the one discussed here, and yet not quite the same. He will be perfectly correct in this; one of the most fascinating things about histories real or imagined (and this is not to draw a line between the two) is how they almost repeat an earlier pattern but never quite accomplish it, like one of those designs in a tessellated pavement which runs out into something else at a corner. Perhaps this is one of the reasons why it is interesting to stare at such a pave or to follow real and unreal history when one is idle of other matters. One is watching for the repeated shock which never quite comes. In our world Augustus-Napoleon does not follow Caesar-Napoleon, however men expect that he will, nor does Hitler-Bonaparte attain the fate of his model.

So in this other world, but that is an off-wandering; the need here is to provide a guide as far as the gate of our history, imaginary or real. A certain Irish chronicler named Dunsany caught some of the news from this nowhere and set it down under the style of "King Argimenes and the Unknown Warrior," but the events he cites took place generations before any told here, and he was only interested in a very small part of them, to wit: the revolt of King Argimenes. The Irish chronicler did not tell that the revolt was against

the heathen of Dzik, who burst in upon the Dalarnan
lands with their gospel and sword in the days when
men were living at peace and their problems all
seemed solved; though he did say that, like all conquerors, these conquerors had become luxurious.

This Argimenes was one of the greatest kings of
whom there is a record and his son Argentarius hardly
less. They ruled over the Dalecarles, who before the
heathen invasion were one people with those that later
come to be called Vulkings (since all their counts
were named Vulk), which is shown by the fact that
their institutions bear so much resemblance. The mountain counties, as Acquilème and the Lacias, East and
West, were corners of Dalarna never under the rule of
Dzik; their people had a certain dark-haired strain in
them, whereas the coastal Dalecarles were, like the
heathen, blond. Therefore the Vulkings held they
were the only true Dalecarles and, after the heathen
were driven from the land, sought to restore it as it
was before, or as they thought it had been, which is
not at all the same thing. Quarrels arose, for if the Dalecarles had been in subjection, the Vulkings had been
kept out of it, which makes men far more intolerant.

Yet both parties still paid respect to the Empire, for
it was by this time an Empire, King Argimenes in his
later years having been wedded with the Princess of
Stassia from across the southern sea that is also called
the Blue Sea. It would be some time before this union
that there was discovered the Well of the Unicorn,
the well of peace, with which this narrative is concerned; the world's wonder. The turbulent Twelve Cities, which had known no master, submitted themselves
to the Empire to partake in the blessings of the Well;
they are east-away and somewhat south from Stassia,
among islands and half-islands, and their back-country
is full of men who wear skirts, take more than one
wife, and do not have the true religion. Even the terrible heathen of Dzik kept the peace of the Well—
after they had been fairly beaten in the field by Argimenes, Argentarius, and above all, Aureolus, that
changed the kingdom to an Empire and its title from
silver to gold.

East of Dalarna lies Salmonessa and its hot dukes (but the maps will show that); south of all are Uravedu and the Spice Islands, very rich, but the commons thereof are blue-faced pagans who wear breechclouts only; north is the Micton country stretching to eternal mists, where short-legged warlocks dwell. At the period of which we speak the Counts Vulk have made good their claim to rule all Dalarna—and the rest is the story.

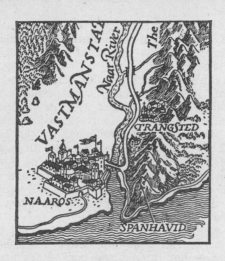

1. Taxed Out

AIRAR COULD HEAR THE HORSES BEFORE they reached the corner of the hedge where the big plane tree was. They were six in number, not talking —an oldish man in dirty blue with a twist-beard, who would be the bailiff; three archers, one of them a dark-skinned Micton man with his bow already strung; and damned Fabrizius in the middle, with his broad flat face and nose held high, well muffled in a fur-lined jacket and followed by a servant on a horse that stumbled.

Airar stood up with the wintry southering sun striking through branches across his face as one of the archers helped his lordship the bailiff to descend, the row of seals across his belly tinkling against each other like cracked pans. He had a parchment in his sleeve.

"I have a mission in the Count's name with Alvar Airarson."

"He is not here. I am Airar Alvarson."

Beyond, Airar could see Fabrizius shake his head —with that expression of decent regret that always covered his baseness.

"Then you stand deputy in his name as the heir of the house?" asked the bailiff, more with statement than question. "In accordance with the statute of the fourth year of Count Vulk, fourteenth of the name, relating to real properties, confirmed by the Emperor Auraris, I make demand on this estate for two years' arrears of the wall tax; and moreover for repayment of certain sums loaned to the estate by one Leonce Fabrizius, the said loan having been duly registered with the chancery of Vastmanstad and attest by the mark of Alvar Airarson."

Airar swallowed and took half a step, but the bailiff surveyed him with the impassive eye of a fish while the Micton archer tittered and nocked a shaft. "I do not have the money," said he.

"Then in the name of the law and the Count, I do declare this stead called Trangsted forfeit to the Empire. Yet as it is provided in the statute of the realm that no stead shall be forfeit without price, but acquired by purchase only, I do offer you the sum of one gold aura therefore out of the Count's generosity, and those present shall be witness. Wherewith you stand quit of all claims against you and go free." He fumbled the piece from the scrip at his side, bored manner of a formula of many repetitions. For a moment Airar seemed like to strike it from his hand; then seeing the Micton's covetous eye fall toward it, reached instead.

"So now this land and house are the property of our Count. I call on you to leave it, bearing not more than you carry on your back without setting the bundle down for five thousand paces." He turned from Airar, business with him done, to look expectant at Fabrizius; but the latter beckoned to Alvarson, who stood a moment with hand on pack, mouth set in a line of mutiny, yet well enough bred to hear what even the Prince of Hell had to say for himself.

"A moment; son of Alvar," said he while Airar noted how the little tuft of fur over his ear wagged as the broad mouth opened. "You have not been altogether well treated, and though you may not believe it, I hold a high regard for you. For as our Count has said, we must all live together, Dalecarles and Vulkings, each giving his best to make one people in this land. So I have made a place for you where you can do better than well. If you will go to Naaros by the dock and tell your name to the master of the cog *Unicorn,* he will make you of his company for a voyage of sure profit. Come, my boy, your hand."

"No hand," said Airar shortly, and swinging his pack up started resolutely down between the hedges wondering whether he ought not to throw a spell, but no, they would have protection. Fabrizius shrugged and turned to the bailiff, but now it was the latter's turn to be busy, signing to the tall archer, the one who had remained mounted, to go with the young man— perhaps fearing some trick of violence like a return along the shadows of the hedge and a flung knife, though Airar carried no other weapon.

As he turned down the road where the hedge fell low, an old brown horse beginning to turn grey at the edges lifted his head and stepped slowly toward the roadside. His name was Pil. Airar looked past him, not meeting his eye, past the house where now no smoke came from the chimney, across the long brown fells rising like waves with crests of brush here and there, till they went up into the rounded crests of the Hogsback, with black trees thinning out to pine and the gleam of snow along the upper ridges far beyond. A door banged sharply in the still air, Leonce Fabrizius entering his new house. Good-bye, Trangsted —good-bye, Pil. Airar shook his head, trudging along, and the tall archer leaned down:

"Cheer up, younker, you have the world to make. What you need is a couple of nights with one of Madame Korin's girls at Naaros. That'll fix you up."

The horse's hoofs went klop-klop on the frozen road and Airar said nothing.

"You get over it. Why, when I was a lad we were taxed out ourselves—that was up in West Lacia in the days of the old Count and how I came into service, scrubbing armor at Briella, when the old man went down there and hired himself out for a cook in the castle, at the time of the Count's war with the heathens."

Not a word said Airar, and the tall archer tapped the neck of his horse with one glove.

"Now take yourself," he went on. "Here you are, a free man, no debts, or service due, and a figure to make some of those court fillies prance to be ridden or a baron glad to have you at his gate. The world's not perfect, but a young fellow is a fool not to make the best out of what he has given him. Set yourself up for an archer, younker, or a billman, which is easier; you'll be noticed, never doubt it. I've done all right at Briella and here I am with a face to scare mice. But you're a Dalecarle, not so? Well, then, try Salmonessa; Duke Roger keeps lively girls there and I have heard he keeps an agent in Naaros to wage men. I'll even give you a word. What do you say?"

"No, bugger Roger of Salmonessa."

"Why, you sguittard, you milk-sucker, if—"

He jerked hard on the rein and Airar looked up angry into a face unlike most Vulkings, long, lean, and lined from nose to jaw. "Oh, sir," he cried, all his black mood running off as soon as it had accomplished its object of reaching another, "I cry your pardon. There must be a doom on me that always I strike at those who would be my friends. But in fact you speak at a hard time when I have lost everything and can gain nothing, being clerk but kept by law from it, nor carry weapons in Dalarna that is my home, nor have even a roof to my head."

The tall archer dropped rein and hand, now mollified. "No matter, younker. I grant you grace. Aye, it would be an ill life, playing tomcat to one of Duke Roger's bawds. Duke! Why, he's only a hedge-duke, or duke of the rabbits, not worth sitting at the feet of a simple count. Now—"

He left it unfinished and for a while they strode and rode along with communication silently established past the stead where the three sons of Viclid used to live. There were a couple of Micton slaves in the barnyard, trying to persuade a bullock to some mysterious doing, trotting around incompetently with many cries, the slow beef pulling from their grasp. The young man thought of these clumsy fools tracking mud across the floors of Trangsted. Presently the place and the hill on which it stood were left behind, the noise behind them still, and the tall archer said:.

"My name is Pertuit. You are for Naaros, then?"

"Where else?"

"Kinfolk there?"

Airar gave a short, hard laugh, like a bark. "A— a—father's brother—Tholo hight."

"No friend of mine. But it is said: long is the street where no sibling sits at the end."

"Aye. Tholo Airarson sits in a street where Leonce Fabrizius' house is and plays his client."

The archer Pertuit whistled. "That's a fine coil. Not that I have anything against Fabrizius, but you were a pig's head sure to be his man, even at the second remove, under the circumstances. Yet what else have you? Hell's broth, it's like being taken by the heathen of Dzik, that offer you a horse—to ride with them to the wars or before them to the scaffold. I was there once, but I found a little black-haired wench who would rather have me play jig on a pallet with her than alone at the end of a rope, therefore escaped."

He shook his head, problem too deep for him, and they came to the crest of another of the long fingers reaching down from the Hogsback. The trees by the roadside dropped away here and a little distance out the knuckle ended, so they could see for miles in the windless clear air out to the west where a clump of wood on the horizon took a nip from the sinking sun. Between were long fields, only a few checkered with winter plowing, the rest brown pasture and animals like toys, moving slowly. Through its center ran the great river, the Naar, dark blue in illumination already becoming uncertain, with flashes of white that caught the last light as ice slid down its floor toward Naaros city.

Pertuit the archer drew rein. "I call this five thousand paces," said he, "and moreover, I'm for supper. Look here, younker, we spend the night at that place of yours, Dingsted or Frogsted or how you call it. But tomorrow I'll be back in the city. Ask for me at the archers' barracks, foot of the citadel, toward evening. We'll toss a pot and think what may be done. You're all right."

He reached down a hand and this time Airar touched it. "Done—at the archers' barracks," Airar said. The archer turned round and with a "Hey Nonnine," to make his horse trot, was gone back down into the shadows of the valley they had just left. Airar Alvarson turned down the opposite slope, alone in the world with his single gold noble, his pack, and his knife, going to the city certainly, but now it struck him for the first time that a city is a big place, not friendly like the steads of the hills, and he would be certain to arrive after dark when the gates were shut with a watch over them. No matter; he had slept abroad before, and in winter, fox-trapping up the Hogsback fells. But it was not comfortable.

So he walked and meditated down into the vale from which the next finger rose to bar the way to Naaros. The sun had gone down, but up aloft it was still bright. In that dim brightness a big owl flew out of somewhere and lit on a long branch that overreached the road. Airar looked up at it. The owl stretched one wing, shifted its claws on the branch, and said abruptly:

"Airar Alvarson."

Perhaps some other might have doubted his own hearing, but this young man had long since reached for himself the thought that the world's not all made of matter. He stopped, gazed, and without showing whether startled or not, said, "What will you have?"

"Airar Alvarson," repeated the owl.

"Lira-lira-bekki," said Airar, and giving a yank to

his pack, which was growing heavy, put down his head and trudged along. When he had gone about a hundred yards the owl swept dimly past him through the gloom and perching on another branch by the roadside, said once more, "Airar Alvarson."

Ahead, down at the bottom of the valley, someone was coming out from the city in a cart, the first person Airar had met on that road. The shape was dim but the horse's hoofbeats could be heard change sound on the wooden bridge at the bottom, and one of the wheels needed tallow. A few minutes more and there he was, an old man with no cap on his white head and a sleepy boy leaning against him, who gave Airar soft-voiced greeting and nodded his head to the return. When he was well past and Airar himself was crossing the bridge, the owl came and sat on the hand-rail at its farther end, once more repeating its two-word remark.

—Fabrizius' work, reflected Airar and began looking annoyedly for a stone to throw, but looking, reflected that one does not get rid of a sending with a thrown stone, so called up his clerkly knowledge to mind. The Seven Powers?—would take a spray of witch-hazel twisted so, and how find it in the dark? Nor the Three Divinities either, which needed a reading from the book, too long to make by any flicker he might strike from tinder there. So he even had to bear the sending, plodding along the road through night now complete with a slice of moon just beginning behind the trees, on the road toward Naaros. It was after all harmless enough to be silly, a big bird that fluttered a few yards ahead to light and again repeat his name with idiot persistence, only kept him from bedding down when he otherwise might.

So they moved, man and owl, over the last of the low ridges above the plain. There was a stead on the far slope with a light in the window behind bushes and somebody singing inside; in another mood he might have sought harborage and been happy, but he was feeling all the world lost with the penalties of the afternoon and the owl hooting round his head, so pressed on down the plain, where the lights and towers of the city showed distant beyond the great sweep of the Naar, glittering faintly under its bridges in the star-shine.

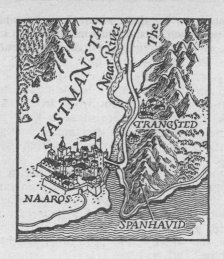

2. The Cot: There Is a Song

THE WAY LED NOW DOWNHILL THROUGH A tall alley of trees with more behind them that concealed whatever view there had been from the hilltop. There were hedges of thorn-apple grown rank, their unfriendly spicules outflung against the night sky, when he paused on the uncertain footing to glance at the odd bird which followed him still. Small things moved among hedge and trees; and they reached a place where a path led winding from the road leftward, not wide enough for a cart. Here Airar looked sharp, for something long and grey scuttled across the path, and through the screen of leafless branches a flicker of light seemed to leap and disappear; not warm yellow, but blue foxfire or lightning. The talking owl swung low past his head, to station itself at the very path, and "Airar Alvarson!" cried, a tone higher. It came to

9

the young man's mind that the bird wanted him to enter by that path, but at the same time thinking—What if not?—he set face and foot to the road again.

At once he had the curst bird in his face, wingtip brushing one ear, as it soared away from his clutching hand, shouting "Airar!" again in the new note of urgency. At the same moment from around a corner down the road ahead, there came a faint jingle of accouterment, a laugh and the sound of voices singing discordantly, where some group came from the taverns of Naaros.

Since there was no great loss of honor, a roof for the night possible and avoidance of the roisterers, Airar let himself be schooled to the owl's path; and presently stood before the door of a house set so close round with trees and bush that one could hardly see how from the window, time and time, came the flash of dead-blue light.

The door had no pillars nor carved name. Airar raised a hand to knock, but before touch it sprang open upon a boy or manikin (for the features were of adult proportion to the body) who gave a tittering laugh in his face. "Airar Alvarson," said the owl from right overhead.

"You are expected," said the dwarf, and bowed not too quickly to hide a mocking grin; then turned and led on soft-shod feet through a room larger than it seemed from outside to another with many furnishings. It was hung heavily with old tapestries worked in a design of frightful beasts and human faces twisted with fear, half visible in the light of a single candle. "Wait," said the guide, snickered, ducked under one of the tapestries, and disappeared.

There was a chair of pretense placed beside a table on which an alembic with a broken neck jostled parchments. Airar avoided it, swung down pack, and sat on a stool. Behind the tapestry to his near right occurred a sound that he, woodsman, identified as like a rabbit moving secretly in brush. The tapestry before him parted and a man came in—medium tall, full-bearded and grey, clad in a robe rather ruffled than neat, stained in front and with a rip in it. Thin white hair made a halo in the rising candlelight and threw shadows up deep eye-arches, but his face bore an expression determinedly friendly.

He sat down in the chair. "You are Airar Alvarson," he said, making no offer of hand, "and I am Meliboë."

Airar knew the name and it was not a good one. The other's expression did not alter at the flicker of muscle round the young man's mouth. "I have sent for you because we can do each other service."

"The owl—"

Meliboë waved a deprecatory hand. "A familiar, and harmless. If I had wished to compel your attendance—" he stood up with a motion lithe for such age, talking as he walked, "—I show you this to prove I deal gently and it is alliance not servitude I offer." The tapestry by Airar's side was drawn back and the rustling had been made by a loathsome great worm in a cage, large as a cockadrill, shining in green and yellow, with pairs of clawed feet where its back-armor ran down in joints. It gazed at the young man with multiplex cloudy eyes and made a small mewing sound, blowing bubbles of froth from a hexagonal mouth. Airar wanted to vomit.

"You perceive I have powers," said the enchanter, tranquilly. "You had better endure an adder's bite than even be clasped by his claws. . . . Tsa, bibé!" He dropped the tapestry.

Airar managed to say, "But why me, of all Dalarna?"

"Ha!" Meliboë raised a finger. "You had a visit from Leonce Fabrizius today, I think?" Against expectation he paused to be answered.

"Aye," said the young man.

"Then you are for what place? Naaros, no doubt? To join your father, son of Alvar?"

"My father—"

"Lives with Tholo Airarson as pensioner of that same Fabrizius. I understand, young man. You are of honor, as noble-born. Most fair; I had not sent for you otherwise."

"The more why me? You have powers and I am friendless."

Meliboë swivelled round to look at him full as though here were something caught to surprise. "It is not less than I would have expected, to find you so acute," he said, "and it does my judgment compliment. Well, since I see you will have nothing less than the full tale, here it is: there are not few, and I am among them, who would be less than melancholy to see an alternation in the rule of our good Count Vulk, fourteenth of the name. Yet here am I, court doctor and astrologer; not Dalecarle by birth. Shall I not need an impeccable ambassador before the Iron Ring?"

There was a moment's silence, no sound at all but an intake of breath from Airar as the last words fell. Oh, aye, he knew of iron ring and iron ring—badge worn by Micton slaves and those sentenced for a time to servitude by the Vulking courts; some words half-caught from behind the door of his lock-bed, the night the stranger in the worn blue coat guested at Trangsted, his father saying—"No and no again. What? Leave my stead and my son's future to [here a gap] iron ring?"—the nine days' wonder of old Tyel, who had hanged himself (men said) in the barn of the upper farm at Grӓntraen, with an iron ring new forged around his neck. But at the market in Naaros, no one would speak of that. . . .

"I do not know what you mean about the Iron Ring," he said stoutly, but Meliboë laughed. "It is as I would have desired. You are a model of discretion. So let us put it this way; there is a certain group at Naaros with whom I am wishful to strike hands, but may not do so in person. You seek employment; I wage you as plenipotentiary before them and will pay well, from which it will grow that either they send you back to me with another message for a second payment, or find employment enough for you of their own. That it is not altogether without danger I admit. Can you do better unhelped?"

The offer seemed fair enough even though (as Airar noted, secretly amused) the remark about danger was made more for encouragement than fairness. But he was of peasant stock. "How great is the wage?"

"I wonder, did you take the Count's goldpiece? I

think you would. No matter; three like it paid down
for this one message."

The sum was princely, yet "Is it enough?" asked
Airar.

Meliboë looked at him narrowly. "Four then. I am
striking too high to haggle." The note was finality.

"And the message?"

"Merely this: that Meliboë, a poor doctor of the
philosophies, wishes them well; and as proof that he
does so wish them, he is full aware of what the syndics
of the guilds of Mariupol propose, but none at the
court knows of it else; that a scorpion without a head
can sting but not bite, but that by certain philosophic
arts one might find a hand to bear a banner."

"To whom given?"

Meliboë twitched lips, but, wise to take substance
rather than shadow, answered: "To a certain group
who meet at a tavern, called Of The Old Sword, with
the arms of the Argimenids before, as though it were
imperial property, but differenced as to color. It is in
the Street of the Unicorn, hard by the Lady-Chapel,
and the hour is one after sunset."

"It smacks of secret. How shall they believe I am
to come?"

The philosophic doctor placed his head a little on
one side, a long forefinger up the angle of his jaw, the
back of his hand ruffling beard under chin. "Your care
is admirable," he said; turning, unlocked a drawer
Airar had not noticed amid the carving of the table,
and drew forth a small ring, intricately wrought in
silver. "This be your passport."

To Airar's fingers it felt wholly smooth. He looked
up surprised and a smile stretched across the limits of
Meliboë's beard. "A small enchantment," said he.
"Look you but now." The parchments and desk litter
were tossed aside till he found a gugglet of water from
which he sprinkled a few drops as Airar held the ring
outstretched. It was plain iron with square edges, but
when the young man rubbed it dry on the edge of his
jerkin there it was again to appearance silver and
much carven.

"Put it on." The enchanter waved hands. "You will

go then to this tavern; if they make difficulties ask for a few drops of wine or water and show it anew. What do you think?"

"Good. But a ring is not always on the hand of the owner."

"That is thought on. There is also a certain song from one of the old tongues before the heathen. How much clerk are you?"

"Somewhat; but not to practice."

The enchanter laughed shortly. "Not for admission to bailiffs, I know. Well, then, one shall hum to you or sing softly,

Geme, plange, moesto more—

and your reply to the same air is,

Dolorosa Dalarna.

Or you may reverse it, offering the first line in challenge."

Airar caught the air and repeated it readily enough, but Maliboë waved hands and stood up. "So for business; now courtesy. You have supped?"

Said Airar, who was in a state to attack the worm and carve steaks from its ribs, "Not I."

"All my apologies." His host pulled aside another part of the tapestry than the dwarf had used when he entered. "Young sir and partner, come."

There was a passage. At the end of it Meliboë ushered him into an apartment where again one candle burned, this above a bed well furnished. He clapped hands. Airar noticed the door had a lock and was glad; the manikin entered, still smiling at his secret jest, and was told to bring a plate with somewhat to drink. Meliboë remained on his feet and so did Airar for politeness, while time paused, from which the enchanter's eyes rolled suddenly. "You are a lucky man and will do much," he said, "but I do not think your luck will hold against that of the three-fingered lord, though he be himself less than fortunate. A mystery."

Airar stared at him. The dwarf, whom it would be more like to call a small man, since he was in all respects perfectly proportioned, came in with a tray that held meat, drink, and a manchet of bread; but at the moment he entered, there was a frightful dying scream that seemed to run through the whole building and rend one to the very marrow.

The little man set down the tray and tittered. "The leopard is dead," he said.

"Ten thousand furies!" cried Meliboë and dived through the door. Airar drove home the bolt before he addressed himself to the food.

3. Naaros: A New Friend at The Old Sword

AIRAR HAD BEEN IN NAAROS OFTEN ENOUGH but never with five pieces of gold and all time to himself, so it was new. He wandered among shops, was beset to avoid slops, took his noon meal in a cookstall where he left his pack in care, and found the temptation to buy strong till the very moment of entering the shop to chaffer. Then he would reflect that he bore his only home on his back, like a turtle; therefore ended by purchasing not even what he might in another mood have wished, like a beautiful little grimoire to fit the pocket, in the Street of the Booksellers. He went near neither the street where his father's brother kept house and artisanship in the name of Fabrizius, nor the dock where the latter had told him the cog *Unicorn* would lie—no, death's resort, both—though from the street of the piers he could see tall masts rising and catch the pungent whiff of spices from Uravedu and the South Isles; and it was of regret that the chance to sail thither had come in such a form.

Without trouble he found the Street of the Unicorn, the Lady-Chapel, and the tavern called Of The Old Sword, marking it well for the evening's use. A black-fronted place, beamed up to a jutting overstory, with a narrow entrance and a somewhat ill-advised big man lounging against it with hair half over his eyes, who made way for nobody. That was behind, it would be toward sunset, and the brouhaha of the city dying toward gate-close when the son of Alvar came upon a street at the base of the peninsula where Naar runs round the tall tongue of rock to outline Naaros citadel. It was an old street that stood on a filled-in moat; therefore zigzagged, the ground windows mostly given to the sale of weapons and such gaudy trinkets as soldiers buy.

Had Airar not been tired with walking paves he would have little paused; had he not looked at things wholly unwanted, the dag whose jewelling caught the last level light had not seemed so priceless good. But so it was; his heart leaped at finding something he could both buy and carry, and he went in. It was a fat man with a squint eye, who with tradesman's deliberation brought the dag from the window for Airar to handle. Permandos work, said he, and the price forty solvars. The weapon was sweetly balanced; at its touch Airar became so eager to buy that he only carried the bargaining down to thirty (though he might have had it for less) and brought out one of his goldpieces. The shopkeeper weighed it reflectively on fingertips and looked the young man up and down.

"Are you not a Dalecarle?" he asked.

"Yes, and what of that?" said Airar, somewhat shortly, having encountered this before. "This is Dalecarle's country."

The man was patient. "May I see your exemption?"

Said Airar, "I do not know that I take your meaning," fearing that he most accurately did take it.

"Exemption. Writing over the seal of our Lord Provost with leave to buy weapons of the classes not by the ordinance to those of Dalecarle blood."

Now Airar did understand with no doubt about it and felt his face flush hot. "If that's your ordinance," he cried, "take your dirty kitchen knife to my Lord Provost and ram it down his weazand with my compliments." He reached for his piece of money.

The squinted eye blinked rapidly. "Young sir, I no more made the rules you live by than I made you six feet tall. It falls hardest on me. Now I must ask your name and to the archers' barrack to be questioned around and around about why you are buying death-tools; or if I fail, then you turn out to be one of my lord's deputies, and where am I?"

The words roused in Airar not only sympathy, but a memory lost among the events of the night. "My name's my own," he said, "but if that's the matter, I'll even go with you. I know an archer who'll make all right."

Squint-eye gave him a long, squinting glance, now clearly confirmed in his suspicions. "I thank you, young sir. You are gracious. But there's none to leave with my shop. You know how to reach it, no doubt? To your right the first street and follow it straight around."

He made a half-bow over a smile of pure malice and it would have been Airar's pleasure to thrust a fist into it, but he restrained and strode out with no more words. The street gave on a wide cobbled square with a stockade at the far end, and the road to the rock of the castle winding up out of it; he had not been there before. At the gate of the stockade a man in jack and sallet held a bill in the crook of his arm and attentively examined some small spot on his hand.

"What d'you want?"

"Is Pertuit the archer within?"

He look Airar up and down as the shopkeeper had done, less friendly, there being no money involved; balanced bill, turned head, and shouted: "Louche!

Louche! Tell old Cowface there's a snotty here to see him." It was Airar's first contact with the guard, save Pertuit himself and the friendly stupid men who kept order at the market.

Pertuit came down capped and sworded, yawning gustily and scratching himself, a burr of new beard round his chin; somewhat shamefast and hoity-toity of look over the glance and whistle his comrade gave to see him called for by a handsome Dalecarle youth. "What's now?" he said, and Airar would have walked away but that there is no loneliness like that of a countryman in town.

"I had thought you might help me find a tavern where we could pick a bone," he said. "Having money—" and dandled one of his aurar.

The archer's ill humor vanished. "Bless you, youn-ker!" he said. "We'll make a Vulking of you yet, that are good to an old fighting man who has spent all his life in service. None has offered any here aught since Prince Aurareus came over in the imperial viceroy's train and sent every man of the castle guard six bot-tles to drink his health." He had taken Airar by the arm and was leading him rapidly across the square from the wicket-guard, who stood looking after with his mouth watering. "Not that—" Pertuit glanced round sharply, and gave a kind of snort. "Ha, stinking Imperials, all perfume. But you never see old Red-beard buying wine for the archer guard and I don't care who knows I said it. Here's a good place."

To Airar's eyes the room stretched back illim-itable, smoking with cressets, deaf with sound. A whole row of spits turned; the smell was delicious. He blinked as the host came forward, smiling at the red triangle on Pertuit's shoulder, but looking with a somewhat anxious eye as the archer said, "We'll have a stall, a bird, and Carrhoene—not the kind with resin, ha? It's all right, the young lord's rich. Show him the color of your shield, Élair."

"My name is Airar," but he clinked gold for the man, whose smile became a smirk as he led toward the rear and a place where the pair could sit beside on a thing like a church pew with arm-rests once carved in the heads of curious beasts, now knife-hacked out of recognition. The pot-boy brought the bottle; Pertuit took a long draft and looked not unkindly at the young man.

"It's a matter of employ, is't not, younker?" he asked, willing enough to pay for entertainment in what coin he could muster.

Airar felt himself blush. "As for that, I'm not so urgent—that is, I would spend a day or two to see—I—"

"Oho, already? Is she fair? Take a veteran's advice and look at the breasts; that's where you have to lie. The face is only the shingle before the shop. Is that her ring you wear?" He laughed loud and now Airar blushed in good earnest, for he was a decent lad.

"Nor that either." Pressed to the point of saying something to cover Meliboë's mission, Airar burst out with the story of his effort to buy the dag, and Pertuit whistled as he took another long drink. "Faith, younker, you fall foul of the law like a dog chasing ducks in a barnyard. Were you truly ignorant of the ordinance?"

"For long weapons, aye, I knew. But a mere dag?"

"A dag is long in Naaros city by order of his worship the Baron Vanette-Millepigue. What's to do on this?" He drummed fingers. "Best devance the matter, say I, by going before a magistrate to confess the fault. But you'll need three compurgators. I'll stand willing for one—swear I never saw a chick more harmless—but where's the rest? D'you suppose Fabrizius would speak for you?"

"No doubt." Airar laughed short. "But the price would be to sail in his curst ship."

"If 'twere to Dzik or Uravedu you might make a fortune, but I misdoubt this Fabrizius trades only with the Twelve Cities, and in essence Carrhoene, where you have as much chance to draw wine from a well as you have to win a solvar. Ah, well, give tomorrow's problem to the dawn, as the song says." He drank another draft, tilted back his head and sang:

"When I was young and in my prime
I thought on age and the end of time;
but now my hair and beard are grey,
I know that time is here to stay.

There are seven other verses, but they all come to the same thing."

The host brought their bird and toothsome it was, with a sauce of little shrimps from the Naarmouth; but Airar found to no pleasure his companion drinking uneasy fast and talking faster even though with the best of spirits and wit. For there were guests in the other stalls who looked and laughed, and the young man could not but think on how he might deliver the enchanter's message at a place where Pertuit would sure be no welcome guest. He was a fool for the invitation and the room seemed slightly to blur as with distance which was a sensation he knew, so at last burst out: "Sir archer and friend, this has been joyous, but as you forgive me, I must even bid good-night. A matter of business—"

"Aha!" roared the archer before Airar could pick up from that hesitation. "The young cock wants to rut." He leaned forward and wagged a finger. "Hark, younker, I'll go with you. Every girl should have two lovers, one to keep guard at the door."

"I do assure you—"

"You assure me of nothing. On the contrary, I assure you against all interruption. What! Am I not an archer of the guard of his lordship, the bastardly Red Baron? Gurion!" He swept up arm in a beckoning gesture for the landlord. "The slate. Pay it clear, younker; I'll leave drink-money for the lad, and let's begone."

It could have been the wine that somewhat dulled Airar's perceptions; yet at the best, what could he do with one so masterful and moreover in authority, but go on and trust that those to whom he was bound would set a guard to screen out archers? He paid then, and rose. Pertuit took his arm, clapped the boniface on the back, saluted some in a neighboring stall, and led Airar magniloquently toward the door. The night air smelled good, with a salty tang the young man remembered coming to Trangsted only when the wind was strong southerly.

"Where are we bound?" asked the archer.

"I go to the Street of the Unicorn. But are you not required to be at the barrack by a named hour?"

"Pish. Never mention it. Is not my trade being guard?" And who better to guard than an old friend at his adventures? I'll answer for all—all, to any night-watch. Does she have a sister?"

The city was quiet and echoing after the noise of the day, the moon low in the sky and shadows everywhere with only a lighted window now and then, so that presently even Pertuit gave over his chatter. They met few and those mostly cloaked, seeming unanxious for company; but as they passed the Lady-Chapel there seemed to be movement among the darkness, and where the Inn of The Old Sword was, one of these shadows stepped forward and from under a cloak thrust a tallow-lantern in their faces.

"Where do you go?" he asked gruffly, and beyond the light Airar thought he caught a glimpse of the surly big-boned man who had lounged there earlier.

"Where I please and answer to none," said Pertuit, voice suddenly metal-hard, and reached round to tap the badge on his shoulder. "Archer of the guard." A light flashed on suddenly within the inn and was quickly out.

"Pass, archer," said the fellow, and lowering the lantern, stepped back a half-pace, but as he did so Airar caught from the tail of his eye a flick of motion that sang danger. Pertuit saw it first and—all one movement with a speed Airar would not have credited in a man half-drunken still—whipped out his shortsword and thrust, shouting, "Watch! Watch! A pax! A pax!"

The big man glided like smoke before the blow and Airar heard a sound of ripping cloth. He half-turned at some touch; at the some moment a laurel-leaf spearhead whipped past his shoulder, the shape forever fixed in memory during that fraction of a second. It dipped and caught his companion full under the shoulder-blade from behind. The last shout died in bubbles; there was a rush of blood on the young man's hand, something clipped him hard behind the ear, and down he went in a tangle with the body of Pertuit the archer.

4. Naaros: Men Meet at Night

"HOLD," AIRAR DREAMILY HEARD SOME-one say in a high voice. "This one wears the ring."

"Give him the question, then." The second voice was gruff from the big man. "No safety for any till we find how he came by that."

There was a light outside Airar's lids, which the headache made as much as he could bear, his hands felt sticky, and he misdoubted his ability to move.

"Nay, Gallil," said still a third. "Here's no Vulking. Look at that hair and those inches."

"By the Well! The question then, for a traitorous lizard. How came he running with the Red Dog's pup?"

Airar opened his eyes and immediately shut them again to the wave of light and pain, but in that evanescent glance caught the fact that there was a circle of faces and he was lying on a floor under a dark, low-beamed ceiling.

"The animal's awake," growled the Gallil-voice. "Question him quick before the syndic comes, or that old fool will be out the door, leaving nothing behind but a bad smell. Naught more ogresome than the thought of death to a man who's near it."

"Nay." Airar tried to sit up and the effort set all the stars of heaven crashing through his head. He lifted a hand, saw that it was drenched with blood, felt sick, and would have fallen back but that one long-nosed and clean-shaven, in the costume of a mountain-hunter, put an arm around him. "Hold the way!" he cried, and it was the third speaker, who had remarked Airar's hair and size. "Some water—or aquaviva."

"True," said a man with a bald head and an iron beard that bristled out from his face like the prickles of a porcupine, passing over a bottle of something that stung Airar's lips. "Let's hear what tune he pipes for himself before making him dance to ours."

Airar coughed, gasped, shook free of the supporting hand, and with an effort heaved himself up, but had to grip a side pillar to face the circle of maybe a score, skeptic to unfriendly.

"Well, man, what's your business, say?" cried someone impatiently, and the hunter: "Give him time for life," but Gallil, "Time for lies, rather."

The son of Alvar looked at his hand. "It's all blood," he said foolishly. "You killed my friend." Then, gaining strength with speed as the sense of danger hit home: "You of the Iron Ring for sure make rude enough welcome for those delegated with messages to your ears."

There was a stir on that. "Messages from whom?" cried one, and "Proof, proof!" another, Gallil threw back his torn cloak to show he was grasping hilt beneath, and a voice asked if the Korosh speaker had come. But Airar faced them till he had all their eyes, having some experience with folk-meetings in Vastmanstad, then hummed through his teeth:

Geme, plange, moesto mori—

letting it drop at the end of the line, and without waiting for the answer, said, "If you'll but give me the means to cleanse myself, you shall hear the rest. Sirs, if I were indeed contrarious to you, would I have come to your meeting with a single archer? It is too many or too few."

The mountain-hunter laughed clear. "Aye, Gallil, there's your proof," said he. "It's a true Dalecarle— bad argument and good heart. Why any archer at all he says not, you'll remark. Let's to full meeting and hear in form this maker of conditions." He gripped Airar by the arm and led him half-staggering through another room, where there was a long table with places for many, to a buttery where he could wash, remarking not unkindly as he waited, "Give them name and station at once; no need to trick out with speech. We're fair to all of Dalecarle blood. I'm Rogai of Mariola." He touched hands for friendship and led the way in.

The group were all in places round the table, as he could see now with clearing head an assembly in all the costumes of Dalarna. This Gallil, now that one got him in the light, was evidently from the peasantry of Vastmanstad itself; there was one who snorted with asthma from a fisherman's beard and a leather jerkin; that tall man with the wind-red face bore a doublet that was surely never fashioned other where than on the boundless plains of Hestinga; and a man with delicate hands on the table, wearing a knight's hacqueton beneath a sharp triangular chin, might well be that Sir Ludomir Ludomirson of whom Airar had so often heard.

The young man gripped the back of a chair. "Sirs," said he, seeing they were attendant upon him, "I will show you my affair without concealment. I am Airar Alvarson, now of no place, being taxed out of my father's stead no earlier than yesterday by Leonce Fabrizius." Murmurs, and the fisher cried, "That's what we're for to cure."

"Well then, as I made my way to town last night,

I fell on an encounter with a certain doctor philo-
sophicus, one Meliboë. He told me you would gather
here tonight; gave me this ring and your song as
passports and waged me to bear a message."

Now there was stir indeed, Gallil leaping up so
fierce his chair crashed to the floor, crying, "Said
I not so? Give him the question at once!" and
mountain-hunter Rogai, pale under brown, "How
came that old vulture by our song and sign?" with
many other confused voicings till the knight stood
up, lifting his hands, and only when there was peace,
saying:

"A moment." He addressed Airar: "Young sir,
this is a very astounding and dangerous thing to
tell us, for among all the enemies of our race none
is worse than this same Meliboë and if he be ware of
our intimate doings, we are not far from sped. Therefore—"

"That is my message. I—"

"You will be still till we give you leave to speak,
since you stand here in no good odor. Moreover, you
will address me as sir; I am a dubbed knight. I continue: we would be satisfied that you do indeed come
as the plenipotentiary of this wizard and demon.
Where did you encounter him?"

"In a cot at the foot of a hill where a small road
turns off, some eight to ten thousand paces beyond the
last bridge as one takes the great high toward the two
Lacias out from Naaros—sir."

"Gallil, you're our delegate of Vastmanstad. Is this
plausible?"

The big man nodded gloomily behind his beard.
"Veritable, even, Sir Ludomir. Few know it, but Meliboë has a pleasaunce there, where he works his dirty
witcheries with the help of a dwarf called Cobbo, off-
spring of a mismating between a sea-demon and a
Micton wench."

Sir Ludomir turned back to Airar. "We will take it as
proved that you have seen Sir Doctor Meliboë. Have
you any proof that you bear his word?"

For answer Airar stepped to the window of the buttery where the water was, thrust his hand into the

bucket, then held it aloft. "Sir, and you, sirs," he said, "I ask you to look whether this be not an iron ring such as I see some of you wear. But now look." He rubbed it dry and threw it on the table, where it caught the light in multiplex reflection of the twined silvery design.

Rogai the mountain-hunter laughed. "Sorcery!" cried someone, but Airar: "I could remove the enchantment myself if I had a book here."

The knight picked up the ring, rolled it between his fingers, examined it closely, and looked up with raised eyebrows: "And the message?"

"Sir, that this Doctor Meliboë finds the world wagging ill under Count Vulk and would fall in with you to change it. As proof of good will, he offers this—that he knows what you propose with the guilds of Mariupol; but says a scorpion without a head may sting but not bite, yet through certain arts he might find you a hand to lift a banner."

Once again there was babble and Sir Ludomir looked forth like a hawk from shadowed eyes. "And what think you—" he began, but before he could achieve the word, there came from the door a knock double and triple. The knight slid the ring down the table to Airar, Rogai-of-the-mountains motioned him to a place, and the portal was unbarred to admit a man.

He was clad in furs, so richly that at a glance one missed the person himself, yet on second sight there was nothing remarkable in this, since it was an ancient, so bleached and colorless as to be without personal existence, with a thin, solemn face, like a priest's.

Rogai of Mariola sprang up. "This is Wigrak," he said in a loud voice, "syndic of the great guilds of Mariupol, to hear whom we are convoked tonight." The old man smiled thanks as Sir Ludomir offered him a chair and said in a voice silver-clear, "With your permission, I will sit and talk."

"We are all one in the Iron Ring, with no rules of sit or stand," said the knight, in the tone of one repeating a formula, which the elder capped with:

"In some measure it is precisely for that that I have come. How long are we of Dalarna to lie under the Mountain? I will give you a hard saying on that if you

are men enough to hear it—till there are rules of sit
and stand, and a captain over us."

He paused for a moment to let them grasp it, and the
prickle-beard man said slowly, "So told us Meliboë
through the mouth of the youngling messenger."

Wigrak did not look at him even. "When's peace and
amity we can talk of no man better than his neighbor,
but, gentles, I do assure you we are now in the midst
of most desperate war, though with no standard lifted,
which will not end till we are all made Vulkings or the
servants of Vulkings—you were not met here else. You
were not else bearing that iron band by which Count
Vulk proclaims that Dalecarle and barbarous Micton
are one."

He paused again. In answer to some signal Airar
had not caught, a chubby girl came in from the pantry and set mead round the table, while one and another exchanged low-voiced words; though none drank
but a stoop-shouldered man near Sir Ludomir, dressed
fancily in the style of the Korsor hills; but Rogai, who
seemed in some sense the old man's sponsor, said:
"And the rest?"

Wigrak raised a paper-white hand.

"Patience," said he. "This is blood and treasure and
more than we own and it is well to think each step.
But here it is briefly—this day one month Mariupol city
throws off the allegiance of Count Vulk and rises in
arms. To you of the Iron Ring, we say—join us; this is
the acceptable hour of the sword."

Now there was tumult of a kind to make dim that
over Airar's message, half the room on their feet and
some of them shouting, so the girl stuck her head from
the pantry, but when they took their places again, the
prickle-beard man did not sit and he addressed the
syndic:

"That is the best of news to all who would see the
Mountain cut down, but our guest has said somewhat of
rules and rulers. Before we pledge heart and sword, I
would know to whom."

"Ha!" growled black Gallil, half under his breath.
"A rat and a Whiteriverdalesman will never cross a

bridge till it is paved with cheese," and Prickle-beard flushed, but Wigrak the syndic signed for the word:

"That is a most fair question, frankly put, and will be answered in the same spirit. Mark you: has Dalarna a leader fit to stand in battle before the Vulking captains—Bordvin Wildfang or even the bloody Red Baron of Naaros? It was our failure at the Red Hills long ago that we had none; and since this matter will come to battle soon or late, the Mariupol guilds have sought champions where they might be found; to it, we have waged the Star-Captains out of Carrhoene to be our leaders, with sundry of their spears."

Airar had heard of those five Star-Captains, each glorious as a trumpet-blast, and had any risen to shout at that word, he too over the thought they fought for Dalarna. But round the table only one or two stirred, looks were less joyous than those of lovers, Sir Ludomir tapped with his fingers, and Gallil scowled darkly, while the Korsor man cried, "What's the wage and who pays?" as he drank from his mug. But Wigrak rushed on like a man used to these checks:

"All's not perfect; that I grant. I have consulted them myself. They're not our blood, something more than a little sly and greasy about them, and they'll want lordships in the land for their price besides driving so close a bargain for ready money that it made some of our guildsmen think twice. Moreover they sit not well with the Emperor himself; may give us trouble there as Vulk pipes the tune of loyal vassal. I grant all this, gentles, and much besides. But does a man cast adrift at sea bemoan the lack of pepper for the fish he catches? The devil of Briella's all too glad to have us meet him polite, reasonable, according to form. We shall lose nothing but our lives if we do. The worst that can be said for these Star-Captains is also the best—that in matters of war and cunning, 'tis they who have bepissed all the trees the Vulking dogs sniff at."

A thrill of laughter went round the board and dark Gallil spoke out of it: "For the Dalecarles of Vastmanstad I say that I like this none too well. But here's no boy's game to run home from if the rules seem counter. Why else do we plot against Count Vulk in the long run, but to war? So I say, haro! Up with the banner of the Wingèd Wolf and out weapons, even behind the scrubbed pigs of Carrhoene. Who follows?"

"I," cried one, "I for Hestinga!" The man from there and Mountain-Rogai, looked round proudly, but Airar noted the voice failed to circle the table. As if weakened a man pretty well fed but with no definite mark of origin in dress or accent spoke out:

"Gallil, all men know you for a generous heart, and you, Sir Syndic, are most urgent, but for me, I am not much taken by that word 'plot.' We of Shalland joined the Iron Ring to keep under the Empire old liberties hard won by our fathers behind King Argimenes in battle. How shall we do that if we revolt against the Emperor's Count under the Emperor's outlaw? For what shield have we against the heathen but the Empire and the Well?"

Old Wigrak raised a finger as though to answer, but another was before him—merchant by his look and gold chain. "You are far from wrong there," said he, "and there's another leg to't as well. Mariupol lies on the very border, in some sense under the arm of the great Duke of Salmonessa, who will never see her down. But who's to protect us of Stavorna, pinched between Vulk's own hold of Briella and the pirates of the north? Nay, let's keep this Count for fear of a worser thing; but make him mend his manners. That's what our Iron Ring stands for."

"Matters are somewhat far for that in Naaros city, where we slay archers," cried one, with a hard laugh at the end of it, and Wigrak looked up startled as though to ask a question, but once again another spoke first, a man as young as Rogai or Airar himself with long curled hair:

"If I may be excused who come from Norby, where we have not all your southern tidings, here's a matter not altogether easy to understand. I was not there at the time of the Red Hills, but as my father has made the tale it was Mariupol city and her guilds in those days that first opened gates to the Vulkings, and not a blade lifted. How comes she so hot for battle and bloodshed now?"

"Because," said the Korsor man, "it's bloodshed or beggary for them. Have you not heard my Lord Chancellor Lannoy's latest inspiration? He is setting up factories with Micton slaves at labor to match the Mariupol guilds in the wool staple of their own town."

Eyes swung to Wigrak. "I will not deny it," said he. "Nor will you, if you look on the matter closely, deny either that what comes to Mariupol today is for Naaros —and aye, for Stavorna and all other cities tomorrow. For it is this Count's evident purpose to pass us through the iron ring of his making by one way or another. Why else all these taxes and sales in the countryside and men turned out of their fathers' steads, that are then grazed under gangs of slaves for owners who sit in the castle?"

He swung to Gallil. "You, sir, are old enough to remember the first days of Vulking rule. How many free farmers in Vastmanstad now to what there were then? As for the admission of the Vulkings to the cities, there were some who thought then that it was ill done, I one of them. But we will not hide behind that, only ask if none of you have ever made a fault and been forgiven. For here is the hour when we must forgive all friends against the enemies of us all."

Airar heard the murmur go round the board and thought the syndic had won them, but there was still the man in the fisher-jerkin, who stood up, wheezing in an accent that turned all his s's to z's.

"I can't talk slick," he said, "to make it sound like I kiss your foot when I mean you kiss my behind. (*Wuff, wuff.*) So with your presence, I'll just hit straight out like us free-fishers always do. It's just grand for a free-fisher to hear that the big men in the Mariupol guilds are friends of ours (*puff*); they never were till now, when they want somewhat. But old Count un sends us Doctor Meliboë to help when we got troubles with the sea-demons. (*Wuff, puff.*) But Count wants somewhat, too, un takes taxes from us, no lighter as he goes, so a man can hardly live. We'd help drown him in Naarmouth if we could get better, we would. But what this syndic wants (*whoof*) I just say is down with one Count, and give us five more, all stinking with Carrhoene perfume, and we just say no, we'll have none."

He sat down. The fat man said, "Shalland will not rise. I could not persuade them."

"Nor Korsor."

"Nor the Whiteriverdales either, I fear."

Rogai the hunter threw up a hand and let it slowly fall. "The old tale," said he. "Five Dalecarles in a room —on what will they agree? On how to cheat each other with the help of a Vulking who comes by the window." He turned to Wigrak. "Sir, there's your answer, and if 'twere better, I'd be a happier man."

The syndic drew his furs round him with a delicate hand, touched his lips to his mug, and in that clear, penetrating voice, said: "Then there is nothing for us of Mariupol to do but draw out of all union with our own blood of Dalarna and submit ourselves to the great Duke Roger. You have heard me most courteously."

He made to rise, but Sir Ludomir laid a hand on his arm. "No!" he cried, striking the table. "No! I, who am of more rank than any here, have kept silent so that all might fully expose their minds without hindrance, but now no more, since you are fallen at variance on a matter of mere words. Look, now; I'm of Gallil's advisement; would have chosen another time and another leader, even another method, for I hold that the path this Count Vulk is following must one day bring him to the crossroads with the Empire. Yet that day may be late; and while we wait, he rots Dalarna with his taxes and his slaves. We must strike before the old edge rusts, nor shall there come again soon so fair a chance, with the money of these Mariupol men and the mercenary spears of Carrhoene to be of our service.

"But you, Sir Syndic, I ask you to mark which delegates have said nay to your way—they're from the Whiteriverdales, Shalland, Norby, Stavorna city, Korsor—all the north. Suppose the war-arrow gone round and the bands risen—think, man, and tell me what your Star-Captains down at Mariupol could do if Vulk or his Marshal Bordvin sealed the passes of the Hogsback and threw their full strength on the raw levies just risen beyond the Naar? Yet, were

Vastmanstad and Mariola in our hands and an army under a good captain marching up the stream, our campaign wears a fairer aspect. Does it not, Vard?"

"I will not deny it," said the man from Shalland.

"In God's name, Sir Wigrak, be not so hasty to leave us. The Iron Ring has given you all you could ask— save Rudr here and his free-fishers, and to him I say that this Doctor Meliboë on whose help he so much attaches is a confessed traitor to his own master by the mouth of his messenger here, so that he is like to have a plague of these sea-demons if he stands by the Mountain. Not that it should keep us from using him —any spade to dig a grave for Vulkings, say I—and I engage you, Gallil, to wait on this enchanter and know his full mind. But most of all I say war; rise; strike now, in the south and along the shore; but let even Hestinga withhold till we are sure of backing her. Is that the sense of all?"

He looked round, gripped his mug:

"The Ring!" he cried, lifting it, and they all stood with him, shouting, "The Iron Ring!" before they drank. There was now a general movement about and toward the door, with tongues clacking and no more notice taken of Airar, who presented himself to this Sir Ludomir, where he was talking with the fisher, and said, "Sir, all my life I have desired to bear a blade against Vulkings, that have been less than easy on my land and kindred. Will there be a place for me in this affray?"

The knight looked him along. "I presume one might be found. Have you a skill?"

"I am thought to be somewhat of a clerk."

"The latter will be needed in Mariola if Bordvin Wildfang takes the field against us—a rare man for enchantments and supersticerie. Go with Rogai."

5. The Road:
Change and Unchange

THEY SPENT THAT NIGHT AT THE FUR-
market, where Rogai had business as a reason for being in Naaros. Airar Alvarson found his companion
an easy and a friendly man, with a streak of masterful
self-will cutting across underneath like a vein in marble
—as when the son of Alvar mentioned his pack where
he had left it, the dag and grimoire he had admired.
For the pack Rogai would do nothing; the archers of
the guard might have traced it down by then, he said,
especially since Pertuit rejoined them not. Dag and
grimoire he swore Airar should have and took one of
his goldpieces, telling him to keep close in the lodging
for fear of the Red Baron's searchers.

35

A boresome day for Airar, therefore; a dozen times he counted the brass studs on the door, trying to make them fall into a pattern they would not, then fell to recalling the spell to put down sea-demons, but that made his head ache, so at last he gave it up and fell asleep on the bed in all his clothes. He dreamed troublously of a pool in a wood where white unicorns came down through a yellow twilight to water and it seemed to him that he never in his life before had known anything so precious as those unicorns; but someone shot a shaft into one. If fell kicking with an animal's wild scream and he woke through a wave of heartbreak to find Rogai shaking him.

The man of Mariola had both book and dag, with food, as bread, wine, onions. There was an uneasy air in the town, he said, and talk of closing the gates for a day—not that anyone missed the archer Pertuit, who might have run from his service, but because of the rumors of uproar. Some said there was word of heathen raiders on the sea, and others spoke of movements among the forces disbanded at the composition of the war between Barbixana and Carrhoene among the Twelve Cities.

"But that's moon-baying," Rogai went on, "and here's the truth: our friend, the Red Baron, has caught some inkling of the Iron Ring and puts out both tales himself the better to trace us down. That's not one born with his head in a blanket."

Airar marvelled how one no longer in years than he could see a way through such complexities; himself would have believed either tale that came last or have been confused altogether, for among the plain farmers round Trangsted it had been accounted mean to bear tidings that were not true and few who did it were guested twice. "Will they not come searching in places of resort like this?" he asked.

"Like enough, if Vanette-Millepigue chances on aught to make him think the trail's warm. . . ." He looked at Alvar. "You are clerk; could you not put a variance on our seeming?"

Airar gazed at him, a little dull with sleep, wondering how to make clear for this young man to whom all enchantments were obviously one. True, he had a book now, but lacked all furniture; and the form-change magic always left him weak as a newborn lamb for two days after. "What's the purpose?" he said at last. "Do they look for you and men in special, or any that hold not by the Count? And if the second, what does the aspect matter?"

"This—that if the Baron gets anything at all, it will be the whole tale. Too many know it; Bland of Sko-galang's not altogether to be trusted, neither Siccald of Korsor—he drinks too much, loses his temper, and is like to fly off. A sharp catechizer could make him betray his hope of bliss to give law to a toss-pot senate. And I'm the Vulkings' daintiest morsel now, being of Mariola, the heart of this whole matter. Ha!"

He stood up, unbelted, and threw his knife with a clatter in the corner. "Keep free of plots and politics, son of Alvar. It's try all and trust none and forever weariness of spirit. I could not believe less in men or more in the Devil if I were ninety."

It came to Airar that perhaps he also rode the ridge of distrust and he said as much.

"Since you drag that worm to daylight, what have we from you? Your story of dag and book is true enough; here they are to prove it, and all else you've said on your movements in Naaros will now stand, for 'tis on the unimportant details that liars fail. I've also seen those two sons of your grandfather with Leonce Fabrizius. But as to knowing gramary, there's only the bauble you wear on your finger and you yourself say the spell was put on it by another. So come, give me proof and set us free to travel, two things at one stroke as the hunter slew bear and bird."

There was no resource but that Airar must then and there make his enchantment of shaping, though he warned it would not last beyond the twenty-fourth hour. He had to draw his pentagram with dust from behind the bed; when they clasped hands and the blue fires started, he was surprised to find Rogai shaking like a cat half-drowned so that he had to brace the book between the chests of the two of them and even then could barely read it to pronounce the dismissal spell. As Airar was no practised strong magician in any case, he had thought it well to call for the shape of an old woman for himself, and for his companion that of a grizzled peasant; and that was well as might be, since (so inexperienced Rogai) they both fell across the figure at the end and lay prone on the floor when there came a beating at the door.

Airar did not have strength to do more for his life than reach out an arm partly to scuffle the pentagram. Rogai heaved himself up, but stumbled across his companion again as door came inward followed by an archer with a brutal red face and a bare shortsword in his hand; behind him the monitor of the fur-market guest house, wringing his hands.

"Arrgh," said the first intruder. "Fool, why didn't you say you had nothing here but an old couple swiving it past their age?" and fetching the monitor a clout, banged the door to again with a final glance of disgust at Airar in his woman's form.

"I cry your grace," said Airar, as Rogai gathered strength enough to help him to the bed. "I had truly not thought the urgency of a search so close."

"Nor I neither." The honest, grizzled peasant face was set with a frown. "There must be famous tidings to make the Red Baron do this. The merchants from the Twelve Cities will not like it—nor hesitate to say so, neither. It speaks sharp danger to our enterprise." He looked down. "Nor can I in this guise go forth for tidings."

Still there was now no question but they must leave Naaros with the day, and after they had talked a little on this and that, Rogai praising his companion for the prince of clerks and wizards, they went to bed, Airar too weary for real sleep. They took the road at dawn as intentioned, Rogai mounting Airar on a donkey while he kept the horse on which he had come, riding somewhat awkwardly as he found muscle would not obey thought with a young man's speed.

At the city gate the guard was double but gave them not a second glance, and Rogai laughed as the donkey stamped across the bridge, pulling rein to say to the seeming beldam beside him that the Vulkings, wondrous race! thought none but themselves could make a millstone look like a circle-cheese. But Airar, still muzzy with the backlash of his spell-working, only grunted as they took the coast road round the foot of Spanhävid mountain into the early sunlight, both chilly and Rogai a little impatient.

It was neither market day nor market season, so they could have expected to meet few; and as a fact encountered almost none, only a shaggy highland farmer with a cart full of beechnuts for the nut-butter that makes Naaros famous. Of outgoers there was a South Mariolan shepherd in his long coat and curled cap, who rode past with his dog behind him, giving them the somewhat surly good-day of those people, who like to keep to themselves. A rabbit came out to look at them, but it scuttled away when the horse kicked a pebble; and that was the only sign of life by land save for the two passengers. It was almost as though some inkling of the Naaros governor's anger or coming disturbances had run surreptitious through the land to keep men and mice alike home-abiding; there was no sound but the beat of the cold blue sea, rimmed with white along the tumbling rocks below and to right, with the scream of an occasional gull—no sight but that and the trees, mixed beech and pine climbing the fronts and draws of Spanhävid to the left, outlining against the sky on some shoulder.

Once and again Rogai burst out with a remark: "Vard's a fool, but dangerous with his talk of reason, reason. D'ye mark how they all tailed to his kite when he spoke about the Empire being so precious? 'Twas he who made the trouble far more than that stinking fisher till Sir Ludomir had to compose all. He thinks wars are made by a decision of judges sitting all in a row on otter-skin."

Or it would be: "Would I knew what set the red dog barking. Whad'ye think, Airar, could your old he-witch have played false?"

Little enough he got out of Airar so weary, who knew nothing of these matters anyway; and they ate cold at noon, where a brook came down sharply from the shoulder of the mountain over stones, bread and

meat from Rogai's saddle-bag. He stood up with an
air of decision when the meal was over. "That nag
of yours," said he, "is something less than a racer,
but you must push her. We have a long journey to
the nearest inn and it's well to remember how sea-
demons beset this road by night."

Airar was willing enough to make speed, but it was
another matter with the donkey, and in any case easy,
with the languor he felt, to lose attention where it
must be kept constantly or the animal would fall barely
to moving while the traveller watched an occasional
gull or the changing shape of the mountain, and his
mind wandered into daydream of what he would do
in the fighting to come, remembering sword-stroke and
bow-pull as taught (keep the left thumb down), wondering whether the tilting he had done astride the old
horse Pil at apples hanging from the boughs would fit
him to use a lance in battle—with a little practice,
naturally—but it was only a matter of keeping the
target-point on a line between spearhead and the
horse's ear, as Sumarbo Bukson of Ivigsted had said
when they tried it together, shouting through the or-
chard in the summer afternoon, and Aslar, the dark-
haired girl, said, "Now I will give you a kiss for a
trophy," but he had thought that only true love should
accept—

"In truth, you work ill," came Rogai's voice. "Were
you the very king of the clerks I would not suffer
it so—not merely to dawdle on the way but even stop,
when there is special need for haste. I'll never be
fingered by sea-demons, my life rather. Oh, aye, you
doubtless feel venturesome; but never pause to think
that I'm a leader, with other men's lives and the cause
itself in some sort hanging from mine."

Airar woke as from sleep to find they were at the
depth of a long swing of bay with mountain going up
sharp to darken the road leftward, while to the right
it went down in tangled rocks to the windless water
where fishing boats lay with nets out and sails in heaps
of red and yellow on their decks. The afternoon had
run well on. "It is my fault," he croaked in his old-
woman voice, "but—"

"So much is clear." Rogai gave an exasperated snort and jerked his bridle so the horse pranced. "Now harkee, young Airar; I will ride round that next turn at my own pace, and wait a reasonable moment. If you come not, then make your way as best you can with your powers over grim things to that inn which is called The Star of Carrhoene."

He whirled and spurred his horse to a trot; little jets of dust leaped up where its feet tapped the road and Airar felt ill-used. Whose fault was it that here he was travelling while in a state fit only for rest but that same Rogai who would hear of nothing but that he must make a magic, and now grew angry with the result? From all he had learned those sea-demons were no such ghastly cattle; more like mischievous vermin. The temptation to let Rogai ride on then held for a moment, was put down, and Airar angrily clapped his heels for speed against the side of his ungainly steed, which laid back its ears, but moved.

His legs began to feel numb.

He had done the shape-changing enchantment not more than three times in his life before, one of those by accident while he was learning, but he knew what this meant: the spell was coming off.

He leaned forward and gripped the donkey around the neck with both arms as the numbness crept up his body, trying to keep it going. Unfortunately the beast was intelligent, and he was aware of it veering to crop a clump of winter-blooming hazel by the roadside. As Airar went swooning, he could no more than half-credit that he heard whoops of "Yare!" and saw men starting from both beside and ahead, where they had lain concealed among the rocks. His comfort was that Rogai must feel the same and would be in the road from his horse's back if he held his pace. Then two of the dream-men, very hairy, gripped the donkey's bridle, and some sort of blanket, stinking hideously of fish, was clapped over its rider's head.

"That's clerk for sure," cried one. "See how un changed look," and Airar was pulled to the roadway. He struggled, the job was being inexpertly done with a kind of rough gentleness that another time might have let him break free to run, but now so weak he could not. "No harm, master," said someone; he was hoisted by four and with a growing sense of ignominy carried arm and leg across the road and down a slope, where they bumped his behind most cruelly on a rock, and so to the shore.

"No harm, master," repeated the spokesman and whipped off the blanket, which had never been more than half on. "You witness now how we don't hurt you or that other one, and don't put nothing on me for it."

Airar spat a fish-scale from his mouth, grimaced, tried to stand up and was helped, but they held his arms. "Why do you take me?" he cried. "I'll not serve Fabrizius." (For he could think of nothing but some trick of that mewling scoundrel to get him to sea as had been wished.)

"That may be as may be," said the other and shook a beardy head, "but we don't take none for Lord Fabrizius or other lords, specially not that wear that." He touched Airar's hand, and looking down, the heir of Trangsted saw that through his own spell or other means Meliboë's ring had become plain iron. "We be free-fishers, and master-fisher he wants seeing you. Now you just get into the boat."

Mind all clear now but muscles like dry grass, Airar looked round at faces turned toward him with a kind of respectful wonder, and reflected on what education will do for a man. He grinned. "I suppose I must," he said and accepted the help of one of the holders to get into the shallop at the edge of the rocks.

6. The Iulia:
First Tale of the Well

"DOWN THERE," SAID THE HAIRY MAN,
pointing to a hole from which came up a smell afront-
ing to a countryman, though Airar had not imagined
the boat so neat a-decks or so compact below; she
was of the type called iulia. There was a passage with
a door that stood open and a table visible beyond it
by the light through a small window at the stern.
Airar entered to find himself, as now fully expected,
facing Rudr the free-fisher, who got up from a bench,
touched hands, and motioned to a seat opposite.

"Make yourself welcome, master clerk," said he,
but Airar:

"Prisoners are welcome always, it's said, to the cap-
tor."

A movement crossed the face of the master-fisher, anger or what one could say not. "You just call it prisoner if you like, but you'll come round to see how we saved life. They Mariupol coggers, they have their mouths open all the time like carp, and they'll just learn (*whuff*) how a man can't do that with old Count hearing. Unreasonable he's called and unreasonable he is, but not silly. That's why I'll have none of this misborn rising, nor let you neither. (*Gruff.*)"

"My deepest gratitude," said Airar, doing his best to make the tone ironic. "It is much to do for a stranger."

Rudr's eyes rolled to a point over Airar's head, he stepped to the door, and in a voice of remarkable volume shouted, "Tholing! Powry! Sweeps and up anchor!" The remainder of the conversation was punctuated with rhythmic thumps and Airar could feel the vessel moving; Rudr sat down and said:

"We free-fishers say that to blow on one, wind must blow on all. (*Mmf.*) Aye. . . . Fair enough, we want somewhat from you; that is, dealing with the sea-demons that plague us. Doctor Meliboë, he's been our man for that, but not so like to be trusted now after what you do say two nights gone and this Mariupol rising. (*Puff.*) You just do this for us, and will lose nought by 't direct besides being clear of this forebedamned rising. There's the thing, straight out as with free-fishers ever. What say you?"

The thought coursed through Airar's mind that this free-fisher had been something less than straight out when he gave quite another reason for not joining the revolt the other night. He said:

"Why, I say shame on any that can see the Wingèd Wolf up with the blades below and not have a part."

"(*Whuff.*) Aye, a deal to say. We have young men like you in our islands, that will fish for the whale-fish in wind and ice, and then I must tell their dandy-girls they're drownded. Have you a dandy-girl to yourself-ward?"

"Not I."

"(*Grmff.*) See to it, now. You have the air of a lucky man and lucky men should have care, which is the making of them. Only those fully selfish can afford to be brave."

To Airar this seemed a silly argument, but he had no answer and merely sat waiting while Rudr stared at him, puffing his lips and blowing through them alternately.

"Aye," he said at length. "Well, I'll not try to talk you out. We free-fishers say a man should keep his own thoughts and damn the world and Emperor Auraris. Small use trying to force you clerk-fellows anywise, that can just say whiff, whoof, done, and catch us with spells like a lobster in a pot. (*Wmff.*) But I'll just offer you fair bargain, one man to another, even be't you don't believe I can vantage you; for I'm an old man that has seen kings pass, and know this Mariupol affair is under an ill star, so it's your life to be out of it. Stand our aid in this matter of the sea-demons till the moon turns green again, which cannot take much time from your war if war there verily be. At that time's end I shall set you ashore where you choose with a band of fifty of my men fully armed, yours to command, with Erb the Lank to rule them. What say you now?"

"That there is a somewhat marvellous change of spirit in this. A moment since and Mariupol was too hopeless to be worth one man, but now you throw fifty into the fire."

"Aye. (*Whuff, whuff.*) I said you were a lucky man and say it still. Have no doubt that when Mariupol bumps, old Duke Roger will be up with a banner for fighting men to follow." He stirred in his seat and Airar was astounded to catch something like a tear on that shaggy old cheek. "Our land—our sea—they stink while Dalarna must bear the weight of the Mountain. Never lift it, nah, with guildsmen and folderol sword-dancers from south; and my people here bear all the undertow and misery when Mariupol cracks, for it's just the fear of revolt, not the thing, that keeps Count Vulk in some kind of bound. But old Count, he'll not dare to go too far while we have a gage with Duke Roger, lest all free-fishers join in. Fifty men to save the rest—save the rest—"

His voice fell off into mumbling and Airar rolled the idea over and over in his mind like a morsel of spiced meat around the tongue and could find no taste but that of honest flesh, with maybe that faint overlying tang at the memory of how Rudr had given a reason, insincere before the assembly of the Iron Ring. Yet captain of fifty! He thought enough of himself to believe he would be a good leader and it ate up all but the last of his country caution, so that he knew his face betrayed him as he said:

"Why me?" and recalled how he had last used that phrase with Meliboë the enchanter.

Outside there were shouts; the iulia began to swing gently as it came from the shelter of the bay into the swell of open sea, and the master-fisher blinked three times like a man coming out of daydream, then turned toward Airar an expression so broad that it could be called a grin. "Because you are not of us, young master. Matter of fishing ground or boat-building, all's well while we free-fishers hold our old custom of every man his say, but not when the wands are set for battle, nah, and free-fishers would no more be ruled by one no better than themselves than would your Vastmanstad farmers. Your task, young man, is to make yourself their master by knowing more than all." He stood up, bracing to the sway of the craft, produced from a cabinet behind him a black bottle and two pewter mugs. "We are at one, then. The Ring!" He lifted the mug, and Airar stood up to drink with him.

These fisher-people, as Airar met them, were not too different from his own; perhaps seeming somewhat less guest-given and more sparing of words, or that could have been because they looked up to him for his clerkship, which had never been the case at home, where they had few bogies of any kind and many who could work the simple spells. Or it may have been that the sea-motion made him queasy so that he himself was not so brilliant as other times. A handful of land breeze was coming off the mountains; not enough fully to drive the little ship or her sisters, but Airar was taken with their beauty as they rocked slowly up and down like stately ladies in their bright dresses of canvas, the crown-sails serving as bodices.

Toward sundown and Spanhävid now only a darker blue at the bottom of the cold blue sky, the wind began to rise and the ladies turned to dowagers with bodices and buttocks of sail swelling wide. Lights were put out; Airar was glad to go below and lean on a bench before a fire on a roundstone, while to do him honor, the fishers produced some of the sweet wine they import from the Twelve Cities, mulled with a hot iron; with which warmed, one presently began to talk of this and that and on Airar's questions how the fishers came by their peculiar charter of freedom.

—A heritage from the Silver Years (said one, and nobody denied it) when Argentarius was King, before the House called itself golden or imperial. That would be in the time when the heathen were still in the land, and of all Dalarna the King had rule of Mariola and Vastmanstad—no more, with the seventh Vulk in his hold of Briella brave as eagles against them and he and the men of the northerly provinces there good friends. This Argentarius was a stout soldier, we were not here else—no man to drink at the Well! Put down the heathen with the iron arm, un did, and won all Skogalang from them, but there's to be said that a's doing was touched with misfortune, win a battle and lose another when a's back was turned. Of those days Stavorna now was just a free city, ruled of three old syndics, Astli, Bekar, and who would be the third? —Derrivont, that's the name. They were the wisest men in Korsor and maybe in all Dalarna; but of them Astli was clearly wisest, so un could understand the speech of birds singing in trees. King Argentarius was mighty advised to bring un to Stassia for adviser in the great court there, but Astli would not; and in an extremity of the wars Argentarius a'self went there to Stavorna to consult him, which is a great wonder with him a crowned king.

"I think that I know this story," said Airar. "In Vastmanstad we are early told the tales of the House and the Well."

—No, no, not as we know it, who saw it all, they

cried. Only hear; and the narrator took up his voice again.—This Astli lived in a house not too great and close by city gate. Un greeted old King well, but like any commoner come to seek an advice, and had nuts and wine set out as un talked. Argentarius put out the case fully before him, holding nothing back—how when un took a town on Skogalang border, the heathen would make a descent into the Whiteriverdales or maybe un be called from a campaign half-finished to deal with pirate seamen of the Twelve Cities. At finish this sage gave one of they long long side glances and said:—There's a cure for all. It's a hard journey thither, but I have heard it said that if a crowned king drinks from Unicorn's Well in the acceptable hour, a's realm shall have peace as long as they both last.—But what manner peace? snaps Argentarius: Could I call it peace while half Dalarna that was my grandfather's realm lies under the dirty heathen and pays the demanded tribute of young girls?—And how is that worse, asked old Astli, than the tribute you now take of young men to die in battles that never have an end? Men accustom themselves to many things, he said, and the clear promise of the Well is that you shall sit in contentment to the end of your days. —Then that end will be soon rather than late, says the King; for I'll sit in no contentment while Dalarna's under the yoke. I did not come here to be told what I know already.—Yet you lack the force to better things, both as to men and leaders, said Astli. Well, well, then I can devise you only to form alliance with your neighbor Damastétil of Scroby, who can bring to the field fifty barons, each with a train of lances and men-at-arms, not to mention a's captain Earl Mikal, who is as good a head for battle as yourself and would be a brother behind your back.

—I have tried; he wants my heart's blood, said Argentarius, and looked at the floor without need to add more, since the whole reason Astli had brought up the matter was that un knew Damastétil's price of alliance was a marriage with his only child, Kry, not young and no beauty neither, being dark-avised with black hair, which made her always look as though she had

failed to wash, a leaving from her mother, who was a
princess of Uravedu. Earl Mikal was said to be in
love with her; why, none say, but it is likely true, since
an approved captain would not have stayed at that
court else. Old Duke Damastétil was a little silly in
those days, and thought of nothing but his daughter
and the marriage she should make, royal at least,
since she was a's heiress; had rejected Mikal in special and many more for her hand, though in all else
he bowed to her. There was never a council when she
did not sit beside him and un smiling say at the end
of presentation—And how thinks my little princess?

Both men knew it; still the sage said nothing and
Argentarius after a minute ground out:—Giving a
word is keeping it and marriage the summation of
love or so my father taught me.—I have heard you
were thinking of the people, replied Astli, whereat
King Argentarius left him without no, another word,
but sent him gifts later, which was considered kingly;
and Tholo Longchin went to make a's suit before
Duke Damastétil for the hand of Kry. It is not in the
story as most people hear it that as King Argentarius
half stumbled from the syndic's room un charged into
a girl who was bringing in a renewal of the wine they
were drinking; bore it to the floor. As un was the most
courteous of kings, un made an apology and helped
as best possible to clear the mess and so doing saw
that she was fair-haired, tall and lovely; Astli's own
daughter to wit, named Lanheira. There is no lack of
girls of such beauty in Dalarna; it could be that it was
merely from thinking on the short, dark, and bandy-
legged Kry that the king's eye fell on Lanheira.

His hand touched hers as he bent to take some of
those things from the floor and in the moment it was
as though poison and burning flame ran through his
veins; but of that, nothing at the time and he went on
to the espousal of Kry. He would not take her to drink
at the Well of the Unicorn on marriage as was the
custom then with the Stassian kings, holding that it
would make him the less a warrior. You may think
you know the story of the House, young clerk, but we
here in the Isles of Gentebbi know it better, for Queen

Kry came here to await her term, living in that old house behind the hill at Vagai. Like all of Uravedu blood, she had something of witchcraft. She was a short woman and few-spoken, who used to be seen on the beach at night. It was said that she talked with the fishes and certainly blue lights blazed round the place, which all thought little canny. This was after Argentarius had lain with her for the perpetuation of the House, you will understand, and she was somewhat changed; masterful still, but altogether after another fashion, so that where she once ruled Scroby in her father's name she now ruled the household at Vagai, inquiring whether two copper ainar or one had been laid out for a cabbage, and forever setting the people to beautify the house with new trees and pleasaunces. Men were happy in Gentebbi in those days; she was open-handed and kindly in spite of her weird doings, waiting for the King.

It would be a week from the time when the last heathen were tumbled down the cliff at Lectis Maxima, not later, that King Argentarius set his feet to Stavorna again and the house of Astli. At the gate the first person he met was Lanheira, she leaning over as though she had only that moment come out from putting away the tray of wine-vessels he had spilled, even the dress the same, which was perhaps foreknowledge of his coming on her part, and shows that even a king cannot match a woman for wit when she has a desire. —You are welcome, said she; it is three years since we have seen each other.—It is too long, said he, and went in to see the syndic.

When they were together:—Is there no day, said the King, when duty runs out? Have I escaped the one debt only by making another? Astli answered nothing for the moment, but sat musing and drinking from his cup of sweet wine till—Vagai is well situate on the Blue Sea between Stassia and Dalarna to be the capital for both; a place of much beauty where two drinkers from the Well might be at peace.

—What manner peace? cried Argentarius as he had at the last interview. With the witchwoman there is no peace but an I give her what is no longer mine to give, which is the love of my heart. Seeing that the old man still said nothing, he cried again after a minute:—Is there alternate choice as the last time?—We grow by always solving the harder problems, said Astli, but I cannot tell you that. You can perhaps tell yourself when you have decided whether you're more king or man.—One may lay down a kingship, flashed Argentarius; Earl Mikal—and then as he saw Astli smile:—No, you are right, he would be in all things her man, and I not the only one to suffer. Is there nothing clean in the world? Astli the syndic still made no answer and he left; but when he went down to Lectis Minima he took Lanheira with him.

Those two dwelt there in great glee and affection for the better part of a year, and she bore him a son who was called Morkar; but at the end of that time there were tidings that Permandos had fallen on a war with Baboi and the ships of both sides pirating those of the two kingdoms to furnish means for their battle. Argentarius struck fast, as always; sailing at once with such portions of his guard as were then beside him and leaving word for the Stassia barons to meet him on the sea. Lanheira was to follow, meeting him at the High House in Stassia when the campaign was over, and Queen Kry was fully aware of this, since the shipmasters of Gentebbi were to furnish bottoms to carry Mariola to the war. She gathered certain retainers of her own, mostly blue-faced men of Uravedu, and put to sea when Lanheira's ship was due. It might be by her magical arts that she discovered when to meet that ship off the skerries of Naarmouth, and there an evil deed was done, for she let slay all in the ship save Lanheira and her son, whom they cast into the sea, then putting about, told a tale of Permandos pirates so that the matter might be blamed on them already at war with the King.

The skerries of Naarmouth are the best of fishing grounds. It happened that certain of our Vagai men found the drifting ship with its dead men and something bright farther on, which was Lanheira, who had contrived to keep herself afloat and the babe wrapped in her cloak. It was the edge of winter and she died of it, but not before they had the full tale out of her. They say that when King Argentarius heard it, he spoke to no man save to give orders till he came to Vagai and set up a seat of justice in the square. Then he only asked the Queen why she had done so foul a thing.—You that were indifferent to my love, she said, shall not be to my hate. It is a good hate; you that would not drink at the Well with me shall have kings and emperors spring from your line, but all hollow, all drinking and drinking to a peace they never win and a glory that is not theirs. But as for these fishers that have betrayed me after my kindliness, they shall know the laughing fear at the hands of sea-demons.

They let her arrange her hair and then they cut her throat; but to us free-fishers Argentarius confirmed forever a charter of privileges. Earl Mikal withdrew from the court and went to build him a castle at the edge of the Micton country; from him is sprung the line of Os Erigu. And this is a true and veritable tale as told to me by my own grandfather, Gyior the Grey.

"And Morkar?" asked Airar.

"Oh, that was a bad line. Un and a's son both were hanged entirely as pirates by the merchants of Lothai in Aurunculeius' reign. Let us go a-deck; from the shouts there Vagai must approach."

7. The Iulia Once More:
Gifts Are Given

THE MOON WAS UP; THEY WERE SLIDING through the entrance to the harbor, over which Vagai Front towered like a sphinx asleep, with its paws extended on either flank, and the water inside still almost to lack ripples, so the fishers were getting out their sweeps. The pale light fell on the fronts of the houses rising steeply behind the quay and gave them a two-dimensional aspect, or as though that drowsing sphinx were wearing a bib. "Behind the hill there," the narrator motioned. "Nobody lives in the place now."

Airar did not answer; was beginning to feel more his own man now with the backlash of the spell wearing away, but lateness and the translation from warm cockpit to cold deck made him yawn. The sweeps rattled, the men had the crown-sails down, and on the quay he caught sight of several who waited, the return of the fishers, standing perfectly immobile, not talking to each other, the tricky moonlight shortening them to figures of children.

He pointed and turned to speak; at the same moment Rudr's eye caught them, too, and "Seademons!" he shouted. "Port helm, sweep out! Sweep out!"

Airar heard the steersman grunt as he flung himself on the tiller and a babble of voices from the crew as they dropped the sail, then all those little figures were off the dock, into the water, coming toward them with heads held high and almost rippleless wakes behind. He felt for his grimoire; it was in his donkey-pack and below. A hatch banged, someone yelled frantic, "No, no, let me in," and one of the creatures came swarming right up a trailing sweep, flinging out a pair of short arms as it leaped toward the unfortunate man who had begged to be let in.

The fellow tried to run; the shape was faster and it gripped him at the break of the forecastle, the fisher gave a great whooping yell of mad laughter that slid into a shriek and took up again. "Come," called Rudr's voice from the cabin, but Airar snatched instead a fish-spear from the rack around the mast as the second sea-demon came over the bulwarks at him. He caught a glimpse of a long low dark wet forehead like a seal's with a pair of burning eyes, of arms outspread with webby hands at the ends of them, and drove the fish-spear at the apparition, shouting (for it was all he could remember) —"Ia ada; ada perdidi! Aulne begone!"

The short arms missed their clutch and Airar drove his spear into the thing's throat, but the hands caught his elbow for a moment and he felt through every fiber of his being a rush of such deadly terror as he had never known while the muscles round his mouth flexed in a horrid rictus. The motion with which he dragged the barbed spear back was less than voluntary; there was a spout of cold black blood all over him and the thing collapsed.

Airar looked around. The sea-demons seemed to be gone, no sign of them now save the little group of ships drifting masterless in the moonlight, their yards akimbo and hanging with sails half taken in. On the forecastle of the iulia that fisher was clutching the mast, his feet beating in a mad dance as he gave peal after peal of laughter which always ended in a scream of fear. From one of the other ships a similar series of shrieks was coming like an echo; Airar saw the madman over there in a high-footed prancing leap across the deck and into the water that cut short his yells. The one forward on the iulia released his hold as a freak of the fit took him, and began to caper toward the bulwark.

Airar jumped for him, all covered with the demon's black blood as he was, hearing only with the memory part of his mind old Rudr's voice from the now half-opened hatch, "No, no, let him be, it is better so." At the very rail Airar caught the man round from behind; could feel how the fisher's muscles were all tied in heaving knots; but he was strong, so the young man had to get an arm round his neck and even then a convulsive movement jerked it into a stifling hold across nose and mouth before he suddenly went all limp and passive—Have I strangled him? (thought Airar) and let him down to the deck.

No; for even in the uncertain light could be made out the movement of hairs round a young mouth with an overcoating of demon's blood already beginning to stink. The eyes were closed.

" 'Tis Visto," said someone behind and Airar looked up over his shoulder, crying for water in a temper thoroughly foul with these men who had so deserted a companion. Rudr's voice came from the background, ordering his people sharp to the sweeps and as the vessel turned so the moonshade fell across the little group on the deck, Airar turned to face him.

"Little use, young master," said the chief fisher,

gently. "We have tried to save those before that were fingered, and always they go numb and die . . . though it is main marvellous you have slain one of these cattle. It has not been so done in the Isles of Gentebbi since King Aurunculeius' day."

Airar felt his anger leave him a little at the sadness in the old man's tone. "Under your permission" (not holding the bite altogether from his voice) "I will still try making him and myself a trifle clean." He sloshed water on his soiled clothes and double-cupped his hands to throw more in Visto's face. The man gave two long rasping breaths, his eyes fluttered, there were a couple of barks of laughter at the edge of hysteria that were cut off with a heave as though he were about to be sick. Airar flung an arm around him and got him to a position partly kneeling. He was sick; the iulia bumped the quay and Airar felt him relax and shiver against his arm.

"Numb and dying?" cried the son of Alvar. "The man's merely cold. A cloak, someone." Before it was brought or anything else, Visto lifted his two palms to his eyes, dropped them, and staggering to foot, proved Airar right with a shiver of chill unmistakable. "I—I'm sound," he said slowly, "fingered but sound," and turned, feeling himself down the flanks as though the sensation of his own body were new.

They started up the steep cobbled streets of the town with the moon shining whitely still on the housefronts where they ran round the bay like the seats of an amphitheater. Not a window was opened nor a toot abroad save those of their own procession led by Visto, with Airar's arm around him and on the other side a black-bearded man—Airar thought it might be the same who had slammed the hatch. Behind there was a murmur of sailor's soft shoes on the stones and an occasional word. At a house Rudr stepped past the leaders and double-knocked; then after a moment's wait, again. The door creaked open to show a girl with one of those boat-lamps from the Twelve Cities in her hand, smelling of fish-oil. She had a combination of snow-blonde hair with dark lashes and black eyes below.

A few moments later they were seated on stools and straw round a fireplace, to wit: Rudr, Airar, Visto, the black-bearded man and another Airar did not know with a long body and Adam's apple that ran up and down. From his size he might be Erb the Lank. The girl brought mead; she was Rudr's daughter, Gython, with whom Airar touched hands, she shy, he not less than bold, for after his victory over the sea-demon he felt strong to battle kings and giants and Rudr was praising him to the company as the warlock of the world.

Yet something was due to mere honesty and Airar could see himself asked to repeat the feat. "No such matter of enchantment, neither," said he. "I did but put a fish-spear through its neck, and it fell down dead."

"Yet you had not the laughing fear, nah," said Rudr. "Man! I heard you shouting words of enchantment in old heathen tongues."

"What says I had it not when that thing gripped my arm?" flashed Airar, shuddering. "It was like all the bogies out of hell till—" He stopped suddenly, mouth open midway the word.

"Till what, say?"

"The enchantment! No enchantment whatever. When the blood of that monster fell on me I was cured and Visto here likewise, for I was all besmuttered with it when I leaned over him. Look, Master Rudr, here's your remedy—" out of the tail of his eye Airar saw Visto's head swing agreement like an apple tree in wind—"let any who be afflicted more by the touch of these demons but use the blood of a dead one as their sovran specific, for 'tis so of all demon-dogs whatever, that the evil they work can be destroyed by their death. Such black spells are a thing so unnatural and against the order of the universe that they must be constantly upheld by those who work them. I did but cry the words of protection that are a help to those beset by witchcrafts; but now you shall tell your people that Queen Kry's curse is overcome."

Rudr drank from his mead. "Aye; and Baron Vanette-Millepigue will send us all sugar-cossets to celebrate his birthday. You be too simple by half, younker. Who's to bleed these grimmish things for their juice, or will they give it down like a cow milk?"

Airar burst out on him that it was a matter of captaincy and finding men who could use a bow well enough to slay one or two of the creatures from a distance—"for after you have so little of this drug none need fear them more," but Rudr snorted on that and Erb the Lank broke in to say that the free-fishers were not much given to bowshot whether for chase or defense, being born to the use of the hand-spear. Whereupon all began together and with so many references to this man or that even of which Alvarson knew nothing that he fell on a silence.

Over against him the girl Gython was sitting on her heels, blue dress in a circle round her, and the flickering firelight on her pale hair gave her a likeness to a lovely flower. Mostly she was watching young Visto, and Airar thought it would be dear to have her look at him like that; but presently her eye came up to catch his own and though the glance was quick withdrawn and the dim illumination left all uncertain, he might imagine she flushed. Again, having himself turned to something said by the blackbeard man, he caught out of the corner of his eye a light movement of her head as she glanced at him again. But it was all firelight and imaginings born of weariness and the lateness of the time, whose charm would be lost if one lifted a finger. So presently it was good-night and good-night all, and they went to rest. But when Airar woke with the day it was to find that Visto had spent the night curled in a cloak outside his door.

There was more talk with Rudr in the morning; he would have his spell against sea-demons and naught but the spell, though Airar warned him it would protect but one ship at a time and that perhaps not permanently—"for I'm none of your strong wizards, only a kind of upland spell-caster who was taught by my father and had not thought ever to use it except against certain small trolls that vex us when we spend a night a-woods. Better your people should be taught how to draw a string or throw a twist-spear and so protect themselves."

"Bargain's bargain enough without more chaffer," replied the old man, evenly; "for the fifty I gave you, you can teach them to draw string of bow or lute or hangman's hang for all me. You be captain; but not till work's done. Might hap too, you could teach my lads a spell or other for themselves."

The end of this, of course, was that Airar must take his book forthwith down to the iulia and make what could be made. He got them all out of the hold with some difficulty (for they were curious and pleaded Doctor Meliboë had never used them so), and set up his pentacle on the roundstone where the fire had been, night agone. As soon as the first words of power were repeated Airar could feel how the whole ship stank of old magics, stronger and more deadly than any he knew. They tore at his throat and entrails as though he had swallowed a new-born dragon-pup; he was not sure he could hold them and sore tempted to dismiss —might have done so but for the half-formed thought he would never get away from here to Rogai, it was carry this through or back to Naaros and be Fabrizius' retainer.

He lifted the spell to the second stage then and they came all round him, yammering horribly just beyond the protective figure, with faces the utmost depths of evil that flavored like soft wax from form to form and always some feature disgustingly bloated or misplaced, promising or threatening to make him cease his runes. The pentacle held tight, but it wrung him through to hear those voices with their high-pitched note like a knife on marblestone that the mind could hardly bear, and when he came to the sobrathim-spell it was all he could do to keep from the yell of anguish that would give them power and him death. Somehow he managed; could feel the protection settling round him and ship in a heavy grey opaque curtain, almost physically visible, with the displaced powers piping and muttering angrily out in the glooms beyond. Sweat came out all over. He could no longer stand, but fainted clean across his figure and must have lain long in that sad state, for when he roused himself to tap on the trap-hatch overhead (having no longer strength to win free by himself), it was to be released on a deck where the sun was bright in nooning.

Airar took this in, with a couple of the fishers sitting by the rail dangling legs as they talked and three or four children squealing over a game of men-at-arms with shells of the king crab for shields; then felt the skin draw tight across his face, and down he went again. The second recovery found him lying in a shut-bed, but it was open, with fair Gython sitting beside it and a bowl of fish-broth in her lap. When she saw him move his head, she offered him from a horn spoon. It was spiced and hot; he gave her thanks and asked for her father.

"Gone." She looked down. "It is no matter. I lost wit, too, the year the quartern fevers came on me. Have you the swaying sickness?"

"No sickness I. It is what comes with the working of magics."

"Meliboë the enchanter always used to make prepare a glass of hot aquaviva for him when he had been casting spells. He put one on a little ape that Erb brought me from the Spice Isles, so it became tame to my hand, but it died."

"Where is this Erb?—Or no: when I try to move my bones hurt. I'll do no more today."

"That is like Meliboë, too. My mother does not like him and when she heard another clerk was coming, she went to visit my aunt over at Linkoffing."

"Would it be the same, think you, if she saw the clerk?"

This time, no doubt; Gython flushed rosy-red. "I—I do not know. My mother's oppositious to all witching, and wars with father on't. She would even have forbade Visto the house when he asked Meliboë to teach him magic. It seems when I was born they called a spae-wife that said an evil should come on me through black sorcery."

"It is somewhat my own case. My father Alvar,

who has astrology, drew a horoscope at my birth and found I should have a great peril necromantic at about this year of my life, which being voided I should find favor under the stars. But before he could cast the horoscope deeper Count Vulk made his decree against all clerkly practices whatever by us Dalecarles, and so as to the nature and hour of the peril I know nothing."

"There are those among our islands who would find the law a light thing to break for a kinsman's life."

"Aye. . . . Are you promised to Visto?"

"No. He is my speech-friend and seat-mate when there are guestings. But now he will follow you to the wars."

"I have no speech-friend nor seat-mate neither. All that might be were taxed out and gone away from our ort years agone."

It was easy for her to flush. "I will sit with you if there is a guesting. It is not just they should unfame you so who only fell on an illness from helping them."

Here was news from nowhere for your Airar and not so pleasant, neither. "Unfame?" he said, struggling to sit upright. "Who's at it and why?"

"Oh—my father, Ové Oxmouth, everyone." She tossed her hands wide so the bowl almost fell. "—That you should be so lightly taken on the road and lose wit over this matter of the spell. They ask a brisker champion for the wars, and some will not go and Visto must quarrel with all, and—"

"And the fiend take them all for mean, ungrateful —your grace, I forgot they were your people."

"Be not angry, I beg. You have right and it is for us to cry grace who have been so niggling after you slew the sea-demon; they mean nothing, but it is but common small talk the more since Erb and Visto are on fire to try your very plan of slaying the creatures by arrow or long-spear." She giggled. "But I am a better bowman than any of them. Will you have more broth?"

"Aye," said Airar with a frown, and then, making his face smooth: "But speech-friends must exchange a gift." He fumbled in his clothes at the back of the lock-bed. "Here, you shall have this small brooch that was my mother's. It is said to be dwarf-work, but I do not believe that."

"And I have naught for you—nay, stay, will you follow our Gentebbi custom and take but a bit of hair from my head? Your knife."

Airar praised that as the best of gifts. "But now you shall tell me of how the fisher-syndic's daughter learned archery and wherefore."

"Oh, no mystery in that. Here in Gentebbi it is the custom for girls to wear in cold weather cloaks lined with ptarmigan down, and I, having no brother, must needs seek my own cloak if I would wear."

"That says why fair enough, but the how?"

—So they talked lightly to and of each other till it began to fall dusky, which Gython observing, with a small squeal rose and cried she must prepare meat for her father who would be back from the fisheries; but Airar lay and closed his eyes, thinking it must have been long indeed that he had been without sense aboard the iulia—that Rudr and his band were over-bearingly unreasonable—yet not altogether regretful for his wasted day.

8. The Isles of Gentebbi:
"It Is Not Fair"

MORNING FOUND YOUNG AIRAR SOMEWHAT recovered, if incompletely his own man yet. The wind had risen during the night and under a grey sky now carried whirls of snow streaming past the windows; from these the ships below in harbor were visible, rocking at dock and anchor, and Rudr, looking forth from his fast-breaking on small beer and oysters, said they would not fish the day—therefore it would be occasion for Airar to disenchant another vessel as he had the iulia. This was flat refused, whereupon the old man fell few-spoken and grumpish, but from his black humor through a day of idleness those with him were saved by the coming of Visto, with Erb and two or three more.

They bore quivers a-shoulder, having come to the idea that exorcising sea-demons by bowmanry in lieu of book might not be altogether worthless; Erb said it was thought that Airar, being from those uplands whose archers are of note, might tell them a trick or two in the use of that weapon.

"The wind's too strong for archery," said Airar. There was a half-snicker from among the group, and Visto lowered, but Lank Erb's face was blank as a cheese as he said that had been thought on. There was a long fish-drying shed at the quay that would give cover and space for their enterprise. Gython went with them, gay and chattering; the air was mortal cold, but plucked Airar's heart and spirits up until they came to the shed in question, when he once more found how the small mice of difficulty can gnaw the foundations of a tall plan. The fish shed not only smelt to turn a landsman's stomach; it was scant of a hundred yards long, no distance at all for bowmen, all cluttered with gear, and there were no butts. Airar was in a mood to abandon all, but not Gython, who laughingly rummaged through the amass with Visto till a pile of old fish-baskets was found and then herself drew the first shaft with them as target.

She hit clap in the clout, but Airar goggled as he saw the first of the men step up; not that his arrow ran somewhat wide, which was a thing expectable, but instead of standing and drawing full to ear, he had come down on one knee, brought his nock only to chest, then pushed out his left or bow-hand, like Gython or any other woman. So now Airar noticed what he would have remarked before had he not been so mazy—to wit, that all their bows were short, like those made from horn by the heathen of Dzik.

"Let see," he begged, and took arch and shaft from Visto to try his own way. The thing had so heavy a draw that it felt like trying to pull down the moon; this made his left hand tremble at the wrong moment, so that his arrow flew off skintling-wise and stuck to the neck in a side beam, whereat someone laughed and another tried to push him aside.

"Stay," said Erb. "The man has an archer-trick and

no question. It turned badly the now, but I think that was because Visto's bow pulls too hard for him. He shall take Gython's and attempt once more."

"Willingly," said Airar. "This curst business of spell-casting makes any man weaker than his sister." This time he lined his feet with care, lifted slowly, and drew with the right snap at the height of the lift. The shaft sped sharp, skimming along the edge of the girl's where it stood, and all but splitting it. From the men there was a murmur of surprised applause; Gython clapped her hands together as Airar turned.

"I have heard they draw a bow that way in the north, at Korsor and Stavorna," said Visto.

"Aye, through all the upland country for that matter," replied Airar. "The hunters that come over the Hogsback from Mariola I have never seen use another fashion. For look you, this short draw of yours and the genuflective posture—it is well enough for hitting small animals of the forest and I suppose of the sea, where the skill lies in stalking so close upon them that any shaft will be deadly. But when you deal with wild boar or bear, not less than life lies on striking them down from far. Still more with the slayings of man or sea-demon."

"But how is your upland draw better?" demanded one. "Continuance not contrivance lifts the 'prentice hand to master."

"But fixity in folly leaves 'prentice 'prentice forever. Look." Airar put a shaft on string and lifted it to his cheek. "You glance along a line; there's naught to do but lift a trifle for distance or allow for windage to one side." He released; the shaft sang into the target side and side with the other pair.

Visto said, "I will just try it," and stepped forward, bow in hand, but he was awkward with his feet and cocked his head over to look along the arrow so that the bowstring clipped him shrewdly behind the ear, arrow flew almost straight up and fell with no force halfway along the shed. All laughed, but it was another kind of laughter than before and Gython said, "Now we shall have no more accidents like that, but you shall show me how to place myself, friend Airar."

He had to reach round her shoulders to place her hands for the long draw. The touch of her body against him was pleasant, and her arrow, though by no means so good as Airar's own, ran true enough to be accounted a good shaft. So now the others in turn must be shown the new manner, and this lesson in bowmanship was followed by all with much merriment and profit till Erb at maybe his third try suddenly caught the hang of it and drew deep to the head. There was a rending crack and his bow split across; the arrow flew wide.

"What's now, young master?" he said, contemplating the two halves dangling from their string. "Where was the fault that cost me a good bow?"

"None I could see but in the bowyer who gave you a weapon too brief for such usage."

"Ah." Erb cocked his head a little aslant and his Adam's apple climbed up and down. "I wondered there might be somewhat like that in't. Now harkee, young friend. I'm heartily beside you in this; it will do our folk no harm to learn a new skill, especially those who are to march under the Wingèd Wolf with you, where the skill may be their saving. But bows that will stand the treatment you give them, have we none in Vagai, nor is this wintry weather fit for cutting wood to make them. I just say wait till some of the ships go over to Naaros or Mariupol and bring back seasoned woods or bows ready fashioned for the purpose, and while we wait, you just make after those sea-demons best you can with your clerkship."

So it sat thus, the whole a trick to force Rudr's will upon him, though Airar as he trudged up the steep street with Gython and Visto, snow blowing thicker round them now, or gathering more than ankle-deep in little drifts against buildings. They two were in a cheerful mood and Gython crowing over the design of a snowflake that caught on the back of her mittened hand. Said Visto when Airar would not be tempted from his glooms: "Come, my friend, a truce to repining. What! You are held the equal of Meliboë and the greatest spell-caster that ever came to Vagai."

"Aye; and unfamed for what comes of casting.

Spells, spells—who ever heard of a golden name that was gained through bugs and bogies?"

Gython bent to look from behind Visto's face. "There's this same Doctor Meliboë. All men think well of him, and has a heart of gold, how kindly he has kept sea-demons from us these years."

"Heart of lead." They had reached the door and stood between its pillars. "He downed and daunted your sea-demons only by conjuring up things more horrible, which in a sense they feed upon as soon as they become familiar, returning after each ejection stronger than before." Airar gestured with both hands. "His curings are like a siren-song, of which one must have forever more, yet have but one end, which is death; and nigh mine he had."

"Crave grace." Young Visto touched his hand. "If I may offer service—"

"Nay, no matter. Naught to do now but stew it through, with this lack of bows and all."

He followed Gython through the door to find Rudr sharp enough because his noon meal was unready, and little wishful to see her so blamed, tried to distract the old man with talk of magic, sea-demons, and the other ships of the fleet. The end of that converse might have been foretold—out came the story of Meliboë the enchanter's double-dealing which Airar himself had hardly realized till he began to talk on it, with the foul things the magician had put aboard the vessels. Now Airar found himself pressed into promising that he would lay protections on all the skonär-ships of the fleet as he had on Rudr's own iulia. The prospect was little pleasing; nor were matters helped any by the arrival during the afternoon of a woman with a lined severe countenance and a tongue that seemed to wag double, who said that her house was overrun with a plague of rats and would have Airar give her a spell to drive them out. The more he tried to put her off, the longer she talked and louder; to keep her quiet he finally inscribed a bit of parchment with certain names of ill omen, as *Angat, Huard, Utesitorion,* with a picture of the unhappy bergamot-flower, telling her to soak it at midnight in the fat of a hog and leave it in a fall-trap.

When she had gone Gython made a face and ran out her tongue, but the master-fisher, in good humor, laughed on Airar's countenance of disgust. "Just see now," he said, "why Erb the Lank's all for wars."

"His wife?" asked Airar.

"Sister. She'll never let un have nor wife nor leman. Eh-ah, boff, many kinds make a world, and we've seen that kind oft before—want you to gut every fish in your cargo at market and then buy a sprat. Women do be so, even of a man's own house. Now my girl Gython here, she's just after me in this archer-affair of yours, no worse nor better than Dame Ervila, and I must promise to send a ship to Mariupol for bow-staves."

"Not Naaros?"

"A piece too much of gate-close and house-search there now. Red Baron's like to come smelling round Vagai if he found us buying war gear, and no mind in me to test the strength of our charter against him."

The next morning came frosty and clear. Airar went down early to the harbor with Rudr, and all the fleet put out but one of the skonäre on which there had been especial trouble of men fingered by sea-demons. The task was hideous bad, only a little less so than that of the iulia before, but now he had some skill born of experience and drove off with far more readiness the gibbering shapes that crowded round his figures. Neither did he fall altogether senseless when the grey wall of his protection rose; but that was slight assistance, for at the end his muscles seemed to melt, he fell to the deck and lay for a long time like a drunken man, mind perfectly clear but quite blank, unable to form any thoughts of his own, accepting the splash of water against the planks and the occasional footfall overhead as soft clay takes an impress. Some of the skonära's people were moved to come a-hunting him in spite of the strict word he had given contrary. He would not speak, and when they haled him up the hatch the light hurt his eyes so much he closed them and thus overheard the babble of his bearers.

"Shall we take this flabbid veal off and give it to Gython or hold un here till recovery?" said one.

"Oh, take un on, we'll none of un aboard," another.

"Did you go to a's archery business, Sewald?"

"Aye. Mind the leg there. Pretty enough with the maid's bow, but could not draw Visto's."

"There's one that draws the ill lot here—with the maid, and Rudr so anxious to wife his daughter among the mainland magicians. If maid she still be."

"You talk like a running stink-pool, Ové. What! Would you not give a thousand solvars to lift Queen Kry's curse after seeing your brother fingered? Never heard of the girl, maid or no maid, worth more."

(Ové; that would be Ové Ox-mouth, the blubber-lipped lad who cast eyes on Gython at the time of the bow practice, and tried to draw close to her. But she would touch him not at all, no more than a slug.)

"And you bark like a seal in heat. Let old Rudr do what he will with a's woman-cattle. 'Tis this matter of fifty that cramps my guzzle. As well call in the sea-demons and make them members of Vagai. There have not been fifty fingered in ten years."

"Oh, as for that, old master's sharp. Knows that once he gets his magic-man in bed with the wench, war's forgot."

"Aye, well forgot. What need we for wars, with our free-fishers' charter and fifty leagues of sea between us and Naaros?"

There was a week of the work and Airar misliking it more as he went on, though never again so heavily beset with shapings as on that first day he threw his protection round the iulia, and coming to recognize what forms the conjurings were like to take and what attack make on his pentacle. There came a certain pleasure indeed in countering their approach, like that of driving shaft clean into a bounding deer on the rise of his spring; though he had to pay for it each time after with an hour or two lying supine, sometimes conscious of what went on about him, sometimes not, with feebleness all the next day so that he seemed to live in sharp passage between sun and shadow.

Gython was piteous kind to him that day of the first skonära, though he was somewhat unresponsive to her gay chatter, wondering whether Rudr meant in fact to set them together and how it would be to live and love with such a one. The thought sent singular tremors, not altogether unpleasant, running the line of his backbone; for the moment he abandoned himself to it, and it was not till another day and a fuller recovery from his befuddlements that he reached considering what would be the price of this lovely and generous girl—to live forever among the small concerns of these free-fishers, making spells against rats, ill spoken of by all but women. Or could he, perchance, win her from there, once the primary step were gained—if she willed, if she was not bound to Visto by something more holding than formal bethrothal?

"The hills of Vastmanstad are not like yours here," he said, on the day he lay in the shut-bed, with her sitting beside it, speaking of Vagai Front in winter and how blue the dark crows looked against it, after he had made a protection for the second skonära. "They go up in long slow rises, and on days like this we used to run ski along them. The snow smokes and we would take darts because there was sometimes game to be had. Would you like to try that sport?"

"Oh, aye. But I would think a bow better."

"It may be I can take you there hunting one day." Airar felt his own face suddenly flame, and half to ease his shamefastness reached forth to take her hand. She did not resist, returning his pressure for a second but then drew her fingers away.

"But you're for the wars and Mariupol city and all. There are great ladies there; when you return poor fishers of Gentebbi will not seem worth a copper aina —if you return."

"Aye, if I return. . . . It has been the fall of better men than Airar son of Alvar that they had not strength to draw a bow or heave a blade when it was needful." The black shadow seemed to close; between despite and sheer weariness of flesh two big tears detached themselves from Airar's eyes and rolled out on his cheek. "What lady great or small would look on me, so little of avail? I am thinking it might be better to let Visto and Erb go to Mariupol, but myself stay and brew potions like a witch in some outbuilding of your Queen Kry's house."

"It might be better," she said slowly, then on a sudden stood up, so rapid and vigorous that the stool whereon she sat was overturned. "Aye, and better still to take livery of petticoats! Visto told me how you were one of dauntless daring that would deal his stroke and never think twice about it, but now it is to be seen that he was wrong and my mother right when she said that all magicians were peeping dastards, only fit to flaunt tricks for children. I'd rather Ové Ox-mouth."

Up went her head; she swept from the room all queenly, while Airar, struggling from his bed as he called after her, found his legs would carry him only as far as the door before down he flopped, muscles twitching like those of a hooked fish.

The next day being that on which he did not go to the ships, he tried to find her, but she slipped him somehow after breaking fast, and when he went in search of Visto that one was gone too. Airar suspected they were together—as why should they not be? he asked himself, but that eased matters not at all. He spent the day lonely, idle, and miserable. It was too chill to wander uncompanioned through town or hills, so he went back to Rudr's house to wait Gython's return. This fell in good season before the evening meal, but she would bring with her a companion, a girl of fat cheeks and no presence, who drew Airar aside, then tittered and giggled maddeningly before coming to the point that she would have a love-potion to melt her reluctant swain.

By time they sat at meat Airar had reached such a peak of reckless resentment that he burst right out across the table and everyone present to know why she evaded him, and if he had done her offense, would offer penitence and explanation. Old Rudr laughed heartily and made some gleeful remark that with women the only wrong is to be right, but he looked hard at Gython, and next morning Airar, coming somewhat late to the fast-breaking, found father and daughter both silent, she biting her lips, he champing away at his victual with a face held studiously blank.

That day was another of the skonäre to exorcise. The usual thing happened; when Airar came to himself in the lock-bed, a mug of warmed aquaviva with honey stood on a stool beside it, but no Gython, so he lay alone and miserable all afternoon. The short day turned dark fast and he drifted into a doze from which he was roused by a sense of chill, to see that across from him the fire in the room had burned low. Beyond the door partly ajar were voices without words— Rudr's slow accent and Gython speaking higher and more vehement, rising and rising.

"—quit you and Vagai and all!" she cried, suddenly clear. There was a moment silence; then banging, a shout, and many other voices. A cold gust from the winter outside swept through the chamber as an outer door was opened; torches were being borne in and in their midst one with a clout round his head and blood dried all down his jacket.

It was Rogai. "The damned baron beat us," he said. "Wigrak's dead and his head on a spike at Mariupol portal. Sir Ludomir's in hiding."

9. Ships Come to Salmonessa

HE TOLD THE TALE BETWEEN GULPS OF mead to a room crowded round a fire brought to brightness. Through prevision or treachery—he thought the latter—Vanette-Millepigue had gained a clear view of the purpose of Mariupol. Or ever Airar and Rogai had left Naaros, his riders carried warnings to the Count's governor in the fatal city. A half-tercia of men-at-arms came down from Briella itself; another was sent from Naaros citadel; so that by time Rogai reached Mariupol the place swarmed with Vulkings in steel, patrols were going through all the streets to make arrests, and the gate-guards had orders to let any in but none go forth.

"What did you?"

"Went into hiding with a certain dame whose establishment is not conducted to the best morals—craving

73

your grace, bright lady—but devoted to the Iron
Ring, and tried to find Lord Wigrak. I found him—
hah! The second day after my arrival trumpets were
blown in all the streets with heralds announcing a
public spectacle in the great square, all persons being
required to attend. I dared not fail, since you must
know in Mariupol they keep a register of quarters,
whereon my name was already inscribed as our
dame's dandy-man. They had a structure there built
up to resemble a mountain all hung with Vulking colors—"

He drank and someone said, "Make honest men
puke to see the curst red and white so exalted."

"Aye, that enough. Well, that bloody Red Baron's
an enormous man for symbols and shows—as he
made clear. When we were all gathered, Vanette-
Millepigue himself pops out from somewhere at the
top of this play-mountain with the Vicount Iselé, who's
governor of Mariola, takes off his helmet and makes
us a talking. It had come to him, he said, that certain
among his good Dalecarles were ambitious to climb as
high as a mountain-peak. He would not deny them
that privilege, only reminding that the Mountain was
the Vulking badge and dangerous for all not of that
blood. On this a trumpet was blown and they began
pushing up their mountain, two and two, a dozen of
the Mariupol syndics, Wigrak among them, with their
wives and children, maybe twoscore persons all told.
As they reached the peak, Vanette-Millepigue and
Iselé sworded them handsomely, by pairs, the women
and children first, then a headsman cut them at the
neck and exhibited the heads to those present. Some
of the children screamed and tried to run."

He gulped and drank again. *"Dolorosa Dalarna,"*
said someone and Airar could see how Gython held
both hands before her face. His own eyes felt wet, to
cover which he cried:

"But the Star-Captains of Carrhoene? Were they
trapped as well?"

Rudr snorted. "Not they slippery eel-fish. More like
wearing Mountain badges themselves now."

"Sir, you are less than just which is less than honorable," said Rogai earnestly. "They could come no earlier; and you know, as I, that no Vulking Lord will take the hire of mercenary spears. Nay, they'll be warned at sea, by one of your own boats, the one that fished me up as I came over the Mariupol sea-wall with my head a-bleed and a dead guard under my arm."

"Ah, hmf, and with a's warning, they beauties will now run for Os Erigu most like, to join the pirates."

"Nay—Salmonessa. It was covenanted if aught miscarried. We retake the war from there."

Airar found voice again. "Then all's not lost?"

"Lost? Lost? We have lost a conspiracy; the battle's yet to begin."

Rudr got up and took a step or two, hands behind, head down. "They young twiggets in Vastmanstad, did they go up or get theyself in Red Dog's trap?"

"I cannot say for certain sure, but my best knowledge is nay. Black Gallil held them for our signal, and there's a hard holder."

"Nah, hah, vmf. Duke Roger, what says un?"

"Oh, he has already sent heralds to Iselé on the ground of his old treaty, the Privilege of Mariola, that gives him suzerainty and the right to sit in judgment on treason cases there. Breathing defiance; means war for sure. I gave the word that all who rallied to my arrow throughout the province should fall in on his standard. We but begin."

"No two ways." The master of the free-fishers drew a long breath. "Mayhap not onc, but such as be, we take. Erb, Powry, summon the fifty that go, from bed if need. They must just sail on the wind tonight for Salmonessa, and young Master Airar, you with a. I'd say more and wish you in better spirit, but now must wait happier times. Master Rogai, you go, too."

Tall Erb goggled. "Tonight?" But Rudr turned on him fiercely. "Aye, no delay. Do you not see, foolish man, that if not the Red Baron of Naaros, then Vulk his master will know Mariola's never be in this alone. We will have their war-cogs here with the day unless storm prevents."

There was a stir. Erb stood up, but a voice deep

among the group: "But our free-fisher charter. We have a charter against such reivings."

Rudr's laugh rang cracked. "Writ on parchment. Just try steel against un one time, as Red Baron's now in mind."

They were all moving now, but—"The sea-demons," said the black-bearded man whose name Airar never did learn.

"Time's enough when time is; all goes down before this necessity."

Visto helped Airar to dress, which he did stumbling and missing getting his points home. He looked round for Gython, but she had clean disappeared, so their final parting must be unfriendly and without farewell, he half-leaning on Visto's shoulder out into a night shaken with winds and low-driving snow. Down the steep street there was a sound of shouting and someone emerged with a torch, words and sparks alike trailing along the dark stormwind. The tempest made it hard to draw breath; at the quayside there was much babble in the bitter cold that cut right through a cloak, and men arriving in twos and threes, companied by torches that threw red glint on a steel cap or caught the silhouette of a spear-point, with cries of "Where's Vardomil?" "Hold there!" "Gone in the skonära *Nedil's Gallai.*"

The ships had all been brought in to lie close along the dockside and each other when storm threatened in the afternoon. They were grinding and pounding together as seas rolled through the entrance between the paws of the Sphinx of Vagai. It made Airar's heart beat to see the gap heave in the uncertain light betwixt bulwark and quay, all slippery with frozen spray, but with Visto's arm and a friendly hand he got across and was led below on the nearest ship.

A fire was already alight on the roundstone. "Keep it live, young master," said one of those who had helped him down. "We be needed above to manage ropes."

"Can I do aught to aid?"

"Not you; you be cargo."

He was left. The hatch closed above, there were

foot-stampings and muted shouts, with presently an
end to the jars from the outer side of the ship, which
Airar took to mean that the vessel next beyond had
pulled out. Now they were moving also, the wild irregular thumping of the skonära giving way to jerk and
come again as she felt the heave of the seas. The
movement turned more intense as they reached the
outer bar; Airar lay down on a bench beside the fire,
all wrapped in his cloak, but no sleep for him, so he
let his thoughts drift idly over the place where he was
bound, what he might find there, and the reason for
Gython's sudden anger.

It made him full sorrowful that she on whom he
had in a measure depended had so failed him, not
recognizing his need of mere encouragement and human sympathy in the black aftermath of his magic-
making. But then he thought—dead and gone now, all
of that, and she out of his life forever, so that he
might look on the matter with clear eyes as one distant, and what did he see? Aye, she had a certain
amount of reason, the more if Rudr had planned they
two for a union. No woman wants her man hanging
to her skirts when strength and valor are praised
—or almost none, he amended himself, recalling how
his own father Alvar had not infrequently wept tears
and was soothed by his wife in the days before she
died and the heart went out of the old man, thereupon to Naaros to join Tholo in the high house on
Leonce Fabrizius.

But this Gython was another stamp—and he stirred
restless, thinking on the graceful cling of her garments
as the wind blew round her. Dead and gone; now
Visto would likely have her to raise a brood of fisher
brats. It had been her fault more than Airar's own
that she missed any higher destiny, but his own for
letting Rudr pursue him into these clerkly doings. Yet
that had been the price of the fifty in which lay his
hope of the future—and what advantage had he over
any of those fifty, save archery (which they despised)
and his knowledge of gramary? Too deeply moiled
and coiled for his working—and Airar, clinging to a
beam against the rocking ship, placed more logs on

the roundstone and fell on a resolve not to make more magic save where naught else would serve. Then his thought fell on a little vein of self-pleasure at what Pertuit the archer might have said to see him going up to Salmonessa, not as hireling but as captain of fifty, and he followed that delight round and round a waking dream of cities and honors and ringing bells till the hatch was thrust back and someone or other came below for a draught of hot drink.

By day the motion of the ship had eased. Airar went aloft to find her running fast northeastward along the flank of the north wind, with the tiller lashed, under a bright sky, climbing flowing mountains of water to slide down the opposite slope without a tremor. Around her bows was a fairyland of fantastic ice-forms; one of the free-fishers stood there, braced and chopping. It was cold.

Airar clutched a rope and looked round; close aboard another skonära swept like their own along the wind, and far out he could just see the speck of a third when the heaving waves brought them to rise together. The spray stung his face; the master of the ship turned to him with a visage somewhat glum.

"Good-morrow," said he. "It would seem we got to Salmonessa with your fifty become but a score."

"How would that be?"

"The *Braihed* shivering on the rocks at Vagai gate and none knowing how many of her people live, while only the *Gulring* is with us, so not unlike the *Nedil's Gallai* is gone, too. Sad voyage for Gentebbi, young master." He finished with a sidelong look and accent on the final word.

"What's then that other ship that looms against the sky?" asked Airar, pointing.

For answer the master looked sharp at him, then stepped to the bulwark, holding with one hand while the other he made a small tube and peep-hole for his eye.

"By the peace!" he cried as he jumped down. "You have right. Draw in the sheets, bear up, bear up!" He turned to the mast and cupped his hands. "Ové, you're a pudding fool! The—the young master betters your lookout watch. Spear and helm all, lest she prove enemy."

But she did not; when she closed she proved to be the missing *Nedil's Gallai,* and she had picked up all but one of the men from the vessel wrecked. So now Airar was much praised for a sharp-sighted as well as a lucky leader, for among all the three ships none but he had spied the rest. They had a good voyage after that across a sea growing calmer, under a high-wheeling sun each morning and a wind that drove them fast, till on the third day toward twilight here was a hairline across their path that grew to a broad river-mouth with a tower bridge standing across it, and in the distance, insubstantial against the gloomy east, towers which Airar knew belonged to the hold of the Bastard of Salmonessa.

The clouds had begun to climb before the setting sun and the river looked like slate as it was down sails and out sweeps to drive into it. Far to west and north Airar could see what looked like waving brown fields of harvest with the road to the towered town running through, but when he said Salmonessa was late with its crops, Visto laughed.

"Aye, if the crop were frog and fish," said he. "Those be the marshes of Salm that run down to Mariola's border," and the *Nedil's Gallai,* was pushed alongside, with Lank Erb in it, crying as they glided that Airar should speak for all, since the Salmonessans set great store by title and ceremony.

The tide was out; the stream ran sluggish, leaving bare long flats of rime-covered mud on either side. Tall piles had been driven so that only one vessel might pass the bridge at a time, and for the moment even the passage of that one was interdict by a rusty iron chain at the water level. As they drew up to it, a head in a steel cap was thrust past a mangonel on the bridge-lip and called, "Who comes?"

Airar waved a white spear. "Free-fishers of Gentebbi to bear arms in the Duke's war."

"Turn again. It is His Grace's ordinance that none may follow his banner but those who follow leaders of birth and not their unruled will, like those haughty

Dalecarles of the west or the barbarous Vulkings that name a man lord on one day and villain on the next."

"I am leader here and I have birth as high as any in Salmonessa. I am Airar Alvarson of Trangsted."

A second head joined the first. "Hah!" it cried, "a Vastman Dalecarle by the sound of the name. What are your bearings, Dalecarle?" The tone was of mockery, and now Airar was somewhat put to it, for his father was not an armigerous man, and though there had been some hint of nobility in his mother's family, the matter was never spoken on at home. Yet he answered boldly enough on the spur of necessity:

"We bear azure, an arrow or in pale."

"It is a coat we never heard," grumbled the second head and both disappeared behind the mangonel for consultation. Presently:

"Have these fishers sworn allegiance in due form?"

Up jumped a man aboard the *Nedil's Gallai* and shook his fist. "Allegiance, nay!" he cried. "We freefishers owe allegiance to none below the Emperor by our holy charter." But Erb pulled him down and shouted back: "It has not been done before among the people of Gentebbi, but I for one will just swear by the Well to look on Airar Alvarson the Farsighted as my liege lord for so long as this war shall last."

"And I!" cried Visto, "And I, and I!"others, and as Airar thanked them, proud for a moment, the gateguards again held parley, at the close of which one came forth to say:

"This is a weighty matter and not to be decided by us but by His Grace's Chancellor, which will need the sending of a message up to the castle. For any matter there is no entry past the gate permitted after sundown."

From this point no argument would move him, nor would he even allow them to tie to the piles of the river-barrier for the night. No help for it; they had to drop downstream and put out mooring stones for the night at the edge of the stinking marshes. Yet it was not too bad, since Rogai came over in a shallop from the ship he was on and entertained them with a merry tale of one of the Viscount Iselé's captains and how he came to partake of the favors of the dame with whom the man of Mariola lay in hiding; how that lord's Micton servant was plied with drink and fantastic tales of evil spirits; how they rigged a device of bellows to cause horrid groans to issue from a cabinet; how the servant had burst into the midst of his master's joyance, crying, "Sword and helm! They are upon us!" so that both fled hastily without their doublets—

"—from which I removed the Vulking badges of leadership as lawful prize and have them here to prove it," finished Rogai, whereat all laughed.

10. Salmonessa:
Now We Have an Allegiance

THERE WAS WIND IN THE MORNING, BLOW-
ing the marsh-reeds flat, with a few flecks of snow and
a hard pull up to the bridge. The Duke's word had
come; they were permitted to enter on condition that as
soon as ever they arrived, the fifty would swear in
Duke Roger's own presence to have Airar for their lord
feodal and he make similar oaths to the Duke. Airar
could see that of the free-fishers, most disliked exceed-
ingly this manner of procedure, and some of them
made objection, stamping to keep warm on the
skonära's deck. Erb settled the matter, declaring that
those who would not swear might have one of the ships
for a return to Vagai; it was clear enough then that all

would rather swallow their pride than face old Rudr
with his instruction unobeyed.

The river Viverrida runs both through and around
Salmonessa, cutting off outside the walls certain sub-
urbs of booths and mean huts, to which in the summer
season (Visto said) came merchants, mainly from Mariupol and the Twelve Cities, for trading in the Duke's
market. Now all these were empty, looking like dead
husks of fruits carelessly flung; from behind them, out
of the flowing moat's slack water the great walls ran up
and up with a slight inward curve that gave them the
more height till the stone wave broke in a tracery of
battlements and jutting turrets, far above. The water-
gate was a tunnel that seemed to run like a cave into
the heart of a mountain; a huge iron portcullis overhung their heads as they entered and there was another at the far end, where they could see nothing but
a wall of cold masonry, pierced by shot-holes.

Once through that lowering portal, it was clear how
this inner wall jutted from the main fence of the city to
stand across the stream just where it made a turn to
plunge through the walls and on to sea, this inner guard
ending in a tall tower. Neither at window or battlement
was any person visible, though a close watcher might
have caught a pair of eyes back in the gloom. The ships
pushed on, Airar's leading. As they rounded the bend
past the tower Outer Salmonessa lay before them,
quays all along the river where it broadened and
slowed, timbered and painted houses standing up over
them, with much people moving about; and behind
these buildings and business, more towers climbing up
a hillside, the steep inner city, impregnable. Airar took
all this in vaguely, for what quickest drew his glance
was the near quayside on the left. A line of maybe
twenty men-at-arms was there, drawn up in order, eyes
fixed before them, waiting. They had halberds all, short
swords belted to their sides, and each a round target
slung over the shoulder of his coat of ring mail, on
which was cunningly wrought the tower and dolphin,
Salmonessa's badge. Their size held the eye; they were
enormous. Airar laughed, whistled, and turned to the

shipmaster, for the others were straining at their sweeps.

"These are surely very pretty men," said he. "I'm no dwarf myself, but the least of them would overtop me by a groat."

"Oh, aye, the shaveheads. Had you not heard of them? They are the Bastard's bodyguard and have first rights in the sack of any city he captures." His voice was indifferent. "But I do not think they are so brisk in a battlefront as smaller men might be, for they come of all races except the Micton and are petted like pigs at a fair."

Now they had reached the quayside and a fisher or two jumped ashore to draw the skonäre to the rings that stood there. A man came down past the giant-guard with little mincing steps, dressed in shoon of plum velvet with the same material showing in the slashes of his yellow doublet; uncovered, but with black hair wonderfully smooth and curled at the ends. From his left hand, where it rested on a jewelled dagger, dangled a ball of scent.

At sight of Airar he swept a bow low to the pave. "Prince Urdanezza," he said in a high, affected voice, and offered a hand for touching. "One presumes it is the most worshipful Airara. I knew at once by the dagger you were he of gentle blood. Pray let me apologize a million times for the smells of this quay." He lifted and delicately sniffed at the scent. "I do assure you we are better at the palace, and His Grace is all afire to see you and hear with his own ears how you have tamed the stiff-necked codfish of Gentebbi into taking a lord. My Lady Malina, as well." He linked arms with Airar and, before the latter could do more than murmur a few sounds which he trusted had the ring of courtesy, trickled on. "You are in favor than twenty-one of the Pillars of Salmonessa to be your escort, which is more than the Bishop of Morango received on his last visit. Will you have your men follow?"

He led past the tall men and stood aside for Airar to crawl into an elaborately decorated litter, with its hangings trailing in the mud of the street. Eight men with shiny black faces, big but not so big as the halberdiers, instantly lifted it to their shoulders, and as Airar stuck out his head to call to Erb, part of the guard fell in on either side, with a simultaneous shout of "Ey—yah!" that set all the passengers looking. Through the curtains Airar caught glimpses of these latter and thought they did not seem so proud as their buildings, but now the vehicle was moving steadily to the rhythmic shout of the shavehead halberdiers and Prince Urdanezza talking:

"—plot, no doubt. Vulk will demand the hand of the Princess Aurea by reason that the old connection of the House in Mariola makes His Majesty's eldest daughter suzeraine there; and this in spite of the fact that her hand was promised to His Grace by the Capitulation of Lectis, seven years agone. Then this Vulkish man will find some means to set Prince Aurareus aside or merely send him the Black Wine and be proclaimed Vulk the First and emperor, and we shall all be under that wearisome Council at Briella with its votings and laws about the number of jewels a man may wear." He yawned. "But I instruct you needless; these things are common gossip."

Airar did not reply and Prince Urdanezza smiled with an exercise of charm that had almost physical impact. "Is there any company now in Vagai to be worth a man's time? I have only seen it once, on my way to the court at Stassia—fish-odored, bat-haunted place, without a single house worth visiting but the chalet where the Knight of Bremmery used to take the waters."

"I do not know. I was only a short time there and was with Rudr, the master-fisher."

"My sympathy, worshipful Airar. You will find it different in Salmonessa. His Grace never sits at table with fewer than twelve lords of blood and ladies in proportion, though I will admit he has had to ennoble one or two of the latter himself. Tell me—" he leaned forward, abruptly confidential, and the litter pitched to the change in balance "—do you privately consider these Carrhoene captains worth places at the high table? The question concerns us much, and I'd fain have the opinion of a Vastmanstad lord. So few from your land have birth that what you say is worth the double."

Airar was saved replying by a loud blast of trumpets. The litter was set down; Prince Urdanezza leaped out and extended his hand, and they were at the foot of a flight of steps that winged nobly up to a high-arched door, with a trumpeter on each step, the fanion from his trumpet bearing the tower and dolphin. All blew again as Airar descended; looking over his shoulder, he could see the Pillars of Salmonessa split to left and right and the free-fishers following up behind, some giggling, most awed, but tall Erb with his face working in agony of embarrassment, and Visto bold and bland.

"His Grace keeps a formal court," said Urdanezza in Airar's ear; "he will expect the full three bows."

At the head of the stairs was a hall of entry with servitors bowing over the tessellated pave; and beyond a pair of great doors, flung open to a point from the trumpets, and tall halberdiers on guard. Beyond, the salon of presence stretched back illimitable, with torch-holders in a tracery of Permandos glass above, not filled now since light came richly through windows of many-colored glass. Lords and ladies brilliantly dressed moved in that changing light along the passage to the throne, talking behind fans; the Prince swept a low bow, nudging Airar to do likewise, and the latter noted that the floor was dirty.

The third bow brought them to the foot of the throne itself, with a big man lolling on it and a lady by his side in a robe that almost showed her breasts. She had full lips and a face that seemed to mean she would laugh easily; he wore a strawberry-leaf coronet above a heavy bristle of black beard and an expression at once silken and surly. When he spoke it was in a voice pitched higher than Airar had expected.

"You are welcome to our dominions, Lord Airar. The more since I have heard of you what will hardly be believed, that you have brought the fishers of Gentebbi to offer their liege service under our overlordship, confirming the ancient friendliness of Dalarna and the house of Salm. Our learned men tell us that we have title valid in law and justice to the suzerainty of those

islands, they never having been of right under the rule
of that King Argentarius in whose charter these Gentebbi men confide. Yet behold our clemency: we here
declare and let all men bear witness that if duty feodal
be sworn to us by you as their baron, they stand released by us of all other claims whatsoever. Is that less
than fair, my lords and gentlemen?"

From the edge of his eye Airar beheld how two or
three near the dais bowed in silent admiration, heard
cries of "Oh, splendid!" and "Nobly done!" and down
the walls of that apartment the patter of hands as ladies let their fans dangle. As for him he was somewhat
at a loss for words, not knowing how his fifty would
take this offer, nor wishing neither to speak against so
high a lord.

"No baron I," said he finally, "only the named
leader of these men, who have come to bear a blade or
two under your standard against the oppressive Vulkings."

The Duke shifted his legs. "We have no manner of
blade-bearing against Vulk of Briella at the moment,"
he said; "nor shall we have ever if he keeps to his de-
voir under the law and the treaty." He turned, lips
drawing back to smile at a man who stood to the right
of the dais, Imperial by the look of him, with dull eyes
and a spatter of hair round the mouth. "This is a matter of service only. As for the barony, you may count
it that our loyal subjects are rewarded. Now we will
have the swearings."

Airar glanced round at fishers huddled a few paces
behind him. Erb was in the front rank, but his eyes
blank and he swallowing his Adam's apple; but Visto
beside him nodded aye and took one step forward, saying, "I will swear."

From somewhere or nowhere an usher stepped forth,
all in tower-and-dolphin livery. "Then you must kneel
before this lord of yours," he said, "and, placing both
your hands within his hands, say the formula I shall
pronounce." There was a burr of conversation from the
walls as Visto followed this saying; but he spoke sharp
and clear enough till the very end, where come the
words with which the subject declares he will follow his

lord to battle. Here Visto checked, gulped, and added of his own: "—for so long as this struggle against the Vulkings shall last." Airar saw Duke Roger frown and lean forward, but one of the lords behind him said something in a low voice; he relaxed as Visto stepped back and another in his place.

"I Vardomil of Vagai do swear—" "I Ové of Vagai—" "I Nene of Busk—" it went, and some were gruff enough, while the whispers around shattered into a laugh somewhere and then into full-voiced talk with the Duke watching silent save for a remark now and again to his lady, and Airar a little unbelieving, hardly noting the faces that came till maybe the fortieth of the fishers, when some vague familiarity of movement in the head-lowered figure with bright hair caught at his attention, and the voice was contralto that said: "I Eythor of Vagai—" All up his back and round his neck swept a wave of hot and cold, he started so violently that he almost jerked the kneeling figure forward and was indeed looking into the eyes of Gython, Rudr's daughter.

No time now to ask or why or how as the formula droned to its close and she, clad in a rough fisherman's garment, drew her small cool hands from his and returned to her place, but he saw Roger, the Bastard of Salmonessa, look sharp from the girl to Ové Ox-mouth beside her and felt a surge of angry fury for no reason. But now another was taking the oaths and at the same time a second Black-staff bowing before the Duke with some message, to which the latter cried above the talk and swearing that it must wait, he was at business. The last man was sworn; the usher led Airar to the foot of the dais where he knelt as the fishers had done before him, and was halfway through the words, when he received the second startling shock of that ceremony. One of the ring-covered hands that gripped his was short by two fingers of the normal number.

His voice faltered as his mind leaped back to the night in the enchanter's cot and the luck of the three-fingered man. There was a tightening of peril in his breast, but he carried it through. Duke Roger left him one hand to kiss, and leaned back smiling.

"Lord Airar, you dine with us tonight. An occasion." He waved dismissal for the fishers. "It is not unlike— nay, stay, hark what's here. I will listen to that herald."

Prince Urdanezza touched Airar's elbow to guide him to the side of the salon, not far from where a dark-eyed girl made room for him in the front rank with a smile that promised all promises, and a herald came down between the ranks of lords and ladies. He was clad in simple white and even without the red pile of Briella blazing on his tabard, one would have known him for a Vulking by the hawk nose at variance with the broad face from which it stood. At the foot of the dais he bowed and, looking never round, said in a voice loud and clear:

"Sir of Salmonessa, I am commanded by my master, Count Vulk of Briella, Lord of Os Erigu and under the Council deputy of the Empire for all the Dalecarle provinces, to bear you this message: that my lord the Count cannot, consonant with his position in the Empire, recognize the right of any outside it to suzerainty or jurisdiction within its bounds, whether conferred by the so-called Privilege of Mariola or other document long since lapsed: that he will act in his own city of Mariupol as he wills: that he does instantly require you to withdraw all soldieries and other robbers from Marskhaun and such places within Dalarnan territory and to pay for injuries you have committed, an indemnity to be fixed by the High Court of Stassia, and to deliver to him the false traitor Rogai of Mariola, with others of like kidney, now sojourning in your city."

One corner of the Duke's mouth curled under his beard. "He did not ask also that I come to Briella with a ring in my nose to make obeisance?"

A great hoot of mocking laughter went up from all down the hall, but the herald's face did not change, and he cried in a voice to be heard: "Sir of Salmonessa, what is your answer?"

"This." Duke Roger leaned forward from his seat, half-rising, hawked and spat. It struck a spot on the herald's tabard and all that hall shouted and laughed again, but the messenger broke his white staff of office and flung the fragments at Roger's feet, crying "Then war!"

Only Airar and perhaps a few by him at the head of the room remarked amid the tumult how the herald lifted the soiled skirt of his tabard in both hands, saying: "'It is grey, but it will be red when washed in the blood of Salm."

11. Salmonessa: The Duke Plans

AIRAR WOKE MOTIONLESS AS TRAINED BY forest, wondering what roused him in dark, then felt again the finger pressed just below his left ear. "Well?" he whispered, and sitting up, swung his feet from bed, then pulled the covers round him, for it was mortal chill. In the thin starshine and icy moon slanting past but not in the window he could make out the sharp features of Mariola-Rogai.

"What's toward?" he asked.

The hunter chuckled low. "D'you like it?" He swept a hand. "This affair of His Grace . . . with lord here and lord there and looking down his nose at those captains of Carrhoene, who must be our leaders if any. I doubt His Grace knows how to stake a field."

"I thought there were but five of them," said Airar, mind leaping back to the day when the Carrhoene ships came in, and they rode through the streets in bright plate mail, with helms swinging clank at their sides and spears behind, all the streets shouting for joy to see them so martial, with that strange white streak in each black head that made them be named the Captains of the Star.

Rogai chuckled again in the dark. "You did not know? The last child of those two triple births was a girl—Evadne. She passes as man, Evander, and follows them everywhere but in the battle front. Your undercaptain Erb could tell you as much—her chained servitor, worshipping from far. But you will be too much a-taken of hiding women for your own to mark that others may do so."

"Who told you that?"

"Sssh, not so loud. We cannot make this conference public game. As to your question, Alcides of Carrhoene, the Baron Basale of another—I do not know. The whole court's ware of your lovesick looks at this pretended fisher over the archery drill. Apropos—you'll make bowmen never from these fisher-folk of yours. They have the eye and hand but no desire to it; will forget all the moment they are pitched into combat where life rests on skill of weapon."

"I—I did not know—"

"Fie, so nice. Forget your upland manners here at Salmoness', friend Airar, or they'll cease belief in your nobility. Love's a sport that all play here—no shame; we think none the less of you for loving well, even among concealments, except they're childish. Look on Urdanezza and the Lady Irene, Alsander and Dalmonea, and even myself having some hope on the Lady Malina of Deidei, of whom it is said the Duke grows weary, having his eyes fixed elsewhither. You are too bishoply by half. It's only a week of sighing to make them feel desired till the trumpets blow battle and we all march, perhaps not to come again. Then they'll relent. But that's not my mission—"

He stopped as Airar laid a hand on his knee for some small sound, but it was only a rat scuttling across the corner, and Rogai went on, though dropping his voice to whisper:

"The Duke—what's he intend? There this matter

of accepting you as noble so he gets a legal title to
Gentebbi—"

"My mother—" began Airar.

"—of Vastmanstad? I laugh." (But he did not.)
"The profit's to your father earlier in any instance.
You make me quit the line. Hark—by what means
does he hold these Carrhoene captains?"

"Yourself said Alsander and the Countess Dalmonea—"

"Aye, and Alcides and his Micton wench with whom
he sits arm around body to dine. The sport of Salmonessa, as I have said. But they're mercenaries, and
His Grace poor as a heathen prophet for all his brave
court. The purse strings are cut while Vulk holds Mariupol; what keeps here those men of the Twelve Cities?"

Airar waited in the dark, no thoughts on the subject,
and the pallet whereon they sat trembled slightly with
the movement of Rogai's vehemence:

"I will say: it smells most frightfully of treachery,
treachery. Why this reluctance to march and engage
with Vanette-Millepigue before he brings all the Vulking forces to the border? Why so slow in bringing the
Salmonessan barons forth? You may think the town
and outside both crowded with men in arms, but
Malina tells me that not one in four of the contingents
has come, and none at all from Deidei, that's her
father's big barony up in the mountains."

Airar murmured that the two slownesses might not
be unconnected, the Duke perhaps wanting full
strength before battle, but Rogai leaped like a salmon
along the stream of his own idea:

" 'Tis treachery; he means to compose with the
Vulkings for a conquest against the Twelve Cities or
Os Erigu with us in the midst."

"Well, then, what's to do? Fly?"

"With all the gates so guarded and my five hundred
exiles of Mariola? Hah! But listen—you're a master
of the art magical. Can you not make a spell to hold
this Duke faithful to his engage?"

"There's no such spell, and if there were I'd never

make it. This working of magics leaves me something less than a man."

"And Dalarna something less than a people when you play at will-not. Tell me, friend Airar, is there not a spell for drawing a man to you and putting his will in your power? I have heard on such."

Airar answered slowly, thinking on the drawing spell and what his father had told him of its use. "Aye. But the spell is of short duration and the man magicked cannot be made to do anything he had not already looked upon with some shadow of desire. Also there is required something from the very body—a nail-paring or other."

"Hah! I'll charge myself with the details. If he but prove false, you bring him to a named place and the exiles of Mariola will have somewhat to say to him."

He glided from his place, pressed Airar's hand briefly, and was gone without farewell. The door opened soundlessly to a streak of light, then closed again, and Airar lay down to compose himself for sleep, trying to decide whether rash Rogai's words were enough to convince him that Duke Roger was indeed false, and so to create that emergency in which he would use his gramary again. Or would that indeed be the crisis if he were traitor? Those who know not physic wish it for all diseases, and what purpose would the death or torture of that false feodling serve?

Sleep came on him in the round of these thoughts and when he woke it was the day when the Duke was to pass his army in review among the meadows before the town and the captains to receive their assignments.

His Grace sat on horseback on a little mound just beyond the bridge gate, with those marmoreal walls behind and his lords around him. The Pillars of Salmonessa were to march first, then form as a guard. Airar, ranking with his own band in the street Azaga, saw them go past, most formidable of look with their long-tailed helmets sweeping down to meet the flaring shoulder plates and a shield on every left arm, marching to their measured shout. He turned, hoping once more with a remark to draw one from Gython, but

as usual she in her soldier-garb had slipped deep
among the rest. There was a tug at his elbow and
Visto said low:

"Master Airar."

"Aye, Visto, what will you have? Does not all go
well?"

"Most, but not all; I'd have a word."

"Say it."

"Need just being private; a long word."

Airar thought: there would be after this inspection
a banqueting, as was the Salmonessan duchy's habit.
"Well, then, tonight when all retire. D'you know where
I lodge? In that north round tower of the upper castle
at the third stage."

"How may I enter? These dukeish people be mighty
choice about setting guards to keep all we away from
those they call noble."

"It is a thing we cannot amend while wanting his
help in this war. But do you mind that heathen bow
with the back-crook that Steen Snot-nose was showing
yesterday? Bring it; tell the guard you've a message
concerning."

Close past them down the main street to the gate the
Mariolan exiles went past with a roar of shout, not in
very good order and somewhat diversely armed with
rusty ring mail as they had come across the marshes
with Vulking pursuit on their heels, but tall men all
and grim of aspect, number over five hundreds. The
Gentebbi fishers followed next, then the spears of Salmonessa city and the Baronial levies, with the knights,
sergeants, and others armed to fight a-horse, in thundering steel at the close of the array. When they had
all passed, saluting the Duke politely, he dismounted
and held council of war on the hillcrest itself, with the
cold grey clouds behind, tracing 'on the ground with
the tip of his scabbard a design so all could see what
he meant.

"Lords and gentles," he said in his high voice, "you
all know—or should—that there be two routes across
the marshes between us and Mariola; the one I scratch
here, running down to Viverrida mouth and so following the shore, and this other across the causeway

straight through to turn north toward Marskhaun and
equally south to join the main route at the shore. Now
the clear expectation of these Vulkings is that we shall
move by the seaward route, since that by the causeway is so narrow to admit only a few abreast, with
quagmires deep on every side. Moreover, my Lord
Moraë, who is warden of those parts, reports his
marsh-fowlers say that Viscount Iselé and his half-
tercia are already on guard at the seaward route, while
before the causeway exit there be only some of those
light-armed horsemen they call *gentours*. Now hear
our plan: it is to leave here this day one week, but
to march by the causeway and so gull them entirely.
But to your charge, Basale, we give the task with certain of your band to go by the coastal route and keep
this Iselé amused so that he become not ware of our
main battle till we fall on his rear."

There was a pause while Duke Roger looked for
applause and indeed received it of all kinds from murmuring to cry; but one of the Carrhoene captains:
"Wherefore the week? Here we are, armed and ready.
What holds us from our war?"

The Bastard of Salmonessa lifted one finger and a
sly smile spread across the full lips. "Because, little
man, whom do we fight? Iselé? He's a sprat; the head
we would see drop is that of the Red Baron, Vanette-
Millepigue himself. Is't not so my lords of Dalarna?"
He looked round to Airar, Rogai, and the one or two
other Dalecarles whom he had counted of merit sufficient to belong to that company, and receiving their
growl or nod of approval:

"Hear this, then. We have advice by way of our
spies that this precious baron with a full tercia marches
from Mariola but today. And whither bound? Marskhaun for certain sure; the city's in revolt against him,
has admitted our aids and flies the tower and dolphin.
He'll wish to punish her—oh, a keen lord for punishments is your Red Baron. Look, then, a week brings
him straitly before the city. As he arrives there we
burst through at the causeway, falling on him in the
one direction and Iselé in the other, destroying both
their tercias. Before they can bring down more from

Briella we'll have all Hestinga in arms; Deidei and the barons of North Salmonessa will be with us; defiance to the world.

"You, my Lord Urdanezza, will lead the advance and have the right wing, with all our strength of knights and sergeants, the Carrhoene spears to follow. You fight the main battle with that wing; the gentours are nothing, break through them. At the heels of Carrhoene will come Gentebbi and Mariola with the young lords Airar and Rogai; your task is to drive off any gentours who remain and those miserable peasantry the Vulkings call allies. Ourselves will follow with the Pillars of Salmonessa and the city bands, preparing to aid you, dear Lord Urdanezza, should your first charge fail, or turn south toward Iselé. Thus we shall split them, shiver them, damn them utterly. How say you, my lords and gentles?"

"A tower!" cried Urdanezza and whipped out with a clang a sword all chased in gold with the loves of the old gods to kiss its hilt before his lord, and others did the like. But it was not a Dalecarle warcry and Airar remarked amid the tumult how the Carrhoene captains, five of them, were a little aside, making many words, their hands moving fast. Duke Roger saw it as rapidly.

"How, you foreign captains, do you not like our plan?" he asked sharply.

One turned. "Sir, we did wish to hear the word of our brother Alcides, who is the man of most worth among us for such tricks and stratagems, as Pleiander is the fittest to command a siege against stone walls and Evides to hurrah men on when the spears are down."

"And where would this Alcides be?"

Before they could reply, "Alcides, ha-ha," cried one of the Salmonessan nobles. "I felt him at the palace playing bubble-cup with that Micton wench of his."

Duke Roger did not change expression. "Now it is to be seen once again," said he, "that a tree is chopped best with one's own axe. So this is our plan; gentle Basale, you leave on the morrow." He signed to the music to blow up, and with the shavehead guard giving a shout, let himself be helped into the stirrups to lead the return to the city. Airar thought the Carrhoene captains none too happy over being left from all planning, but no chance to say to any of it with the trumpets sounding, horses prancing, the shout of the guard and the procession moving into Salmonessa, with himself forced to ride a distance from Rogai, to whom he would willingly have talked. There was feasting after, formal in the Salmonessan manner, many courses from half-reclining couches, and he as a womanless man must share a place with the unlovely daughter of some petty baron from the hills against Hestinga. His eyes were elsewhere and mind on Visto; but between eye and mind, he noted that Roger the Bastard for the first time seen had no one on his couch.

12. A Night in Salmonessa

AIRAR WAS WELL ASLEEP, BEING SOMEWHAT fuddled with the dinner wine, when the sound of the man of Vagai struck through to his consciousness. Visto flung down the crook-bow with: "It's just be-damned that the people of one blood cannot speak without excuse in this place." He looked very sharp.

"Nay," said Airar, "be not wroth. One may use even a poor knob to beat a pig; and it is in my mind that this Duke may turn not so poor a knob, neither."

"Aye. If knob break not and pierce hand."

Airar sat up, trying to shake from his head the fumes of wine and sleep and the thought that here was a second midnight warning to a purport heard before, though how could one ask more of Duke Roger than his proceeding at the muster? "What's here?"

Visto peered round. He had brought one of those small lamps called chrysma that are the specialty of Phyladéa of the Twelve, and as he glanced across it suspiciously toward the room-corners, the light threw up in his forehead wing-shaped shadows from his eye-brows, giving him an appearance almost demoniac. He came closer. "Before too much be tangled, one question, Master Airar, for asking the which I crave grace: you are in love with Rudr's daughter?"

Airar felt the red creep up his veins and found it hard to meet Visto's gaze. "Is it contest between us, then?"

"Oh, nay. We're childhood friends and long com-panions, but—"

He paused and now himself went wordless, so that Airar, to hold his small advantage, said: "But you are fixed elsewhere?"

Visto moved; light and eye-shadows flickered, con-cealing expression: "Not I; but 'tis my own affair. Yours is that your sweeting is threatened where only a lover can save her."

"Lover? I? She'll barely speak to give me the greet-ing of the day, and then as soldier."

"Then a's not just indifferent since a holds you high enough for anger. Hark: d'you know why they call this Duke Roger the Bastard?"

"Because he is one, I suppose. No despite to him for that."

Visto snorted. "If it were but the one. But I have it that the whole custom of these Salmonessan dukes is never to wed, succeeding bastardy with bastardy, and the Church likes it little." He snorted. "No more does Baron Deidei, I hear, with his daughter the Duke's mistress-in-title, which he holds as disgrace."

Now Airar caught some glimpse of what was for-ward and half rose in his bed. "How is this—?" he cried. "Say on, say on."

"Well then, this Duke has sent his word to my friend and your darling, Gython, that by her feodal duty she is to come and lie with him this very night."

A push of pain touched Airar's heart and for a mo-ment he found it hard to breathe. "I'll slay him," he growled, hands twisting the blanket for a moment, and swung his feet to the floor.

"Not just easy to do that with they big shaveheads all round."

"Will she go, then? She's but to refuse him flat, and I as leader will guard her with our fisher spears to the last. This dukeling will change his tune, I warrant, when he begins to hear the swords play breakhead around his own halls."

"We have talked on that, and Erb. She will not have it, saying it is all Dalarna's war gone down and her father's death to jig it so."

"But that's moonshine and madness. This Duke will never alter his whole politic to make of a sweet girl a bonaroba. Is there none to tell her so?"

Visto shrugged and the shadows danced again. "Not tall Erb. He's been consulted, say's a's right, to have her at the court will make a bond which keeps Salmonessa forever faithful to the project of this war, and when men give their lives to bring down the mountain, a woman can afford her body. I'm none so sure but I am with un, yet thought your interest should just have its word to speak."

"But, Visto, what's then to do? We must fly, leave this accurst town tonight—no, the bridges are up, there's been no ship from Gentebbi since ours, the Vulkings are sure in possession there. Hide, that's it. But where? . . . Marry her tonight, no, she'd not have me, and no bar to this Bastard's lust in any case." Airar was pacing the floor, barefoot and in agony. Visto watched across his chrysma. At length he said:

"I'm not one of they lawmen, Master Airar, but is it not that a owes no duty feodal save through you? In our swearing we never said no nothing about this Duke."

Airar whirled. "Aye, say that to her, will you, Visto? It may serve. Go quickly, tell her that. He's merely overlord and may not enforce such orders unless I grant it."

He was wrenching his hands with impatience, even before the door had fairly closed on his visitor, running to the cabinet for a light and his grammarion, full aware that Duke Roger of Salmonessa would never be held from his peculiar passion by so tinsel a cry of law, even did Gython choose to employ it. He had not so been withheld from the daughter of that Baron of Deidei. No—the girl had right; any contest over would set Roger together with the Vulkings and down Dalarna as Rogai had foretold. No—this was that ultimate hour of peril to all he held highest when he must use his father's art and call on powers beyond his own.

He found charcoal in the fireplace and, half-naked as he was, traced the pentagram with hurried fingers. "Ia, Ia, Sabachthani—" moved the drawing spell, nor did he forget to include in his lines the lock of hair she had once given as a friend's gift. Outside the dull day had become black night, black and cold, with only a gleam here and there from windows in the town far down. Unlike there would be any aboard to remark the blue of his own devil-fires when they came up with the pale lost melting faces among them. Done—"so now I order you by the Seven Powers that are my servants and your masters to lead her from whose very body this token came to me and to subject her will most utterly to mine." Done—and the blue fires died, young Airar hastily blew out the light and began to dress himself in the dark.

She came so softly he could hardly hear her step at the door; in the half-light of a dying torch set in a bracket round the corner, he could see she bore a woman's garments again. "Gython," he whispered and drew her in by the hand. It felt flaccid. "Shall I make a light or will't be seen?"

"As you desire, my lord," she said, so he struck it from flint and steel, twice missing catching the spark, and there she was in all her loveliness, but the robe was a hideous pink rag with an open fente before that almost showed her breasts, clear enough Duke Roger's gift.

"You are safe here," said he. "Will you sit?" (For the after-rush of the enchantment was upon him and he was like to give at the knees.)

"I thank you," she said, and, taking the cross-legged

chair he indicated, dropped her hands in her lap and looked straight before her, though not unfriendly.

"You are safe here," he repeated. "Salmoness himself will never invade this chamber—if he knows where you are. You may hide here as long as you wish." But she did not reply nor move the muscles round her mouth, and after a moment, he said again: "Gython—I offer you all apologies and crave grace. I'll make no more magics nor do aught but as you desire, to be your friend and comrade again."

"The grace is granted. Have I not sworn allegiance to you and to be your servitor?"

"That was Eythor, a spearman of the free-fishers."

"But it was Gython that swore it."

The words were warm as one could have wished, but the tone cold, cold, and her hands did not leave her lap nor the dumb look her eyes, and Airar in despair cried out:

"Would you really have gone to this Duke Roger the night?"

"If I thought it your will, Lord Airar."

"Lord, lord, I am no lord, but your playmate and gossip of Vagai as well you know." He was on his feet again, pacing, weariness forgotten. "How shall we solve this lecherous duke? For to hide here's slender device, he'd find you by some servant's tongue and call you again."

"I'll never go to him if you say nay."

He had reached the side of the room where the fireplace was. Now he spun to look on her unmoving as ever in the cross-legged chair, beautiful and passive. "Can you think of nothing, say nothing?" he cried and before she could answer was across the gap, had swept his arms round her and was kissing her on the lips, the first time without reply, but they melted under his touch and with a little contented sigh she relaxed in his arms and drew him closer.

"Gython," he whispered again as they drew breath, and kissed down her throat, and she made a vague movement toward the light so that he released her long enough to blow it out.

She gave him passion for passion unsparing, but as

the world broke in a surf of delight he felt her suddenly tremble, and then she could hold it no longer, but burst into rending sobs. "Dearest," he said, lips close to her ear, but she turned her face:

"If it were Visto, if it were only Visto," she said in a new voice.

The next day Duke Roger showed himself only once from his apartments, and then with a frown portentous.

13. The Causeway: Battle

ALL THE TRUMPETS BLEW TIRALIRA AND
the host went marching to the bridge-gate in the opposite order to that from the day of the weapon-showing,
knights and barons of Salmonessa first, their pennons
moving to the south wind. There had been a light
snow for two days past, but now it was thawing and
underfoot treacherous where the way was paved, so
that horses stumbled to be pulled up amid the ring of
steel, with many a sweating from their riders. Urdanezza went past in his gay armor that seemed more of
tournament than battle, yet Airar must say he mustered them in all respects like a man of war, with
"Ho, there!" and guidings to bring his heaviest armed
to the head of the array, where they might bear the
jar when the foemen were met. The Duke had lent the
tallest man of his tall guard to bear the banner of the

realm before this company; but his personal standard was farther back, where himself rode among his shaveheads.

There was this and that last preparation—Nene who had some broken scales in his mail-coat, and only on Airar's own intervention would the smiths' guild repair them without the laying down of money; Berni that had a cause of some sort with a merchant of the lower town—so there was no moment for Alvar's son to search for his heartbreak love among the spearmen, where it had been covenanted she should take her place. She had remained in his chamber mostly, but after that one night, he on the floor in a cloak, and few were the words spoken between them. But now the trumpet blew up and up, coming when far with a note of sadness in the mild winter weather; the gates were open and the spears of Carrhoene riding through. Alcides was at their head this day; Airar thought his dark triangular face looked sullen in the helmet-gap as he went past, and the hair with its white streak was hidden by the sallet. Lank Erb plucked his young leader's arm: "Master Airar, we lack a man. Ové Ox-mouth is missing, nor can anyone find him."

Now the call was for Gentebbi; Airar swung into his saddle and lifted an arm as the free-fishers shouted and began to march behind. They were armed with their own spears, rather short than long, and could be used for casting; steel caps; target shields; and bows the gift of Duke Roger, who greatly favored Airar's plan of teaching them to shoot, since he had not overmuch archery of his own. They marched then, the gloomy tunnel of the walls echoing to their calls, out into pale sunlight beyond, and past the merchants' booths to where the march causeway runs through walls of giant reeds, higher than a man.

Once and again there was a halt as something or other checked the riders ahead, for they were in number above seven hundreds. A sergeant broidered with the Keystone of Carrhoene dropped back to grumble it was always so with these baronial people: they were already a watch late along their route and the sun would be westering before they reached the Mariolan fields—"and how is that time enough for full victory before dark?" At the next halt it was Visto:

"Where would Gython be?" he asked. "Not in the band."

Airar felt a catch of dreadful fear. "You were to be her guide and guard!" he cried. "I hold you account—"

"Nay, that you may not, master. My care was to begin when she joined us, and I can find none that has seen a do so. Your charge till then."

Before more could be said the trumpet blew again from Carrhoene ahead and once more the host began to move. Airar had only time to fling over his shoulder that Visto should drop back to seek for her among the exiles of Mariola, she might be in that next company behind, and led on again with a heart full of trouble and doubtful surmise. There was no chance, no possible chance, of himself turning back. Along their flanks by the way the red marsh of reeds had given place to quagmire pools in black ooze with tussocks growing out of it, no path there and the causeway backward crowded with men. The fishers round him were mostly in a high humor, with laughter and wild jest and a catch of song, though for most as for himself this was the first approach to battle; shouting greetings, as "How now, master magician, have you a spell to stop swords?" with other things not so gentle. But he could not share their mood, and though feeling clearly they might think him afraid, nothing he could make of the matter.

The pale sun drove toward zenith and passed without any other event than both red marsh and black fell away at their left to a region of interlocked lagoons, with a low island standing out from them at the edge of sight, and a house on it before which stood a woman to wave and wave as the companies went by. Shortly thereafter word came passing up the line from the Duke that all should pause and break bread. Airar got off his horse, somewhat stiff at the joints, and sat down with the Carrhoene sergeant, who grumbled again over a demi-bottle of sour wine from his own nation, "That it were never so if our Captain Evimenes had the ordering of it. A march is a march and means of arrival, of which a sharp foeman will haply be aware. Why, I remember how in the war with Poliolis we marched a day and night long till a man could hardly sit saddle—aye, and fought a battle at the end of it against—"

He stopped; here was Visto. "Not there, master, and seen by none, though this is not just positive, since so few among them know."

"But it could be," the Carrhoene sergeant went on, "that these Vulkings are not so quick warriors. I have never fought them. Their foot, mark you, they carry that big round shield with the spike in the center long and keen enough to jab a man. If one thrusts at you with his sword, beware that; the next stroke will be from the spiky shield and on the wrong side. Much adroit at beating off archery as well. They open order in pairs, and while one covers both with the big shield, the other casts those throwing-stick javelins, all advancing till they have driven the archery apart, which must needs hold together for effect."

Visto had waited. "Master Airar, what's to do?"

"Search, ask," Airar moved his hands and lurched to his feet. A thought struck him. "Ové Ox-mouth—where's he and who has deed?"

A messenger came down the line from forward, crying that Alcides of Carrhoene asked haste, for time pressed. There were shouts and movement, Airar could hear how the wave passed along the marchers, not himself giving true thought to anything but Gython and where was she. But now all moved again and the trumpets sounded—not so cheerily as before, for musics like men had marched along. At the side lagoons vanished; there was nothing to see but cold marsh, reed and tussock alternate, either with little joy, and Airar thinking bleakly on the Salmonessan Duke and his devices.

There was a sound of shouting up ahead, not unmingled with hoots, and down the causeway, pricking his way along the edge, came a man in a long white robe, with a circlet of gold on his head and bearing a carven chalice before him on the saddle. Behind came

a second rider in ceremonial garb, in whom Airar
thought he recognized that same sheep-faced Imperial
he had seen at the court the first day in Salmonessa.
The leader stopped him, bowing in saddle, and asked
whether he be captain of a company, but when
Airar said yes to that, he held the chalice up:

"Then I command you in the name of the peace of
the Empire, which is the peace of God, that you drink
from this veritable water of the Well of the Unicorn,
as earnest that you will drink of the Well's self with no
less than Count Vulk, the deputy of His Serene Imperial Majesty Auraris. Thus this impious war and man-
slaying shall be laid aside. But if you will not, then
you shall be under the ban of the Empire and its luck
of the Well."

Airar would not say yes or no to that, but bade the
embassy pass on to Duke Roger as his liege lord,
whereat the messenger, as though his blank face expected nothing else, urged his horse to push a way
among the spearmen. The sheep-faced man turned
in his saddle and crossed his fingers back, crying,
"Ban, Ban!" Lank Erb, striding by Airar's saddle, said
that was the worst of luck, but the young man was
shaken by his own concerns, and what could he do in
such a press under the near approach to battle with
bad luck spells or good, as he said.

The day wore. Words were now falling thin, there
was around only the tramp of marching men and
spears held at various angles, so that Airar had time to
wonder whether he and his band would bear themselves well in combat, a thought which would not come
clear but mingled itself somehow in his mind with that
of Gython. If he had not been thus concerned he might
have noted more clearly how left and right little mammaries of solid ground and passes that might have
been made by men's hands sprang here and there
among the reeds, promising an end to their desolate
march.

These bits of land were not less than numerous
when the trumpets ahead called him from his reverie,
blowing all at once, thrilling and discordant, with a
sound of confused shouting under their blast. Airar

could see the men of Carrhoene just ahead snap down their vizors. Erb came. "Tell them to dress bows," said Airar, feeling his own voice at the edge of cracking at the arrival of this long-awaited moment, "and push out where there is hard ground flankwards, since we are the cover for the Mariolans as they for the Duke."

It seemed that he turned his head but a tick of time to say this, yet when he turned again, he was as though alone. A few backs of the Carrhoene riders moved ahead where the causeway was suddenly a causeway no longer, but a road bending northwest across a rolling slope, with shout and weapon-clang coming across it and a single flung dart pinned high by the eye against a red sky. A startled marsh bird went past with a long peening squeal, almost brushing his head. Someone plucked at his foot; he looked round again to see the fishers running out leftward among scattered boscage, some pausing to string bow and all confusion, but the man was pointing—"Look! God's name, look!"—and over the rise between a clump of willows at the marsh-edge and the northwest turn of the road came a clump of riders at a hand trot, with gay plumes in their headgear—the gentours.

Airar reached aback for his bow, being armed like the rest. "Stand!" cried Long Erb's voice, "and draw!" and Airar's bridle was being jerked back toward bush and reed, as on the other side he caught a glimpse of the first spears of Mariola lowering and heard the shout of the men that drove them.

The gentours did not draw back but spread, each striking his horse to gallop with a quirt he held in his left hand as they came in, at the last moment wheeling to fling javelins from throwing-crooks. Arair could not manage to wheel his horse and to nock shaft together. He saw a ragged volley of arrows go past from his fishers, badly drawn, with the darts coming low and very fast in the opposite direction, and it was more the animal than he that swerved to avoid one. There was a cry like *"Aurrgh"* by his side and the gentours were turning away, one with a great bound as an arrow stuck in his horse's rump.

The cry was Vardomil, that friendly man; he had one of those spears through his throat and was tearing at it with both hands, blood all over him and his face a mask. Airar went sick in the realization that war was no dainty sport as he had been taught, but horror and pain and the death of friends. Yet no time for that; there was cry and cry among the fishers in reed-clump and bushes, and he turned again to see coming across the rise a Vulking tercia.

Though he might outlive the ancient spider, it would not be to catch a grimmer sight; for they came not running, but in a quick-step march of utter confidence with their little flutes piping, straight for that joint where causeway became road and Rogai's Mariolans were spreading from march to line. "We are betrayed!" cried a young voice, going high. The Vulking line was long but perfectly formed so that all those fighting men seemed to move to the will of a single mind. They had helmets that flared up and short horsebrush plumes thereon; their shields were in order and so were their blades. From around behind them, pouring down the slope, covering their flank, followed a great river of people light-armed with a few bow-shot among them that paused to throw a shaft or two, but mostly they rushed without pause toward the free-fishers.

"Back!" cried Erb's voice. "The Vulking allies are too many," and Airar lighted down from his horse just as a shaft stood quivering in the ground by his side. That deserved a return; with a sudden great swell of anger drowning his horror, he pivoted to draw to the head and saw that the man who stood before his shaft stood no longer, but now all those Vulking allies were right upon him while from the side came a high shout and clash of metal as the spears of Mariola broke on the tercia's shields.

He felt Visto jerk his arm. "Back, back, they are too many," and was in a half-stumbling run among the bush and tussocks. An arrow hit a man of Gen-tebbi, but it must have been near spent, for it bounced from his armor and the man only stumbled, going down on his face with a splash in the oozy ground. Visto paused to reach him a hand; Airar set both feet and whirled round. A half-dozen of those allied men were close on their heels, but the nearest had a broad-blade spear, and as he paused to set both first to the ungainly weapon, the young man had just time to speed the arrow he already held in hand. A poor draw, but it served, given the distance and the fellow's rush; it took him right in the face and down he went, with the one next behind stumbling across his legs, while of those still coming, one went to knee and threw up a shield and two or more dodged behind clumps lest another of those fell shafts should follow.

"Will you not stand?" cried Airar, but Visto: "No, no, they are too many. Come!" and he was running with the rest again, not knowing whither. But now the ground ahead grew so boggy they made poor work of it and presently right ahead was a patch of tall reeds that must be skirted on a path of ground spattered with foot-trodden dirty snow between reed and black marsh. Behind was one of the small hillocks. At its foot half a dozen of the free-fishers, most standing, but one lying flat on his back and another sitting his haunches with face buried in his hands. None had their bows and the sitting man neither helm nor spear.

"The pursuit's a-distanced," said Visto and made to kneel before Airar. "Master and friend, here is a second life I owe you."

"And I another," said the second companion, in whom Airar now had time to recognize one called Svarlog Longarm of Mjel; but one of the others growled sullen, "No lives owe we. Without un's womanish nonsense of archery we might just fight them down."

"Aye," cried Airar, "and with the hearts of something more than chickens you might have done so regardless. Twice now have I seen you free-fishers run, and each time from something that could be stopped with a little courage and an arrow. Nay, if you will finger your weapons, I have still a shaft or two left." He set his feet, but the sitting man looked up:

"The sharpsighted has right, Sewald," he said, "and

we were more to consider returning than blame un
that would keep us there. How goes it now?"

None answered, but glancing from face to face
Airar could see all the fear that lay behind his own,
but all knew it was not here at the causeways they
should have met a tercia. "Fear not well," said one.
"Hark!"

From afar yet somehow near a shout rose up and
fell again, but it was not the "Ullu-ullu!" that the men
who followed the Wingèd Wolf of Dalarna use in victory,
nor yet the measured bellow of Duke Roger's halberdiers, and on all faces there was less than cheer.

"Man does what man can," said Airar, "and I'm
back to see what's done. Look you, men of Gentebbi,
I'm but your straw leader and have no such skill as
your own Erb; but being your sworn captain, I say
this—that Sewald, who is bold and brisk as any, shall
run ahead; while I who am the best archer, shall
cover him from some twenty paces behind, with Svarlog and Visto to guard me with their spears from
close onset, and the others after, since here there's
naught to gain by staying."

He looked round and there was no naysay, so gave
the word to move at once, Sewald for shame's sake
leading. They switched round the pillars of red reeds,
and keeping twilight on the left (for it was now falling
dark) made gently toward the causeway. A pool of
black marsh sprang up on the right and Sewald went
softly, bending low; Airar kept a shaft on string, but
nothing for maybe three hundred paces and then only
a man evidently Mariolan by his colors, who had an
arrow through his back and falling face down in the
water had so died. The sight was not gladsome, but
nothing was visible from the left, the west where the
Vulking allies were, and but few sounds, most of them
somewhat muffled under the evening.

Another clump of red-tuft marsh sprang at them.
Sewald leading circled southward around it, and there
was a scrambling sound while Airar held an arrow in
leash till a voice cried, "Who lives?" It was Gentebbi
in accent so he himself answered, "The ring!" and

half-drowned from wet and hiding came three more men of the band.

"Have you seen Erb?"

"No, nothing; but one of Mariola passed running."

They pressed on. It was now fast toward dark and none could miss that this was defeat and no mistake. A little later one of the flankers hauled another man from behind a bush at the edge of black marsh. He was a Mariolan upland man hight Tholkeil, who said Rogai had ridden into the Vulking swords at the first onset and been slain; the Duke was fled and Evimenes and Pleiander of Carrhoene both fallen. This depressed all mightily till Airar reflected the man could not possibly have seen so many things and said as much. But now it was falling full dark and Sewald came back from leading to report he could no longer find a way. They had best stop and gather round a fire for the night.

Now they were some dozen together; all cried out at Airar that fire would bring the foeman down on him, and he could but agree, but a search of pouches brought forth three bottles of aquaviva, with which they comforted themselves. As they talked, there was a hoof-splash in the mire, a voice called, "Who lives?"

They readied spears. "The ring," said Airar, looking up toward a tall armed shape on horseback against the sky.

"The iron ring!" replied the other in a voice Airar thought he knew, and the stranger pushed up a morion, dropping hands to side and leaning down for them to look at as he approached. It was as visioned; the face belonged to Meliboë the enchanter.

14. A Night in Mariola

"IT IS NO LESS THAN I WARNED YOU," SAID the man of magic as Airar held bridle and he dismounted while the others nudged and murmured. "Your luck runs thin beside the three-fingered man. What think you of your prospects now?"

"None so unhappy. The Carrhoene captains —"

"Are broken; flying toward Hestinga's mountains. Alcides is slain and Evides the Marshal Bordvin's prisoner."

"Bordvin Wildfang?" gaped one of the fishers.

"Aye, Bordvin. Thought you that tomtit, the Red Baron, would deal with such a war? These are high matters; the marshal has no less than three tercias in presence, and all your armies are overthrown, your Duke of Salmonessa will be duke of his own castle by another dawn, ha, ha."

For answer Sewald whipped at him with a hand-spear but it glanced harmless from the magician's good plate and he laughed.

"Free-fisher, no patience. Noble Lord Airar" (there was an accent here at once of mock and menace) "pray your servitors not toss their pricklets on me, lest I loose against them something worse than sea-demons."

"Noble Lord Airar," mocked Sewald in return, "just tell this frog-spawn sneak un has the count of seven to quit our company or try whether we cannot dig un from shell like a lobster, nah."

"There are certainly one or two words to be said if he wishes to prove himself friend," said Airar, thinking sourly on the horror he had found aboard the fisher-ships.

"Tsa, young man, I thought you clearer-minded. If I could find you alone amid these boccages, could I not do it with a deese of terciary soldiers at my back, or a wing of gentours? Yet here am I, solus."

"Might hap un just got separated from a's people," growled Svarlog from the back, but for that the magician had not even reply. "Look now," he said, "I'll give you conviction of friendly purpose. What's your plan and whither bound?"

"If we have one, why give it to a lord of the Vulkings?" answered Airar, fingering weapons, but then reflecting how little could come of cross-purposes in such situation: "Yet since it tells nothing, none. We did but scout toward the causeway to have a full tale of what passes on which to reach decision."

"Most wise, O puissant young leader, but—"

"There be friendly folk among these marshes," cut in someone, "that might help us reach the sea."

Meliboë turned on him. "And whither then, foolish man? Will you swim to Gentebbi?"

But Airar, his thought jerking back to Gython and anxiety: "Rather we're for Salmonessa if way can be found. There the center of hope still rests."

"And somewhat additional, nenni, young man?" Airar felt a sting at the enchanter's sharpness. "But it's not to be thought on. The town's become a trap for all against the Mountain. Will you drink again of the Duke's luck, that has laid you so low today?"

"Where then? You close all roads to us."

"Not I, but Marshal Bordvin. If you'll but hear me, there is even a route through this snarl. Yet first, have some of your people gather the dry heads from these tall reeds and strike a fire. This ironmongery is chill to a man of my years."

"The Vulkings—"

"Bah, have you so poor an opinion of my philosophic powers, young master? I'll make myself answerable they never trace you. If you doubt, set a man with a dag at my back and I'm the first to fall if it goes awry."

Airar gazed a moment at his unflinching eye and gave the word; the light flared up redly on intent and gloomy faces, Tholkeil of Mariola shivering with cold and wet, and for that matter, Svarlog. There was a search for food and under-voice talk of it as they made places, with the tall reeds looming behind, and the colloquy went on. But it was Airar's friend and not himself that opened the next chapter:

"Sir, I am Visto of Vagai, that would have been your pupil there, and am sworn to obey Master Airar like the rest here, so his decision will stand for all; but would just have a question if permitted. What's your interest in us poor wolf's heads and fugitives, under the ban of the Empire?"

"Hah, and the beldam prevented the 'prenticeship. I call you to mind. Is she dead yet?" the enchanter asked.

The fire fizzed and crackled, running in the heavy reed-tops, still half-damp with snow. There was a silence for a moment as the magician gazed across it, and to Airar it seemed (though he could not tell surely in the moving light) that Meliboë's eyes held the same distant expression as on the night when he had spoke of the Duke's luck and things to come. "Your question is not truly put," he said slowly. "You would know why I, loving ease and with a court at call, fall in with you who must wander. Put it thus— that I'm a faithful son of the Empire, no Vulking by blood, and would not see this Count swollen so great he could pull down the House of Argimenes."

There was something like a snicker among the shadows, and though Visto lowered his eyes, he made a little sound like clearing his throat.

"You will not credit it so?" Meliboë. "Then say I have a private grief against the Count, who would forbid the study and practice of the art necromantic, save as it directly serves his court. The worst the gods can do for a man of mind is to make him dependent on such a dolt. . . . Or say that I weary of meeting none but easy problems, as a glutton wearies of eel-pies. All would be true; and maybe more besides. Man's reasons are mixed and mine own not less than the rest. Take it only that I'm here to save your lives, not needing gratitude, and let's fall to more profitable discussion."

Said Airar: "Would it be profitable to inquire whether we shall then set our courses for this great Baron Deidei, who was late for the rendezvous, but still must have great force?"

"You will lose only your lives and your war if you do. Deidei's the cleverest scamp in the dukedom, therefore like to be the head of it before many seasons turn; bitterly hating Duke Roger for the whoredom of his daughter Malina; sold out to Marshal Bordvin and the Bishops, who mean to put him on the chair of Salm in their interest and so end the bastard line, that Church has never loved."

"Another road closed. You lead us with a nosering. But whither?"

"Stiff neck makes stumbling foot. But no need now conceal your case is so bad that in all the lands north of the great sea there is only one power at hostility unalterable with these Vulkings, and that will be Mikalegon of the burg of Os Erigu."

"Oh, oh," around the fire and a hard laugh and again and someone let slip "Mad!" But or ever the matter could be carried beyond, a man on the outer circle leaped up, lifting one hand while with the other pointing. More than half hidden through the screen of reed they saw a torch of lanthorn flicker briefly and die; it might be moving toward them. There was leaping to feet and Sewald saying low and fierce, "Now, sir magician—" but Meliboë threw up a hand to ward distraction and Airar saw that he was moving the fingers of the other hand as though feet in a complex dance on the soft ground beside him, meanwhile with a long rimeless whistled tune that rose and fell.

"Hush, be quiet all," he broke off to say. "Not a word or sound if you wish your skulls to hold brains instead of mead for a Vulking banquet."

Airar motioned them to obedience, which warning was in truth not altogether needed. It was a magic he had never seen before, and there was a tramp of feet that seemed approaching, but beyond the walls of reed it halted and there was whisper, whispering which broke in a downright shout: "Nay! That I will not. Be damned to the deserion; the place is not canny. A moment since we saw that campment plain, now it is gone and see how those glittering foxfires run, and whence comes that evil whistling moan? Come."

They heard the steps turn a pace or two, then a cry swelled—"Nay" and "Nay"—and run. The wizard's mouth was twisted into his beard in an expression too savage to be called smile. All breathed deep; there was a sense of crisis overcome, and little question to taking Meliboë's advice. But most now were willing to leave the question wholly to Airar, being much fatigued with the long march, battle, and escape, whereas there was little meat and they remembered that sleep will do for dinner where naught else is. They began to compose themselves; Airar set guards in pairs, and the magician like the rest unlaced his armory for sleep.

For Airar himself rest was distant long, his mind running round and round like a rat in a cage till toward dawning, when he fell on a doze, fitful and marred by dreams of the clash of arms, with spears breaking and worlds shaking. It seemed to him in this dream that he should but could not turn the course of his thought on Gython—for even in dream was ware he dreamed—and was somehow disgraced by not doing so. At last with a mighty effort he brought the name to the front of his mind, but with no image save that incongruous of a white unicorn that sniffed among green leaves; then woke with set face, trying to remember how his love had last looked.

Dawn was sliding in under cold blue clouds, a wind driving the red-grey reed-tops, and someone had caught a pair of ducks that were being prepared for a meal. Meliboë the enchanter stood leaning his back against his saddle, a cloak wrapped round him and the wind playing in his beard. His head was sunk on his chest; the horse sniffed and nibbled unhappily at the dry rank marsh-grass of their little island of solid ground.

"A new day and new cheer, master," called Visto, not ungaily, who was building up a fire; somewhere he had found sticks. Meliboë lifted his head, gave a glance from another world, and—as though this were a signal for which he waited—squatted and began to draw a pentagram on the ground, presently sifting onto it through his fingers a quantity of certain particolored powders he drew from a pouch. It was a divination—to what purpose Airar could not guess, for there was no smoke. The men of Gentebbi huddled for warmth around the fire, glancing over their shoulders and talking in low tones as the appetizing odor of roasting birds floated along the gust. Magic and meal were done together; as they took their places to try a hunter's fare, Airar asked the magician which way it was in his mind to travel.

"I have looked in the seeds. There is no danger for you this day but toward Salmonessa; therefore, as you please if you follow your own thinking—but if mine, southwesterly and away from this causeway toward the shoreward march of Mariola, thence back north and westerly toward the foot-path passages through the Merillan Heights, where they fling off from the Hogsback, and so on into Hestinga."

He traced out a simple plan with the end of a duck's thighbone as he spoke. ". . . Always avoiding Marskhaun, which will be under deadly siege, with the gentours scouring the country." Airar might have caught from the tail of his glance a certain stir and fall of faces among the men, but none said a word as Meliboë looked on his drawing melancholically. "Oh, weary—what it costs a man to have unease in his vitals." He swung to Visto: "Sir 'prentice unpreniced, find a stupid wench, marry her, settle down and raise cabbages, thus guarding your happiness in what you do. You can be happy or heroic, not both; but no use saying so to this young-blood leader—he's of the kind must stir up wars and kingdoms; but if such found fewer to follow them, we'd all live long."

Visto laughed. "Would not be better to seek content; the others are all for renown and never happy till their robes be trimmed with kings' beards, being worse than stirring men, since they make all men stir. . . . And she, she; there's a strange fate for you."

Sewald growled that the magician had small experience with dames to say so. And they took up their journey soon after, moving on much the same order as the night before, with Meliboë riding among the main group; he had taken the pennon from his lancehead. A few flakes of snow slanted along the air and it was better to be walking than standing still.

They had gone maybe an hour in this fashion when Airar's quick sight caught on a hillock that rose above the weeds to marsh-bush leftward something that moved contrary to the wind. This could never be foemen; he cried halt and sent four by a circuit round a patch of reed to see whether it be friends, or some animal that would make a dinner. Some were found to grumble about the delay, but all were soon glad of it, for it brought back no less than Erb the Lank, with a group that brought their numbers to a score and two. His ugly face wrinkled when he saw Airar; took the young man's hand in both his own and tears came out on his cheek.

"My shame that all ran," said he. "Free-fishers have never done so before, and now you shall make me bow-bearer or other menial behind you."

"Nay," said Airar, "you no more than the rest. We ran all. They were in truth too many, and their over-captains with a closer thought on plan than that bastard three-fingered Duke, hiding among his shave-heads. As for bowmanry, I have thought on the matter—" (which was not true, it came to him only

on the tongue with the need of saying something)"—
to this end, that a man is born to it like a stal-
lion to studding, but must learn through long years; so
that from now your free-fishers that remain in this
venture shall be spearmen while I lead. Though I cannot but think it the worser weapon."

All now praised him for the best and most generous
of captains, saying they would follow him to the end
of the world and back. Erb touched the hand of Meliboë, it cannot be said with any great pleasure on
either side, they eyeing each other like uncertain
hounds. Erb said Airar had done well to set a picquet
before the band, but that if it were three or four
men strong there was no need of second cover, and
the arrangement was thus altered.

The snow had begun to come thicker now, all the
landscape driving with it; fortunately, the previous
day's thawing had left the marsh so damp the flakes
would not catch, so they had but to follow the path
of growing white, but direction now became a problem
and the air was bitter cold. Airar walked not far from
the enchanter, well coddled in his cloak and unhappy,
while the free-fishers treated it as a jest, speaking of
ice about the mainhaul, or shouting for an imaginary
lad to bring hot spiced wine.

He was not done marvelling how readily all had
followed on this unknown adventure and said as much
to Erb, who replied that it was no marvel whatsoever
but old Rudr's good choice, who had found for the
fifty to Salmonessa men without ties to keep them at
home—"Saving myself, that must just come as captain, though I have a sister in house, much in need of
man's helping"—whereat Airar thought of the harri-
dan Ervila who had come to him for ratsbane, but
dared not laugh, for Erb was blowing his nose with
thumb and finger.

Now they were on harder ground, with bush, as
marsh-edge thorn, low juniper, and an occasional yew,
frosting fast with falling snow. Airar called in the
picquet and a consultation was held, with some for
camping against the growing blast, but Erb said gentour parties would be across the whole countryside

when the weather cleared, seeking wreck and plunder from the battle. Press on, therefore, in a tighter knot; but as the hour drew maybe past a noon that none could see, it was clear that press on could be carried little farther and Svarlog had the shivers.

They stumbled on a cow-track. Airar said take it, though it led as near as he could judge southward from their true direction, meandering crazily along rising ground. His thought bore fruit; the path took them to a byre and beyond that down the hill a little to a cot around which snow was already drifting onto the old snow that had lain. For a time there was no answer to their knocking, but when Erb said in a loud tone there must be none within and they had best burst the door, it sprang open. A carle stout and wide-shouldered stood there, not very high for a Dalecarle, hooknosed and sullen of countenance, and the more so at the sight of so many armed men. He let them in with an ill grace, naming himself Britgalt. As Airar brushed past through the door he sunk his voice low enough just to be heard and chanted, *"Geme, plange, moesto mori—"* but there was no response. The place had but one room, which they well filled; there were two sons, as sour-mouthed as their father, but no women visible.

Airar bustled Svarlog into one inglenook and got water boiling to give him a hot draught. Meliboë took the other unbidden, dropping his armor in a pile on the floor, and sat muttering to himself with his cloak half-wrapped round his head, dabbing a finger in the ashes, while Erb and Airar were persuading Britgalt to sell a pig for a handful of silver ainar and sent Sewald and Visto out with one of the sons so they would have to eat. Not much was said.

The pork was already in pot and a savory odor coming out to mingle with the steaming smell of wet clothing when Visto looked round to ask where one of the sons was, that had been with them to the pig-yard.

"Un came in with you, when you brought the ham," said Sewald, but Visto:

"Nay, I left un; turned back."

"Where then? Could un be lost in storm?" Visto got upright, but there was almost a smile round Britgalt's lips before Meliboë lifted his head in the dark corner and said:

"He has gone to warn the gentours of your presence."

Their grimly host reached to his belt, but tall Erb got an arm round his throttle and held knifehand with hand, there was a yell and tumult, the other son snatching for a boar-spear till thrown down by numbers crash among certain objects in the corner. The wizard stilled it with uplifted hand and another word:

"Nay, take your meat undisturbed. Not for nothing have you an enchanter of your company. I had marked these for Vulking allies from the first moment, so that when this one passed I but touched him with ash and a small spell your young captain knows of. In this weather he will wander at fault; they will find his body or if the wolves come his bones, in the spring."

At this the man Britgalt's eyes seemed like to start from his head; he got breath to yell a slobbering curse and struggled so hard it took all Erb's force with another to hold him. The tall man said:

"Undisturbed we take meal, but sauce we just must have, and the sauce is that these two false Dalecarles be hanged to the ridge-pole of their own byre before we sit at meat."

There was so loud a shout of approval that Airar, young enough to be tenderheart, gave over before bringing to speech his thought of protest. Meliboë the enchanter looked at him as the pair were led struggling out.

"I have heard of those so gentle they will not squash beetles," said he; "mainly they turn religious and live by cozening women."

But that night he thought of Gython and lay awake long among the snoring men, wondering if it were possible to die of heartbreak alone; and of Rudr's people under the iron rod of Briella.

15. Hestinga: It Is Another Day

THE STARS WERE ONE BY ONE TWINKLING
into light and the moon not yet risen when young Airar
came forth to look on the west's last paleness. They
had that day burned old grass from fallow land for
the easier planting of grain; the smoke still clung along
windless levels and mingled its scent with that of things
suddenly green. Out toward the ricks a colt capered
beside its dam.

He drew a long breath and looked round; north
and west the steeps of the Dragon's Spine climbed
brokenly to snow, their peaks still catching the last
faint dayshine and seeming so near they might be
reached in an hour by a man not of the most brisk
afoot. Said Erb the Lank:

"What think you? Who be they riders that comes
past elm clump there? You have the eyes of me, Mas-

125

ter Sharpsight; but I make it too many for Holmund and a's band."

Airar turned long and lazily, stretching his arms. "Belike the men of that Hrappsted twenty leagues away south," he said. "When they guested here they would join us for the journey over the mountains at the break of spring, and lo! it has come." He looked under a hand; "Nay, Erb, you have right; these are far too many and not of the right fashioning; I see a gleam of steel. Cry sword and ware."

Erb turned; even as he did so there came a shout from the man who stands always in the spy-post on the rooftree of those Hestinga steads. Now there was hurry and barring of doors, with even the cook who was a Micton serf called out from scouring pots. In truth as they drew near it could be seen this was not a little company, though maybe their numbers were made more in the dying light; fully armed all. Bows were ready at the overhang windows as they approached and spearmen in the watch-booths along the stockade, but the leader of those who came rode in with one arm uplifted, crying, "Ho within, is this the stead of Sedu?" and when he had a somewhat surely answer, instead of answering again, sang out in a high voice:

"*Geme, plange, moesto mori*—and have you one here called Airar the Farsighted of Vastmanstad?"

"*Dolorosa Dalarna!*" shouted Airar down in return and ran below to be embracing Rogai the hunter in a moment, with "What tiding?" and "You come escorted for sure," and "I thought you dead or sieged with the Duke Roger."

"Aye, there was the worst man in the world, but dead and gone now and can make no defense or himself, so no more on that, but let us in and we'll fall to a change of budgets."

Now Airar must vouch for Rogai and his train to the overseer of the stead of Sedu, Holmund the horse-master being absent. They crowded through the gate to the number of some thirty and there was a busy confusion with torches brought and serfs running about to care for horses, while fresh meat was set out in the long hall. The first that came in beside Rogai were four like as peas to peas, with black hair bearing a wisp of white above the brow and long, thin visages. Airar went shy at once on seeing face to face those famous Carrhoene captains. With Rogai it was all ease; he named them—Alsander, Pleiander, Evimenes, Evander, the last with no hint of hair on face, who must be the concealed girl.

"Great joy," they murmured at the naming and would at once have taken the places flanking the high-seat, but Meliboë already had one seat there and Erb stood behind another, so with slight frowns and Evander making a mouth at him they must follow Rogai around the table to the seats facing, while Airar last of all slid into his accustomed chair to the right of Holmund's high seat. As soon as they were down and the servants busy, Rogai said:

"Now, Master Airar, you shall tell the tale of how you broke half a wing of gentours with so few men, then vanished like a worm in bark; since it must be a story marvellous to make so much said of it in Vulking camps this winter and the last."

"No marvel whatever beside that of how came you in Vulking camps to hear say."

"Nay, that's but a small tale. Evimenes has a better—"

"Mmgrowrr-uff," said the Star-Captain named, with his mouth full, then clearing it with a gulp; "I boiled a Vulking viscount, ha-ha. Legs like those of a lobster."

"As we have heard," said Rogai with a sidelong glance, but the Carrhoene captain banged his mug on the table as though for attention and rushed on:

"It was while I lay hide-o after the curst battle in Countess Dalmonea's gard, up near the Deidei border, with my skin all stained with nut-juice and hair clipped short to be a bastardly Micton slave. After the fall of Salmonessa this viscount came up to clutch the estate for Vulk; her husband, d'ye see, had fallen in the city. It took him no more than two eyes to see that she would be a bouncing bed-companion, as indeed I found her. She played at melting, but told him he must have a bath first, and I as serf made it. When the stupid bastard was in the bath-house what did I do but bar the door from the outside and then drop hot stones more than he wished in the reservoir at the back. Squealed lika hog in heat before the steam finished him, ha-ha-ha-ha-*ha!*"

"Aye," said Rogai with another of those side-glances, and Airar might have conceived that all was not harmony in this new band; "aye, and you left her to bear the pains when they came inquiring, if I mistake not."

"Glmff," said Evimenes, chewing again. "What would you? A citybred dame, no person for a flight with gentours riding behind. Women's security lies in their legs, but not by being used for running."

"Oh, aye, the gentours; that is precisely what we wished to hear on," Rogai cut in. "The tale, Airar—" The one named Alsander had moved not a muscle of his face; but Airar could not think how small any doing of his own must look to these experienced swaggering captains with their cold, hard faces masking cold, hard minds, and moreover wanted to cry at Rogai: You have been in Salmonessa; where is Gython? He looked into his drink and said only, "It was that Doctor Meliboë knew they would come, sirs, therefore we set an ambush in a defile."

At this the enchanter lifted his head. "Gentles, I ask you not to believe too closely the account of this young captain, as much a paragon in modesty as he is in deeds. I am only a poor doctor of the philosophies, who lack understand in intricate matters of war, but to me it would seem more honorable to slay five and twenty enemies in battle than one in a bath."

"To you, old man—" began Pleiander, but Evander-Evadne, the girl beside him, laid a hand on his wrist and said: "Oh, peace, brother. I'd hear the tale of this pretty young captain." Airar looked up; her voice was in her throat, almost like a man's. "Say on, sir doctor, with the tale, since he will not give it himself."

"Why, then, it was so," said Meliboë. "As we journeyed north through the Merillian hills toward Hestinga, I became aware through certain of my arts that these gentour people were on our slot. We were mounted, but the worst of us not so well as the best of them, so that soon or late they must overtake some in a race. We of the philosophies are never for strife where smoothness will serve, and I was for giving them a false shape or seeming to follow, but not this young war-leader here. He recalls that we have come through a defile shaped crookedly like the hind leg of a dog, I do not know its name."

"Stone Pass," said Tholkeil the Mariolan from down the table.

"And well named, being set with boulders, much hidden under snow. The young lord here turns the whole company back and sets some down at the upper end of the pass on foot among the boulders, some more at the lower end before the crook where it is narrowest, and more along the sides. When those gentours have all entered in, moving fast as they may along a clear trail, he let stone and spear come down from their flanks; nor could they up-slope at the end against the spearmen among the boulders, nor down at the gut where Master Airar slew a couple of horses with his bow to block them, nor up the sides neither, all slippery with snow and steep. When some five and twenty were slain the rest cried quarter."

"It was Erb—" began Airar, but "Poh!" said Pleiander bringing his fist down. (When one saw them together his face was a trifle more heavy-jawed than the rest, though with the same nose and curious chin— round seen in profile, but pointed triangle in face.) "Well enough if you like, but a common little toad-catching ambush. Why, in the War of Poliolis our brother Alcides—"

"Nay," cried Erb across, his Adam's apple working as he lifted an arm for attention. "It's in what un did after ambush that our Master Airar comes captain. You lords of Carrhoene must know I'm just a free-fisher; have traded to your Twelve Cities and was even at Poliolis dock when Captain Alcides led that great ambush beyond walls on which you speak. But that was for battle; after the trap sprung all was over, no more to be done. At Stone Pass having won we had all to do—make across great Hestinga with prisoners almost to our own number or feed them to the sword. Been me, I would ha' sworded a; mainly heathen from Dzik in they gentour bands, nohow. Not our Captain Airar. He just played on a for all's safety, keeping a by for two-three days, pretending to debate death and by arrangement talking on the best way to reach the highboard for Deidei. Then he lets a slip one fine night to carry news. A carried it, ha. Three days from the time we turned off in other direction we had a Hestinga man of the fellowship of the Iron Ring leading us here to lie in cover, tidings spreading as Master Airar thought. Did news come to Salmonessa through the siege even?"

Rogai: "Oh, aye, just before the turn of the year and after the Duke was stabbed across his own dinner table by the Lady Malina of Deidei when he shook her off to take a new mistress—that same whiteheaded damsel, good-looking and dressed as a lad, to whom you sang roundelays, friend Airar. I saw the downfall coming then and slipped out; with the set of Vulking badges I stole at Mariupol, passed myself as one of them till free. They do say Marshal Bordvin nigh bit himself with fury over the tale; not so much at the loss of the gentours at Stone Pass as letting Doctor Meliboë slip through his fingers, whom he holds for his worst enemy the now. He's no small wizard himself, Bordvin Wildfang, and has made his protection against all sorceries; conceives you must have found a new magic he does not know."

"No magic at all, only adroitness on the part of this young captain," said Meliboë; "though I will not say but it would have been better had magic been employed. For now they know themselves gulled; but if it were a doing beyond human power, they'd have no choice but submit."

But Airar, who had gripped the table edge till his fingers seemed to sink into the wood, asked as soon as he could gather breath:

"Where did she go?"

"Malina?" said Rogai, at whom he looked. "They stoned—oh, the girl. I do not know; they say she was asking a let-pass that she might go to Stassia and drink at the Well. They hanged that man of yours, though —Uffa—Ové. He was held to have brought on the evil luck of Salm through fetching the girl to His Highness and so driving Deidei to the side of the Vulkings."

"My lords," said Airar, pushing back his chair to fall, and even to himself his voice rang so strange that he did not wonder all dropped out of conversation to look; "my lords, I have done much today and would retire. Do not stint your nutriment, I pray, and on the morrow we'll talk of what's toward."

Eyes followed him as he reached the door, almost running. It was all over; the world was shaken with sobs which he told himself unmanly but could not hold till he felt a hand on his shoulder and roused from his bed to find Meliboë the enchanter gazing at him not unkindly.

The old man said nothing. After a moment:

"Have you a spell for broken hearts?" asked Airar.

"Hearts do not break; or knit again quickly under the poultice of new springs. I would have said the warrior-lass looked kindly on you, and did mark how her voice touched some string in that heart you call broken."

Airar reached out one hand and let it slowly fall. "If I had followed mine own will and not your divination and gone to Salmonessa, I might have saved her."

"From what? She goes to the Well and will find peace. Your love is of self only if you do not wish her the best. Touching the divination, it does not lie; and said clear that for you, all your hopes and projects were in deadly danger in Salmonessa."

"Rogai won free."

"Aye, not being mixed in this coil of loves and hates and stabbings of crownèd dukes. You have no vengeance but on two men now dead—to wit, this Ové and the Duke's self. All tasks are done there for you; it is time to be a full man instead of one half-made, and think on greater things than a comfortable bed-fellow."

An impulse to strike him chased through Airar's

mind, was driven past by the thought—Why? and his face distorted as he cried wildly: "You are unfair, you do not—Nay, I'll never do it, I'll follow her to Stassia—"

The magician sat down. "As you will . . . and if you can reach one of the ports, as Naaros or the lesser Lectis . . . Young sir, you are reasonable acute; will some day learn that to run the race of this world in pairs is to go halt-foot both. . . . Oh, aye, pain of loss. But what loss? . . . How much did you ever really have of her or she of you? Ask of yourself. . . . The loss that cuts to marrow is that of a companion through years, with whom are no new discoveries. . . . I could conjure you up a shape would give you as much brief pleasure or pain, but brief only, long loves are not so made. . . . What you have lost is a pleasure of possession, as of a horse or red jewel, no more. . . . Look now:"

He drew from his pouch something that flickered bright in the single low wall torch the room held, snapped his fingers, and murmuring, moved both hands as a weaver might at a loom. Before him Airar saw a shimmering faint shadow against the wall, growing more solid till it was verily Gython, Gython. But her face was fixed and distant as on the morning she flung out at him so in the lock-bed of Rudr's house at Vagai; and it came to his mind that she would always be thus for him, the very he without aids from beyond the world; and for no other reason had she come with the band of fifty under his command then to avoid being wedded to him by authority of her father—"If it were only Visto!"

The vision failed and he realized he himself had cried aloud the words or others like them. A smile that made him look like a devil played half an instant at the corners of Meliboë's mouth.

"Good-night, fair young sir. Tomorrow is another day and there are wars among the hills."

16. A Judgment in Hestinga

HOLMUND THE HORSE-MASTER CAME HOME
the next day. One might have said he was none too
well pleased at being so stormed with guests of such
quality; but it was a tall, reasonable man, with a face
lined and impassive, who sat down to discuss measures
and war-movements as calm as though it were points
of a mare. Rogai was in that council and Airar of
course, as leader of a numerous band; Meliboë for
his divinations, and the Star-Captains with their sister; but not Erb, though Airar asked for him, feeling
much in need of his experience.

But: "Here we are in a circle of foes," said Rogai,
"and I've no mind to show them our projects, as did
Duke Roger. Oh, your Erb's a true man, yet like others, ourselves not less, needs a tongue-guard, and the
fewer tongues to guard, the better purpose is kept."

It seemed to Airar a hard rule to hold a man ignorant that must do much, but he could not protest when Holmund turned as self-denying with his own son: "Nay, when you're elect horse-master, you shall sit in my room; till then you're but another of the stead."

As to the purpose itself the Star-Captains were not less puzzled than Rogai. They had lain over the twain winters at various parts of wild Hestinga (except Evimenes), being led up to the Stead of Sedu by men of the Iron Ring who knew Airar was there with Meliboë and the most considerable band that had escaped the rout at the causeway. But that could be no more, as Holmund said; Marshal Bordvin could be counted to send strength through the horse lands when the ways were clear to hunt down just such as themselves. As for wandering peregrine:

"You are too many or too few," said the horse-master. "Too many to live like the outlaws who nest among gaps of the Dragon's Spine and raid our herds; too few to rouse Hestinga round any standard for a war against the tercias that have broke down Salmonessa."

"All might make submission and appeal to the Empire," said Rogai, and looked at the men of Carrhoene to see how they would take it.

"Not we, who are under its ban," said Pleiander shortly, and Alsander:

"Count Vulk's the deputy. 'Twould fall on his hands for judgment and he'd twist our guts out round a tree. You talk as though he were gentle or yourself wantwit, Sir Rogai."

"Nay, brother," said Evadne the girl in her whispering voice. "Do you not see this was said to try you, whether or no these half-castrato Dalecarles may trust on us? Hark!" She swung to Rogai. "Now no secrets; our case is too evil to be served by less than the full trust of all. We brethren fight for honor, and beyond that, pay; yet of either, there is little prospect in your lost war here. Nor is it to be denied that we made an effort at a composition with Count Vulk on the term that we'd withdraw forever from his lands in exchange for the release of our brother Evides. But these Vulkings are not of the polite people; they said nay, nothing but full surrender. So now we are yours without fee, since there's no place in the Empire whcre we may go, and will not go to heathen lands. . . . But I have no thought on what's to do."

Rogai smiled, all pleasure at learning what he wished, then shook his head. "Wrap our helmets in clouts and lift the green flag of Dzik for all I can see."

Now Meliboë threw on the surface of their talk his thought of making through to Os Erigu, as he had exposed it that night among the marshes.—No, no, cried all, it would never do, the man Mikalegon was a mere reiver and rover and his hold at many leagues of distance; but none could think of an alternate. At last Alsander:

"It is reported that after a battle all those under his standard share equally in plunder; an open-handed man."

The other Carrhoenes nodded, and now one by one those present gave reluctant adhesion to the plan except Airar, who had been over this ground before and, never saying a word, sat wrapped in thought, mainly to the end of how futile this fell on his ears. So it was to be Os Erigu and join their fortunes to the Earl there, who would have them for sure, since Rogai said all the talk among the Vulkings was that as soon as ever Salmonessa became quiet, Marshal Bordvin would lead the tercias north for a blow against Mikalegon and a great conquering in the Micton lands beyond, to gain serfs for the new estates. But now arose the question of how to reach to that north country with so large a band. Holmund Horse-master had the word:

—The ways (he said) spread all east and south from the Stead of Sedu to reach the main highroad from Briella down to Marskhaun and Mariupol. There was one turning faintly east of north through a pass in the Dragon's Spine to the upper reaches of the White River, but the vale through which it ran was narrow there, with another main highroad from Briella running through it down into the Whiteriverdales and so to Naaros. It would have castellas and patrols of the Vulkings; nor would escape from that vale be easy save along its length, for north over it stood the mountains of Korsor.

—Westaway (he continued) was another gap in the Dragon's Spine, not much used by the men of Hestinga because its steep slope made it all but impassable to horses, "and you know we Hestingerne are accused of being bastard to the Centaur." At the head of the pass was a little villa alone, not much known, called the Count's Pillow, for that the ninth Vulk had laid his head there and was thought to have buried treasure; the pass takes its name from the villa.

—It led straight down into the Whiteriverdales, the route meeting indeed the Briella-Naaros highroad, but in country much broken by ravine and sudden forest, with numerous outlets through the High Hills of Froy still farther westward, where a pursuit would find it hard to follow without falling on some such ambush as that Airar had given them at the Stone Pass. (Here Holmund paused to give Airar a glance, not sorry to praise a Dalecarle by comparison with the lords of Carrhoene.)

—Once through the hills and into Shalland, they might press to the shore and find boats for Os Erigu; or bend sharp north toward Stavorna, the city aloft in the Brenderhai. The Iron Ring was strong in those provinces; they would be passed through.

"With sixty men?" asked Pleiander, his tone skeptic.

"Were not sixty brought here together?" asked Holmund, but before the other could answer again, Evimenes (who of those Carrhoene brothers concerned himself with marches and movements) began to ask about distance and where they should find victual. Young Airar schooled himself to listen, though with the back of his mind his party was being taken —he would never love woman more save chance-met —Madame Korin's girls of Naaros, the archer had said on the first day of his journeyings?

Thus it was settled; the gathering rose and, it being full moon, postponed till after meat the mustering of their little host. They were sixty-six against an Empire when the tale was all told: twenty just of the free-fishers, twenty and two of the Carrhoene sergeants including those brothers, most of the rest Mariolans, who naturally chose Rogai for their leader, or men native to Hestinga who fell under him as the better-known Dalecarle, not liking to serve a foreign standard. But three fell into Airar's band, and that night came three more from Hrappstead, very stout lads, which gave him by a little the largest of the several companies.

The next morning they set out. It was the first day of the Month of the Wolf-cub, and this was held the best of omens to Dalarna's ancient emblem, though it rained. Airar and Rogai rode together at the head of the march, with a guide of Holmund's, who saying much as the horses plodded beneath the streaming skies through a landscape rolling featureless as the long waves of an ocean. They went slow pace; yet the riders must keep a good rein to prevent their mounts from stumbling on the burrows of small animals. The free-fishers were clumsy horsemen still, even after practice during the time. Meliboë had dropped away from them, shivering and querulous as always when the heavens frowned. On one side they passed a dolmen of piled stones, at which the guide looked up, waving a hand.

"We have little land-title here in Hestinga," he said, "but it is considered that from this point the Sea of Sedu marches with that next west. Under that monument lies the Abbot of Stavorna, who was slain here by Count Vulk the Ninth at the time of the lifting of the Lady Deodata."

It was a tale Airar had not heard and would willingly have shortened the ride with, but could not put in a question before there was a squawk and shout from behind and a horse without saddle or rider came charging past. He and Rogai both turned toward a group milling confusedly behind the curtains of rain, but Airar's horse caught a foot in a tuft of animal-hole and pitched him off on his nose with a shock that left him dizzy. A moment later Visto helped him up; while he gathered sense and felt to find himself unbroken, the hurlyburly broke out more furious than before, and Airar thought he could see someone on the ground among the horses' legs.

"What's toward?" he asked.

"Some broil of the southerners."

They hastened toward it just in time to see Rogai whip out a sword and cry furiously, "If that's your mind, draw off your greasy-guts and we'll even try handstrokes."

Slim Pleiander reached to his saddle for the mace that hung there, and Erb threw himself as though to protect Evadne with upraised spear, but Airar launched at both bridle-reins, crying, "In heaven's name, have we not enough to fight without each other?" and the thing was not gone so far but that both could pause, growling like dogs. The man on the ground sat up, holding one hand to his head, the rain washing blood down between his fingers. He was a Micton and, to judge by his dress, serf.

"What's the variance, and can we not compose—" began Airar, but the girl Evadne moved her own mount forward.

"He has right, brother," she cried. "Here's one not concerned in this contention and of good thought and heart, as we have said. I propose we handsel him a judgment; or if we will not take his word, then we shall draw off our company from the rest and go another way."

Pleiander growled again in his throat and his face held a half sneer, but Airar saw his hand relax. Rogai put up his sword.

"Come," said Evadne again and reached down to touch Airar's hand. "As one of the six brothers of Carrhoene I swear to accept the judgment of Airar the Farsighted in this quarrel or else to separate our people from these Dalecarles and never to disturb them more."

Alsander started forward to do the like, when Airar drew back gulping down his heart (for these were very great people, though their present case was low) and said: "No judgment on terms. I'm honest or no; if so, will have full judgment without retreats, but if not, why, choose another."

"Here's a breeches-wet justicular," snarled Pleiander, but Evadne: "Brother, you're a poop, and he has nothing but right, for did we ourselves draw from your company when you bade us tunnel under the outer tower at Phyladea against all our own wills? For my part, I'll seal judgment to him in whatever form desired."

Evimenes followed her, Alsander after Evimenes, and Pleiander came last of all, scowling still. Rogai and one of the Hestinga men next; they too were in this cause as Arair found when he asked, and all began to talk at once, while the Micton with the bloody head was being helped by another.

Said Evimenes for the Carrhoene captains where Airar could get a clear word: "A matter of horses; we've not enough for our men and all the package if any be lost in this pass, as seems most like, that is, no reserve. Here we met some running loose, and would take them as a dozen times before in these plains where they run wild. Up comes this mere serf squealing and howling in a language nobody can understand and seizes our brother Pleiander's bridle, which he'll not brook from any serf nor I either. So our brother clipt him, as any man of spirit would and should. Then up comes this other which Master Rogai, taking the serf's part and crying about thievery, which is a word we think too highly of ourselves to take without blood or boot."

Airar swung. "A fair statement, Rogai?"

"Aye, if it be foul to call black black, or name a thief for thieving. I—"

Pleiander gave a shout of rage and urged his horse forward again, but Airar held an outstretched hand against him and to Rogai cried: "No more of unfaming, or I call all against you! Now, sir, you whose name I do not know, what's your tale on this?"

Holmund's man rubbed a bristled chin, shining with wet. "Why, master, it's most like this outland lord make it, but he not saying Ruzi the serf told him these were not horses of the common store, but tamed to labor and so marked in the ears, and Ruzi did but seek to keep the goods of the stead, as taught."

Said Airar to the Star-Captains; "And you truly did not know the custom of these Hestinga lands that some horses are privy and hence nicked in the ear?"

Evimenes drew black brows together, but said "Honor of a soldier." Alsander lifted a hand.

"Then I find that the first fault is of ignorance, though a tort to those who have guested us well. It falls to the ground. Have you money?"

"Somewhat," answered Evimenes.

"The horses we need if you say, for you have much experience in these matters. But for each of these trained animals taken, you shall pay not less than half a piece to Holmund Horse-master's man here. Is not that a fair price?" and as the man nodded; "Whereas for the broken head of the serf, there shall be a fine of thirty ainar, paid to him."

Evadne said, her fine lip curling: "It is not the custom in our country to pay guilt-fines to slaves."

"But in Dalarna it is, for we hold a serf a man who has come to that estate more through misfortune than fault. Yet it is not our custom neither to unfame a man to the edge of blood unless blood's to be drawn, so for that there lies a guilt on Rogai toward you; and for that I fine him other thirty ainar, to be paid with such words of apology as Pleiander of Carrhoene shall ask. And this is my judgment."

All took this well and Airar was much praised for his justice throughout the band as they took to move again. But of this he knew little (since he rode with the guide and Rogai as before) till they sheltered for the night on cold food in one of those stone-and-sod huts with which the plains have been dotted by horse-masters, and Meliboë the enchanter came in. A fire of twisted grass burned, only enough to keep them from shivering; the magician worked himself into the best place before it and said low to Airar at his side:

"Now it is to be seen how far we can go together with my philosophy and your quality, fair young sir, and how little I was wrong who saw at first seeing that you would be an adroit and a lucky man. I have given you the test before them all and they see what a leader you will make if you but keep that charming boyhood simplicity."

"*You* put me to the test?"

"To be sure. Who do you think contrived it you should stumble out of that quarrel and so into judgment upon it? Or, for that matter, the quarrel's self? Those Carrhoenes can no more resist stealing anything that moves than an eagle can resist raping a rabbit, and someone must draw free horses under their eye."

To this Airar made no reply. He thought how happy life might have been had Gython been as kind as rude-tongued Evadne of Carrhoene.

17. The Count's Pillow: Second Tale of the Well

THE NEXT DAY WAS DRIPPING STILL, BUT from high clouds that showed a desire to break in streaks. They crossed a stream running swiftly between steep banks and began to climb, with hills throwing up on either side and small patches of wood, as pine or locust. Evimenes rode up with Airar at the head of the march this day and brought his sister, whom he addressed as "brother" and "Evander." They were gay and chattering; full of tales, and it flashed across the son of Alvar's mind that those four captains might have taken counsel the evening before and found him worth conciliating. But their talk was of useless wars and politics among the Dodekapolis, mainly to the point that all in the People's Party which stood for the Imperial interest were traitors and villains.

"The dog-smellers—for it is so we call them—rule everywhere but in Phyladea now," said Evimenes, "and there's no gain for us, since Phyladea hates lovely Carrhoene and joys to see her cast down under dog-smeller rule."

"There's Permandos," said Evadne.

"Our hope for a glad tomorrow. Aye, they'll not bear it there forever."

"Bear what?" asked Airar.

"The procedures of knavish Sthenophon, whom they made their leader in pulling down the true government there, and who has made himself into a mere spadarion and tyrant, with man-slayings by order and no law. . . ." He looked up shading his eyes. "Ha, it's in my mind the sky is breaking. Why, look you, Master Airar, his rule's a madness. Began by confiscating goods and properties from the families of the guilds that made and kept Permandos great, with their ships and caravans, putting down piracies and standing for honest dealing. But picking other men's pockets is common dog-smeller rule wherever it be. What marks this Sthenophon is that now he must run to confiscating lives, with horrid tortures, even among those who once helped him, for no other reason but that he finds their beliefs tainted by those of the party of the Guilds. A careless word at dinner, and you're for the rack."

"It was never so done among the Twelve Cities in the old time," commented Evadne.

"Nor even among these rude Vulkings," added Airar, "who let all believe what they will, so they give obedience to orders. I do not see how he's to know what's in the mind."

"No more can he. Ah well, 'twill not endure in busy Permandos, where they remember well the mild rule of the Gulds. The'll rise; and then, Evander my lad, we'll have a Permandos alliance and see olive trees again above Carrhoene."

"They grow like green smoke across the hills behind the city at the shore," said Evadne. "Hills not like these brutal and lonely mountains, but with round tops and sharp friendly angles and little bowers and springs where the heat of the day is sped with a bottle of wine and music. It may be we can show them to Master Airar one day."

Airar looked quick at that, which seemed to jangle some memory he could not fully form; but as it eluded him, said: "Sir, I beg you instruct me how it is that the Empire sustains the hold of this People's Party among your cities, whenas here in Dalarna the Imperials are all for the Lords Vulk, and down with everyone less."

"There's a good question," Rogai cut across. "Sir Ludomir Ludomirson's the only one of the kindred ever to be received at the court. The Iron Ring brought me a word from him, by the bye, Airar—he's somewhere in Skogalang, keeping touch with the Ring in Naaros city as he waits happier times. The Vulkings have set a price on his head."

"As touching your question, I do not know," said Evimenes. "Never thought on't. Those Well-drinking eunuchs are all for order, order, peace, peace, and let nothing change but the rates of tax, and they forever upward."

Said Evadne: "May I speak a word on this, brother? For I think I may unravel it by saying you have hit the target but only at the rim. Look you—if it were but peace and order these snot-licking Imperials sought, could they not have it from the Gulds of Carrhoene or these Dalecarles in their own country? Nay, here's no desire for peace general, but peace of one kind—namely, which has no change or conflict, or dignity but the Empire's own. Nay, for that, brother, they in Stassia know that change is never wanted by men secure in their daily bread, though they be chained to the stones that grind the meal. Where's the difference there 'twixt dog-smellers and Vulkings? Different, aye, in manners, but alike at heart in that they put out of the world all that does not make men as sure of their places and as stupid as so many sundials."

"Ha!" whooped Evimenes. "Brother, you talk like

that mangy philosopher with the moth-eaten beard."
Whereat Evadne flushed red, calling him a cow-pimp
with other foul names till Airar would have ridden
apart from them had there been any way. But this
was difficult, for their journey imposed less speed upon
them, the pass having become steep indeed, the horses
labored with bent heads as though dragging heavy
loads, there were cries of urging among the men behind, and on either side long draws ran down toward
the way from overhanging peaks with dirty snow pock-
marked by rain under the trees.

There were more of these trees, now nearly all
dark pine; they crossed a low ridge and, coming down
the backslope, found themselves cramped by trunk
and rockshelf to the very edge of a whirling mountain
stream. Here their guide dismounted; so did Rogai,
and Airar when he saw the experienced mountain
hunter do so, though Evadne the girl sat her horse
waiting with a smile that might have been half-sneer
for their weakness, but that it was kind. The Mariolan
picked out a pair of darts from his saddle-bow, saying
that in such weather they might chance on an early
bear, savage with hunger, or one of those great mountain cats that would be attracted by the smell of their
horses and not hesitate to attack. Airar slung quiver
over shoulder and took down his bow, holding it in
one hand while he led the horse with the other.

Nothing of that sort came on them the day, but it
was a hard climb and a long that brought them, come
early twilight under grey skies, to a place where the
way suddenly became easier and they were in a bowl
of ground with peaks all round. The trees gave back;
here was a meadow containing one or two trees, out
of which against the dark forest on the opposite slope
started a villa with two or three barns, all built
peasant-like of outlandish woods, and painted: The
Count's Pillow. Alsander and Pleiander came up to
ride with the leaders, a goat bleated, a bell tinkled,
and a man came out of the dry grass ahead.

As they drew close all saw he wore the red badge
of Vulk, and a glance whipped from eye to eye; but
it was a very old man, somewhat vacant of face, who

greeted them with the Peace of the Well, offering forage for their beasts with straw in the barns for the men to sleep on, "but I do not know that I have provision for so many, provision for so many," and shook his head.

Evimenes bade him give no concern to that, and having signed Evadne to hold the gaffer under observation (lest there be some secret treachery intended) they went to see the men disposed. Fires were lit under the darkening branches; there was jollity and exchange of favors, for the Hestinga men had brought proviant of dried beef as was the custom of their country. But before Airar or Rogai or the Carrhoenes could think of their own night, here was Evadne back with word that the old guardian, too dim-wit to be dangerous, had told her stablished custom called the leaders to lie at the villa, and was preparing food.

"Could it be poisoned?" said Rogai, and she laughed. They went in presently, taking Meliboë. The Vulking served them with his own hands, in silence and from good plate, a roasted kid with garlics, then sat with them before the fire and gazed around from somewhat lackluster eyes.

"Sirs and gentles, I ask your indulgence," said he, "to the hearing of a tale; for I am set in this place under an ordinance as my father and grandfather were before me, pray everyone that comes to hear this tale, which is a memorial of the blessed Count Vulk, the ninth of the name, and now I have no son or grandson, but am the last of those called Boulard, so that who will keep the memorial beyond me, I do not know, yet—"

"Well, then, the tale, old man," said Pleiander, "and let it be brief, for we must seek our rest, since weary men march ill."

The ancient lifted both hands before his eyes clutched at something invisible and drew them down, trembling slightly.

—I crave your grace, gentle sir, said he, I do not mean with mine own affairs to interrupt this tale, which is a very moral relation and of great profit, as you shall see, therefore it is no small matter that it should be lost to the world through the failure of my flesh. This is the tale of Count Vulk the Ninth, the blessèd, and the days when the heathen were still in the land, against whom he bore his banner with the love of the Church, and made much slaughter of them down among the Whiteriverdales, as has been told, but that is not this tale.—

The door opened; Erb came in, and would have spoken, but Evadne motioned him silence, and made place for him next to her, which he took sheepish as a boy, but without halting the flow of words.

—Now you must know that the Count Vulk was at this time young, having been elect to his dignity by his eighteenth year, which is a thing almost unheard-of and only because of the great valiancy and the high name of his father. It is said also that he was the handsomest of the Vulks, tall as a tree, with hair smooth and black like midnight, gay eyes and ever a laugh in his voice, a very fortunate and perfect prince. After the great battle in the Dales, he went up to Stavorna city, where thanks were offered in the church for deliverance, and there was a banqueting afterward in the hall of the syndics. Oh, the bright plate and the clean white napkins and the brave meats they served, with music among a thousand candle-flames at that banquet, and young Vulk the merriest of all, leading in song.—

The old man cleared his throat and in a voice so quavering it could not be said to make a tune, intoned:

> *Let us drink, drink, drink once again,*
> *Drink without thought of tomorrow;*
> *Let us love, love, love all the night,*
> *For love is alone without sorrow.*

—Sirs and gentles, you may easily believe that those of the Church who were present were not so well pleased with songs of this nature, for it has ever been the office of most holy Church to restrain the loose illicit passions such singings would encourage. Now fortune willed it that there should be seated at the left of the Lord of Briella a nun, it being the custom in those days (though the Church has a different rule now) for these brides of God to go forth into the world on such occasions as feasting, that they might learn the nature of the sins and temptations they were required to combat, and all the arts of the Devil, that they might the better refute his arguments. Moreover, this nun had by two a reason for attendance, being Egonilla and the daughter of the great Earl of Os Erigu, who had taken her residence in the monastery of Stavorna for the fame and holiness of its Abbot.

She had to now been merry as any present, her heart being good and filled with the love of God, though without joining in the drinking. But at this revellous song she signed herself and cast down her eyes. It is related that Vulk looked at her in his grey mad humor and marked how long the lashes lay on her cheek.

—By the Well, cried he, here's one that could love all night! How of it, sweetling, shall we make the song came true? And he clapped his arm round her— an evil deed, sirs and gentles, but he was young and without thought and from such we are given to learn.

—Sir, she said, I love all the night and the day, too, the perfect love of God; and for that you have clipped me, and so introduced to my thought, even if only a little and for rejection, the touch of another love, I must be on my knees. Therefore I beg you withdraw your arm.

—The greater the temptation, the greater the victory, said Vulk, but he took away his arm and turned to answer someone who had pledged him a cup, but as he took his eyes from the bottom, the fiend sent him a thought and he turned again to Sister Egonilla.

—Look you, said he, you of the monastery come from time to time to the world to learn what you cast away. I call that true philosophy; none so good as those who, knowing all that evil offers, will sell themselves at a higher price. But there's a flaw in your practice: if you know so little of secular love that its touch is sin, then say I, you are not good, but ignorant. Or riddle me, were you born of your parents' sin? For union is a sacrament, no sin.

—Sir, said she, the sin of our first parents into which we are all born, yet through the blessed sacraments obtain absolution.

—Yet if the sacrament itself lead to further sin, the absolution is not real, said he, and they debated thus like doctors in the midst of the banquet to the exclusion of all others, which conversation being reported to his lordship the Abbot, he frowned and looked exceeding grave, declaring that the young Count was not far from horrible heresies. Yet shall one quarrel with the sword of the Church? He gave her permission to convince Count Vulk of his theological errors, she being of all the ladies of the monastery the most sweetly persuasive, and of rank sufficient.

. . . Meliboë the enchanter laughed. "I can see what is coming," he said, but the old man only looked at him with pain as Airar thought the horse Pil had looked at him when he left Trangsted.

—Sirs and gentles, the ways of God are mysterious and not to be accounted for of our poor minds. The Count and the lady met in the reception room of the monastery, agreeable to the rule, speaking across the gate-window in the wall. His Lordship the Abbot, thinking to take some part in this discussion, entered unannounced, and what did he find, O ta-li-iddle-daly? He found them kissing and fondling through that window. To her cell with a heavy penance he sent Sister Egonilla, while himself sought sweetly and with love to reason against Count Vulk. It was to little purpose; the Count did say aye, aye, but soon he was gone, and then she too, he having convinced her that she must first sin to be forgiven, as though the sin of our earliest parents had not convicted us all. The Count let build this villa even as it is here now, and on this very floor before this fire has sat the blessèd Count Vulk, domptor of the heathen but unblessed in those days, with the damsel Egonilla.

Sirs, that was a grievous time in the land, for if the heathen were dompted, the Earl of Os Erigu not so, an old man who held that his daughter had been raped away to the utter disgrace of his house, as the bishops and abbots held it was the disgrace of the

Church. Therefore Os Erigu stopped the trade of the two cities Lectis, threatening war; and there was fire on the rooftree in Norby, where he let loose the barbarous Mictons that are for neither God nor man. Oh, sirs, a grievous time; up out of the Whiteriverdales and down from Briella by the long road came divers to this place, with protests of this and that, and embassies from Os Erigu and the Empire, till the lovers could not spend a night alone, and at last the Chancellor of the realm himself, who said Os Erigu would have his daughter back or war, and at that Egonilla, who sat with Count Vulk, twisted in his arms, saying:

—My lord and love, this is his death, his very death, for my father is old, and I know if you are forced to the field against him, it is he will fall. And she wept; oh, the tears of the lovely lady Egonilla on these very planks and stones.

—Death and life and we two (said he). I have given my hope of greatness to find peace with you, and shall I now not have it? Nay, I'll lay down the courtship.

—It is the same. Do you think my father could stand against who would be chosen the tenth Count Vulk?

Vulk's brow went frown and arms relaxed.—There is the ninth Vulk and I am he. But the Lord Chancellor cleared his throat.—I am he, he said again, and will not make wars on the father of my love. I'll raise the standard—

—Against whom? said she, sliding wholly free from his grasp to stand.—Now I will give you a choice; nay, an end—I'll not be kissed from my purpose. I'll give you a choice and there is no third way. Either I shall return forthwith and accept whatever penalties are due for this sweet sin; or we shall go and drink together at the well of wonders, the Well of the Unicorn, so winning its peace.

—I am a warrior and by office leader of the Vulking tercias.

—A moment since you had left hope of that greatness for peace with me.

Now it was she who had the better of the disputation, and though he might turn from storm to pleading or play cold, the end was that he must give way. The Vulking lords thought ill when they heard of him going to the Well and there were not a few that wished to unseat him and sweep Os Erigu into the sea, but there were enough of the other view to withhold them this time, and the more so since the heathenry saw in the land's troubles their delight and began a raising of diversions. Of those pilgrims to the Well, it is told that they were received with all honor in Stassia, and did drink as others before them; yet, when the draught was drained, could find themselves no different in thought or condition, so that when they voyaged back there lay upon them a certain strangeness and expectancy of what this peace might be that they had won.

There were few to greet Vulk when he finished that journey, and when he came again to this very villa of the Count's Pillow none but my grandfather and a single guest, the Abbot of Stavorna to wit, that saintly man. It is not told what was said at first among them, but no word of return to the monastery and the Abbot gave them joy of their new peace, whereat a shadow crossed both their faces together.

—It is a long voyage, said the lady Egonilla, and Vulk:

—With a cold welcome here. Where is this peace? With Os Erigu still threatening wars, but now it is the lords in council make all the answers and I am as good as uncoronate.

—Yet the promise of the Well is sure, said the Lord Abbot. Did you not on the ship hither find that peace and joy together which you sought?

—Oh, aye, said Vulk and seemed about to say more, but let his voice drop.

—The promise is sure, but you shall not say what manner the peace may take, said the Abbot, for that is to presume to dictate to God how He shall accomplish His ends. It is for us to seek what way He would have us go.

The lady Egonilla had said nothing since the first. Now she looked up and there was a light in her face.

—I see it now, she said, and it was the lack of it that has turned our love to weariness and ashes. There is no peace or love but the perfect love of God, which is the essence of every other. Father, forgive me; and she knelt before the Lord Abbot.

Sirs and gentles, my grandfather (who was in the room) said that Vulk's face flushed like wine and he seized out a deadly dag, crying—You shall not take Egonilla from me or I will slay her and you too.

—Hush, said the Abbot, there is no Egonilla here, and taking a vial of holy water he sprinkled her where she knelt.—I give you a new name, he said, that is Deodata, which is given of God and to God returned. As for you, Sir Count, you may indeed slay us; but remember that you have drunk from the Well, seeking peace. Peace you shall have; but if you will not have it, be beaten with whips and rods till you accept your gift.

Soon he was gone and Deodata, too, as Egonilla had gone from the monastery, Vulk left alone. But is told that he, somewhat repenting of his fury, rode after to give her some token or small object of farewell. Now the gentle Abbot was an old man and the way down through the Whiteriverdales beset with landslides, therefore he and the lady had taken the easier route, east into Hestinga. But when Vulk reached the first crofts in the dales and found they had not passed that way, all his devilish rage came back on him, doubled and trebled.—I have been tricked, he cried, and they think to escape me with another trick, but it is not so. He turned rein and rode like a madman across the Dragon's Spine up the brakes and down the other way, and coming on the Abbot and the lady at the issue of the pass, struck that good man down out of hand. Oh, sirs and gentles, the Abbot lying with his blood all spattering the horse's back! But the lady Deodata looked on him coldly, coldly.

It is not told what was said there or if he besought her to return to the Count's Pillow. But if this were the case his beseechings were without success, for she rode on and away. And now came troubles manifold on Count Vulk and his realm, since the Empire placed its ban upon him for that he had violated the peace of the Well, and the Church its excommunication for that he had slaughtered the good Abbot, and the naughty Dalecarles rose and some Vulkings fell away to join them, and when Count Vulk buckled on his harness again, he that had been so mighty had no more heart nor hand for war, so that he was driven back at last to the home counties. There was a battle in North Hestinga, which battle he lost, and flying into the Korsor hills saw one after another of his men drop away into the hands of the pursuit till at last he was left alone and they ranging on his track. It would be toward evening that he saw what might be a faint path leading to one side and following it, came to a cave with a fount running down beside it. His horse was wholly spent, he unbridled it, and thinking he might find some defense or means of escape at the cave, went toward it, but as he did so, a hanging at the entrance was drawn aside, and he found himself facing the nun, Deodata.

It is said that she was even more lovely than when he first had seen her, yet now with an expression of joy and calm that was somewhat disturbed at seeing this armed man she had known in another world. —Can you not let me live my life as I have let you lead yours? she said, but he laughed bitterly.—You are as ever, too vain, he said. Would I come for you wounded and alone, from a lost battle? Stand aside and let me fight for my life; is there another entrance to this cave?—A shout was borne to them from down the valley; she looked at him for a long moment and said,—Will you have peace? He looked at her a longer one and saying aye to that, dropped to his knees before her, where those who followed found them.

—Lady, they said, for all in that land had respect to the holy nun, now let us take this Count Vulk, this most approved traitor, from your sight.

—Be still, said she, there is no Count Vulk here, and taking a handful of water from the spring, she sprinkled it on him. I have given him a new name, she said; it is Theophilon from the old tongues, which is to say the lover of God. They were of the Bishops' party and did not offense her, so left them. It is told that after Count Vulk entered the Church he became no less famous than she, like one of the blessèd saints; but there was an ordinance made that this place should stand forever as a memorial, with one to offer guesting and the tale to all who came through the pass of the Count's Pillow, and that is my narration, O ta-li-iddle-daly.

18. Issue of the Pass: Captains Gather

THE DESCENT, AS NOT UNEXPECTED, WAS far worse than the climb, for they had not only the height of the pass itself to lose, but all that of the high plateau of Hestinga, so far upborne on the bones of the Dragon's Spine which look across the rough Whiteriverdales. One or two horses were lost on the breakneck ledges, as Evimenes had foreseen; but Rogai of the mountains, now thoroughly at home, rode forward to survey each passage and, at one where the way went round a cliff with a steep to water far below, had his Mariolans set stakes interwoven with branches at the edge, so a chance step might not send a man down.

How could he foresee, as they camped in a cleft

and owls ghosting past the fire, that Evadne of Carrhoene would rise from her place and motion Airar to follow? Should he go? But indeed, why not? And with a murmured word to the rest about taking an easement, did step after her. Among the trunks there was flickering light from the blaze; not too cold, for it had cleared during the day, and even at this height all the buds were shouting spring. She led the way, they both stumbling, to a tree-root for sitting, and "Hark, friend Airar," she said, "what do you seek in Dalarna?"

"Why, liberation from these Vulkings. They are not our blood, yet rule over us with a hard rule. When I was a lad, the steads around were happy, with good friends and honest neighbors and gatherings on the holidays. But now? Ours was the last, all under some Vulking magnate now, who lives fat and lets graze them with Micton slaves."

"Ah, tsa, you preach like a dog-smeller. It was yourself I meant on? Whither are you personally bound?"

He was a long time on answering. "Truth tell, I had not thought of it, and—"

"You'd have me credit that you take up these wars for pure highmindedness and others' benefit, like a priest or an Imperial? Come, no cant; give a true reply. Are you for a coronet—to be a fighting man and daunt the heathen—or do you war some lady-love and you two apart, like the foolish Count in the old dodderer's tale?"

Airar felt himself grow warm, then chill as though the perspiration froze in the dark. "I have no love," he said in a strangled voice. ". . . And in Dalarna we care not overmuch for coronets, but hold that men should meet together and follow a leader of their choice for each enterprise."

She laughed like a fox's bark. "A good rule if all were peasants. And you, you're like the general, no purpose but live till tomorrow." The nightshine was not so faint that he could fail to see her head turn from him a trifle. "There might be those who could help you find a higher goal."

Her knee touched his; a thrill ran up his spine at

the contact and the low husky voice, yet not so much
of a thrill but he could think that if he knew more of
courts and places, he would know whether he might
take her in his arms, and the same time that he was
a fool if he did not; yet dared not for fear of her anger and that somehow his sword was sold to Carrhoene for an aina if he did.—A whirl of thoughts
unclear and paralyzing, so that a sigh came from his
lips.

Evadne of Carrhoene turned toward him and
laughed again. "Now it is easy to see, Master Airar,
that you know less of people than of pigs." The half-
formed thought of lost opportunity swept through him
and he lunged to grasp her, but momentt and mood
had passed, she slipped him easily and stood up, leaving him ridiculously asprawl across the tree-root.
"We'll talk on this another time, my—"

The word cut off short as the big cat dropped. From
the tail of her eye the girl had caught just enough of
the motion of that dark avalanche as half to avoid it;
only a hind paw caught her shoulder, driving her to
the ground, rolling over and over. She screamed. Airar
whipped to his feet all one motion with the dag of Naaros in his hand, but before he could reach where the
animal ramped round on its haunches against her,
out from the shadows leaped a shadow with head
low and spear level, that it took it through the guts,
visible even in the shaking light. The cat's fierce squall
mingled with Evadne's second scream; it ran right up
the spears, slashing in agony with armed claws, but
now Airar leaped, slipped once on smooth fur and
metal muscle, then got a grip and drove his dag home
at the throat. Warm blood hit his knife-hand; he
rolled clear, into a tree, and now it was shouts and
men bearing brands from the camp.

Airar stood up. Alsander was of the group, crying,
"Brother, brother, are you hurt?" in a voice of real
fear, astounding for that cold captain, and Evadne
with her hand on brow, saying no, it was but a blood-
scratch. It was surprise to see the man who drove the
spear: Erb the Lank, his face all puckered, blowing
his nose between two fingers to keep from tears.

"You have saved only my life," said Evadne, and offered her hand to Erb as the beast was borne away with shouts to be skinned for a trophy. But to Airar never a word, so that he felt the countrified larrikin that ever was as he took his station by the fire and began composing his blankets for the sleep that he felt would be late coming to his eyes.

Meliboë the enchanter had the next place, and was already lapped in, nor had stirred for the disturbance. He cocked an eye from his place. "Did you lie with her before you brought her back?" he asked, and Airar would willingly have fed him six inches of the bloody dag, but the warlock turned his back and fell to snoring, real or feigned.

Morning come, they were on the road again and a hard road, with pents and shoulders. A croft was met by noon, high in a vale with goats grazing round. It had a thatched roof and a vacuous-faced master, who stared at all these armed soldiers in company, and would say few words to them, nor answer when there was chanted:

Geme, plange, moesto mori—

but looked honest, and his hair was blond. They camped there thus early on Evimenes' advice (for the Hestinga guide knew his way no farther), throwing out scouting groups of Rogai's men in exploration, since these best knew such country.

There was talk of this and that, the adventure with the cat, and Meliboë drew Airar aside a moment. "Hark," said he, "must I forever school you? Your luck lies with the damsel; I have taken the divination. Yet you have somehow faulted the chance I made for you, and I cannot continue to make a woman's eye fall on a man, but once he prove cold, the hardest to make her forgive."

"I do not want her," cried Airar, his mind leaping to the tale told aboard the iulia long ago of proud Queen Kry and the unhappy king.

"Bah. Bed her, not wed her, she's a Carrhoene. A little of your time to make the usual protests of love undying, a pleasant diversion, and you have the services of those captains and all their crew. They'll deny you nothing on their sister's instance."

How explain to this cynic philosophical doctor that he would be self-betrayed thus to betray, so that though he might win the Carrhoene swords, they would gain his soul? Meliboë would daunt such objection down with his metaphysic, as Astli the adviser had talked down the ancient king. Another reason, then. Said Airar after a moment: "Not I to deny the divination, in which you have such skill; but it might be that an alliance so lightly made could be as easily broken."

"What then? Seek another. You reach the heights only by springing up stairs that shift and break beneath the feet. If it's security you ask, go drink at the Well—or serve Leonce Fabrizius with your father." The enchanter turned to go on some other concern, but Airar could not forbear plucking at a furred arm to say: "Well, then. But one thing I will have, and that's a truce to all this magic, magic, spells, spells to make me a mightier man than I am. What? am I to be but the sport of the Seven Powers and do nothing for myself?"

"Do all," flung back Meliboë over his shoulder. "I can but offer you occasion." And now the scouts were coming back and there was a call for the leaders to hear their say.

People lived for the most part quietly and after the old fashion among those Whiteriverdales next to the Dragon's Spine, there being little to tempt Vulking cupidity save in the north part of the province, where the silver mines were. The scouting parties' tidings were somewhat scant. That to southwest had followed the track on which they stood to a hill overlooking a small market town, and brought no news save that of watching from a screen of trees how people went about their wonted business. Evimenes praised the spies for not pushing on and announcing the presence of the band—"there would sure be Vulking Allies there, and we can do without a pursuit, ignorant of our way, so far from the coast and safety." The party westward had come on nothing but a scramble over rough ridges, rocks, and screes; the direction was right, but the way clearly not to be taken save in an emergency, because of the horses. North the slopes ran high; the three who had taken that direction brought only a brace of game they had shot.

The scouts northwest were last in, and they had a man with them, a Whiteriverdalesman clearly by his costume, bearded and burly, who looked round, suspicious as Rogai at seeing the Carrhoenes in their strange armor. He had the iron ring on his thumb; Tholkeil of Mariola, who was of the scouts, said the man had addressed them first with the password of the song, yet the song was not all he had. When a little reassured by the tale of what had brought them there, Salmonessa and Airar's battle at the Stone Pass, he gave them in exchange the news of the Dales.

They knew something marched strangely in the south (he said), but little, for tidings come to those shut-in valleys chiefly by way of the Naaros and Stavorna merchants for the wool markets, of which that in the fall had been normal or nearly so, and the spring market not yet due for another week. But the Vulkings had forbid the usual winter folk-meeting at the northward turning of the sun; brought Micton laborers down to build new castellas in the chain along the great highway that cuts across the eastern dales from Briella before swinging south to pick up the Naar on its journey through Vastmanstad. Latterly also a thing never heard before: all persons of Dale-carle blood had been taxed out or bought out of one of the dales, Godmansdale, and in their place had come colonists—veteran terciary soldiers some of them, but others accompanied by women, smallish of stature and dark or sandy of coloring, with skins always looking unwashed. These had disgusting table-manners, lying down to eat, and spoke with an accent that turned everything to a-wa-wa-wa, like mewing cats.

Glances ran round the circle. "Salmonessans." And Meliboë said that when he was last at the Vulk's court, the council had talked on this new policy, to keep all conquered lands secure by settling in them people from the rest, who must be faithful to the Vulking rule for their lives. "Why else, when all in this realm runs to Vulking benefit, do they promote Dalecarle argosies to the Twelve Cities, with factories set up there under his protection? The day comes when he'd have them fight for him inside Carrhoene—aye, and Permandos, Berbixana, Poliolis, and the rest."

"They were as well not to try it," said Alsander, dryly, and then thinking deeper, flashed out to know more of this design, but the rest hushed him to hear all the Dalesman's narration.

He was told (he said) that the band here was either for Stavorna or for the coasts of Shalland, and on his word they would take the former way, for, though it might be difficult to swing so large a group round Stavorna city and castle with its Vulking garrison with only one road splitting the Korsor heights, the High Hills of Froy, through which they must journey, were wild indeed, and the Iron Ring was not strong in Shalland, where Vulk gave some security against the sea-pirates who vexed those shores from heathenry and Os Erigu.

"But it is precisely Os Erigu—" began Pleiander, and was stilled by a grip from his sister. But the adviser had not noticed amid the babble around and evening fires lit, and rushed on, having a thought to ride:

"How much of proviant you have I do not know, nor how long you can maintain yourselves among the Dales without discovery, seeing you be so many. Indeed, you are likely seen already, for we be woodsmen in these parts, who could count every man's shoe-buckles in this band without being detected; and among those that would have seen you there are like to be Vulking Allies. If I were you, I'd fear, for just beyond that wooded shoulder" (he waved a hand) "a thousand paces or more runs the main highway with its castellas, and a word has reached us of the Iron Ring that there's a Vulking deese afoot on the road due to pass here tomorrow day. Nothing so likely that they would come hunting Dalecarle rebels if they knew."

Rogai gave a long whistle. "What manner deese?" snapped Pleiander.

"A full one, newly out of Briella. Five-and-forty armed terciary men-at-arms, with due complement of Allies."

"And we have not over twenty. Pest! It is many." Pleiander frowned. "Too many," said Rogai. "Let us rather melt into these slopes and forests, back to Hestinga side if need be. My men are the more part mountaineers and will price their heads that no harm comes where they guide."

"What of our horsebacked sergeants with their heavy mail?" asked Alsander.

"Lighten it off; a life is worth more than an iron shirt, or a horse either."

Pleiander's hatchet face darkened. He burst out: "Nay, here's too much from any Mariolan dog-smeller! Always the same in this Dalarna, brothers —some new way to make us weak. After the old warlock's saying here, I begin to see a pattern. What have the arkons of Phyladea promised you for the bodies of the captains of Carrhoene?"

Rogai rolled over and flashed to his feet, hand on dag, but before he could make the quarrelsome retort that bubbled behind his lips, Airar jerked him off balance by a cloak-tail, and Alsander: "Brother, there's no treachery in this companion, only a fool's reasoning by what he knows. We had better stand our ground here, hoping they pass without action, or somehow tempt them to an ambush. But hold." He swung to Meliboë. "Cannot you, sir enchanter, lay some blindness or weakness of spirit on these people so they will pass us by?"

The magician shook his head gloomily. "If terciary soldiers, they'll have a full protection. I taught Bordvin Wildfang the manner myself, and aught attempted against his men would recoil only the sender."

"Would we had Alcides!"

Evadne swept back with a hand her hair so little longer than her brothers'. "Here's one who most thoroughly ambushed some of these Vulkish men at the Stone Pass. I'd listen to our long-legged frog here, who leads the largest band of all, but has said never a word."

"Because in these matters I'm a child to all present," Airar replied. "What can I say? . . . Yet will say two words, of which one is that all talk goes merely round and round till the decision's made—if to fight or to run."

"Run," said Rogai. "No disgrace before these so numerous and better-armed."

"I would also say to keep from this shock, masters," said the Dalesman, but blinked and they could all see he was unwilling to have fighting brought down among those peaceful dales, with the vengeances that would come after.

Alsander, slowly: "You have right on the first point, Master Airar. What's the other?"

"There's need for lean Erb here, the best planner of any."

Carrhoene faces looked dark and Pleiander under his breath said something of peasants, but Evadne cried aye, and when Erb was summoned, drew him down by a hand to a place beside her, with a remark about his strength that made his face work like a boy's.

Alsander was fingering his sharp chin thoughtfully. "It is the wrong thing to run. We have run and run from these, with no profit, d'ye see? Wars are not won that way. Nay, more—Here's as it were a test set to us. Be sure that the noise of this transaction will run though all this Whiteriverdale country. If we run now we mark ourselves forever too low in spirit to meet these Vulkings save with advantage on our side. Most men still follow the strong, and however little you Dalecarles like the rule of Briella's Mountain, they will make themselves a way to live under it and be faithful to it till their children have no other memory, if we fail here for lack of trying. For us, the four, it does not matter; we are Carrhoenes and only follow the drum till we come to our own sweet land again. But for you Dalecarles I say the test is not of your arms but of your souls."

Airar heard Meliboë snort from where he sat, chin buried in cloak. Said Evimenes: "Now it is seen that as always when there is long planning to be done, you are the best of us, brother. There is only one small question—how to set forth a battle against these very mighty men."

"How would this do?" spoke Pleiander. "Let certain of these Dalecarles set themselves in the path of this deese, bearing signs of peace, but with weapons concealed. They shall make semblant of wishing to join the allied bands of the Vulkings. When they have broke formation and clustered round, let all on a given signal whip out and stab the nearest enemy. We shall have a watch at some convenient place among the trees; when the commotion is sighted, we of Carrhoene will out and fall on them with the lance before they have time to form again."

Meliboë raised his head and seemed about to speak, but "Well thought on!" cried Rogai. "Truly, you are less of a dolt than I had conceived."

The plan stuck in Airar's craw, though he could not quickly say why, but, seeing the Dalesman frown and Erb clear his throat, motioned the latter to speak.

Said the lean man: "We be just free-fishers and have not all they fancy manners like Dalecarles from the mainland, but I do say that if plan like that was put up in the isles of Gentebbi, we'd have none. Because it's just treachery, that is, and sets against who tries it all they bishops and Sons of the Well."

"True—" began the Dalesman, but was devanced by Pleiander's snarl: "What! You peasants are too hoity-toity dainty for wars, where nothing's held back. Would you perfume piss before using it to put out a fire?"

Airar held up a hand, thinking fast. "Yet there is another objection. The scheme's too fine-cut. What if the signal to strike is missed by some, or by others seen before really given, the which is almost sure to happen? There are we Dalescarles without armor and only dags as weapons among men fully plated, having swords. I do not see that however fast your lancers ride, they can be our aid before most are cut down. I'd seek a plan that gave a better chance of life."

"Offer one, then," flung Pleiander, mouth atwist.

"I will," said Airar, and stopped. Evadne laughed, but Alsander said: "From the principle upward. Our strength lies in the mounted men and their speed to move"; and that supplied the clue he lacked. He swung to the Dalesman: "Is there not some point farther up the road where another wooded shoulder or cliff overhangs it?"

The other combed his beard with fingers and said there might be; at a place called Crow's Tower, some eight or nine thousand paces distant. "The road runs an S around two such juttings, and on the opposite one, but a good distance farther, stands a Vulking castella."

"The castella is certainly a difficulty, and the distance is somewhat great, but I think not to harm. I say let Rogai take such of his Mariolans as are mountaineers and move at once, tonight to the Crow's Tower, where they shall lie in covert. They are all bowmen; when the deese appears, let drive at it with arrows, but most specially against the accompanying Allies, not caring whether few or many be hit. They'll not bear it meekly, and that is the design—to send these light-armed furiously on your pursuit, so their band remaining on the road will be all terciaries. Therefore let them pursue, but if they design to turn again, rally and give them another shaft or two. You run small danger. I vow there be few among those Allies who are hillmen, whether they be Salmonessans, Mictons, or traitor Dalecarles—but you'll need guides."

"The Iron Ring will furnish those; we can gather them on the way," said the Dalesman. Airar's strong confident air had washed away his scruples and he was snapping his fingers for excitement.

"Done, then. Here at this shoulder we'll take our stand, the free-fishers with their spears for throwing, and when these terciaries come, nag them again. It is in my mind to have heard that when attacked so by missile-weapon men, their custom is to spread out in pairs, one covering both with his shield, advancing and using javelins till the attack's broken. Now then the knights and sergeants of Carrhoene will issue round the shoulder when they are thus opened; or if they close up again, the better target for us."

Evadne clapped her hands. "Did I not say this was Alcides come again? We must take him into the family; if he will not speak for himself, brothers, I will speak for him and make him my future."

Pleiander seemed to be chewing his tongue, silenced, unforgiving. Alsander said: "And if we lose?"

"Rogai's resource of the hills. Rendezvous at the Count's Pillow."

The Carrhoene passed a hand across his mouth. "The plan is good. It leans heaviest where we are best —though much rests on you exiles of Mariola."

"I am of one mind with this," said Evimenes, "for even if they have been warned and close rank to go marching past without a battle, they will have lost much glory by the acceptance of our insult, and what they lose, we gain!" Now Pleiander must also give in his adhesion, but Erb the Lank said: "Forgive, Master Airar, and you captains, but though I think this plan is just the plan of a master like King Argimenes a' silver years, man would not be man not finding one flaw to alter, thus under leave—"

"Get on with it," said Rogai.

"Just this, then. You have two-three Mariolans who are horsemen, not hillmen, and there be two-three more of Hestinga. Why should a not stay mounted and move light on the flanks of they Carrhoene riders like they there gentours to pick out the loose men?"

"I accept that," said Airar, "if Evimenes will lead this band, who knows all his way in swift movement." The conference broke up, Rogai to rouse his people and depart with the Whiteriverdalesman, since a march of eight thousand paces is not an easy one and they must be posted by dawn, whereas it was already falling night. Airar told Erb to set the watch and himself lay down; but not before Meliboë the enchanter spoke sidelong: "Young sir, you have done

well. Oh, not your plan, which is mere battle and bru-
tality and will succeed or not as fortune wills. But
you have the sense of a very pretty philosopher; I
marked how you rejected the argument moral against
Pleiander's plan, yet destroyed the same plan with a
plea rooted in pure reason. It is false philosophy, for
it began with what you wished to prove and worked
back to the proof empirical; but for method, well done,
excellently well done."

19. The Whiteriverdales:
Spear and Shield

"RISE UP," SAID VISTO; "TODAY WE GO TO battle," and Airar rolled wakeling from his cloak, all at once clear, though he had spent half the night talking to his free-fishers, group by group, to tell them how much hung on the fray and how they should place themselves. There were but one-and-twenty when the Hestinga men left them to mount, and one was detailed with other ones to take the horses back up a draw and keep them there. Erb had set a watch; they breakfasted meager and in haste; then moved out along the hill-shoulder past the mounted men, half of whom were already a-horse and armed, lest the enemy surprise them by too early coming. The rest took their meal. Meliboë

was back with the horses; Evadne came to make fare-
wells before joining him, but it was Erb she embraced,
only touching Airar's hand, and he felt a twinge of jeal-
ousy even without desire, that made him wonder at
himself, but there were too many concerns for time to
spend on that.

This would be his third battle-day; and though not
confused with the wild turmoil of the first, he found still
the same strange emotion, almost as though he were
falling into the arms of a fair maid, and remembered
the song of a harper who came down the road long ago,
when Airar went to the stead of Sumarbo, where he
tilted for apples on the old horse Pil:

> *Give we again   ourselves in surrender;*
> *Gather for others   the fruits of tomorrow,*
> *Holding that life   is the hostage of time;*
> *For those who know but a little of what have spent or*
> *shall spend.*

"Malediction," said someone as a branch ripped his
sleeve; the day was breaking grey with a promise of
rain, the slope was steep, and the trees around mainly
beech hung with last year's brown leaves and birch
touched with the green of new. Beyond the crest, on
the face toward the west, the underbrush was thick, tall
bushes with arms abroad and holding fresh little leaves
in their hands (for there was more spring down here
than on Hestinga's tall plateau), among which a discordant chatter of birds disturbed by the passage of so
many armed men. Airar looked northward from this
screen; there was the road, sweeping down to make a
long graceful turn off to south and west; and the
market-town the scouts had seen, fine and firm with its
cobble-blocks; and on the opposite side a rising wood
like that in which they stood with the stream round its
feet. The careful Vulkings had cut everything back a
hundred paces on either side to prevent a sudden onset
from thickets—O excellent engineers.

"Spread out, spread out," tall Erb was saying, and
bidding the men lie down, well behind the screen of
bush. "Now when we sight them coming at long dis-

tance, a shall rise and crouch to a single knee, but no more, on life and all, till Master Airar's bowstring snaps, which is our signal. A shall not fear to run out then and get a good cast for the first flight of spears— or back after, for 'tis our design to make them open out and follow."

This had all been told before. Said Airar: "I would have you all to lie down now, then at a sign from Erb come to the crouch and hold there while I watch from the road. All rests on their not catching a glimpse of us."

It was as well he thought of that. Burly Sewald had chosen a bush too small for his frame, which quaked clear as he rose; and Nene of Busk had on a damned red tunic whose sleeves showed bright from underneath his mail. When these matters were cared for, not without protest from Nene, who said the tunic was his luck, here was Visto to remark they had no banner. It was all one to the son of Alvar, and there was no way to come by what might stand for the Wingèd Wolf of Dalarna's wars; but perceiving his fishers held much by a symbol, he said that they should set on a pole the head of the cat killed overnight and follow that; "for it is as cats that we spring here." All applauded this design, and now there was nothing to do but wait, with rustlings as a man or two shifted position, but not many words said, for not one there but remembered the last time they had faced these terciaries at the causeway and the upshot of it, with the other good companions of the fifty gone, all dead or sold serfs now.

A little after, Visto was back with the cat-head on its pole. Airar's keen eye caught distantly where the ribbon of road flowed down between the hills a glimpse of movement and "Down!" he cried, but it was only a single man horseback and moving at a fast canter. Airar let him pass, hoping the Carrhoene riders farther down would stop him, for the speed of the man's progress and the cut of his gear suggested a Vulking messenger to warn the posts that Rogai's band had attacked the deese. Then he began to wonder if he were right to have acted so, and wormed down the line toward the other end to ask Erb.

"—different this time—" "—voyage to Uravedu; but when he came back, not one of the family—" "—let you use the left-handed stroke—" he caught fragments as he passed along, and felt well to know the free-fishers were of good cheer. But, when Erb was indeed reached, here sat the tall man on his haunches, arms around knees enclosing his spear, and head down.

Airar touched him. Erb looked up with tears on his cheeks. "Are you low-hearted?" asked Airar, not knowing what else to ask, and Erb:

"Oh, aye. But not for battle or wars, so under your leave, young master, you shall not lower me from my lieutenancy to make me a spearman, since this time your dog will cut off a's feet rather than lead out of the fight again, like at the Salmonessan causeway."

"We'll have no talk of dogs," said Airar, liking little this form of address; "but what's the trouble, then?"

"This—" He blew his nose, looking round. "This woman or witch, the Carrhoene. Master Airar, you be of an age when wenches bed-willing, but what's an old poop like me to do, that has never played with a dame in a's life? From first sight there in Salmonessa I thought her just fine and wonderful, like a queen or fairy fay; would ha' given seven lives to serve her; but now here this morning, a embraced me and thrust her paps against me, and now all my blood feels like turned to water and a man burns inside and thinks how un may be slain in the battle with never having dandled her—and yet she does not mean it at all."

Airar looked at him sidewise, feeling himself somewhat flush, and to cover it said: "But she's a Carrhoene, and I have heard that those of that race are not above granting favors for sheer delight—nor below it, neither."

"But if that, then for a young master like you, who'd bump her happily," said the tall man, and ended his saying with a sob.

Now Airar realized quickly he had but repeated Meliboë's thought and could hardly bear to look at his man. "Oh, take—" he began, but someone exclaimed, and looking up the vale, he saw them coming, still a dark mass under the dark clouds of distance, and now it was too late to get back to his chosen place at the other end of the line, so there he must stay, taking arrows from his quiver and sticking them in the ground all in a row.

Right on they came; closed up tight in marching formation, six abreast across the front, full-armed and in the Vulking quickstep rapidly, shield on each left arm and watchful, with the soft-pointed Vulking javelin in every right hand. There was no dust; the red triangle bobbed on its pole in the center of the group and behind them the deserion rode, with his red cloak flung back across his shoulder and helmet off in defiance of the world. There were two other men on horseback behind him, staff or messengers, but their mounts were ordinary, and it went to Airar's heart that when he loosed shaft, it could be against no target but the splendid brown animal the deserion bestrode.

Yet there it was and must be. Along the line as far as eye could see among the boccage they were all on one knee. The Vulkings swept down the long curve, neither left nor right looking, with clang of arms and heavy steps, a touch of russet in the center showing there were still a handful of Allies with them. As they drew abreast and all had their left sides toward Airar, he hove up slowly as by a machine, set his feet and drew to the head, holding between the crotch of a branching dogwood with its blossoms inconsequently noted. Deserion and horse came into line; he released, and releasing, shouted he never knew what. The arrow flew true; for one flicker as he bent to pick up the second he saw it standing feather-deep with red blood spurting and the horse rearing. Airar nocked and loosed again as the fishers burst from their cover and the startled Vulkings turned; the shaft caught a shield-rim and glanced upward, a miss, as he drew at the third; but now there were free-fishers all across the rank dry grass, shooting with their stick-spears, and a side-rank Vulking went down with a clang as one of them took him through both calves. There was no clear sight; Airar was running forward with his sword out.

The Vulking trumpet blew two discordant notes,

their own javelins were in the air, and Airar saw their formation dissolving, spreading out into pairs as had himself predicted. He ducked a javelin; one of the men was right upon him, faceless beneath the dished-out helmet, and he cut backhand at the fellow's right arm to gain space, but the blow was caught on the iron edge of the big circle shield and Airar thrown off balance. In a moment of dreadful pale fear, Airar saw the man's companion reach round with a hand-held javelin to strike, but before he could do it, someone at the side drove a spear into the spearer's armpit, and down he went with a scream.

The first Vulking whirled and Airar remembered he was a leader; ran back a few steps as the trumpet sounded again and found himself all alone at the break of the slope and end of the undergrowth with men dead and dying out before, one of Gentebbi with a Vulking javelin standing right through his armor and another's face smashed in by the short enemy sword, legs twitching; two or three terciaries down and russet Allies, while left and right the free-fishers were running with Vulking pairs in pursuit. But the trumpet had not blown for them; it had blown for the sight of the riders of Carrhoene, sweeping down in a tight squadron with lances all in rest.

Those Vulkings were soldiers of the best, and not over half their number had spread. Those still on the road faced round at the trumpet-cry and formed steadily, the front rank kneeling, with their javelin-butts on the ground, the loose flankers to that side still looser, running forward to take the little tight knot of horsemen from the flank.

"Ullu—ullu!" shouted Airar. "Come on!" and not looking whether he was followed, ran forward to strike at any cost the Vulking ranks from rear, out of the tail of his eye seeing one horse go down and the terciaries running forward to pounce on the rider. Then a flash and a crash and lancers were in on the deese. A javelin caught one horse in the side and at the same moment another was jabbed between his legs to bring him down, but they were too close in for this to be of service to the defense; horse and falling rider slid and pitched upon the doubled rank of foemen to scatter them like a stone from a giant's catapult, and the Carrhoene lances took the rest. For one moment there was a wild tangle of horses down and men down and then everywhere across the slope, along the road and into the water there were Vulkings running or throwing down shield and holding javelin high in token of surrender.

Airar saw a Carrhoene sergeant drop his lance and smite down one such with a blow of the mace from his saddle-bow; leaping forward, was just in time to go hurtling to the ground atop another before that one too was slain. "I give!" cried the man beneath in a muffled voice; a horse missed them narrowly, Airar rolled over and was up, jerking the fellow after him, and a glance at the silvern badges told how it was the deserion himself that he had caught. He looked round to see whether there were more he might save. But he'd no device for calling the sergeants to heel, and their Carrhoene blood was up; all across the road to trees they were butchering the last of the terciaries save a few who had given themselves into the hands of free-fishers —or three to be exact, as was found when all gathered round to reckon their victory and its cost, lay out the dead, and congratulate each other.

Of the Carrhoene sergeants, the two who had pitched from their horses were killed and another had a broken leg; so furiously had they smashed through that not another man was more than bruised. In Airar's band there were four gone, but only two of them freefishers. Several were more or less wounded, one so badly in the leg he could not stand; he had been hamstrung. All in the council of leadership were agreed they could not remain close in the neighborhood, ignorant what force the enemy could bring against them and how quickly from the nearest castella, and indeed it appeared that the riders had already estopped two or three travellers coming north out of the market town before the fight. But there were their own dead to give honest burial and the bodies to pillage for whatever they had, chiefly weapons. There was praise to Evimenes for bringing the extra horses, on which the loot was loaded; the Vulking shields were well smashed and a litter made for the wounded man, on which the prisoners were bedded to carry him with their hands bound to the litter.

The sun behind its clouds had now well passed zenith and no word from Rogai. On Alsander's word they sent ahead, north along the road, a pair of the well-mounted Hestinga men, whose dress might make them seem to belong to the Dales. Their weapons were covered. Now all took that same direction, since they knew no other direction to take, with a pair more of scouts dropped behind.

A little after this march was begun, a slow drizzle started, and Evimencs swore a good deal about what it would do to his armor, which he had ungreased for the battle. They had not gone much above the two thousand paces that carried them to the break of the next big curve in the highway when a self-possessed dog with a curly tail came down the road to accost them, and country-bred Airar said that meant a shepherd was not far off. Sure enough, there was instantly a faint whistle; the dog cocked an ear, stepped intelligently on stones across the water, and trotted off up to the left, westward slope among the trees. Airar, with a word to his companions that guidance was most needful, dismounted and climbed after, up the steep slope, slippery with wet, following the dog by sound through trees and crashing underbrush across a crest to find himself looking down on a little open vale.

There were fat grey backs on the far side among the trees, but no sign of shepherd, nor did any answer when Airar whistled the *"Geme, plange, moesto mori."* He ran down the slope, crying, "Peace and good will to any here," and presently the man stepped forth among his animals, a surly, loutish-looking fellow, handling a nail-studded cudgel, wet dripping from a leather cap. Airar spoke him fair and gave him the tidings. The man only grunted at the tale of the deese wiped out, saying there was no sure way through the High Hills of Froy into Shalland till one came to Crow's Tower; this vale led up only into a false pass. Then, melting somewhat as the thought of the victory over the sons of Briella reached his slow mind, he suggested the vale as a good place for nighting, since hidden from the road, and agreed to exchange a pair of his sheep for some of Airar's silver, that the company might dine.

On Airar's return one can imagine the Carrhoenes looking a trifle glum over his having changed single-handed the general plan for a march. But Rogai was still unheard from and they were men of war enough to see that under the weeping skies there had come on all the dreadful weariness of after battle to make it feel less like a very great victory than a defeat. Picquets were set at the road to watch for the return of the Hestinga scouts; the company toiled up slope and into the vale, and with some trouble got fires going and the sheep a-cook. The forage for the horses was but poor.

20. The Whiteriverdales: Debate of the Deserion

Said Pleiander: "Let's have that bastard of a Deserion here and sport him for sweets to our supper."

Airar would have said no, thinking it less than high-minded to deal so with a surrendered enemy, but the girl Evadne clapped her hands. Meliboë's lips twisted in his beard, and Erb said: "We might have from un a tale of some use."

They had the man fetched. He stood straight in the campfire light before them, rain striking down across his bare black curly head; short, hawk-nosed and well-built, like most Vulkings of the upper class, a certain dignity or insolence in his manner. Pleiander looked him up and down.

"À pax, à pax!" he sneered with the Vulking war-cry. "Gay times will be had in Briella when you come again with your victory. How do you like to command a deese?"

The deserion said nothing at all.

"No answer? He does not like our humor; let us take him at seriousness. Were you bound for Naaros city? And how many men in the castella at Crow's Tower?"

Not a word from the deserion, and the Carrhoene captain gazed at him intent for a moment before saying:

"Your life and freedom may hang on what you say; or be forfeit, you bastard, if you do not say."

The deserion shrugged to indicate life and death, freedom and unfreedom were all one to him.

"Us you may slay," he said, "but you shall not so murder all the Vulkings; nor have I yielded myself to you, so there is no duty on me to reply to your questions."

Airar saw Pleiander brace himself to rise, and was before him with a question:

"I am your taker. Your name."

"Luronne the junior, of Anné in East Lacia; deserion of the 12th." The 12th was the new tercia, recently organized.

"You are a taken prisoner and may be sold for a serf like a Micton. Now you shall tell us the force of the castella at Crow's Tower."

The skin round the man's eyes crinkled in the ef-fort of thought, the firelight throwing shadows there. Then: "I will not. It would be contrary to my military oath."

Now Airar was taken aback, unwilling to threaten or sneer like Pleiander. There was a chuckle from Evadne, but Meliboë the enchanter lifted his silver head.

"You have wrong," said he. "I know that oath; it was to serve loyally for the advancement of the realm of the Vulkings, and how can you render such ser-vice, being dead? Why, this is disloyalty; not to men-tion that it involves the lives of your three as well.

Were I still in Briella, I could have you prosecute before the baron of court for as much."

"Not I. It is an order not to name the force of our armies nor their placing. The true treason would be to disobey, the more since the tale would be given to most approvèd Dalecarle traitors."

Now angry words trembled behind Airar's lips, and Pleiander's dark brow was turned sneering on him, but Meliboë motioned silence, and as light as though the deserion had made a jest, said: "Traitors to whom, pray?"

"Why, to the Count Vulk, under the Emperor, ruler of this realm."

The enchanter squirmed in his cape against the rain. "Is the last duty, then to Vulk? Do not men also owe somewhat to God and His church? Or to their own inner souls, which are God's reflection? For it must surely be very clear to you that this fine body of yours, now so near dissolution, can have little commerce with the eternal and infinite except by means of the soul. Yet here you unfame these Dalecarles as traitors because they follow the leadings of their own inner souls, not orders from Briella; nor will yourself cross these orders, or what you conceive them to be, to hold soul and body together. Has a man no duty then but to the county?"

Luronne the deserion raised a hand as though to scratch his head, then lowered it again quickly. "Why, sir," he said, somewhat slowly, "I do not know that I have a soul, except that the priest says so, therefore it must be true; but I have never seen it. Yet this I do know: that in soul or mind, I can never be secure till I have found what all others of the kindred are thinking and by thought or act brought myself closest to the general. For look you, sir sophist, man is an animal that lives in assembly, and cannot do by himself no more than a sheep, or else is an outlaw for every man to slay."

"And therefore," said Alsander judgmatically, "must take orders like a sheep from the nearest dog. Is't so?"

"Nay, indeed," replied the deserion, earnestly.

"What would you?—that one should say his soul told him to take my goods while I am abroad on a campaign? It is prevented only because the general voice in the realm will not have it so; that is, under the County Vulking, we live safe. All who wish otherwise are at bottom merely desirable to gain with the strong hand against all law."

To Airar it seemed that he had never heard anything so terrible as this man talking against death, yet nothing so soundly put forth that there was no flaw in it, and he must concede everything Luronne said was true as true. But Meliboë the enchanter only smiled in his beard with red lips. "You are palpably a very good reasoner and philosopher," said he, "as was only to be looked for from one who has had the instruction of the Lyceum of Anné. Yet I would ask a question: who is it determines what the general will of the Vulking kindred may be? Since yourself cannot go from one to another citizen and ask his desire on every topic where all must act together."

"Who else but the Count Vulk himself? Since he is elect by the common will of the people and must be the full expression of their will."

"Ha. True. And if he expresses his will down through his chosen deputies it is still the will of all, since he is chosen by all. But how if this be untrue? How if evil men in the state have made a combination to advance one of their number for mere power and glory?"

The face of the deserion looked merely unbelieving. "Why, sir, who would make such a combination? And if 'twere made, what then? The power and glory of the Count is the power and glory of all the Vulking kindred; since all association exists only at the will of the Count and for to do his desires, which are those of the realm in general. None will have it other but certain of these Dalecarles, who would see our strength fall away into mere worship of the Well and the Empire, while every day the Micton and heathen crowd in as we quarrel with one another. Fie! Realms have no pause; they gain or go down, and we gain because we Vulkings are one, giving to all who fall in with the kindred this sweet unity."

"And how for those of other bloods?" Meliboë glanced round. "The Carrhoenes—are they part also in the sweet unity you name?"

"Unity with them? With them? It would pollute. Whatever you find of low and filthy, there's one from the Twelve Cities at the bottom, like a maggot in a stinking corpse. Why, sir—"

Now Pleiander did leap up with a cry half-articulate. So sharply he could not be stopped, he flung himself on the deserion, and with one arm round his neck, stabbed him quick and deep, three times in the side. With a kind of gurgle Luronne the junior folded down in his blood; Airar caught the glint of an eye-white as he died, and Pleiander stood over him with the bloody dag in his hand, mouth working. "Diades! take this away. Where's young Visto?" Meliboë laughed, but none other had a word to say, and presently it was time for all to seek rest.

Yet rest was far from Alvar's son, to whom the after-battle weariness that made the others sleep so sound came in a form that flogged his senses full awake. Wind sighed among the branches above; big wet drops drifted down to plash on the wing of a cloak he had flung over his head, and his mind trailed across and again the events of the day, seeking for a reason why he should feel a sense of crisis more intimate than that of war.

Why?—why? There was Evadne now, the Carrhoene, and her open speech of making him her future, barely heard in the haste of preparing to meet the deese, now risen to plague his midnight thought. She was older than he, aye; yet the dusky olive of her skin and swelling breast it would be sweet to press —or would it so? Something deep down recoiled with a crawl, as though an enchantment lay on her to counter desire, not that which Meliboë had placed to draw her to him. Or that itself; a pang of pain and the thought of another drawing enchantment he himself had raised (he resolutely kept his mind from forming the name), and how he drifted along the thought of

these magics, magics, and how ill each had sped at
the end—the shape-change that brought Rogai only
into deadly danger at Mariupol; Meliboë's spell, with
death for Britgalt and his sons in the snowstorm; the
evil fate of the enchanting and disenchanting of the
ships against sea-demons; the night of the tower in
Salmonessa (a white flash before the eyes and one
must not think of that) . . . was any of all the magics
good? The night in the marsh when it saved them
from the Vulkings—No; for that was a treachery by
Meliboë on those who trusted him; and the divination
of that night had held him from going to Salmonessa,
where he might have saved *her*.

Now Airar, turning over uneasily, began to wonder
whether there were not some element of spell in the
debate of the death of the deserion. One would think
it so—and a mean end to a man, black Vulking
though he was, to perish because Pleiander could find
no answer to his saying but a blade. He was my prisoner—and Airar began to know a bitter resentment
toward the whole Carrhoene tail, about whom the unfortunate Luronne had not been too far wrong that
they had a touch of rough and foul—Evadne's loose
language and easy caress for Erb, how Evimenes had
been all too willing to steal the horses after hospitable
guesting, and most of all that Airar did not like: Pleiander's cry for young Visto after he had done the
murder and the way he fondled the lad. That Visto
was less than he had at one time seemed (regret
and resent mingled here below the level of Airar's
thought)—oh, faithful and willing, but in a pinch a
poodle-dog, who'd follow where finger snapped and
make nothing of himself, nor offer that exchange (except as a woman might, an inferior) which might
have brought him to the level of the friend Airar at
another time thought he might have found in Rogai,
about whom there was something not merely chill
and distant, but hurried, as though he had no time for
friendship. This, then, would be why there was no contest from Visto—the slight sarcastic tone with which
he had referred, that night in the tower, to "My
friend." Why he had held it so light a thing that she

should go to the Duke; yet come to warn me. Oh, no true friendship in Visto; only this—this wish to be dominated. I have no friends. No friends, no true friends, they do not like, but wish to use, me. Must I be friendless forever? And again he twisted on the ground till the other thought came that here once more was the same self-sorrow that had cost him Gython's—

Not that. Well, if Visto wished to live that way, 'twas sure his right. No; disgust. Luronne the deserion had right, men live with others and must match their doings to the general will, or here's untame Pleiander, with his man slaying and catamite-making. Or for that matter, Duke Roger, living beyond law by his single will. Yet no, not he—he was under a kind of law and it had caught him at last—law not written, but with boundaries nonetheless against the pride, injustice, and hardness of heart with which he enforced his bastardies and presumption, so that at the end his own people fell away, when these brought down on him first the arms of Briella and then Lady Malina's dagger. For a moment Airar played with the fascinating game of speculation—did the law run inexorably against a single fault? With either his war or his wooings the three-fingered duke might have succeeded but for the other—or would some different conjunction have brought him down if this had failed?

But then, but then, the law's more than human, and our laws can but pattern forth this universal rule—this over-law that will not let a human enactment be set up in opposition to it. The law of Duke Roger's house was to keep Salm alive by bastardy succeeding bastardy, and the house fell through this very law. Now young Airar found himself on the horn of his crisis, for sure, Luronne the deserion's desire for the voice of the general, and sweet unity in Dalarna of Dalecarle and Vulking, stood in violation of no law natural or divine. How's this? (he asked himself) do they have right, and we wrong to wish our freedom? Does that not make us one with those of the quarrelsome Dodekapolis? He could see no way through; the idea was so disturbing that he bounced himself upright (touching a branch and letting a curst trickle of water up his arm) to find Meliboë the philosopher and persuade him to unravel the problem.

Out in the clearing there was the faintest trace of false dawn beneath skies still weeping, but among the trees none. In the blackness Airar's first step brought his foot against someone that snarled "Who lives?" in the voice of Alsander of Carrhoene as he came afoot, and when Airar had identified himself, said angrily he did not know where the old man was, but better occupations might be found than stirring one from his sleep. Airar gave him right and apology; while the grumbling Carrhoene was about composing himself again, there was a speck of light not from the sky at the opposite flank of the vale, and here came the outer guard they had posted at the road, bearing a candle-lantern, with the scouts sent toward Crow's Tower, and another man besides.

The tale was they had spent the evening and part of the night wandering in that neighborhood without finding much trace of battle or any of Rogai, not too anxious to approach the Vulking castella, where there were watchfires and much activity. They had resolved to camp at the tower itself, an old ruinous structure once builded by the heathen, keeping watch and watch. To them came this other, a Dalesman of the Iron Ring and Rogai's messenger, he having guessed that if all went well in Airar's battle, a contact would be sought at the tower. His own attack had gone by plan except that the Allies accompanying the deese were more numerous than expectation and had swung round to take his little band from the southern flank, so that he could in no manner make down toward where Airar was, but had drawn his enemies off into the pass that leads through the High Hills of Froy. Since they were so deep on that road, he had decided to keep to it, sending back this messenger. They had but two men slain and very few hurt, the Allies of the deese proving mainly Salmonessans who lost heart utterly when their leaders fell.

Alsander heard most of this story from one man,

but toward the end he stood up again. "How many men in the garrison of the castella?"

"Not above a rank, which is less than half a deese. Master Rogai—there's a captain for you!—debated assaulting it, and if you have men-at-arms in full proof, as I understand, you could do it with ease."

"I did not ask your advice. What force have the Vulkings in the Dales altogether?"

The man's face was somewhat sullen in the lantern-glow. "We do not know for sure. A good part of the 8th tercia has been spread among the castellas and latterly some deese of the 12th have come down the highroad; this was the third such which you have fought, bound we think for Naaros city. It is said that most of the 4th is at Stavorna, but of that nothing sure. The wool-merchants have not come."

Alsander turned. "Master Airar, we had best rouse the people and move at once, before break of day, or we shall be in a trap."

"How so?"

"This matter of the castella all watchful the night, which I do not take to be their custom, and Rogai's retreat through the pass. Is't not clear that some of these Allies, cowardly bastards, have run and warned the place? Then the whole news has spread—I will not say how, but in all directions they'll gather forces to cut us off, this 8th tercia from its posts and the 4th down from Stavorna to bar our path."

21. The High Hills of Froy:
They Ride

THE DALESMAN GUIDE RODE BEFORE
them, and it was as well, for though the dawn broke
clearing, it was plain that the pass by Crow's Tower
had no true road, only a track through a forest now
very thick, no longer with the steep pents and cliffs as
in the eastern Dales, but winding and winding among
round mammaries of hill. Evimenes dropped back
among the pack-animals to hurry these slowest of the
march; Alsander and Meliboë were in the main guard.
Pleiander rode at the head with Airar, cheerful as
a lark and a little lark chanting the coming day, but,
not getting two words from the childe of Trangsted,
soon fell to whistling one of his tuneless Carrhoene
airs, himself clapping hands and giving little barks

when he came to the refrain. They crossed a brook, with the horses stepping daintily; on the far side Evadne spurred up through the press to join and laughed as she brought her horse alongside Airar.

"You have a song—do you not?—of dolorosa Dalarna; and dolorous is this ice-bound land where you have wind instead of sun. When comes the spring?"

"Why, it is spring now," said Airar, weary enough with his sleepless night and hard thinking to fall into her bantering mood. "What would you? Two seasons only, of ice and hot sun? Here in the north we may grow slowly to love; but it is forever and does not burn out."

She clapped her hands. "Courtier, courtier. You could do no better if you sat in the high horse of Permandos with Sthenophon and his ladies. Not so, Pleiander?"

But Pleiander, as in obedience to some unseen signal, had dropped aback and did not answer, so she went on: "Nay, truly it is a dolorous land, and you must leave it when you have your profit. Here's Alsander my brother, gossip and merry companion, and what does he do? Ride back there with this long-bearded doctor and babble-babble, gabble-gabble, whether this business of war is more an art like a painter's, or a science, as astrology and mathematic, as though there had never been a bird on a bough."

"Now that is a very doubtful question—" began Airar, serious again, but she laughed out merrily, and said, "Master Airar, the frog, you will never in your life be a philosopher and resolve such questions no more than me. Give it up, be gay and live longer. I marked how you were ready to abandon all last night and turn to join that Vulking louse as he farted by the mouth, till Long-beard spoke. Perhaps it is so still."

"Ah, no," cried Airar, his mind splitting suddenly to note how much in word and phrase her address to him was like that he had used with Gython (no downing the name now), but she treated his sudden check only as evidence she had his whole attention, and rushed on:

"It's as I told you under the tree, where you and Erb slew the cat. You Dalecarles would live two ways at once, like the man-fish, or those demons of the seas round Gentebbi. You'll have no birth nor privilege nor leaders permanent—oh, no. What's then? Why, these beasts of Vulk will always do you down with their dumb obedient union, if only that they come always full strength to the trial while you have but half yours, there being some who do not choose to join you."

"Is it so indeed? I would not like to think it."

"Master frog, master frog, you will never be weaned till you can look a fact in the face, here's one for you to gaze on: how all that call themselves Vulking come skilled and full armed to every battle and with certain of your own people as allies. They are clearly your betters there."

"I had not thought to hear you praise them."

"Praise—praise, who spoke of praise? I'll praise the great cat his claws. Any fool or frog can see what's amiss with these people and their ways; for ensample, no music or delight, and not even their barons secure in that dignity but must be made afresh by their Council each year. Why, it's no better than the regiment of the dog-smellers among our own cities! But when you've an enemy it's needful to know the length of his arm. I say these men are very good soldiers, brave and loyal. What makes them so masterful, answer me?"

Airar thought a moment, riding between the trunks, and from behind came a bump and a laugh as one of the free-fishers, poor horsemen still for all their long riding up through Hestinga, fell off his horse. A bird flew across their path; Evadne made a motion with her hand like the curve of its flight and hummed three notes. At last he said; "Why, this is a question for Doctor Meliboë, is't not? And one I meant to ask him no longer ago than last night. A deep matter. Yet here's how I'd read it, if read it I must: that the more part of these men are sottish, with no more spirit nor desire of renown than—than—"

"Than what, good frog?"

But Airar's mind had suddenly jumped to his father and how the old man had even praised Vulking dealings as honest and honorable, making all equal and to all giving the chance to rise high in the service of the realm; holding the realm and the race themselves high, free from the pollution of blood of Micton or Carrhoene.—They hold the future, old Alvar used to say, and we must follow it; our race cannot stay fixed no more than stars in their ride across the vault, but must rise or set like them.

"I do not know what there is better to offer sottish men than Vulk gives," he achieved lamely.

Evadne laughed. "So you'll turn Vulking—is that the tale?" and through his "No, never," caught up again: "Hark! Among our cities is the story of certain dog-smellers that sailed to seek the Well in a ship all together, but, being dog-smellers, could not agree that any should have more power than the rest, so kept watch turn and turn, and all handled ropes. Now there was one of them an approved sea-captain that could read the stars, but when a storm blew he was worn with much watching and asleep; nor would any rouse him, since that was held unfair, so the ship ran on a rock and everyone was drowned without their ever getting to the Well at all."

"If what you are saying is that there should be a captain for every voyage," said Airar, "why, I do not know who will deny it. Not we of Dalarna. But it is precisely on this question of captains that all turns, and I am harried with the thought that these Vulkings may have found the better way of choosing them."

She laughed again. "Who praises Briella now? Frog, frog, I said you'd never be a philosopher. Nor a true courtier neither, since you have to learn that one should argue with a woman no questions but those of the heart. The point was that the captain came to the ship a captain and the only one there, no matter whom the dog-smellers might call by the name. Even so we six have little inheritance from our father but our place in the Guilds and our skill in war. Come, is't not reasonable that a shoemaker's son, brought up to the smell of leather, should cobble better than a man whose father burned charcoal? So you have the choice, you of Dalarna that are yet young in politic—to follow Briella's path or that of Carrhoene."

"I'll never agree," said Airar, and she: "Ah, poh, it is only a boy after all, where I had thought to find a man"; reined round to ride in anger back toward the rest, whereat the day seemed to Airar less than cheerful.

A little beyond this they came to a sign of war, where a track led from the way across a clearing to a house that had been burned and only the gable ends standing, quenched with last night's rain and still smoking. Several rode toward it; there seemed no sign of life about, but as Airar turned back toward the band, there came a small mew and he looked down to see at his feet a kitten that cried toward him with a small pink triangle of mouth, unafraid. He lighted down; the little beast had stripes down its back and round its tail and came to his hand to let him feel that there was a cavity under its ribs where its belly should be. "Poor kekki," he said and picked it up. It began to purr, and thinking how ill its fate would be in those wild wet woods, with master slain or driven away by the Vulking Allies, he lifted it to the saddle with him and made a fold of his cloak where it curled contentedly against the warmth of his body.

They were still sloping upward, with the streams running south and easterly to join the affluents of the Naar, and near one of these rills stopped for noon meat, packing up into a closer group among some shelving rocks along the bank, where the wet from the previous night was less. Airar snipped off bits of his meat for the kitten, which ate greedily, where Evimenes found him. "I do not like it," said the Star-Captain, with puckering brows. "It was full light when we passed the castella and surely they saw us. Soon or late, if that leader knows his business, we shall have gentours on our track, riding light and faster than we, with our wounded men and baggage cattle, their object being to annoy and delay till the heavy-armed come."

"Shall we then set another ambush?" said Pleiander.

"We have that master of strategem, the Dalecarle."

Airar flushed, but Alsander said serious: "Nay, for that is to delay, and what they desire—in war, as any contest, the will of one party being enough for the other to hate a thing. What counsel then, brother?"

His frown had not left Evimenes. "I would we had more bow-skill or these Mariolan mountain-men who know how to hide in crannies like spiders. A pox on this restless Rogai, so avid to increase his own credit, but leaving others always the unseen difficult task! And these Hestingerne can ride like the wind, but what use here among the trees? Nay, brothers, I say this Master Airar and his fisher spearmen are our best guard in this juncture and, if it's your will, shall ask them to lag behind the column with half a dozen of our sergeants to sustain them against charges, while the pack-animals move up ahead. If the gentours follow, the fishers shall light down and fight afoot, always rallying on the heavy-armed."

Airar said yes to that and it was a risen meeting. They rode. The High Hills of Froy were now all round, a country little peopled save by charcoal burners and such shy folk, so it was not to be expected that many would be met; yet it was somewhat grating to have no further word from Rogai. The night camp was by the earliest of those lakes which fill all the bowls of the hills, the more particularly westward toward rainy Shalland. Guards were set well toward the rear, and next morning, as being somewhat short of victual, the more part kept camp while the rest went out to see what could be had among the trees. Airar's own bow brought in a wild pig, and there were other small items, but it was long before noon when all let themselves be engaged by Evimenes to take the trail again. Summit of the day and pass came together; now they were in Shalland, and a little beyond the way swung left between a pair of hilltops to open out a lake with a lawn beside it and a house set midmost of the lawn, not very great.

Airar was back with his rearguard when the place was reached, but hurried on in answer to a message that Rogai had left another of his Whiteriverdalesmen guides at the place. The Mariolan himself (said the guide) had pressed on with his men, being confident the main band held the trail. He was scattering his men abroad, north and west toward Stavorna to feel the temper of the country and know what force the Vulkings had there; would meet them all at a place called Gäspelnith, which was no more than a tavern on the road that runs south from Stavorna towards the borders of Skogalang along the edge of the foothills.

Alsander was heard to grumble over this arrangement, but there were no two ways about it, they must follow the line as it lay. Debate was brief; the foreguard and packs set off again with the Dalesman guide southwesterly toward this tavern of the wild-goose nest just as Airar's men began to appear among the trees. Now his band must wait while the rest gained, and progress was poor for the day, with less meat than most of the men liked. Airar gave another nibble of his to the kitten, which crawled close under his chin at twilight and kept him awake with its stirrings till it had purred itself to sleep. He could not seem to think of a good name for this first true-love friend he had ever had.

The morning it began to rain after the persistent Shalland manner, straight down. One could almost see the tender green leaves jump up under it and flowers growing by the way, but few had eyes for that, now being hungry and more than a little fatigued with much travel. They rode. Every league or so another little lake or pool was brimming, with a brook running out of it. There were more open places scooped out of the hills around these waters, and the route clearer marked, with tracks of carts, leading off through fields where flax had grown to visible farmsteads. There was something peculiar about these places that touched Airar below the surface of his thoughts (which were all of the dilemma of Vulk and Carrhoene, with maybe a day-dream or two) till they reached a place where three of these cots stood together, with a heavy-faced man who leaned on a mattock as they passed, nor gave any answer to a greeting. Then it pushed to the

forefront of mind that among those Shalland homes
there had not been a person seen, nor a wisp of smoke,
nor cow nor dog nor goat, as though they were a conquering army whom all men had fled.

This seemed so strange that when they camped
again (and again at a hungry camp, after passing a
ford through a rather biggish stream that got their feet
wet as well as their heads), he rode forward to consult.
The Star-Captains also had remarked the want of men
in Shalland, the more since they had tried to get food
at two or three of these places, but found only some
horse-grain in a barn. Said Alsander: "The worst is
we do not know whether it's this foolish Rogai's doing,
or something of the Shallanders themselves, or the
Vulkings somehow to trap us. I like not this running
a blindfold race. We brothers give full confidence in
all our transactions, but confidence is of knowledge,
and here's one that commands us all without agreement, yet hides his purpose from them that have a
right to know."

"The blind man complains that he is led by one
lame," said Meliboë the enchanter, for which he received a glare, but Evimenes:

"I remind you of our old rule, brother, to bury the
past and think on the present. This matter of Rogai
may stand till a fairer day, but what's to be done now
of these long marches and short rations that have already so worn our people I doubt we could fight another such battle as that four days since?"

"It would be right," said Alsander, "to hold here,
sending scouts for food and to pick up these over-
nimble Mariolans at the rendezvous." His tone was
gloomy. "But what say you, Master Dalecarle?"

"I say—" began Airar, then, "Nay, I'll not say at
all till we know more. Where's the Dalesman guide?"
The man was brought. Airar made him sit, and in
answer to questioning he said Gäspelnith was better
than fifteen thousand paces farther; that it lay at a
quad-road in the midst of a rich district of dairies and
was a great resort of drovers so that whatever tidings
were toward could be heard there ("Aye, and tidings
of us passed to the world," grumbled Pleiander); that

it was a wood-built garth with shingling also of wood, in a hollow and thus not too easily defensible (the question had been Pleiander's); but with a grove close and open ground around, not easy to approach against lance-armed mounted men (this was Airar's). Of the disposition of the boniface he knew nothing; which was to be expected, since the Whiteriverdalesmen are a home-loving race, little given to guesting or aught concerned with it.

"Then here's my word," said Airar; "that we should push forward at once and any cost; for we shall find food at this garth and either encounter Rogai and his by which our strength is greatly waxed, or have quick warning of danger and so be the longer on the road toward any security."

There was a brief babble; somewhat to surprise Airar found Pleiander backing him and only Evimenes oppositious; Evadne somewhat frowning and biting a lip, Alsander judicious, but so much inclining to Airar's side in the words that were said that it was just about decided for an early start and a hard march, when Meliboë stood up on the other side of the group, where fire sputtered through wet wood. He had been moving his fingers in a kind of measured step through tall mosses there, clucking at the kitten, which had crawled from Airar's cloak when rain ceased, and taking this for some new game played with the magician's dancing fingers. Now Meliboë dropped the bundle of fur into Airar's lap.

"Of all animals," he said, "cats are the most near to men's minds. Young sir, I'm no war-master nor strategist and cannot tell you what you should do, but I have taken the divination and do assure you there is much danger for you at this place of Gäspelnith. You should seek another way."

There was a silence. "And for us, too?" said Pleiander in a voice so shaken that Airar felt a start of astonishment.

The magician's eye rolled and his voice went up half a tone. "Danger, aye, but none so great; your fate's another. This relates to the young master here in his proper person."

Airar felt skin tighten on his face. "Then if it touches myself alone, I say again—march. I've followed this danger-divination before, and the last time it cost me . . . more than I wished to lose."

So it was decided. Meliboë left his place to walk with Airar back to where he would sleep among the fishers, and on the way told him he was too forward— "not that you refuse the divination; men of your metal do that ever from time to time, since they're at war with the world and all compulsions. It is no more than the flout a philosopher attends. The error lay in saying it sharp and public, just after Pleiander announced himself fearful. This Evadne loves to think on you as not so harsh as she is; destined, but of more delicate temper, that she can cover in some things, so you will keep an edge to cut through the cobwebs that plague all bold and daring women. If you show yourself hard and masterful, you'll lose her. Do what you will, but more subtly."

22. Shalland: Evil at the Inn

THEY RODE. WITH SADDLE-SORES AND HUN-
gry, they rode; few were the words that were spoken,
and those mostly of a quarrelsome kind, so that Airar
must intervene to keep one of his men and a Carrhoene
sergeant from blows. The day had cleared, so they
lacked the rain that left them so miserable yesterday,
but the march was a hard one even without that, and
the only interlude to the dull grey of the journey was
when the kitten squirmed and had to be set down to
do its duty. The small animal raced away into a clump
of weeds and Airar was much put to retrieve it while
Carrhoene sergeants whooped at him and his face
reddened.

In another mood he might have remarked how now
around the country showed less of trees and more of
farms, with here a man or two visible, and cattle; but

196

he did not, therefore was surprised on turning a corner again to see at the crest of the next slow rise the others gathered in a group, men off horses and waiting. It was Gäspelnith beyond, lying below down a noble slope of lawn, a long one-storied building not very large, nor very clearly visible either because of the tall oaks that stood it round. There were rooks in the oaks, to be seen even from here, and tall barns for the drovers' convenience; but over the heads of barns and trees, far away through the next sweep of the rolling sea of land, Airar's sharp sight caught a silver gleam. That must be Vällingsveden, the river of Shalland and the reason why the inn had been set here; for up that river came ships from the lands to the south and down it boats from hillset Stavorna. The spectacle was so gracious that he answered but absently to comments (which in any case had small importance) as they rode down the slope, with weariness redoubled by the near approach of peace.

Three or four men came out to watch their arrival and from the distance they looked like nut-brown Mariolans with their mail-shirts off, a thought which confirmed itself on reaching near enough for speech. One was Tholkeil, whom Airar had seen long since, shivering in the marsh; he had a tale to tell, but must keep it till all dismounted stiffly and as many as could be crowded into the tavern, where the host with two or three wenches and some Micton girls was setting out hams and drawing beer. Airar did not much like what he saw of this host, a burly man with a fat face and hair so cut that it stood straight aloft at the front of his head, who ran around like a dog, alternately barking at his underlings and sniffing of his guest's feet. He liked it still less when Tholkeil said the fellow was neither of the Iron Ring nor of the Vulking Allies, but had taken priest's orders, the better to run his inn without molestation in the midst of alarms. His name was Vindhug "—and there's a fine priest who'll sell you the service of any girl here and never think twice about it."

There had been some complaint (continued Tholkeil) from the country to the Bishop of Shalland, but the lord was a Vulking, and not too sorry to see Dalecarles at outs with their religious, which meant they must go for marriages to the Vulking courts and for heart's comfort to the Well; thus the Bishop did nothing, while Vindhug prospered.

Now that hunger had been appeased it was possible for the leaders to dispense with the services of this hedgepriest and his wenches and gather in a corner to hear what Tholkeil had to say. This was in part what they already knew: that, having slain or driven off the Vulking Allies at Crow's Tower, Rogai at the issue of the hills had split his band in groups of three or four, spreading them across the countryside. The new was that these had orders to say frankly who they were, but that they were only the vanguard of a great host of Hestingerna and Salmonessans, who had won a victory and were marching to free Shalland.

"What gave the fool that senseless inspiration?" rapped out Alsander.

"Why—" the Mariolan looked surprised. "They have a full tercia at Stavorna, with gentours and Allies. Master Rogai thought to make them keep their seats and let us through by making them think we are the more. Is't not well?"

Here was the reason why the Shalland farms stood empty. "No," said Alsander, more than a little grim, "but say on."

—Well then (Tholkeil continued) he and his own little group had cut straight west toward Glos, the walled town standing where Vällingsveden spreads in many mouths to run through fertile deltas to the sea. They gave their false tidings till near the gate of the place, and, taking a night's guesting, came here to meet the rest. The tale was that the night's guesting had nearly been their last, their host proving traitorous, and setting fire a-night to the old hayrick he gave them for sleeping. "What's worse, the scoundrel slipped our vengeance, but as he liked bonfires so well we made one of his house for him."

"You may join the others," said Alsander shortly, then turning to the leader-group: "Here's hell's broth and no pepper for it. I do not know too well these Vulking ways of war, but from all I've seen of them, the commander of this tercia will do the same thing as myself in such a case—march fast with all his strength down to hold the gate of the hills against the issuance of this imaginary force, and so come on our heads. We're in a trap."

Evimenes: "This afternoon and night of good rest will make all so much new men that I think another forced march can be dared; but how we are to outstrip these gentours with the heavy-armed and the fishers that can only half ride, I do not know."

"Then it's outlet by sea if in any way possible. But where boats? I would we had a faithful Shalland man to advise us, but would trust the dragon of Phyladea as soon as our host here."

Said Airar: "Rogai is of the Iron Ring and when he comes will perhaps know someone who can aid us. But there is one thing very curious in this, and that is why a tercia should be at Stavorna city at all. I do not know if you have remarked, but the people of these northern parts are mostly not too comfortless under Vulking rule; yet for Mariola, all rebellion and independence, they had half a tercia only on guard, while a whole one here."

Alsander: "The question's doubtless keen for you Dalecarles but has naught to do with present necessity. Was not there something about a movement against the Earl of Os Erigu?"

Meliboë the enchanter, who had listened silent as his custom was, now lifted his head and hand. "You have wrong," said he, "and the young master full right, who has learned that all which does appear and has to do with present necessity is made up of what does not appear and has to do with nothing visible. But if you say this is metaphysic, then let me show something forth. Your hopes are set on this Erigan Earl, not so?"

"Nay, on ourselves and nothing else," cried hot Pleiander, but his brother the strategist: "In some measure, I confess."

"Good, then you take him for a skillful man in war?"

"Aye, that certainly." Alsander made a mouth. "Had't not been for his reivings, we'd have more time to spoil these dog-smeller uprisings. . . . But no malice, d'you see? He plays his game, we ours, and will strike hands."

"I have no doubt; you out of the Dodekapolis would strike hands with the Devil to make women wear tails. That's not my story. If he's a fighting man approved, not like that piddling duke, then there's a better chance than no that he's ware of the storm that gathers in the tercia at Stavorna, not so?"

"I will give you so much." Alsander fingered his chin, then slapped his hands together. "Ha! I see; you will now say he'll devance them as I myself would—strike first, to wit."

Evimenes: "But what if he's decided to strike by the Iron Mountains and down through the northern provinces by land?"

Now Meliboë laughed and Airar too, for both thoroughly knew that the Os Erigu pirate Earl from his almost-island by the shore had story and glory only on the sea. Alsander of Carrhoene grinned. "Well, then. But what's the service to us?"

"I can tell you that," said Airar. "The service is we seek the shore and put out, not with many ships in flight, but a few to find the enemy of our enemies on the water and make common cause. But 'twill not sit well with these Shalland men."

Meliboë looked at him indulgently. "Fair young sir, you are a lucky man and not without talent; yet at every point so ready to concede this free election of the will that I wonder on you. The end of giving every man his choice is in Vulking rule; but you look toward putting them down in name, only to yield to them in spirit."

Yet was it decided to reach for the sea as soon as men and wounded would and could be moved. The distance none knew nor did they like to seek counsel of Vindhug, but the Whiteriverdalesman guide, being called on, thought it might be twenty leagues

or more. Now came the matter of Rogai, for whom
the Carrhoenes would not wait, but here Airar became very strong, saying this was another such test
as the battle at the pass; they dared not abandon any
who held to the cause, whatever their fault or trouble. Inner and outer guards were set and the men
sought rest. It was considered that Meliboë had spoken well.

Toward dawn of the next day another of the little Mariolan groups fell in, to rouse them early;
they had three-four young Shalland men with them
to join the rising, who had brought their own horses
but were without swords. These last knew the country
enough to solve the worser difficulties of guidance,
saying the road west from the inn touched a ferry
across that branch of Vällingsveden not far from
the point Airar had seen from the hilltop, approaching. Twenty leagues downstream to the sea would
about hit it (they agreed), but the chance of boat-
finding there was not great, since few fished that
shore and the ships of commerce went ordinarily
upstream to Glos and its market.

Now it came out that the difference all had thought
settled the night before was by no means relieved,
for Evimenes wanted to march on the minute, seize
the ferry and transport all overstream to the bogland
of the delta, where they would have the broad water
betwixt them and Vulking pursuit; while Airar had
understood they were still to attend Rogai at the inn.
There was some pretty hard talk, turning to as near
a quarrel as any point yet reached, and Airar looked
in vain to Meliboë for a composition, who only
listened, drawing his fingers through his beard; but
Evadne settled it by taking Airar's part with:
"Brothers, I no more understand this flying in the
face of sense than you do, but it is said that wars
are not won without willing hearts and we shall never
have willing hearts from these Dalecarles till we yield
on this point they make." The other Star-Captains
at once gave way, as always for her, and there they
were for another day as Gäspelnith.

Airar separated himself a little from the rest and

played with the kitten while trying again to think
things through—none too happy over carrying his
point in this manner and with this help. It seemed
to him the Carrhoene damsel had said her words less
out of honest belief than to gain his own approval,
and he did not like owing her debts no more than he
cared for this kind of double-dealing, which was not
the way men behaved in his part of the country.
Out of all this grew a sense of being trapped, too
deep for thinking, and he let his mind run idle. Toward evening, the coil of troubles turned worser, for
down the north road Rogai came riding with two
more Shalland men and a feeling of self-pleasure;
there was contest between him and Alsander till
Airar bade the Star-Captains remember their own rule
against bringing past into present. The point was
granted but then all turned grumpish. There was no
word of stir from the Stavorna tercia, but Rogai said
the roads had been mostly cleared, at Glos the gates
closed, and the soldiers had been withdrawn from a
castella on the road down.

The plan was still for the ferry then, as soon as
all might move. Rogai solved the question of bringing in the rest of his scattered men by sending one
of the loyal Shallanders with Tholkeil to a post above
the hillcrest for guiding late arrivals to the ferry as
they came, with a signal by smoke or torch, and—

Just at this juncture Pleiander looks up to see the
glowering Vindhug, standing close with his mouth
half-open, as though to take in their talk by that way.
The Carrhoene leaped from his place and gripped the
fellow by the collar.

"Here's one spying who will sell us for an aina
and our plan, too," he cried. "What, brothers! Shall
we not slit his throat and stuff the coin in it to reach
his fat belly quicker?"

"Aye," said the other two Star-Captains and
Evadne with them; the Shalland man who sat with
them aye, that the animal had lived too long. Vindhug went to his knees despite the choking grip, with
tears on his cushioned cheeks, beginning to blubber
and cry he was a priest, they would lie under the

curse of the Church for this, and be sure he would say no, nothing, if they only let him go. Not a whit relented Pleiander for that; he would have dragged the whoremaster priest to the door and finished him, but Airar lifted hand and said it should not be so done in Dalarna. However little one liked a man's manners, he did not die from them till it were proved they stood contrary to the law of the land and of God; but nothing was yet proved on this one.

Many of the men had crowded round from down through the long inn building at the squall and babble, but the Carrhoene sergeants had mostly gone back to their drink and dice at seeing it was only their leader punishing a desperado, so those who stood by were Dalecarles. Airar, remembering how rude they had been at Britgalt's hut, was now surprised to hear them murmur approval of his saying, and so was Pleiander, who gazed round in a startled sort of way, and then released his hold. Vindhug, still on his kneebones, crawled toward the lad of Trangsted and tried to nuzzle his hand; Airar kicked him lightly in the belly and told him to begone.

They moved at night under flickering torches. It had begun to rain again and the horses tossed their heads, protesting as horses will at having to work when it is time for sleep. In the dark and wet the way seemed longer than it had looked by daylight and Evadne sneered at Airar for taking the kitten, asking whether he were "like Pleiander, that had a taste for other meat than that of woman?"

"No," said Airar, "but the cat is my fortune that protects me from whatever might wish to have my soul; my luck and banner." He gestured toward where the cat-head followed on its pole (all on the spur of the moment, for he had not thought on it at all and was desirous only to silence her), borne by the free-fishers since the day of the fight at the road. She gave him a very strange look and drew apart; the enchanter was nowhere.

When they reached Vällingsveden, there was no ferryboat or ferryman to be seen, nor did torches and shouts bring him from the rolling water, a good thousand paces across. Some of the free-fishers, who live wet like otters, volunteered to go fetch him. The Shallanders, who use those short fighting axes forged head and haft in one piece, had down a couple of light trees, and three of Airar's men wove trunks and branches into a kind of raft on which they set out, while the rest of the band lay down to comfort themselves against the rain as best they might and wait for daylight or a return.

The latter came first, though after a wait half through the nightwatch, two of the fishers rowing a leaky shallop, while the third alternate bailed and talked with an old man they had found in a sod cot beyond the stream. He said word had come three days before from the priest of Gäspelnith that invaders were in the land and were to be held at the stream-bank till the terciaries came. The way of the saying made it seem that the invaders must be heathen from Dzik: none thought of Dalecarles out of Vulking law. Therefore the ferryboat had been taken upstream to Glos. Pleiander rapped out that Vindhug the landlord now stood convicted, but Airar that this was by no means true, it might come from the spreading of Rogai's tale; and Evimenes that if true, then the more need of haste, to go back for a pleasant vengeance might cost them all their lives. The old Shallander, being further questioned, thought he knew of a kind of barge that lay at a place a few hundred paces down the stream, and as it was beginning to grow light, some went off to seek it, while further trees were brought down and rafted. With several of the horses swimming, these ungainly craft began the voyage. Another of Rogai's Mariolan groups came in on the main band in the midst of this; they had been pursued by gentours and had ridden all night, with one of the horses foundering so two men had to sit another.

This pressed still more the need for haste, and when daybreak brought the searchers with their barge, bad and leaky though it was, they began to move the unswimmers and some of the animals into it at once. The sun rose behind mist through which rain continued to drizzle, and none had slept, while there was little on which to breakfast, yet Airar felt oddly elated and began to sing:

There is a river to the sea, to the sea,
And 'twill bear my love from me, love from me;
But though it bear her far and far away
Nor she nor I will lose this day.

                                  Fare thee well!

At this point Visto, who had not yet crossed, pushed up to end the singing with a word that this was a mighty bold and daring undertaking (though many were like to suffer therefrom) and Airar the master of the stronghearts, who had brought it through and should take the cat for his badge and warcry, never minding the old Wingèd Wolf under which Dalarna fell. Airar now went thoughtful. By noon they were all across but one little knot of three of Rogai's men that had not come in. As they stood together on the low farther shore, they could see some gentours caracole and brandish spears on the bank they had left.

23. Shalland: Debate
of Meliboë the Enchanter

THE COUNTRY NORTHWEST OF VÄLLINGS-
veden is low and boggish, with huts built of sod and
little of value in them because of raiders from oversea. The Shallanders of this region are not esteemed
the highest of men, but will live no other place,
partly because the ground is exceeding fertile and
partly because of all Dalecarles, they are the most
stiff-lipped race. One or two Vulking castellas stand
near the outer shore, but these are gentour commands of men who can ride fast when the sea-rovers
come. There is much tree-growth of willow and similar; the roads wind greatly. The bands now united
pushed southwest down one of these through the

afternoon and they were better than seventy strong
now, with additions from the Dales and Shalland itself, maybe one or two young men from the bogs
falling in, but not many, since in that country it was
not considered a disgrace to go for a Vulking Ally.

Toward evening they reached a bog village of low
huts set along the central road. Men fell asleep almost at once, some hardly waiting for food. It was
now a question of speed and the hope of Earl,
Mikalegon's coming from the ocean, for they were
clearly caught else, though it would be as hard for
the Vulkings to cross Vällingsveden as for themselves,
and no one feared gentours, not with the armed riders
of Carrhoene and the light horsemen of Hestinga
under their standard. The cries of dirty children
roused them early. The villagers were merry with
them as they left, offering the local liquor made of
roots and stored in skins—but at a price.

Airar was fain to leave the kitten now; for which
he foresaw but a hard life, one of the bogwomen
desiring it. But she was a slattern and he could not
bear to give up his little friend to sure mistreatment.
They rode; now it was through willows and mist.
The way was not good underfoot. Evadne came up
to trot for a while beside Airar and to say he should
be of good cheer—this was hardly as bad as the
time when the People's Party in Carrhoene had triumphed and there was talk of hanging the six Star-
Captains out of hand, when they had won mercy only
because messengers came from the Mariupol Guilds
with offer that they should adventure to Dalarna.
"Even dog-smellers could see that to the major glory
of Carrhoene. Yet I do marvel," said she, "on you with
so much faith in your luck. With us it is that he have
a surety of being right and knowing in the end we
must triumph, but here are you with no thought of
right, only your own luck to guide."

He would have replied, but just then they reached
another bog village, so there was a question of tidings
and the conversation fell. Then came Erb, joining Airar
in highest humor with a hail of "Up, young master!"
and a word of "They Vulkings that be so great of

the sword in their own mountain will now know what it is to do by sea with Earl Mikalegon on a, and maybe we shall pay a debt or two"—till Airar could not but question why a man in flight should be so gay.

The Lank took his steel cap off and scratched his head. "Now there, Master Airar, you just ask me questions like my own sister Ervilla or the priest, and I do not see how man can find an answer, but that we go where there is salt in air again, and we can sniff it now, after all they mountains that never move, but make a badge for Vulkings."

"They are the hills of Dalarna."

"Ey—ah—aye." The tall man's face contracted with an effort at thought. "But Dalarna under Briella Mountain, and Mountain over Dalarna hills, and so many like that man Vindhug that just be happy slaves. We Gentebbi folk be main poor, but 'tis better than they rich Shallanders."

"And Earl Mikalegon?"

"Oh, un most of all. Hark, Master Airar; we free-fishers understand little of this politic, we just make Rudr our Master-Fisher, and there's a long head, but I have talked to one-two, all saying we might make worse than have this Earl for our duke or king. A's free-handed man and a lordly bold one that stands against Vulk and the Empire and all."

The idea was new. "Shall we go pirating with him against the Empire, then? Why are we against Vulk but to lift Dalarna, not to drag her down?"

"Down how, then, young master? With Mikalegon, that's not down. Un lives free in a's tall castle there by Erigu rock; and a's people, too. They say 'tis hung finer than the high house in Stassia. Un never sits down to dine with less than six meats on table and dancing girls every night with the free choice of them to those selected most valiant in war."

"Like Salmonessa." (Airar thought of Gython given to the Duke.) "It must be splendid. And the dancing girls, what's their choice in the matter?"

Erb turned to him a face of honest incredulity. "Choice? A be dancing girls. 'Tis just by election a follow such life. . . . Nay, Master Airar, forgive an old man that's never been young, I did not know you so churchly minded, but say as you will on dancing girls, there's still this—that in Os Erigu no man lowers his head before other, and Earl, he beats off Micton warbands and holds they heathen at bay without leave or help from Empire. There's a life a man can live gaily, with enough fighting in it to keep from going fat."

To this Airar had no reply as they moved along with the metal flash of the river occasionally visible leftward (for after making from it they had now approached again). He had begun to think that perhaps with Mikalegon was the middle path through his problem of Briella and Carrhoene; yet this was a thought unspoken, he being sharp-minded enough to see that what if all Dalarna went pirating with Erb and Earl Mikalegon? And pirating even from each other? A case for Meliboë (he thought); thinking so they reached a place where the willows went low and faded out and the west was lost in mudflats mixed with sand, then sand alone and sea, where from the left hand brown Vällingsveden swept to slip his waters almost secretly into the blue.

Here was the crisis of their voyage. All the riders came to stand while Airar shaded a hand and turned his sharp eyes out to look across the water toward where Earl Mikalegon and his ships must be if they were to win free.

"They are not there!" cried Evimenes in a raging voice, but then Airar: "Nay, look to the north far away, how at the horizon there are specks of light that flash and go. You seamen can say if those be not sails that catch the glare of the western light and vanish as they turn."

"I do not see it," cried one, but Erb, "By the Well, it is so!"

Now silence; and soon, as the view grew, all were agreed that here was Os Erigu upon the water and no mistake, the armada drawing nearer. Most of the men came down from their horses and rubbed stiff leg-joints or searched in pouch and saddlebag for meat and drink. There was converse among the leaders on what's to be done. Alsander said that the Earl had made a descent already up the coast, or this was his first adventure—"but if the latter then he will take us who stand in arms at the shore for levies and gentours warned of the earlier coming, and is like to land or attempt something on such; while if it be his earliest approach, more like to think us the terciary band from Stavorna and draw away without touching ground. It's a man who understands war and now all his force is in movement by ship to strike unattainted; will not fight straight-up battles, d'ye see?"

Airar thought that a man who warred like this was less than knightly, and said as much, but the Carrhoene laughed, and Rogai remarked between his teeth: "Knights are like Sir Ludomir Ludomirson, with a price on their heads, or if they get fat, turn into Dukes Roger. But what of that? Here's our instant question, to get word to those ships that we be not foemen; and even then I misdoubt how we will be received."

That was a question now that he put it, and no wavings from the shore were like to be of service, since they were like to be held an indication of Vulking ambush. The Shalland men were confused; they thought it might be possible to find one of the coracles used by the people of these parts when they venture on the water, and went off to try it with Erb, a couple of fishers, and Rogai as ambassador. Evadne said it was Airar's place to go, but now he was suddenly stricken with shyness over meeting to the person, and when so much hung on it, this renowned warrior and champion of Os Erigu. He made a ridiculous excuse about the kitten. Pleiander sneered, which Evadne saw and a moment later she picked up some remark of her brother's so the two began a pointless wrangle that drove Airar apart to seek Meliboë, while all round the men in little groups sat down to chatter of this and that and their hopes.

The philosopher was set on a slope of sand with his back against a brush-clump and his cloak arranged to keep him clean. He was not wearing armor and his eyes were fixed out toward the sea, where ships were now clearly visible as ships, so graceful. Said Airar:

"There's a matter I'd have you unriddle according to philosophy, for I do not like neither answer I can get by myself."

"Well, then?" The enchanter's tone might be somewhat short.

"Well, is't true there are no paths to follow but those that lead to Briella or Carrhoene?"

"Fair young sir, your trouble I may unriddle, but not your riddles. What is you would say?"

"Why, 'tis this and concerns me much—" Airar watched his kitten that scampered after a leaf while he sought for words. " 'Tis this; is there no way for men to live but to submit all one's self to the voice of the general, as that deserion said whom Pleiander slew? I'd rather be a pismire, running blind. Yet here's Evadne says there is but one escape, and that's to follow the rule of Carrhoene: let all beg whose fathers were blind—which is clean against our Dalecarle rule."

From off at one side there was a shout, men began to run and point. Airar stood up; down the stream the coracle came loping crabwise and rocked when the ocean swell took it. Rogai put his head over the side; there was laughter when men could see the movement of the craft left him little well. Meliboë did not turn his head:

"They have found a boat? Then our lives are safe from both and I think for this time also your Dalarna will be safe from both these things you fear. But in the long she has right, the lass; as those who have right who say there's no escape from the old man that mows. For see—all's well to be free and labor together (this is the thought forward on which you look, as I take it); all's well when it's a matter of two or three to build a byre or hunt a bear, but when there are foemen in the land or something other where each man cannot see for himself what's to be done, why then all must take the guidance of a man they never have seen nor perhaps heard on.

Can any give more than his own arm and confidence? Can any have authority to himself? No."

"I do not see—"

"You do not see, you do not see. Son of Alvar, I can but give you the book; read in it. Nay, I'll spell it but for you, rather." The magician lifted his head and beat with a finger. "Suppose then this leader for war has been chosen—no matter how. Here's your fountainhead of authority; but he's not immortal, and should he fall in battle, then all's broken unless there be another with authority to step into his honors and no delay. So there's your government permanent and paramount with authority atop and confidence below, and I know no way of keeping it so but the ways of Briella and Carrhoene. Ah, you'll find tricks and devices, given names in the books—that is what books are for, to call names—but it comes to the same in the end. There's a rule arbitrary for choosing your head, such as that he's of a certain family—that's Carrhoene, or the Empire, for that matter. Or there's no rule and the head's a figurehead and you have Briella. In either, those below are less than free."

"There's Earl Mikalegon," said Airar, who wanted to ask which choice would be Meliboë's, but durst not for respect and shame.

"Aye, there he is in his ships and see how they crowd toward the coracle. It must be clear that she bears tidings. Fortunate son of Alvar! There's your man that's free and all beneath him, with full choice to go elsewhere if the prospect not please. Mark him well."

Meliboë leaned back against his bush and turned his eyes seaward. The conversation was ended, but Airar made one more effort. "And the danger of Gäspelnith?"

"A thing has been done that all your life will not be more than enough to change." He waved his hand and would not answer more, but chucked the catkin under the chin when it came to him. Out on the water the high ships crowding round with painted sails obscured the coracle; some of those sails came

down and the ships stood still or moved so little
that only by one could it be seen how another's position changed. A trumpet-sound drifted elfin across
sea and shore. Airar wrinkled his eye-muscles and
could see black specks move, the quarter-boats handled and now these separated to come flicking toward
them over the wavetops like water-beetles. One of
the Star-Captains shouted his name. He was a leader
again and here was Sewald with a sore foot, and
Gynnbrad that claimed another had taken his dag,
and there was pressing to the shore, with Evimenes
shouting and men taking the packs from horses.

This was Airar's second sea-voyage but the first
in so big a ship and he not a little bewildered on
coming over the side to find stairs down and stairs
up into the poop, men all round the waist of the ship
and a very martial aspect, like a city afloat.

"Mark the third step," said someone, but not
quickly enough, as Airar stumbled on the broken
tread. At the head of the stairs, with the grasshopper
legs of a ballista rising behind him against the sky,
a big man stood with his suite round him, and was
made even taller by the fact that Airar came up to
him from a level below. He was armed in rusty
chain-mail with a couple of torn links at one shoulder, as though his massive frame had bulged right
through it, seeking escape; uncovered, with a mat
of rough black hair that hung loose to his shoulders
and a beard that bristled in every direction back
from a widespread nose and bushy brows.

"This," said Rogai's voice, "is Master Airar of
Trangsted in Vastmanstad, of noble blood, a very
notable captain in battle, who has now done twice
what the Star-Captains of Carrhoene could not accomplish the once—to wit, bring the red triangle
down."

"You are welcome," the big man boomed and
came three steps forward to touch Airar's hand, as
though he were a prince. "Not that to outdo Carrhoene is so very much, for I have raided their cities
myself, but it is a good cragsman can climb over
Briella Mountain."

"The Carrhoene captains——" began Airar, but before he could go farther in their defense or his own modesty, the great Earl was already turned aside to see who came next to his place of command and it was Alsander to speak for himself. "Ha!" shouted Mikalegon, not touching this hand, but taking it in his. "Here's one that needs no herald! Old Bag-of-bones, we have spent one or two strokes on each other and I am happier to have you with me than opposed. Where's Alcides, that owes me good ship he took from me with his tricks?"

"The damned Vulkings slew him." For the second time Airar was surprised to see a Carrhoene captain show heart; but now there were greetings to all to be made and returned and bustle across the decks, with sails set up again. Yet almost before the ships began to move, here came a hail from a vessel beyond and then one from their own masthead, and Airar, following the direction of fingers that pointed, could see where Vällingsveden wound back among its willows, all the flood dotted with small shapes that moved.

"We made good our retreat none too soon," said Alsander with a meditative air. "It must be a very good baron who leads that tercia—who would have thought to see Vulkings afloat?"

"Not I," said Mikalegon. "Yet you shall now see some aswim, to remind them whose element they tread. Shipmaster, ho! Bear us in toward those galleys if the wind will serve, and cast loose the catapults for using!"

There were shouts of "By the left, rudder!" The sails flapped and the ship came round; but as she settled to the new course it was clear that the commander of the row-galleys had discovered his danger, for they were turned to shore. Earl Mikalegon stamped the deck. "We pay for our good luck with bad," he cried, "and here's an end of this raid, for they're ware of us at Lectis Minima, and I doubt we can reach Smarnaravida before news of our coming. Shipmaster, set our course for homeward—and you, sirs, follow me and be shown what I mean."

24. The Northern Sea: A Bond Broken

HE TURNED BENEATH THE POOP STAIRS to a door so low that even Alsander, of far fewer inches than the Earl or Airar either, must stoop to enter. They were in an apartment from side to side of the vessel, with fenestrations in the walls and built-beds beneath them. An amass of gear clattered about the deck as the ship moved to the breeze. Earl Mikalegon ducked under the beams of the deck above and beat on a further door, "Wake, all!" crying. Airar heard no answer; but what there was seemed to satisfy; Os Erigu flung open the portal. Crowding behind Rogai and the Carrhoenes, Airar caught over their shoulders a flicker of color in the light from the stern-windows; Mikalegon swung to one side, bowed and swept out an arm like a showman:

"The sea-eagle feeds on golden pheasant, oh-ho-ho-ho-ho-ho! What? Down to your knee-knuckles, lawless dogs! Do you not know the most exalted Princess Aurea of the Empire?"

Airar caught a glimpse of a tall fair girl with a spoiled mouth and a green-and-golden gown, a small red gold coronal atop piled braids of pale gold. The color of her lips was not her own—but so much of the old Imperial reverence held that Alsander went slow to one knee and Pleiander and the rest, so that Airar could not avoid imitation, at the price of being boorish.

She laughed like a tinkling bell and her voice had an edge of sneer. "I thank you your obeisance. If 'twere meant, I'd say out sword and cut down this famous conqueror that wars on women, but that's too much to ask, not so?"

The big man laughed in his beard. "They had as well not. Or is there a champion of the Empire here who'd give me a knock? I'll offer him fair duello, man for man and no interference from any. But before the play begins, mark that you fight not for the Empire, but for the affianced bride of Count Vulk the Fourteenth, the Unreasonable. Ah, bah! These debates eat our hours and should be conducted by glee-singers. Come, doves, chicks—a promenade a-deck for you, while I've a word or two to say to these masters."

"No courteous thing to order women so," began the blonde girl and stamped her foot as though to go in a tirade as the Earl firmly gripped her arm, but Airar missed half of what was said, for he had risen like the rest from knee to feet and at the plurals looked—then lost his breath. For there was another girl in the room besides the princess, and as he saw, he knew that all his life long he should follow that other, feeling in a flash that this was somehow infidelity to Gython and his life's ideal, yet—false though it make him—he could not deny that this was his hope forever. . . . Not tall, yet not so short neither, and eyebrows that missed the perfect arch over eyes whose color he could not have named; a

fine, thin nostril, a shapely chin—no, no, can one
tell the form of the lightning-stroke? A tune rang
through his head:

> *How shall I know her? What shall I give for her?*
> *Lift your eyes to her eyes and sing—*
> *Many will die that a few may live for her—*

Oh, yes, and yes; if the Earl's challenge had been
for her it would be easy to fight him and his ship
and his whole fleet; or if she were the damsel voyaging to wed the Count of Vulkings, it were time to
abandon all Dalarna and join them to serve her.

"Mi-e-e-e," wailed the kitten from in the pouch at
his side.

Just brushing past she turned. "A kitten! May I
see?"

Trancelike, Airar fumbled the pouch fastening
open, conscious only of the perfume of her nearness.
The small frightened animal leaped past his groping
hand with claws outspread; past hers, and in another leap lit clinging on the bare arm of Evadne of
Carrhoene.

"Phlegeos!" cried the shield-girl, flinging her arm
round furiously. There was a thud as the kitten detached was thrown against a beam. Evadne was nurs-
ing a scratched arm, mouthing curses, and Airar leaping across the room, not noting how a light-brown
head was beside his own as he picked up the poor
little body that kicked twice and went limp in his
hands. A mist of tears swept past his eyes and his
jaw muscles set; the girl beside him gave a wordless
cry, and from behind the mist Earl Mikalegon said:

"Noble sir, sorrow that you lose your pet through
accident in my cabin; but neither mice nor men are
immortal and now we have men's work to do."

"No accident!" cried Airar wildly. "This was pre-
pense and I'll have repair." His hand was on his dag,
hardly noting how the Earl did frown.

Said Meliboë the enchanter: "There is something
more in this than a small matter, my lord. The cat
is in some sense Master Airar's luck and banner,

his people bearing the head of a great cat before them to battle, so that to lose this small one is not merely of evil omen, but despite as well."

"Ha! So? There must be satisfaction." The Earl slid behind a table bolted to the deck and beat his fist for attention. "My judgment: you, Evander of Carrhoene, shall make full acknowledgment of fault, paying such fine as Master Airar shall fix; or, since here is a question of more than value, lowering your standard to the cat-standard of Trangsted; for he has noble birth and you none. Or if Master Airar will not accept this, then both parties shall take weapons and fight it on the deck of this vessel till blood is drawn according to the rule of the free company of Os Erigu; but afterward, all shall touch hands and be friends."

"You are somewhat free with your judgments, Lord Mikalegon," said Pleiander. "Who gave you authority to judge over us?"

"None, truly enough. All are free to go their own path among the free companies. Do you wish it? I'll call the quarter-boat and have you set ashore again where you were found."

Pleiander looked black murder and Evadne too, but neither of them had more to say. Evimenes had out a kerchief and was dabbing at his sister's arm, but could make little of that, for the wounds were truly scratches. Said Airar, brushing the edge of a sleeve across his eyes: "I'll take no fine; not a fining matter." He reached a hand to touch that of Alsander, but Evadne did not offer, nor he to her, for it seemed that if he did so in such a moment, he must either have screamed or driven a dagger into her to break the peace.

Now there was a council, with the reflected light from the water swaying back and forth across the ceiling as the ship moved. The travellers exposed all their story and Earl Mikalegon listened as the tale shifted from one to the other, tempers somewhat cooling as each remembered the good help the others had given in urgency. Os Erigu heard them more

quietly than one would have looked for in so booming a man, at the end, saying:

"That you may know what passes in the world
and how these come aboard, I'll say: we sailed a
raid, hoping to harry the trade that passes up the
rivers toward Briella. Well, off the capes that shield
Lectis Minima, what do we find? A great nef be-
calmed under the lee of the land, bearing the Imperial standard. I rowed over to make my ruty, but
found the shipmaster an ill-conditioned rogue with a
cast in his eye, who warned me away and hove up
a cantle of stone to drive it through the bottom of
the shallop. 'Tis not so done in the waters where
Mikalegon rules; one of my people let him have a
crossbow bolt through the shoulder to teach him
manners, and I went aboard, with a few of my brisk
boys behind. As soon as we reached the deck there
was a hurry like a hen-yard under hawks, so instead
of making bows and taking leave, I'd a look around.
It was not long before I discovered these two pigeons
and that brother of theirs—what's his name?"

"Prince Aurareus," said one of the Earl's officers.

"I name him Pretty-boy. He's forward. Well, as
soon as I found him, there was weeping and wailing
that an Imperial ship with the members of the family
in it needed no let-pass from me. Though in Os
Erigu we care not much for the house of Argimenes,
we keep the peace of the Empire and it's true enough
no harm comes from me to Stassia; but it failed
explanation of why there was such eagerness to keep
us distant at the beginning. Pretty-boy would say
no more, so we went back to the shipmaster, and
between his wound and an applied bowstring, he
turned reasonable enough to tell us the tale, which
is that this Princess Aurea was given in marriage to
Count Vulk. His possession, not the Empire's; therefore I seized the ship and its cargo. Lawmen may
argue the point; I'll take that up when Vulk sues
for peace and his bride."

Airar swallowed once and said, "Who is the other?"

"What other? Oh, the lesser girl that took your
fancy and made you gawk so. She's the cadette—

Argyra. Be warned; she's proud and contentious like
all the Argimenids; has refused a marriage with one
of the greatest lordships in Dodekapolis, which is
why she was sent hither—in the hope that she might
marry off one of the Vulking counts or barons, thinking to spite her family, whereas it is precisely what
they wish. I joy to be a daughterless man; but now
you have all my tidings and there's much mystery in
these muddy waters, though mayhap one of you can
see the pearl-oyster at the bottom."

"Where's the mystery?" asked Alsander. "It seems
a plain tale to me."

"Nay, Bag-of-Bones, cozen children with that
sugar, but not your old opponent. You know as well
as I it's more than strange that the great County
Vulk affords no convoy to a ship that brings him a
bride Imperial."

Alsander looked down with black lashes on his
cheek, but it was Meliboë the magician that spoke.
"I can tell you the reason for that."

"Say on, old man. Pest! If I'd a beard like that,
I'd paint it to give at least the appearance of life.
What says your woman when you bed her?"

"There are those who would think white hairs
came with wisdom. . . . But touching the other, here's
the thought: who's Chancellor to this Vulk that is
so unreasonable as to have it for a by-name?"

"The marshal, Bordvin Wildfang, unless there be
a new one."

"And the Vulks are counts elective, not so?"

"It is thus credibly reported."

"Good. Suppose Vulk wedded to this proud, fair-
haired girl."

"I suppose it. What then?"

"The next in line of succession to our good prince
and Emperor Auraris is—"

The Earl jerked a thumb. "Pretty-boy forward,
Prince Aurareus."

"Is he like to leave progeny or even sit well on
the throne among the hot lords of Scroby?"

"Ho—ho—ho, I see where you lead. Aurea and
her man heirs of the Empire! That's clear from the

start. So you think she's delivered to me, as 'twere, by Marshal Bordvin to make it sure there's no Imperial dignity between him and the title of Count Vulk the Fifteenth? But is that not a long way to go? Pretty-boy lives in health."

"Aye, and was sent with his sisters to the court of Vulk the Unreasonable. Sad if he met accident there. . . ."

"Which is to say our good Emperor Auraris prefers a Vulking heir to the one of his body."

Alsander cleared his throat. "Or that the lords of the Empire would throw it into a collateral line, grasping true power for themselves. Is there not a cousin-german or something of the sort?"

Mikalegon brought his fist down again. "In fine, here's the fact among these lofty matters: Vulk seeks to be emperor, Bordvin seeks to be Vulk, and the Emperor seeks a sword that will keep the peace of the Well in his house or domains, whatever Dzik or the Dodekapolis may do. But we hold the ruling piece on this game-board, and 'tis check with the queen, ha, ha. But you masters of Dalarna, what is your desire?"

"Freedom from the Vulking rule," flashed Rogai, and Airar nodded, marking from the corner of his eye how there was a twist round Meliboë's lips.

"So do we all," said the Earl. "What! What! How would it fare in Carrhoene, once a Vulking prince sat in the high house of Stassia, with his claim to be lord of the Twelve Cities and no sons of the Well to rein him in?"

"I do not think you or we need crack our brains on that," Evadne said. "Even the dog-smelling People's Party—"

"Faugh, they'd be the first to hail it," said the Earl. "Why, 'tis precisely as the party of the whole people that these Vulkings rule, with neither lordships nor baronies of heritage, but with these dignities held from hour to hour by will of the Count and council. Nay, you brethren of the sword are deeper caught in this coil than the Dalecarles themselves; they'd but have freedom from Vulk the single man, but for you it's root up all the Vulks and the rule they live by."

Again Meliboë shot Airar a glance that might have said this was the choice of Briella or Carrhoene in new words, but no one added another voice. "Bah!" continued the Earl. "This politic wearies a man more than battle, and it's with battle we must concern ourselves the now. Old man, I'm told you have been somewhat in the counsels of our foes. Think you they mean a crack at our hold of Os Erigu?"

"Sobeit Count Vulk has his way, and not the Marshal—but that's an idle question now. By stealing the bride you have touched Vulking pride and made the contest certain." The enchanter drummed on the table with his fingers. "Bordvin has the lesser ambition for himself, but the more for his race—or mayhap it would be the other way round, I do not know. 'Twas a matter of debate in the lyceum of Briella till Vulk the Unreasonable made his decree against magic and closed our doors. Bordvin's way is to conquer all in the Vulking name, Salmonessa and the Twelve Cities; Vulk would seize all in the name of the Empire, then the Empire itself. So that as matters have fallen out you have admirably brought both parties to agreement against you, for Vulk's hope of the Empire rests on recovering the Princess, while to Bordvin it will surely be clear that he dare attempt no great wars while there sit at his back in Os Erigu such mischief-makers as these young masters of Dalarna and the Star-Captains of Carrhoene—not to mention myself, a poor doctor of the philosophies, though somewhat skilled in gramary."

Os Erigu's brow had puckered in the effort to follow. Now his countenance burst in a smile of animation. "Ah! I had forgot you were a warlock and foreteller. Show me my fate—I've never had it told but by a pretended spae-wife at Lectis Maxima when I went there in disguise once. She said I was a wool-merchant who should have great success in the sale of woven stuffs, which was not true at all."

Meliboë plucked his beard. "Lord, the fate of us

all is death, and no profit in learning its manner, for
'tis not to be avoided.'"

"Nay, I'll not be so put off. The fate of this war
in which we are engaged, and whether there's peace
and a good life for me short of a draught from the
Well of the Unicorn."

"You'd have it shown before these others?"

"It is my will."

The frosted eyebrows of Meliboë the enchanter
flicked once, but without more words he drew from
his compartmented pouch a pinch of each of parti-
colored powders, and mixed them on the table, biding
Earl Mikalegon strike a spark on the little pile from
his own flint and steel, while he himself traced a
pentagram around, and bringing out his grammarion
began to read certain spells. It was the great divination in form, Airar recognized, though he had never
before seen it done by a master magician. As the
spark struck, a tiny line of smoke curled from the
powder like a waking serpent and, without dissipating,
rose to a point just above their heads, where it gathered in a gray cloud that hung motionless, with all
in the cabin swinging beneath it to the heave of the
sea.

"Amador, volador, amblysecton," intoned Meliboë,
and with every eye fixed upon it, the cloud turned
translucent, seeming to boil within, then hardened
till at its center there grew the likeness of a fairy
castle, hanging in air, pillowed on the cloud. The
cloud was sea; an ocean washed round the fairy
castle's foot, and it was as though the building turned
or the watchers sat in a heaving boat offshore, moving past while every aspect was presented to their
gaze. Was it night? Did twilight seem to fall on tower
and wall? There were lights at the narrow windows
high aloft as though a banquet took place within,
though no movement of guests was visible across the
tracery of bridge-arches that led to the castle's gate.
Then, from one of the windows as they watched,
the light burst forth as no light but a bright, stuttering
flame that licked a gasp from those who watched;
window after window shot forth its tongue of fire to

join the chorus, the roof-peak of a tower fell in with a silent crash, and a wild cry of rage burst from the lips of the Earl of Os Erigu, but Meliboë signed him to silence and went on:

"Eperuatorion modocaccus." The cloud whirled round the doomed castle and hid it, then thinned again, and now at the center there was a blaze of light as bright as the eye might bear, and to Airar watching it seemed as though he were looking across a floor as though from a prostration. The floor was black and white marble; in the background were visible skirts and men's shoon and the feet of pillars richly carved. The view shifted; a manikin strode across that rich pave, and it was Mikalegon of Os Erigu, walking proud as a prince, in plum-colored hose, with golden armor and a white surcoat bearing the black sea-eagle of his badge and a sword by his side. It was to note that his hair was not storm-black as now, but touched by grey; men and women gave back as he marched, the view following, till he reached the steps that led to a dais or throne, where he went to one knee and bowed the head. One saw, as though walking round to the back of the man bowing, a golden coronal upon his hair, and for a moment it seemed to Airar that the face of the queen on the throne could be none but that of the Princess Argyra—or was it dark Evadne?—but the mist swirled in fast, the cloud vanished, and Earl Mikalegon boomed:

"Is that your divination? I could make a better one myself."

There was a smell as of something dead and rotting foully in the cabin; it made one ill and weak together, as though this were an illness to be cherished till death's release. The enchanter shrugged and blew a little puff of dust from the table-top. "There's no compulsion to follow such a road, and the will is free. I but show you the most favorable; all other ways lead to an end of less delight. I am faint; have you to drink?"

"The man to whom I will bend the knee is not yet born," said Earl Mikalegon, "and before any shall burn Os Erigu, they must break not a few heads of myself and the free companies. But a pox on this madness for children; let's talk of present necessity. They strike up then—but who and in what strength? That's all we need to know for tomorrow, not so, old bag of bones?" He threw the question at Alsander of Carrhoene, and that one replied:

"A fair case. It is all one needs for war."

"The 4th tercia, certainly," Earl Mikalegon went on, thinking aloud. "It's at Stavorna and it's Count Vulk's own. That I count upon; we can meet it in equal battle. But what of the 8th, that used to be in the castellas of Norby and all down through Shalland and the Dales? Does Marshal Bordvin's influence run so far that he can hold it back from this attack? Does this new 12th tercia replace it, or is it gathered toward the south for some move overseas? We'd be farther forward if we knew these things."

Said Airar: "There is one very sure way of finding out. At the battle on the road of which we told you, there were three men taken who belonged to this new 12th tercia. Let them be brought and questioned; I have found it already that such men are often wiser than their captains."

Alsander said: "As to those three, Master Airar, we have them no longer. I let slay them all when we left Gäspelnith, for fear of betrayal on the forced march we made."

"Which shows one should not discard even a copper aina lest it be the fee to heaven's gate," said Earl Mikalegon. "Well, let's to meat; our mystery's for the term insoluble and the old spae-man lolls in his seat."

Airar said nothing at all. Alsander, too; and Alsander had been the best of them.

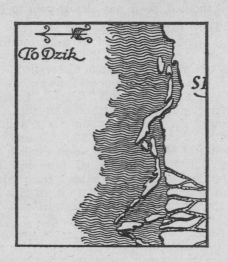

25. The Northern Sea:
Third Tale of the Well

WHERE THE PLANKS OF THE SKONÄRE OF Gentebbi had charged creaking into the sea, these sang. Airar could have picked out their tune from the thuttering blocks that formed a bass. White water gambolled from under the prow and away in diamond spray across a sapphirean sea, above the straining sweep of crimson sail.

Said she: "It is hard to lose a friend; yet what's this friend that you have lost? A presence physical, or the friend's love for you—and yours in turn? If the former, why, all tears will not restore it, but if the latter, it was never lost to my way of thinking, since love's lost only when self-betrayed."

"I thank you, gracious lady," said he. "You are most kind." (And beautiful, beautiful, the back of his mind shouted, so it was almost pain to be beside her.)

"Nay, if you'll play courtier, go make attendance on Aurea. She feeds on speeches; but I was brought up peasant in the Scroby hills and like a plainer style."

"Well, then, it's not so much the loss of the little cat itself, but to lose it so. It would have been better to give it to one of the Shalland women. Oh, you say you're peasant-fostered, but I am peasant-born, and in our country we'd treat no friendly creature so. . . . And there's that manner of luck and symbol, that Meliboë spoke on. Such gramary as I have does not see so far as to say what it may mean."

She let him finish. "I would not know of your gramary. It is forbidden to us of the House by the rule of the Well. But you would say, I think, that what the Carrhoene did was careless-cruel."

"Something like that. . . . Tell me, bright lady, an you will be so kind, how is it they look on these Star-Captains of Carrhoene from Stassia?"

"Oh, they are surely the greatest war-dukes and champions that ever lived, but troublous; not of our time, but the silver years, when heathen still raided. We'd rather the People's Party, that believe in the Well and the sons of the Well. . . . Or so says my father."

The ship heaved and her shoulder touched his under the brilliant sunbeam; chill though the day was, he felt a flood of warmth all down the front from chin to knee. But she was a princess! He moved a little and in a moment found words: "The Well, the Well, and ever the Well—do I make it from your tone that all's not smooth therewith?"

She giggled, but it trailed off laughing-serious. "Will you catechize me? Fie! Your wits are of Uravedu, the country of my great-grandmother whose name was Kry, and she more of a peasant than you or I in spite of our upbringing. But here's my brother, seeking as usual to keep me from the hands of evil men, I think."

Airar started round. This prince at first glance might be older than himself, but after a moment one saw it was youth spoiled by petulance and eye-pouches. He had the broad jaw under thin head and darkling hair of Uravedu; was small and carried himself even on the heaving deck well back under his yellow cap of pretense, so that he visibly strutted. The Princess Argyra made a curtsey; Airar swept off his hat and bowed, but heard what might have been a laugh from the shipman at the tiller behind.

"I present," said she, "Master Airar of Trangsted in Vastmanstad, a most loyal servant of *the* House and the Well and all."

Prince Aurareus made a gesture dismissing legions. "Our liege servitors shall always have our eye," he said in the form, and Airar remarked a mincing lisp. "Sister, my puss, our good friend and well-wisher of Os Erigu conveys messages, and it is a question of what to say. Will you wait on our sister?" He turned, with the girl following him, then turned again, and looked Airar down. "You are a very well-built man. You will wait on us in our apartment at twilight."

"There's no punishment if you avoid him," whispered the girl behind her hand, stuck out her tongue at his back, and hurried.

But Airar did go, more from curiosity than else, after he rose from evening meat. The Prince sat cushioned well; there was an odor of southern island incense in his cabin which room, though not wide, was yet large enough to permit that two blond young men, muscled like tree-trunks and stripped clean naked, wrestled against each other at one side, after the manner of Stassia, arms up at length before them and fingers locked with fingers. When Airar was admitted Aurareus clapped his hands:

"Done," he said; "and I do name Balinian winner by two bouts to one. Now leave us; we would speak with this heart from our dominion of Dalarna."

"I would have beaten him the second time but for

the throw of the ship, graciousness," said one of the young men sulkily, picking up a shift. "Let me try but once again."

"Another time. The sport commences to weary us." The Prince waved a hand gracefully. The other wrestler was climbing into his clothes and Airar's wandering glance surprised on his face a look of pure and petulant hatred that filled him with amaze. When they had gone:

"Trim the chrysma," said Prince Aurareus. "Your name again, Dalecarle?"

"Airar of Trangsted, son of Alvar—sir," said the young man, none too pleased over this Prince's lofty-from-above manner of address after the ease of the Star-Captains, Earl Mikalegon, and even the Princess Argyra; but he supposed it to be a matter of the form of the High House of Stassia and would not appear impolite.

"It is easy to see that you have been little near the golden court. You should address us as 'graciousness,' who are to be your emperor and ruler. What is your art, Airar?"

"Graciousness, I know something of the art magical, but it is an art I prefer not to employ."

"You have right; the forbidden thing. Come here." He pinched Airar's arm. "Ah, well-thewed. You might throw Balinian flat on his back, and Garrus, too. Have you another art besides the dark one?"

"Only what little I know of the war-art, graciousness."

The Prince's smile was meant to be kind. "Among civilized peoples we do not count it an art but a barbarism to wreck fine bodies so that might be better used; hence our law holds that arm-bearers may not sit in high places. You will have to find a new art after coming to the Well. What can we do to please you, Airar? How came you by that name, among other matters? It might almost belong to the House, and we are not sure it is permitted."

"Graciousness, it is an ancient name in our family," said Airar, avoiding the first question with an answer to the second, for there was something about this Prince that made his short hairs crawl.

"No matter. We grant our permission as to the name." Aurareus smiled and shifted his position so that his foot came in contact with Airar's where he left it; but with the next move of the ship the childe of Trangsted made that he had been a little moved from balance, and drew away. On the Prince's countenance the smile remained as though graven. He said:

"You have not answered on how we can please our subject and servitor—our delight, to bring new blood to the old lands, even it it mean the ennoblement of Dalecarles, who have no blood noble whatsoever in their provinces." He paused to let the suggestion drive home and Airar thought in a hard momentary flash on how Argyra and those others had referred to his birth, which must be something they had caught up somehow from the rest, leading back to that rash statement at the gate of Salmonessa which he wished he had never made. Prince Aurareus smiled with a steady determination. "They are not a few estates in Scroby that want good masters. Come, we'll have a bottle of wine and discuss pleasantly on't."

He lifted his hands to clap, but Airar stopped him desperately with: "Gracious lord—"

The smile changed. "Speak."

"How could I hold an estate in the Empire, being under the ban of the Empire?"

"You have not drunk?"

"From the Well of the Unicorn? No, graciousness."

"Then it's a matter easily amended. Once you dip there, all bans fail. But we'll converse on that at ease."

The place was not warm, but Airar found himself gently perspiring down the back of his neck and in the palms of his hands. "Graciousness, I cannot the night. My men—"

"You need not fear Balinian. He is under my orders."

"Graciousness, I—"

Prince Aurareus signed and relaxed among his cushions. "Another day, then. You have our leave to withdraw."

The sun was already westering next day before she came to the place by the bulwarks. She girded him a little for his glooms and few-spokenness; it was several minutes before he could be brought to say that her brother wished him to take the service of the Well, since he would not give the true reason. Argyra twisted an invisible something impatiently in her hands. "It is a service I would not have you take, nor any," she said, and now came her turn to fall silent while he looked interrogation; for he like all in Dalarna knew how that great wonder was the luck and foundation of the House of Argimenes. But out of respect he forbore to ask, till at last she:

"Shall I say why?"

"If you will, gracious lady."

"No titles. Aurea . . . but hear——" and she told him that tale, seating herself on the low bar of the big ballista with her back to the rail, wrapped warm against the fresh sea-breeze that ever and again detached a lock of her hair across her face, which she put by without seeming to notice.

——The Well, the Well of the Unicorn, it is the profit of our kindred, so that you nobles of Dalarna look up across the sea and think how splendid it is for us to hold this treasure that is the heal of every unease. But at what price? Peace to one may be another's misery. I had a brother once, a little older than I; he was merry and gay when we were children together. According to the rule of the House we were brought up by peasant fostering, westaway in Scroby; for it is the custom among us Argimenids that those who are to rule must so learn the people and their needs. In those days it was planned for me to marry some great lord abroad, but for Princess Aurea my sister no marriage was seen but in the home counties, she being heir after my brother, and the House loves not to have its claims of inheritance spread abroad. Yet now it is a question if the House itself keep the inheritance.

The stead was among the rolling low hills where everything is green—have you seen Scroby?—and the bonders who kept it were good fosterers, treating us in all respects as their own children, so there were even duties for us. I have played milkmaid—these hands have drained the warm white milk. My brother tied sheaves with the reapers and came in singing with them to drink cider when the first fires of autumn were comfortable at night.

We were happy then! For the winter festival, which is the turning of the sun, it was mostly that we were taken back to the High House. We would ride through the snow on sledges with bells and an escort of horsemen, singing all the way. I mind once, when they let Bardis go up to the court with us, how he stood in the sledge as it dashed along and loosed an arrow that brought down a snow-fox that hurried from a thicket when the dogs barked. There was a splash of red on the snow and white fur, the only color in the world as it seemed, and my brother called out how it was lovely, but Bardis gave the pelt to Brodry and not to me. I was unhappy and cried to myself in bed. Certes, I would not do as much now; but I think that far more than Bardis, it was being in the cold marble hall of the High House, with its carving and tracery, lying on the great brocaded bed, rather than back where I had come to think it home. My mother was gentle, but always stately; she did not seem to listen when I spoke of the stead, and Aurea used to torment me, calling me her Sister Miaouw, and saying the only marriage I would make would be with one of the white heathen princes of Dzik.

Airar made a movement.

—Oh, Brodry and Bardis—I did not tell you of them. He was the son of the stead where we were fostered; I thought him more splendid than all the lordlings of court, so strong and fine, when they could only dance and giggle and say silly things to make a girl conceive they thought her a beauty. I knew I was no beauty—a gawky wench, as Bardis was gawky in his dealings at the High House. Aurea left me no doubt on my shortcomings, as legs like wheat-straws and the brown skin of a peasant—and Bardis gave the fox-pelt to Brodry.

She was Bardis' own cousin, from the stead nearest by that where we were fostered and there was much visiting and exchange of labor, as at seed-time and harvest. My chiefest friend among the girls of that part of Scroby—many a night have we shared the same bed, and all our secrets. One of those secrets was that my brother would oft be lover-like with her, as holding her hand to cross by stones in a stream, or lingering on the kiss of greeting when stead visited with stead. Such things girls do mark on; she used to speak of them and what she would say or do if he burst out with some word of love.

—For he is a prince with a coronet and will be emperor of us all, she said.

—Do, do, I said to her. What do you wish to do? If you would love him and bear his children, there's no bar. You know the law of our House that has stood since Argentarius the King, that the heirs shall never make marriages for policy alone, so that our mother the Empress was daughter to the poor Knight of Bremmery.

—Ah, she said and flung her arms round me in the dark. If I but knew! Argyra—I think I am in love, but I do not know whether it is with your brother or Bardis. Is this not a very strange thing?

But that I could not tell her. My brother so gladsome and gay, who could read and cipher better than a magician and knew old tales—many an evening did we sit round the fireplace of the stead eating nuts and roasted apples till long after the hour for rest, nor marked the hour while my brother told some story. Yet he was not behind in other things; I did not see how anyone on whom he cast his eye could fail to love him. I would go so far in my thoughts and then see how Bardis, too, was so desirable a companion, and Brodry the luckiest of women, while I must go and wed unloved with some faraway lord. All four of us did in truth hold each

other dear and could not bear the thought of choos-
ings among the fellowship.

So matters rested and no more said till after the
sun-turning festival when Bardis gave Brodry the fox-
pelt. We were all sad as we homed to the stead, for
we knew this was the last time we should be there
and together, our fostering being done with the seed-
time moon of spring. My brother would go on some
embassy to learn court manners while I must sit at
home and wait for the coming of some princeling
who would swallow a gawky peasant girl if she were
sugared with an Imperial dower. We were not long
at the stead this time before I marked how Brodry
was changed, no more giving me her full heart. Oh,
nothing to make reproach on, but now when she
spoke to me of Bardis or my brother, it was as
though a bar came down and she spoke of almost-
strangers.

She has made up her mind (I thought) and does
not wish to tell me which it is, lest either choice
give me a hurt. But I was wrong in that and only
right in seeing how a mist of some kind had clouded
the friendship of us four. There came a day at the
break of spring when my brother had gone early to
the stead where Brodry lived, while I had some
small task that kept me, and Bardis, too. We started
out to join them not long after nooning, taking a
path through a little wood on a hill between the two
places, and it was that hill that kept our voices from
sounding. As we topped it and came round an old
oak-tree, here were Brodry and my brother in each
other's arms and kissing, while from one of her hands
there trailed crushed to the ground the violets she
had been gathering.

She saw us first and pulled free, then stretched a
hand to her cousin.—Oh, Bardis, she said, forgive
me.

—Wherefore? asked my brother. Is it not a joy
to the friends that friendship is made forever by two
of them? Nay, I publish it before the world and all.

He reached for her hungrily, but Bardis went on
one knee and I noticed how his face was white and

strained round the mouth.—You are my lord and prince and I rejoice for you, he said.

But Brodry broke free, crying—Nay, nay, what have I done? and put her hands to her face. Forgiveness is needed (she said after a long minute while Bardis remained with his head bowed down), for now I have given my pledge of love to you both; and it can be kept but to one ، . . but which one I do not know.

I could see a change on my brother's face; never did one see such a change.—Is this true? he asked Bardis.

—My lord, he began, but my brother interrupted him.

—Nay, I'll have no rank; I thought we were friends. But you—he turned fiercely toward Brodry and I thought he would strike her, but she looked on him so proud and pitiful together that his hand lowered. He said,—No, you have done this in honesty, that I see; which is to say that the friendship has been true. But now the friendship's broken.

None of us said so much as a word, but he after another minute—You set a hard problem to your prince, friends. Then somewhat hardly to Brodry—Well, have you now made your choice, now that you have your woman's victory of breaking friends for you?

—No victory, she said and shook her head.

—Even that I almost credit; and believe me it is no victory I seek neither, but the keeping of the friendship of us four, a precious thing if we may keep it. Now there is only one resource that I can see and that is we shall all go to the Well of the Unicorn forthwith and drink a draught together.

—I know, you are for renown as a soldier and champion, to fight along the windy borders of the world. We have taled on it together. Here's the choice then, which will you have? School me if you can see how Brodry falls to either of us without breaking the fellowship unless by the brink of that Well where the unicorn will dip his horn.

—It is true, said Brodry. It is my fault. I will go.

—And you, puss? My brother spoke to me.

—If you desire; but am I a party to your trouble? said I.

—You could be a party to the curing of it. I saw how his thought was that the peace of the Well would turn Bardis to me instead of to Brodry. I knew how little was the hope of such an issue, but—I will go, I said.

Now Bardis had risen and stood frowning.—It is in my mind (he said) that this is not a lucky enterprise; for love's a thing not changed or commanded even by the Unicorn's Well. But I will not hold back when you three go forward.

We made the pilgrimage in spring. Under the marble arch we four joined hands and drank, sipping from each other's cups as the regulation is; and afterward we sat at the gate together and made a plan, which was to let all lie till my brother returned from his embassy, when the wondrous water should have worked in us. I remember how we were calm and happy, all contention spent, and sure of a glad issue, except that perhaps Bardis did not quiet believe, for he was less spoken than we others and we chided him for it. Unjustly—for that afternoon by the gate of the Well was our last, and I never again saw my brother—

Said Airar, amazed: "But how can that be so? I have never heard that the Well gave death for peace."

"Death, death, who spoke of death? The embassy was to Naaros and that foul court of Salmonessa, where my brother Aurareus caught such manners and airs as you have seen, and came back no more my brother at all, but a stranger—so little an Argimenid that there's talk (though he does not know it) of setting aside the succession and making Aurea queen."

Airar searched for words of sympathy and could find none for such a case. "But the rest—did not you and they draw a better peace than that from this draught of the Well?"

"Bardis and Brodry are wedded, I think. I have

not seen them since Aurareus came back from the embassy. As for myself, the matter's not decided how I shall find peace. It may be I shall have it when I make my marriage— or that I have it in not making the only one yet offered, which is with Sthenophon, spadarion and tyrant of Permandos. I told them I'd slay myself before I'd be given to him, and they sent me on this voyage, which is no more than an exile."

26. Os Erigu: The Cup of War

Os Erigu climbed slowly out of the sea at them, a shadow first on the horizon rim and then a grey finger pointing skyward, with the shore-line behind a lighter grey. It was the castle of Meliboë's picture in a dream; the sea-waves washed round its foot and one could hardly tell which was man-made stone and which the rocky promontory from whence it sprang. At its rear or eastward face piled rocks lay in a waste with water lashing through them, but above against the middle wall sprang joyously a bridge poised on slender arches, and midmost of it was a draw. This was lifted, thrusting a blank outstretched hand toward the land. Earl Mikalegon frowned:

"It could be that we have unwelcome guests," said he. "The order was to keep the drawbridge down."

But Pleiander of Carrhoene gave a long breath of delight. "I have not seen your hold before, Lord," said he, "but I am thought to know something of buildings and siegecraft and will say that this is surely one of the notablest and stoutest castles within the ring of the world."

The wind came down from the east; the ships swung to it round the seaward face where the wall was lower and waves leaped up. Above the inner buildings rose step by step to the tall baillie at the citadel's heart. It was all built of black ironstone from the mountains behind and seemed to leer, squat as a huge dark toad in the clear sunbeam, though the height was far from small. No banner flew as they swung past the cape and fell into the calm from the rising hills landward, with in sails and out sweeps for entrance to the bay on the northward face where ships are sheltered.

A quay had been built there, also of the gloomy dark stone. Against it stood a dismantled ship, her upper masts down and deck piled with loose sails and uncoiled cordage. On the quay itself a bale had been broken open, then forgot; an end of the rejected stuff trailed disconsolately down the quayside in the water. At its landward end the pier had a water-gate like a portcullis. Earl Mikalegon went ashore first, surrounded by his men of war, and let blow his trumpet as a signal for arrival. Airar noted they did not march in even ranks like the terciaries fo Briella, but rambled carelessly. Visto was among them. The prisoners of the Empire were a group; Airar tried to work toward Argyra's side, which he did not accomplish, and saw how Princess Aurea looked niether left nor right, but Aurareus leaned on the shoulder of now one, now another, of his two bully-boys with a whisper and a titter.

The courtyard smelled like a pigstye and was littered like one. When Airar followed Erb to see what accommodation his fisher spearmen had in booths along the northern wall, he was less than pleased; but that night there was a kind of banquet in the Earl's long-beamed smoky council hall by the edge of the keep, with great collops of meat borne in and rivers of drink for all. Mikalegon boomed and bellowed in the high-seat; Alsander sat on his one side and Prince Aurareus on the other, the second not taking much food. There were no women, even Evadne missing from the Carrhoenes, who might have been thought fit to stay in any company, but Airar thought he understood when he saw how the Earl chucked his young cupbearer under the chin and Aurareus looked moon-eyed on Pleiander. (It only proved how wrong are the judgments a man can form.) The servants were mostly Micton and a villainous-looking crew, with even a few of the fantastic head-dresses of Dzik; they plied the cups rapidly, but Airar forbore to drink much, misdoubting what was coming.

Here also he erred; what came was a glee singer who wetted his whistle and sang a long chant of Os Erigu's glory, where men were free. Earl Mikalegon himself joined the refrains, beating with his knife-handle; when the singer had done he gave a shout and stood up:

"Drink! to the old gods of battle and an end to the cursèd Well!"

The singer struck a sounding chord from his harp; all down the hall men stood and shouted, disorderly and discordant. Airar stood with them but barely touched lip to his own cup and sat down with a tingle in the hair at the back of his neck, for this was only a little less than sacrilege. The man on his right marked this, one of Mikalegon's officers, with a lined hard face and a scar that almost involved an eye.

"No disrespect to you Imperials," said he, friendly enough; "it's but our custom on the peak of Erigu when wars begin."

"I'm a Dalecarle."

"Sssh. Now comes the word and the swearings."

Earl Mikalegon's cup had been filled again; he beamed through his beard with mountainous jollity. "We are besieged!" he cried. "Beyond our bridge there sits Baron Catiná with the 4th Tercia of Briella and will have only this eagle's nest itself, no compromise, war to the end. His summons came this morning, his messenger hangs by the neck over our outer-guard at this hour."

He paused to let them shout again and, when they had finished, lifted his cup;

"Now we swear. I swear by the cup of war that I will make no peace with any, nor give any quarter, till this fourteenth Count Vulk is pulled from his place and his Baron Catiná slain. Let all who would hold to the fellowship of Os Erigu follow me."

He drank; all down the table till the torch-flames rocked, the fighting men of Erigu, aye Dalarna and Carrhoene, leaped to their feet and roared with brandished weapons and this time Airar fully joining. But as the shouting somewhat died and men were seated, Scarface beside him remained on his feet, cup high:

"By the cup of war I swear," he shouted; "that I will follow Earl Mikalegon in this contest to its very end; and I will not sleep under roof till I have met Baron Catiná in personal combat or till he is dead." He drank; the hall sounded again (not so loudly as before, but as in politeness for a thing expected) as Alsander of Carrhoene rose:

"Though I be a stranger and sometime your foe, I will swear with you by this cup of war to be in this battle with Earl Mikalegon; and not to know peace or take peace till he gives peace, and I swear it not for myself alone but for the six brothers of Carrhoene, born in two births miraculously. But as for our own dear land ever unforgotten, I swear that I will not enter the High House of Carrhoene till the leaders of the People's Party have cleared the floor with their beards. This I swear by your cup of war."

"We swear it!" cried Pleiander and Evimenes together, and before the hall could shout at them, the last raised up his hand saying; "And to it I add that I swear to slay Sthenophon of Permandos and lie with his sister Lycaoniké without his permission."

Now did the hall roar again, with men beating on

the table, pledging cups to the Carrhoenes and saying that had sworn well as the cupbearers scurried, for all that these northern sea-kings were wont to speak less than good of the captains from the isles. Into that sound others leaped up to swear by the cup of war, free captains of Os Erigu—one that he would plant a white spear on Briella's topmost tower, which was thought to be a boast and not a good oath; but another that he would bring home the triangles of three Vulking deese, and that was shouted at for the best. Rogai stood up; he swore on the cup of war to serve Baron Vanette-Millepigue as the Red Baron had served the syndic's children of Mariupol city, and his voice snarled as he said it, so the hubbub drooped a trifle. Erb would have risen; but Earl Mikalegon motioned him away and waved a hand at Airar.

Though Alvar's tall son had taken so much less of these strong northern beers than some that this business of swearing and shouting to do what would be done in any case came to him somewhat silly as he saw wizard Meliboë's lip curl, yet drink and excitement worked high in his mind, and there was no escape:

"I swear by this cup of war," he said, "that I will not leave this war till Dalarna's free as Os Erigu—" he checked and for a moment all waited, and with sharp inward surprise young Airar heard his own voice shout: "—and that I will love and wed no woman but Argyra of Stassia, and she shall escape never though she flee across the world!"

There was the shout and they pledged him cups, but over the sound out bayed Earl Mikalegon's laughter—"Yee-ha-ha-ha-ha-ha!" Aurareus' face set in a nasty sneer, Pleiander looked like a sulky boy, and dark Evimenes flung back so fast his seat was upset and he half rose, one fist on the table and eyes intent. Airar caught a glimpse of Meliboë; beneath his beard the enchanter was looking down thoughtfully and it might have been a trifle sad.

"Well pledged," said Airar's seat-mate, and another of the Erigan free companions stood to swear to eat naught but stockfish till he had fed a deserion to the fishes. Sound filled the hall like a tide; the place seemed slightly to sway by a pivot as the word swept round, one and another swearing some deed, but Airar of Trangsted wondering whether he had done well or ill.

The siege began in effect next morning, when heads were still thick and tempers short from the waters of the night before. At the shore end of the bridge, where the westmost tip of the Iron Mountains cascades down into the rocks out of which Os Erigu presently rises, a road winds among pine trees round a peak to reach the span. Here a man as sharp-eyed as Airar might see at dawning under the drizzly spring rain the red triangle of Briella flame on its marching-pole; and if that same had ears as good as his eyes, might have heard, through the mist that deadens sound, the thin high piping of the Vulking flutes. The terciaries marched. "What will they do?" growled Mikalegon. "Leap the gap?"

But they had better thoughts than that. Airar caught how the metal gleam muted by rain spread along the opposite peak. Down the road came a train of carts drawn by horse and mule and bullock, with laboring people and Mictons in them and men pressed from the countryside. As these reached the bridge they halted; the workingmen leaped on the carts and began to heave their burdens to the rocks below— trees with branches, cut down anyhow, clods and stones. It did not need the mind of a master to see what was meant: they'd build a causeway across the neck of rock to reach the castle attainable in no other way. The distance was too long as yet for Erigu's engines to reach them.

The leaders talked of that and what the counter-move should be. Mikalegon was all eager for a swift landing from boats among the rocks to break down the nearer arches and so make their work the harder, striking at night when they would not be ware. Alsander was with him. In any trial of war (said he) the first need's to win by surprise a victory however small, which the leaves the foemen uncertain and

dreading. Pleiander say nay; if the Baron Catiná
knew his business, "as I take it he does or no Vulking baron," he'd count on such a move; have engines
and archers ready and firepots to throw down by
night against any who attempt to spoil the bridge,
"and they'll shoot down on our heads where's no
reply. All chances of your first victory lies to them."

Now the Earl in his morning-after-drinking mood
glowered and shouted he'd not be ruled in the case
of his own command by some damned people's par-
liament; but he yielded. It was decided to send the
war-cry of the Ring through the Iron Mountains and
all Korosh; the miners, being great friends of Mikalegon's house and knowing well they were sped of Os
Erigu, went down. They should be urged not to rise
in full arms but in little hill-bands, to harry the
Vulkings' trains which would incline them the more
to the war through good prospects of plunder. (Alsander brought forward this thought.) Airar said
there was none like Rogai of Mariola for quick and
secret daring, and besides he was known to all
leaders who wore the Ring of Iron; he should have
the mission. It could be seen the Carrhoene captains
liked the plan of Rogai none too well; complained,
indeed, how he had sped in Shalland. The Earl
shouted them down, which they took in good enough
part, perhaps more willing to be ordered than convinced in a matter not their own doing.

The man of the mountains gladly took the task,
asking only that the shallop set him ashore northward,
at some secret place. "In the Fjord of the Bear?"
quoth the scarface captain who had sat by Airar, and
then looked as though he might have bitten his tongue
out, for as Evadne snickered the Earl bellowed ob-
scenities at him, and the conference broke up.

The Carrhoene girl did not speak to Airar. He
wandered near the apartments assigned to the Imperials, not quite daring to ask after the Princess
Argyra (after his doing of a night agone), yet by
no means unwilling to meet her if chance offered and
so deliver various pretty speeches of exculpation he
had planned out in his head. The trouble might have

been spared; she did not appear, but the scarface captain did, looking glum as could be. He touched hands, naming himself Poë—"Or as it will now be put, Poë the Witless, since the fine case I have made of myself with our lord and leader."

"How would that be?" asked Airar, one eye over his shoulder toward where she might come and not deeply interested, but in order to have something to say.

"Slip of the tongue; it's all a man needs here in Os Erigu to turn his futures into pasts. Another might have challenged or the old Earl would have shown me forth for it, but not our Earl Mikalegon. He's crafty; will put upon me in ways, till it's not to be borne and I leave the fellowship of my own free will."

"For mentioning Bear Fjord only? But that's a little thing—"

"You do not know the tale behind it." Now it was Poë's turn to look over a shoulder in search of who might hear. "Hark! It was nigh on four years ago when our lord and leader bethought himself to go up for a few days' fishing in a little decked shallop with one man, and he was from Korosh. I misremember the name—Partén, or something like that. They were sailing up the fjord finely, a good breeze behind and this man at the tiller, when our lord spied a fine bear swimming, and, thinking what a grand thing it would be at the castle yard if taken alive, ran and sought a coil of rope while his man bore over toward the beast. No great trick to drop a loop over the animal's neck; but instead of choking it dumb, the pressure of the rope only roused Master Bear to anger. It swam up the wake of the boat, and the shallop being low-decked, the first thing his lordship knew, here an armed paw came over the stern and then the animal hauling himself up.

"His lordship had not brought a sword, only a little fish-trident, with which his man made a dab at the monster as it came over the stern and began to drive them both in a morris-dance round the mast, with the tiller let go and sails flapping. At about the third round, his lordship's man, not having so much beef to carry, reached the hatch and got it open. They tumbled down together, arse over ears, and one or t'other managed to get the bolt home before Sir Bear could overcome his hesitancy about going down the hole after them. But now they were no better off, for they as good as in a dungeon, the beast lord of the deck, unmindful to continue his swim, and the shallop drifting to and fro.

"His man said later that Earl Mikalegon used such words that he feared lightning from heaven would burn them both to a crisp, and the bear too; but after a time they began searching the underdeck for weapons. There was a gird or grating at the after part that gave them a little light; from time to time the bear came over to it and snarled at them or tried to reach his claws through after the manner of such animals when they fish. The best they could find for arms was a pair of old fish-knives, not very sharp. Earl Mikalegon fixed them at the end of the poles and both men tried to jab the bear through the grating. But the grid spoiled their stroke, the knife did not bite on the bear's hide, and he clipped one of them with his paw, so the pole broke and knife was knocked across the deck, adding to which they could now see that the rope was somehow caught in the deck gear, so that even if the animal wished he could not quit them.

" 'What's to be done now, lord?' said the man, being in spite of their plight so shaken with inner laughters that he could hardly speak—though he knew better than to make his humor open before Earl Mikalegon.

"The Earl cursed him for a fool and said did he know any magics or spells? The man was a Korosh, as I have said, where all learn a little gramary because of the Mictons and their troll-raising; he said as much, but also that bears were beyond him. At that his lordship burst out that he'd have the lout's ears unless whatever magic he knew were tried. It was needs must for him, over protest. In the midst of this spell his lordship huffed and grunted so that at

just the wrong time the man could no longer hold
his laughter and the spell was broke in the middle.
I have said it was a troll-magic? It summoned them
finely, in the form of nixies, which are a kind of
troll marine we have here in the north. They swarmed
all over the shallop and garlanded it with seaweeds
and pine branches; making a pet of the bear and
gambolling about the deck the more Earl Mikalegon
roared with fury, for it is the nature of these nixies
to joy in mortal misfortunes so they be not grave
ones.

"The nixies also kept the ship from coming to land
and the two aboard were held awake all night with
their gibberings and racket. His lordship was not
rescued till next day when some at the castle became
anxious of a Micton raid and went seeking him. When
the story was known they laughed at Earl Mikalegon
from the mountains of Korosh to the Isles of Gentebbi, and he swore a great oath against any who
should lower the dignity of Os Erigu by mentioning it
again, and woe's me."

27. Os Erigu: Generosity Rejected

HE FOUND HER THE NEXT DAY, THOUGH, walking the battlement at the sea-face, a step behind Princess Aurea who, when she spied Airar (he could see it from far), turned, drew her sister's arm, and said something to her with a laugh. The golden quean was nearer as they passed; Airar could barely catch a glimpse of Argyra's face. He made to bow; Aurea noticed him with the coolest of nods, his dear spoke a greeting he did not hear.

All the night through, the Vulkings had worked under torches that one could see spattering in the tender rain, the carts rumbling as the cargoes were hove down. Pleiander said that far though they yet were from the walls, there should be strengthenings, and Earl Mikalegon had what stoneworkers were in the place to build up a block from the south end of

248

the wall, where the bridge sprang through, to the
central baillie, and from thence again to the harbor
face, making a demilune. Airar thought the men
worked slow and clumsily, showing little spirit for
the task to match the fever-pace of Lacia's progress
with the causeway. They paused often to take drink,
laughing and hooting.

Earl Mikalegon came to that face of the battlements and had one of the catapults loose a stone
ball. It fell well short of the enemy work-spot; he
growled and turned away. Later the same day as
Airar watched, Rogai came to him, dressed in rough
clothes like a miner but prancing as a ram, happy
in his mission, on which he would set forth the
night. Count Vulk's baron had done well with his
building (he said) against no opposition; but his men
had not begun to tire or hunger; it would be different then.

Airar roused himself from thoughts of what the
cut timbers there on the growing causeway might
mean (too many for engines of war) to wish the
Mariolan godspeed, and turned again to the castle's
lower court with some thought of seeing, if not
Argyra, then Meliboë, invisible since the night of the
cup of war. Instead it was Aurareus, pacing with one
of his bullies—Balinian, Airar thought his name. The
Prince did not seem in a good mood, and neither
did his companion, who looked away after a head-
movement to indicate he had heard Airar's greeting
of the day. The young man would have passed without more; the Prince seemed at the rim of doing
likewise, when taken by another thought he turned,
and in a voice dripping with honey bade Alvar's son
have no shame for his oath over the cup. It was
an acceptable sign of love for the House Imperial,
however overspoken:

"Though if you are a gentleman armigerous, as
some claim, I doubt you would make names to be
bandied about, except those of enemies. It is a gentleman's joy ever to hurt only those he hates."

"I pray you, make mine apologies," said Airar, "for
it seems I stand under her avoidance."

"You are to call me graciousness. They're not needed. She's your partisan—and will see you herself, even though her taste in colors is all gloomy hues, like a peasant lass of Scroby. Our sister seeks to fix attention by other means. Has she told you how she swore to die rather than wed with Sthenophon? I perceive she has—already! It is danger; we fear for you." He laughed on a high note.

"What to make of such a farrago? Airar said nothing at all.

"But do not despair. Our sister, Master Airar, is not taken too seriously at court, even by herself. But tell us—are you in comfort? We will say so much for this Earl here, that we will let him be hanged with a silken rope when the time comes, for that he has given us a splendid apartment with service us befitting, so there is even space for our friends." His Graciousness waved a hand, Airar answered that he was already well lodged, and the interview ended.

The day dragged into another and another, while the Vulkings brought their loads (but they had still a long way to go with their causeway) and tempers shortened in the castle. There was word by a little ship of what passed in the Isles of Gentebbi; Bordvin Wildfang himself had gone to Vagai, cancelled the charter, made a slaughter of those contrarious, and was building a castle. Alsander said two-thirds of war and all of victory lay in knowing how to wait with patience till occasion ripened. Over mugs of ale one evening clever Pleiander thought aloud how a big trebuchet might reach where Vulking catapults would not and annoy this trespass of the enemies. Two-three of Earl Mikalegon's men were dispatched northaway up the coast to get timbers—"Not that I've confidence in't as plan," Airar heard the Star-Captain say low-voiced to Evadne, "for before we build the thing we'll be at handgrips. But 'twill sweat them finely and leave a sense of something done, which is the crucial point in sieges."

Airar would have harked to more, for this seemed to him of importance, but Evadne had caught how his ear was cocked, and turned to ask how progressed

his suit for the cat of the Empire? and had he stroked
her fur as yet? Clear he was one of those moonshine lovers who'd touch nothing else unless a girl
raped him. She laughed at the blushes he could not
hide; and as he turned away, he saw that Meliboë
the enchanter was crooking a finger, which he took
to be a sign for privy speech. The old man left the
table somewhat early and as Airar came from the
smoky council hall to the paved court with its rows
of huts over beneath the wall, here the warlock was,
pacing under the starshine, hands behind back.

"Young master," was his greeting, "you are more
to me of trouble than of gain; yet if 'twere I gain
nothing, I'd trouble with you still. A mystery."

"That has been said before," quoth Airar, somewhat roughly, for he felt alone, by all avoided, ready
to nip his best friend; "but if there is something new
I will hear it."

"Tsa, patience built the spider-web and spiders
can catch wasps, young master, I have been at much
trouble for you." He took a few steps. "I do not
know if your luck is strong enough to bear the
weight you put on it, but since you point the road,
I can but furnish the horse. I have undertaken certain matters for you and it has not been an easy
task. If you knock at the door of her apartment tonight, no less than Princess Aurea of the Empire will
receive you."

"And what use that? I have been received by His
Grace of Salmonessa."

"Nay, nay, no tempers. Aurareus turned as he is,
and the old man doddering, she's the true head of
the House."

"Well, then?"

"Well, then, if you desire your fancy-girl, fail not
the rendezvous."

Check a moment to regain temper. "What hour?"
asked Airar, Alvar's son.

"Ha, it begins to bite, does it? Say a turn of the
glass from now, when Earl Mikalegon has drunk
himself senseless and is borne off to bed, and the

others are busy with their dancing girls. You know the where?"

"The green-thatched house at the base of the baillie in the angle. Look! One can spy the light from here."

"I have your look to say you have reckoned the number of steps thither. Knock then, and make your treaty; I'll attend."

Airar had twice to take a water-easement while the time wore, and was not even then sure of his hour. Once from up behind the hall there came loud voices as one sought rest, and a torch or two threw off little rivulets of light. When he tapped, the glow within went dead. "Who comes?" said a voice, and he knew it. "Airar of Trangsted," and it was indeed she, with a friendly hand-touch, too much of friend and not enough of else. She led through a shadowy small room, calling to Aurea that all was well. He heard the clink of stone and iron; the sister-princess had stood to strike a lamp, but sat as Airar entered, he managing some kind of bow.

"Welcome, Lord Airar," said she, all graciousness, and offered a hand, at which he went warm all over, not knowing whether to touch or kiss.

"No lord," said he and kissed. It was the wrong thing; he could tell by the slight movement round the flawless lips.

"Would you sit? What I have to say is somewhat long." The golden princess looked round and, as at a command unspoken, Argyra whisked through a door and away.

Aurea watched her go, then leaned forward with both hands clasped round her knees and to Airar's astonishment her face melted human as could be: "The old wizard is your embassy. I did not know you were so well thought on in Dalarna. You would benefit us by your counsel."

"I—I thank you, bright lady." (It was a phrase he had caught from Rogai.)

The mouth flicker again, and what should he have said? "What think you of—our friend?"

"Earl Mikalegon? He seems true enough?"

"Aye, when he cannot help being so. His free companions had overthrown him in a breath had he not given you shelter, with so many fighting men and the captains of Carrhoene to aid him in this war. But as for other matters—did you know he takes your man Visto to the Black Tower?"

Airar felt his face flame. "Every man is free at Os Erigu, I'm told, Visto not less than the rest."

"Ah, Master Airar, for each freedom you have someone who pays with a loss, not so? One day your Earl will go to walk the ridge of the moon, whether in these combats or by a mere straw-death—and what then for Os Erigu and all its freedoms? There's a flaw in all this Earl does—had you not marked it? So with his continuance; there's no heritor, nor is this place of the Empire, where it could be adjudicate without battle. I fear many will lose freedom before another coronet leads the free companies and many lose life in trying to set their peculiar freedom over those who wish the dignity."

"I do not think I shall trouble about that as yet, bright lady."

"But I shall. That is—" she checked in mid-speech, and Airar, wondering inwardly whether this were real or a manner, looked expectant. "No matter. I suppose it was done in a moment, for those who overheard, and not really true."

"What not true, bright lady?"

"That you swore on the cup they drink in this place to have my sister by fair means or foul—enrolling yourself companion of Os Erigu. I do not see what withholds you now. Use your means. You're in some sort a captain here, and we your prisoners to order as you will."

Airar felt himself go cold and warm but steadfastly enough answered: "Part of it is not true by any name. There was naught of fair or foul in what I swore nor of membership in this free company. I did swear to follow her to the world's four corners, but in all honor and affection. I—I'd not have her other than freely and to wive."

She placed one finger on her chin and the other knuckles beneath it. "High and romantical. You do not lack for wings to fly from your little lordship of Trangsted to the House Imperial. Are all Dalecarles like that? I remember one Sir Ludomir Ludomirson of your land when he was at court, a very stiff-necked man. Still—" she sighed "—the daughter's daughter of the Knight of Bremmery cannot say too much on that, and the old wizard declares you one of the most destined of men. But you swore also, as I am told, to let Dalarna out from under the rule and tribute of the Counts Vulk, our deputies. If that's held to, why, you make yourself my foe— when I am wedded; and my puss of a sister would be my foe as well should you win her."

"You are not wedded yet," said Airar, but the words lacked fire.

"Why, for that matter, you make yourself my enemy and my sister's by the oath you gave. She is a child of the Well and the Empire, and you are under its ban." She looked at him.

"I had thought—" said Airar.

"Nay, as I feel it, you had not thought at all, or only thought of lording it over these free companies of Os Erigu, cut from the great world. You are a very romantical thinker, Lord Airar. Who seeks his bride among those born to politic must deal in things political."

Airar gathered himself desperately. "Bright lady," said he, "do you tell me my quest is vain unless I give over my hope to see all that I love free and happy?"

"By no means, silly fellow. I am your advocate as much as the old wizard." She reached forward to tap his wrist, and there was another knock at the door, a double rap. Argyra flashed by as Airar looked at her hungrily, there was a low murmur of voices at the outer door, and Meliboë the enchanter slid in along the wall, the low light from the lamp making him look as though his eyes were closed. He did not speak. The Princess Aurea gave him a glance of recognition and once more addressed herself to Airar, Trangsted's son.

"In politic all can be done. I tell you secrets which

you must never breathe—" she looked at him closely "—but the chancellery of the Empire is none too happy over the dealings of this Vulking lordship. That they should make conquest of foul Salmonessa was well done. Even the bishops applauded. It is tolerable that this hold should be assailed, since our persons lie in it and the place not under Imperial allegiance; but there was no right to such dealings as were held at Mariupol city, and in the Whiteriverdales—nay, nor that this matter of Os Erigu should be carried through by the strong arm with no negotiation."

"But this is all the doing of Count Vulk, is it not? I have heard they—"

"Nay, but that half-attainted traitor and very perfect scoundrel, Bordvin Wildfang, who intrigues to be himself the count. So we are allies after all, you and I, our enemy's the same."

Airar would have said, but could not find to say.

"Why cannot we have then an alliance in form? For the honor of the House my sister must have an Imperial dower; why not that city of Mariola where Bordvin has behaved so ill—with whatever suzerainties in Vastmanstad are needed to uphold the dignity? Look how this ruins Bordvin, while my intended stands on the gain over Salmonessa and nothing has been lost. We become kinsmen, you and I—a pleasant thing."

Said Airar: "What of Earl Mikalegon?"

"As Count of Mariola, you're his equal. Treat with him as one. I'll warrant composition; remember that he wars for gain."

"And Hestinga—the Whiteriverdales?"

"You bargain too close, Lord Airar. I cannot but feel they must remain in the Countship of Vulk and Lacia."

For a moment he contemplated the dazzling prospect of Airar the youth taxed out of the little stead, Airar leader of fifty, then Airar Count of Mariola, with more than all, husband of the Princess Argyra, and his mouth came open a little. Then his thought slid past Rogai, past his own father and

Leonce Fabrizius (and here it burned) to old Rudr the free-fisher. He closed his mouth to lip-biting.

"No," he said.

"Nay—" she began, but before another word was interrupted by Meliboë, eyes closed against the wall, speaking without accent or tone:

"Some philosophy is needed to see why patriotism, though praised as a virtue among men, must be so carefully inculcate in children before they will have it. Indeed it is not a natural virtue at all, but only a substitute for that love of mankind which the bishops recommend. It's a love which recognizes only one kind of man as man, have he blond hair or a dialect of Lacia."

Said Airar: "I will not, though you make me duke."

Aurea's face, the princess of Carrhoene, surprised by holding less of anger than of rueful smile. "One might say—" she said; "—that is, it's well we did not fall in with Lord Airar's hint of a city greater than Mariola. Patriotism, you named it, sir wizard? I call it a small and narrow thing, not worth such high names, which speaks the interest of a little part of Dalarna against that of the Empire, great and universal."

"Bright lady," said Airar, stoutly, "can the whole be great if the parts are broke?"

Meliboë the enchanter, in the same voice that had no change of sound: "I told you he would not."

"It is true? You will not, really?" Aurea came to her feet in a swirl of garments. "You have our leave to withdraw. My sister will be sorry."

Meliboë stood still as a blank-eyed statue as Airar brushed past, burning hope and wild despair a whirlpool in his mind. "My sister will be sorry—" he clutched at; was it true? Or was all lost, not only the unaccepted proffer? She did not come to let him out; behind, as the door left him in dark, he heard only a step and the bar fell behind him. Off to the northern, seaside flank of the courtyard a girl's voice ran on a trill of laughter to high point before breaking in a little squeal. The moon had gone; the keep toward which he turned stood outlined against the intricate summer stars. A moment he gazed; something touched, then gripped lightly his arm, and he swung round, hand on dag. Little mice ran up and down his spine at the realization it was herself. Argyra.

"What will—" he began, and saw her hand flash white to cut him off as she spoke hurriedly: "Lord Airar, it is not just. Only I must let you know that my sister's plan was none of mine. I do assure—"

Now 'twas his turn to break in. "Hark, no lord I," said he, almost fiercely, "but a simple peasant of upland Dalarna; yet one that dares to say he will love you more than a day, as a mole may love the star it cannot see."

"You hurt my arm. I know—they use the title to make you of their party. I'll call you so no more." She turned, held out her hand again, which he felt slightly quiver, and in the dim starshine her head was lowered, though feet shifted in eagerness to be gone. "And I do accept of your true service."

He held her yet. "I'd lineate the earth for you, halt Saturn, steal a horn from Capricorn, or raise the ghastly dead with Mercury—"

"Now you do unconvince me. No need for all these flowers if you're sincere; only falsity needs poetry."

"Why, love—all love itself—is poetry, and here—"

From beyond the keep came a booming thud, then a shout muted by obstacles, and another. They turned; the thud again. Someone waved a torch against the sky at the keep, and a trumpet cried harshly across the thick dark. The siege had truly begun.

28. Os Erigu: Ramp of the Cat

THE VULKINGS HAD MOUNTED A HEAVY
catapult behind cover atop the wooden tower they
were jacking forward at the end of their growing
causeway. Airar stumbled over a smallish stone, with
shards still clinging of the clay ball that had been
baked round it, to where Pleiander stood by one of
their own catapults in steel cap and target shield.
His face seemed to change expression as the torches
moved. Os Erigu's riposte had fallen short and the
men were toiling at the windlass.

Another of the balls came past overhead, crashing
against the pave and a man of Carrhoene clutched
his wrist with a cry. Pleiander rapped out an oath.
"They shoot for the lights," he said. "Diades!
Gonatas! Take a pair of those torches a few paces
down the wall and fix there to give 'em a target.

Come, lads, pull her home merrily, hai! hai! Are your muscles made of water?"

"What's to do?" asked Airar.

"Arm yourself if you'd stay here," snapped the Carrhoene, short and savage. "This is long-range work; idea against idea, not crash to crash; he wins who rouses dismay with a few hurts.—Release!"

The Vulkings had a light up there behind their shot-window. Airar saw it occluded as those within let go another of their stone-hearted balls. There was a wait, then the thud-shatter as it struck down along the battlement where the torches were placed, with mocking yells from the men of Carrhoene. Pleiander was unpleased. "They overreach us from their height," he cried. "Relax winding! Astyanax, get me three or four crossbow bolts; we'll leash them together and try a fire-shaft from the catapult; the wings may carry it high enough to tiddy them a trifle."

He turned, saw Airar: "What, still here? Go, I said; begone until you come caparisoned. All lives are valuable, even yours, since that Baron Catiná yonder's evident a pretty fellow that knows his leaguers, and there'll be sword-play for all before we're done."

Someone laughed among the shadows. Airar turned away, half-consciously in his irritation twisting fingers and pronouncing the first words of a spell that would put an itch on the Star-Captain, till he remembered and stopped just in time. His conscious thought was all brimming with the glory of Argyra, the peasant-fostered princess, and whether she had meant it as he wished it to be meant, saying she did accept his service. No use to the wall again; he sought bed and lay long unable to find ease, his mind going round till the window above turned pale grey and there was a truce to the clamors exterior, when unexpectedly and for the first time since parting with Gython of Gentebbi he found himself in the land of dream.

A single star rose over a twilight sea, while somewhere a bell rang slowly. He felt a rush of what must be mighty wings and the ground of the dream shifted, so that he was no longer rocking among sea-waves, but in an immemorial colonnade of trees that pillared up to make another and perpetual twilight on the forest floor. Far among those lofty trunks flashed something white—a unicorn that galloped, lifting dainty legs high. To Airar in the dream came the thought that only a virgin may tame this beast, yet he desired it much and called to it, using the words of old tongues that are magic for friendship to all enchanted creatures, as his father had taught him. The unicorn halted, sniffed the air friendlily, and then came toward him; but as it approached, instead of a horn in its forehead, there stood a naked sword, and he was being shaken by Erb the Lank.

"Come, young master, there be council for all but slugabeds."

They were already together when Airar arrived, with the air of men among whom previous sayings had not gone well—Pleiander by a window, hand on hilt and humming one of his Carrhoene airs, Alsander looking at his shoe-tips, and Evadne staring straight before her with a spot of red in her cheek. Just opposite was the Earl; he was gathering handfuls of his black beard in one fist to stuff them in his mouth and chew before he spat them out again, an odd habit indeed (thought Airar) but one that made him look ugly enough to bite a viper to death. Poë was not among the captains who watched him. At one side a peasant-looking man with a braggart-cap in his hands shifted feet.

"Here's now your famous captain and justiciar," sneered Evadne. " 'Ware him, though; he'll sell you all to Stassia for a milkmaid's kiss."

"That was not well said, brother," said Alsander. "This sits on all our shoulders." He turned to Mikalegon: "May I set this matter forth, lord?"

"Bedamned little to say. Unresolvable. Hell's fires—"

"Under your leave, lord—" Then to Airar: "Os Erigu's master and commander here; so grant we all. Yet by his own rule are not we free companions?

Now we are split past curing on how to save from these Vulkish men, hence would exercise our freedom to withdrawn even into Micton country. But his lordship says an obligation taken must be worked out to the end, even free spirits depending on each other till obligation's over. Where lies the line? Can you but point?"

Airar could have wished to be anywhere but there. "Will you handsel me a judgment?" he said.

"Not on the terms of that among the Hestinga mountains," said Evimenes. "This is too deadly."

"Nor I," said the Earl, spitting out a tangle of beard. "What! What! Handsel in mine own castle?"

"The freedom of your free companions must be a very little thing then," said Airar, "if 'twill not bear the first stress put upon it."

"I do not know for that," growled the Earl, "but I do know I'll have none of oath-breakers that run yammering for help with mouths full of promises, then say nay, when all's not as they wish."

"Oath-breakers!" cried Pleiander, his sword flashing out like blue lightning, and up leaped all the Os Erigu captains with a metallic clang, but Airar's listening had brought him between the two parties, and he held up both hands to keep them back.

"What's here?" he cried. "Handsel or no, they beat with stones on the wall there, and now's the time for composition within. Who gains by hard word or sword in this room save those curst Vulkings?"

A little silence in which muscles almost creaked, relaxing. Pleiander put up his blade; Alsander spoke:

"Well, here's the thing more closely: our brother Pleiander, who knows more about siege than any other here, says the castle must fall unless somehow we make an effort naval. Yet Earl Mikalegon will not waste his ships."

"We have nothing but by sea," said Mikalegon; and "If they reach the walls with their tower, we're sped," Pleiander together with him.

"I am uninstruct," said Airar. "Will not firebrands from your catapult hold them at bay?"

"They've hung the thing with rawhides; will not bite."

"Rogai in Korosh on their rear?"

"Ah-wah-ha-ha-ha-whoop!" roared Mikalegon, fingers in his beard. "Here's your Korosh man; quiz him. Nay, saves time to tell. Your Rogai has the mountain men up, but now two tercias and a half are before us; another half in march. Their convoys are too strong to be cut, all provisions come down from Briella with full guard and grisly enchantments to make the Korosh tremble in their shoon. Little help there."

Pleiander added: "They build faster in wood and rubble than we can with stone within. Overtop us; clear out battlements with catapults. A ram—"

"What's then to do?" asked Airar.

All spoke at once, but out of the babble a certain sense. Earl Mikalegon's will was to give up, go, all ships to sea and make a new home, Uravedu or the Spice Islands, where the blue men would be easily dominate, or Dzik if need be; but Evadne, no, it was stand or fall here, Carrhoene would never forgive their defeat—

"Nor Dalarna ours, neither," said Airar. "What do we fight for? Our advancement or the hope of the land?" and if Mikalegon thought elsewise, he was ashamed to say. Airar waited across half a minute of silence and added: "Yet I fail understanding how you'd beat them off with a sea-effort, Master Pleiander:"

"Clear enough," the Carrhoene. "Load our people in the ships with scaling ladders, bridges, and similar; run them against this causeway, carry it with escalade and burn their tower. Belike part of the causeway would go down, too; there's much timber in it and binding the flanks. But attack we must, or a long good-bye."

Earl Mikalegon growled. "It is just this plan that's not to be thought on. For look—they'll knock my ships to pieces with their stone-throwers and firepots before we ever come close, not to say that we can only reach the causeway by bridge or ladder that

every boat's bottom would be beat out on the rip-
raps. Even so, burn me the tower; such a thing might
daunt play-warriors from the Twelve Cities, but Vulkings are made of stiffer stuff. They'll build anew,
and where will we be then with no means of egress
from here? If that's the sole plan this famous siege-
captain can make, I say damn all and abandon all.
What?"

"I would hear Alsander's word on it," said Airar.

Evadne made a sound but Alsander cut across it
to say: "In point of planning, his lordship's most
reasonable, since we shall soon be penniless if we
must spend the fleet for the tower, which cost so
much less to build. Yet reason's self turns coward
before necessity."

"Not if they may touch hands," said Airar. "It
seemed to me his lordship said a thing that showed
how this might be done. The causeway reachable by
a ship among the rocks, to wit."

Earl Mikalegon called peace to his beard-chewing
for the moment and all stood dumb to hear Airar's
word.

"Would we put men on the tower? Nay: fire.
Then why not use a single ship, build out your
bridges and ladders, but let them at the outer arms
carry pots of combustible, so when the ship's driven
there, these pots would ignite the tower? If she's
brought home fierce enough they may attack and
take her as they will, but can by no means pry her
loose."

"I'll do it!" cried Mikalegon. Pleiander, more cau-
tious, fingered his sharp chin with a scowl of
concentration and said after a pause he believed the
trick might be made good, but not alone—it would
require an annex of other attacks, as one by small
boat and ladder against the flank of the causeway,
another across the broken rocks and archers under
mantlets to what remained of the high bridge con-
necting Os Erigu with the mainland. He was much
taken with the deep draw of these northern bowmen,
never seen in Carrhoene.

Now the Earl's voice boomed hearty again, giving

detail to his captains for carrying out the plan, the selected ship in the harborage to be screened by others while she was prepared. They let him make the plot precise, which in truth chiefly made itself with a word from Pleiander now and again on some such small matter as substituting for Airar's firepots baskets in withy wood that could burn through and shed their cargoes. Airar found himself with the fisher-spearmen assigned to one of the most singular parts of all—the advance in small boats to cover the flank of the fireship, since his men were good boaters. There was not much of pitch or like material in the castle but it is a thing the men of the Iron Mountains make when they are not mining; the Korosh messenger said such should be collected at the Fjord of the Bear if a ship were sent in a week's time, which set the date of the effort at a week plus two days. With this messenger, Meliboë the enchanter held long converse for the finding of some protection against the witcheries by which the Vulkings surrounded their road convoys.

Airar did not hear how this was done or if it were done, though it interested him much, since a protection general could not be laid in such a case through any magics he knew; but he had more urgent affairs in hand, to wit, seeking Argyra. In vain that day; the nest and next there was war-work to do, for every hand was now in need at the wall, where Catiná had more than one catapult going and the tower closer daily as his men poured more on the causeway from the shelter of the machine's lower levels.

They were firing balls of stone now, that crashed furiously against the outer battlements, where the dark stone chipped to a tattered aspect. Men were hurt and on the lower wall an engine or two smashed when clean hit—even a pair of Os Erigu people dashed down to lie like twisted dolls from where they labored on the demilune within by a deadly crack that came from high. The Earl would have ceased the task; but never a whit for that did Pleiander relax urging men to walls and engines; or the castle armorers to hammering in the court, at work on long steel shafts. With Airar's sharp sight and acquaintancy of bowshot to guide, these were flung by catapult at all that moved on the growing causeway, sometimes through the ports of the tower; and not unwounded went the sons of Lacia. Once as those enemies changed a guard a lance was driven through two together to leave them like larks skewered for roasting, and there was a shout of triumph. Even the magician Meliboë came to the wall, as drawn by the wave of spirit that welled from the Carrhoene captain; he had a handful of little wooden images made with long spindles thrust through their guts, to be flung over beyond the Vulking tower to their causeway. Count Vulk's men might have protections (said he) but the laborers not so, and in this war of walls a working man's as worthy as a fighter.

There were blue balefires in and round his hut the night he made the enchantments for these toys. The sun had quenched beneath the sea and Airar was abroad with witless Poë, only coming from the wall, weary as though they had marched ten leagues, and a stout of wine desiring. Poë made the sign of the true faith and his voice was unstrung as "Master Airar," he said, "let us bear rightward here and mend our pace, if you'll accept; for I am not so poor a man of war as must fail admitting when I'm gripped with cold grue."

To change route so was no joy for Airar, who had taken this way that it might carry him once again nearby the door of the Empire's daughter; but he was at the edge of consent when from the shadow came her laugh and she was beside them: "The physic for that, master free companion, is to drink at the Well where all enchantments fail."

"Not I," said Poë shortly. "Under leave, I will begone," with a glance at Airar, who hardly heard or remarked him, eyes only for Argyra.

"I'd have a word," said he; and "I am here; say your word," she. But now he fell tongue-tied, the speech he had all planned to make driven quite from mind by delight and tremor of her presence, with Meliboë's witch-fires playing from distance on her face.

"What, no word? Then I'll have one for you. Hark, Master Airar—d'you know the little tower that overlooks the sea-face, the one with the balcony round it? And its purpose?"

"Aye," said he, and flushed under the dark at how lightly this girl could take such things which himself hardly bore to think on, for this was that Black Tower where Mikalegon took his sweethearts male.

"Well, then, and for your needs I tell you that the Earl led your young man Visto there last night; but Pleiander of Carrhoene is now betaken with Prince Aurareus."

Airar felt a surge of anger; high love brought low. Was this bit of gossip all—? Am I to weep?" he asked. "I'll have no part in such a game."

"Nay . . . I do but warn you, and at some cost to myself from my sister." She laid a hand upon his arm. "If I have made you wroth, I'm sad; but men will still do and say strange things for what they call love."

"You do not believe, then, that when I say I love, the love is true? I'd pull the stars from heaven to make a wreath for your hair—"

She laughed to stop him. "I am not sure I'd want so many. Nay, you must let me go. My sister—"

"What can she do to hurt you here? Ah, if you'd thought on her at first, you'd not have come at all —for this small matter."

He had gripped her hands. Now they went sudden unresistant and she leaned soft toward him: "This is no less than true, master logic-chopper. But for tonight no more—we'll speak again when you have daunted down the Seven Powers—for oh, I'm of the Well, and you're a clerk."

She tried to twist away, quickly, but he held one hand and was about to lift it to his lips, when she grew close again, he staggered with the quick kiss, and her last word as she fled—"A token. Till then."

What did she mean? Down Meliboë the enchanter and his works? But that was long ago done
—nay, I'll have no magic more. It could not be that;
Meliboë himself is for the good cause. How shall we
damn him who serves as well as he may, even if
that well were less than good by some thinking of
the sons of the Well? The Well, the Well, which she
herself denied on—and nothing one can say for
sure.

How daunt the Seven Powers? Too deep; his
mind slid off on the thought of give all up, go to
Dzik and wind a turban round his head to have
some sweet submissive girl like them of that land,
and never care a care. Trangsted's heir lay wakeful,
thinking so, and how useless is life and sore the effort
—for what? To rise a-mornings and make another
effort more. Futile; life's a round without an end . . .
Yet somehow at the back of his mind a hope and
joy that did deny the thought he formed—a hate,
too, for how ordinary these were around him, with
wood-block face, and might not he, Airar, be somehow better than they? Visto to the Black Tower!
There's your free companions who escape one con-
trol to fall on another and worse.

Now came the wave of gloom again; how his
high thought were vanity only, and he'd naught to
give a king's daughter. Even her token might be no
more than a clever girl's escape from insistence. So
it was, after all, Briella or Carrhoene, and his thought
whirled round to Dzik and beat its wings against the
cage till the hope and joy of the kiss filled him again,
and (knowing he would not keep it) promised fiercely
to himself to down all common moral, and another
night bridge the gap between them by having her
body whether she would or no, for the mind would
come after. So Airar drifted into tumultuous sleep,
all tinged with sudden pain over this new thought
—that but for his father's magic and Meliboë's
(an accident) he'd have kept pure and there would
be more to offer Argyra than the leavings of Gython
of Gentebbi and of a lawless union a Salmonessan
might make. So now there swept over him the old

sense of anguish and irreparable loss for the lost one, though he had already found a sweeter. . . .

No more of that now. With the first dawn of day came a ship from Bear Fjord with materials needful, and it was all bustle while at the battlements the war went on. The ship *Nolbärn* was chosen, with long booms lashed to her yards and baskets as Pleiander prescribed. Earl Mikalegon himself would have commanded her, but gave it to one of his captains when 'twas represented that one must keep general direction of the battle from where all could be seen. Pleiander to command the rush along the stump of broken bridge; Airar and his to come against the causeway from the north, the harbor side.

The day of enterprise came bright and clear, as was to be hoped for, therefore a good augury. All were afoot with the sun, but the dawn breeze was onshore, so the tall ships must beat against it round Erigu's castellated cape. Earl Mikalegon, rather splendid than other in his rusty armor with the seaeagle surcoat, did swear and stamp the deck. Up along the causeway the Vulkings relaxed their shooting when they saw sails rise, and Airar could make out how heads were thrust forth the shot-holes of their tower, doubtless in wonderment at what this move naval might betoken. They tried one shot harborward from their high catapult, but it fell short; men hooted and the Earl broke out his banner. Airar and his hundred or more—for he led Evimenes with many Carrhoenes the day, and some of Os Erigu, whatever the boats would hold—lay at watch under the shadow of the pier, waiting till the sails should show southward through the arches of the broken bridge, which was to be their sign.

A long wait, and not an easy one; all had the discomfort of approaching battle. The free companions growled and grumbled how Erigu's Earl entangled them in wars of no profit, when he might easily have reached composition on some term that would send them forth to raid Uravedu in the Count's name.

"What if they did call us their allies? The profit

would be ours, with swords to keep it? All that's
a-need is a little grease in the knees of that fine Earl
of ours. Too stiff to see beyond his own belly-pot,
is he."

Airar would have replied, but tall Erb's Adam's
apple began its up-and-down and he spoke first:
"Aye, that be just what a want you for to do—make
all they hard wars and earn profit so a can take it
away with a bailiff and a piece of parchment."

The man growled unconvinced, there was this and
that babble on it, somewhat wearisome, till one
shouted from the castle flank of the pier that the
ships were coming. So they were in truth, sails belly-
ing little in the light air, but coming along well
since the wind was full fair for this part of their
approach. Os Erigu's Earl did handle ships like a
craftsman, with *Nolbärn* in the forefront, to be known
by the singular cant they had given her through
weighting aft. Airar looked to the causeway; there
was hurry there, the catapults against the castle had
ceased, the sound of a Vulking marching flute was
faintly borne along the air, and he saw a red triangle
dance.

"Boats all!" he cried, and Nene of Busk held aloft
the standard of the wildcat's skull. There was a
briefer wait while beyond the bridge-arch a splash
of water went sparkling into diamond sunshine as
Catiná's men loosed a stone at the onrushing ships.
Then *Nolbärn* was driving in, a great tear in one
of her crown-sails; he, crying to strike out, looked
back and saw a small figure that waved a hand and
he knew it for the Princess Argyra wishing luck to
his blade. When he tried to recall her face there was
only a flash of light in his mind and he could not.

Ahead, the view of the hasty craft was cut off by
tower and end of causeway. A lance from the castle
catapults stood quivering in the Vulking structure;
the Carrhoene trumpet called as Pleiander led his
sally. Eyes went forward; with a crash and splash
a big stone dropped in the water before the boats
to say they had been marked and were opposed.
The craft rocked.

"Pull harder!" Airar, for she seemed not to move at all, the next descending missile drenched half his crew and there was a shriek as the next again struck in one of the shallops near Airar's own and a man was hit, all bloodily. He was not the only or the worst, for thrower after thrower took up the tale against them, the curst stones came storming round, one of the boats was hit fully and burst, with men in the water trying to aid comrades who ran red.

The pace slowed. "They are too strong for us!" shouted someone, and Airar, fear dreadful in his heart, shouted discordant as he tried to stand in the swaying craft to urge them on, as stones from hand-slings began to fall among the larger weapons. But before he was up a sound burst from all lips, the rain of missiles round them began to relax, and one looked aloft to see just past the tower's edge a long boom with blazing fire-basket held and spilling, while those within the structure tried to fend it free and around them rained the sharp steel lances from the castle.

Among boulders the boat grounded and careened. Lank Erb cried "Ladders, ho!" Ahead a man stumbled across an obstructing rock and a thrown stone from above cracked his helmet like a nut. But now a passion of fighting fell on those men of Erigu and Carrhoene and Dalarna as they saw flame catch the Vulking tower from one and another boom, with men giving back from it. The ladders were set, they went up and up, nor was the slope so steep but that a few could climb by hand, reaching the crest to cast spear or strike with sword against the backs of those who still strove to work engines against the oppositious ships on the other side of the causeway, or to deal with the mounting flames. The tower burned in three stages; men leaped from it screaming to fall by spear or arrow or merely amid rocks; quarter-boats were putting out from Mikalegon's fleet to aid the attack; and there were those who threw down shield, holding arms aloft in surrender.

Airar turned. At the shoreward end of the cause-

way he could see how a few of the Vulkings were
rallying to line, led by a man with gold badges on
his armor that named him a high officer, his morion
up. At the line of engines on the cliff a few had not
fled, but were slowly loosing missiles on the ships.
"This way!" cried Trangsted's son, at the height of
his voice. "Before they come again."

Nene of Busk heard him for one and bore the
banner round. The free-fishers followed it and, as
the word spread, so did the wise Carrhoene men-
at-arms, but few of the free companions. Airar led
toward the rallying foemen, a Vulking spear-cast
whirring past his ear and another fixing in his shield-
edge to be shaken loose. A terciary went down; someone had made a good cast. Their line was but forming, forming, and a trumpet brayed. The officer
turned, and next moment it was cut-and-thrust all
along the break of the causeway, spear and sword
against shield and shield, and Airar caught a flash
of dark hating eyes out of the face inside the helmet
as he found himself engaged.

The officer was as good a master swordsman as
Alvar's son would ever meet; with difficulty Airar
held his blade from being beaten down, gave back a
step, another, thought now without fear but only an
intense curiosity that this man was too strong for
him. There was a shout in his very left ear as he
half spun to the force of a blow, feeling it would
be the last time ever; a giant arm with a starry mace
at the end of it swung past, and down went the
Vulking leader, wallowing in blood. Before them the
foemen hung a minute, then broke again in dismay
as they saw their captain fall, one with a spear in
his back.

Airar turned; Mikalegon of Os Erigu was beside
him, with a booming laugh in his helmet that ended
in a cough as a tongue of stinking smoke rolled past
them down the breeze.

"I thank you," said Airar. "I am now half quit
of my vow," he, snapping up the visor for breath.
"That was the Baron Catiná, but Vulk survives!"

Down the smoke rolled thicker, but these Vulkings never give up, and back among the trees someone was seen trying to rally them once more, as Airar faced westward, lifting both hands:

"Back to the boats!" he shouted. "We have won!"

29. Os Erigu: Treason

Enter Rogai of Mariola, all radiant
and with a batchet of news. He wore a leather coat,
like the Iron Mountain miners. The command ashore
there was by name with another baron, he said
—Viyar of the 8th Tercia, but Count Vulk himself
was in transit from Briella, where he had sworn a
great oath in the temple to take Os Erigu, though
it hung by chains from the starry sphere and could
be approached only with wings. Their loss was a
full quarter of a tercia, six hundreds of men besides
all the work undone. Vulk had called the 3rd Tercia
and the 7th out from the home countries: the Lacias,
Bregonde, and Acquilème.

Korosh was all aflame and the Iron Ring holding
its own courts by night in Norby, setting Vulking
judges at defiance; the barbarous Mictons in their

skin caps were raiding West Lacia, surprised at having Dalecarle allies. Bordvin Windfang? In the south,
'twas said; had been in the Isles of Gentebbi, where
his procedures were wild, making more disorders
than they cured and the Count furiously dissatis-
fied with him. Some whispered he had been fingered
of a sea-demon at Vagai, and in spite of all protections was no little witch-struck thereby, so he had
flung a shot-spear through one of his own pages.

They were drinking as Rogai told his tale, and
greetings cried along the table; a few with bloody
clouts, but the great Earl in huge good-humored
laughter over his own lewd jests as he shared his
sup with Visto. Airar caught a glance that might
be hatred or a tear from the young cup-bearer toward that latter and thought for a moment of what
Argyra had said; but this was swiftly driven out by
the sight of the four Star-Captains with their white-
streaked dark heads together and the speech of one,
to wit, Alsander.

For their parts (he said) the captains of Carrhoene
failed understanding of how men who'd win a war
could be so neglectful of the means. Here was a week
passed in little but silly roisterings and now another
banquet for the coming of Rogai. Those enemies
labor, toil; whereas but yesterday, when Pleiander
would have had some of the free company to the
upper wall for work on the trebuchet, not one would
go, no, nor let their castle servants neither. "In Carrhoene, we'd hurl down from spadarion a leader
that could not make his will obeyed, or that saw so
little to the future."

"Aye, and there's why you are not in Carrhoene
at this hour!" cried the Earl; "instead of beggars on
the charity of freedom's hold. Go rule your southern
slaves and see if they fight for you as these brisk
lads have done for themselves."

He was drunk enough to be shouting-disputatious,
so there was a great deal more, but in so good a
mood over his victory and his Visto that Airar could
see nothing would come of it but windy words, no
danger; and rose to slip away to the night rendezvous

his darling had given him. Yet as he did so caught the flash of Evadne's eye and the sneer of her lip fixed toward him, and in a moment, as though they had communicated thought to thought, knew this was not for his going, but to cry that here was the old difference. Briella or Carrhoene! For surely Earl Mikalegon's way was wrong as merely war, however it might maintain piracy; the thing had been to follow their enemies hard, strike them while reeling from the one defeat. Yet the Earl had flat refused a plan to raid by ship Naaros or the Gentebbi Isles to draw off the assembling foes.

This was still uppermost in his mind as he met her, and he gave it voice: "Tell me, you that have been taught to rule, is there no weapon to make men work together but the lash?"

She laughed. "What, are you now turned politic?" When he had explained (without saying it was Evadne's dilemma he presented, for a reason he could not have told): "Nay, I'll humor you thus far," she said. "At Stassia in the High House, they say there's no solution but the Well alone; and sure, naught but the Well and the treaty of the Well has held the peace between our Empire and the heathen of Dzik, that would make most horrible wars. Briella or Carrhoene? I do not know; but sure there must be other means of reconciling man to man than their two alone. Our Empire is one such; I have heard even that you Dalecarles have another, with your masters, as the Forest Masters in Skogalang and Master Fishers of the isles."

"Aye, but—Doctor Meliboë, that is a philosopher, says that it comes to the same thing in the long, Briella or Carrhoene."

"It may be he is right, Yet I can say what is wrong with the rule of Briella."

"That they will give full life to none but those of the Vulking blood? It is the thing we war against; I have been taxed out of my heritage."

"Nay, let me have my little say. Does it not hit you strangely—you, who were taxed out and are despised, at war to bloody death with them—that in their system of the voice of the general you can find no flaw?"

"I place myself in your hands by so saying—but not I."

"Think on this—perhaps their plan has none. . . . I mind when I was child in Scroby. They taught us to spin, but threads would twist, and twisting, break; and I cry to Mother Valana to know what was amiss, whereat she, setting all right, would say that naught was wrong but the temper in which I had done it. So I think it is with these: that Carrhoene or the Vulking heritage, if their rules were changed, would be still the same, for it's the inner spirit, not—"

"Argyra," said a voice loud and clear, and it was Aurea the other princess, who looked on Airar coldly, as he could see even under the dark. "I have heard," said she, "of nobler deeds that nobles did than try to take the prize without the price. Sir clerk, can you find no better target for your drawing spells than a poor silly child who purrs when stroked, like a kitten? Ha! Try them on my lord Vulk, when he comes with the fleets of the Twelve Cities."

Not a word for a moment said Airar of Trangsted, then he saw Argyra hang expectant and realized in a clear desperate thought, though without words, that here it was, the crisis; if he spoke not now for his love the chance might never come again. "No spells!" he cried from the pit of his agony. "And what so wrong, bright lady, in us two speaking here? Nay, more; I'll dare declare my love for her, though empires fall. Would you make me recreant to that love because I will not be to Dalarna, and so strike down our happiness?"

Argyra spoke: "I have drunk from the Well, and magics have no more bite on me, not ever."

The tall princess merely sniffed. "A fine gesture, Master Airar. I'll certify you a part in any company of mummers you desire. But here's the Empire's daughter; barns will burn and people die if she choose not wisely, whether in love or out. What's the happiness of two beside a thousand? Nay, do not try to halt me. I know what you would say—to give all up. She cannot change her birth, the blood is there in spite of all renunciations. How would you like to see her broken on a wheel to clear some other's path to a throne, and all because she played at love with a foolish lad that captained twenty vagabonds instead of twenty thousand?"

Airar was left, and to cruel reflection. He had not dreamed the proud Aurea could clip so close. Why, so even Aurareus, the pretty-boy of the Earl, might have in him some dash of the iron blood of old Argimenes. So thinking, so avoiding Aurea's thought (there must be a flaw in that, could he but trace it), he sought across the castle-court to Meliboë's dwelling and the comfort that could be had from his philosophy—though that might be somewhat small.

By no means; the enchanter was just speaking to Poë the Witless at the door, he welcomed young Airar as with delight, and led him to where a pair of candles shone across a scroll opened, waiting for the junior to speak. This was less easy to do than might have been thought; Airar for a time could but gaze, and 'twas the old magician broke silence with: "I do not believe you came to look at my beautiful eyes, young master; or if you did, there are better to be seen in the dancing girls' pavilion."

"Nay, I . . ." The voice stuck.

"Truce. I'll not sport. You look forth as a soldier come from a defeat. Is't not that you sought the love of this high lady, but she's proved harsh, as with the Lord of Permandos? Or nay—your sorrow would stem from her sister, that would have won you to the Vulking alliance."

"She said I dare not think on one of the House, lest there be a battle of succession, and all that destroyed which I would most preserve," said Airar miserably.

"Therefore you'd give up hope, let her and the world and all go by default, so that the onus of these future wars rest on some other who'll lead her to the bridal bed. Yet you will not do that neither, till you've come to make me see and say how high-minded you be. Not I; Master Airar, you speak like a priest, that is, selfishly. While you have that priest's small self-content in avoiding answerableness, you do not care what happens else. Is that not it?"

"Oh, nay." But he felt himself flush. "Aurea the princess said it was but selfishness to think on her sisters, when so much of what will come to other people of Dalarna and the Empire lies on how she weds." He checked. "And besides, I am not sure she'd have me if she were free."

A smile played across the crest of Meliboë's beard. "Touching the last point, which is the first of your importance, I'll go warranty for you. But as to the first, which is the body of the argument, what duty do you owe to the Empire or Dalarna, or she either, for that matter? When you wear a crown imperial, with its power and glory, then you have a duty; that is the price you pay for baubles. But till such time you have only the same duty as any other man, that is to find what happiness you can; and she, like any other woman, only the duty of being bedded by a youth who'll beget lusty sons upon her body."

Said Airar: "Owe we nothing then to others?"

"Aye, if you'll take the way of Briella, and be a grain of wheat in the sack. No man's born to duty. Has only those assumed, in change for some value— as now there is a duty from you to those fishers whom you have led so far from home that they might cry your cat-cry and further your projects. Duty, duty carries with it the surety of knowing always what's best to do for another. Look—are you God? Can you tell always what another needs? A count rode by and saw an old woman digging in a field. Thinking her lot hard, he gave her a silver aina to relieve her poverty. So she ceased digging and missed a great treasure that lay beneath the ground; but when she had gone to the city with her aina in her hand, was soon reduced to lower beggary than before."

Airar drew a breath. "Then you'd advise I made flat contest with the Princess Aurea on this?"

"I advise you nothing, having learned that you

take little advice, young sir. You can look for advice only inside yourself, from which point the world is other than through these eyes. . . . There's another answer on your duty, duty, among the rest. Duty to whom? Not to those you think; you have only the report of eyes and ears on them, which say nothing of the heart, where lies the true man. For that, duty why, Master Airar? Would I could teach you from that idea; for duty to those you have never seen is paying obligation not to men that are ponderable, but to some principle and loose idea—as honesty, or what you will."

"Why, yes, and wherefore not?" asked bewildered Airar. "I had hoped to be honest."

"Ah, bah, young master." Meliboë reached over and began to roll up the reading scroll. "Honesty's but agreement with the common thought of where one dwells. I was an honest man when I made enchantments at the lyceum of Briella till the decree forbade. Suppose that decree had been passed at the moment I was in the sobrathim spell. Before it's ended I'm a villain, so have my choice of bringing it to a halt and being torn by demons or of turning contrary to law."

"I do not think so, sir, not by what you lately said. Is that not disallegiance to a law merely, not honesty or any other thing that lies beneath the law? Why, I break Vulking law myself, and hope to see it overthrown."

Meliboë smiled with one side of his face. "What, then, do you live by, Master Airar? Say principle, and I'll laugh. You have no test if principle be true or false, save that some man has thought to put it into law for others to live by. Even your true religion —which I doubt not you believe in without thinking on't, as the young ever—it's but a kind of law, is it not? To wit, you must accept another's word that it's right to believe thus, and wrong to believe so; and all the rest flows from that, including your very principles, to which all lesser arguments return, as kittens finding the world in the tips of their tails."

"Sir," said Airar very earnestly, "you may talk

wonderful logic from the schools and put me down, but—"

"But I'll do so no more this night," said Meliboë, rising. "I'd not confound you, sure. Do but wish to make you see that you must do as you please and not think too much on that gold-haired princess, whose true metal has not a little brass."

This was good speech-strengthening, surely; but Airar thought as he left across the dark courtyard, how could he bring it to the market where sale would be of most avail, with Argyra, Princess of Stassia? Time proved him right in this doubt; the next day she was not to be seen, nor the next, nor did any message sent bring return. It seemed clear she had fallen in with her sister's view, while in the castle men lived easy except the Carrhoene sergeants, always at it in the tilt-yard under Evimenes' glowering brows, whom Airar found a keen man with either lance or sword. Ashore the Vulkings toiled at some mysterious concern, it seemed half-heartedly renewing their causeway a little. It would be some sight of this, mingling with his effort to review the past for what else could or should have been said, that brought Airar up short—some effort to fix clearly a thought nagging at the back of his mind. Once again he saw the scene and heard the elder sister cry—"My lord Vulk, when he comes with the fleets of the Twelve Cities."

"What's here?" he asked himself and sought Alsander. The Carrhoene was not less struck than himself and the two went at once to beg Earl Mikalegon for a full leaders' council, though it were barely noon. They were assembled after much shouting and scuttling round the court. Airar told his tale of the chance phrase while Pleiander picked his lower lip and the black brows of the Earl drew in to frown. All tried to speak at once; Mikalegon brought down his fist:

"What's there in't, Bag-of-bones?" he said to Alsander. "Could and would the whole Dodekapolis rise on us? I am half ready to believe it. There's a sort of friendship between myself and the lords of

Phyladea, which you will not like. It is in my mind that the ship I sent there to buy for our needs after we broke the damned Vulkings is not returned and may be held."

"It could be," said Alsander slowly. "Though I doubt the trouble lies in Phyladea, where they have little love for the People's Party, and so for the Empire. More: Phyladea would hesitate herself to oppose Os Erigu; she's not a power maritime. Or Berbixana leads this, or Sthenophon of Permandos—"

Airar gave so vocal a start that all heads turned on him. "What's it, young Eyebright?" demanded the Earl, twisting his fingers in his beard.

"Sthenophon of Permandos—he is just the lord whom the lady Argyra refused in marriage, and I have heard he took it ill."

"Ho! Then I can smell a rat as large as a fox," quoth Evimenes. "Vulk and Sthenophon, each searching an Imperial bride within these walls."

"And I can smell another," cried Evadne's husky voice, cracking high. "Brothers, think on this: if what's said here be true, why, there's communion clear between our enemies without and within this place, so those within have tidings before ourselves. I cry with that hatchet-faced Mariolan, 'Treachery, treachery, dirty treachery!'—and know where it lies."

She halted for effect, and "Where, then?" the Earl shot into the gap, peering round as though to spy a red wool bogie in every corner.

"It starts and grows with these Imperials, the women, that need a little breast-dandling with the red-hot tongs. Hah, shudder, you eunuchs, you farting men, that look on Argimenes' House as holy and live in yesterday's world. If you're too awed of shadows, have those wenches in, and I'll get a tale from them before your eyes."

She had come slowly to her feet; her eyes rolled and Airar wondered how he had ever thought her pleasing to the gaze as he stood himself, hand on the jewelled dag, crying confusedly that before they put Argyra to any Carrhoene tortures they must strike a rap at him; but—

"One word."

It was Meliboë the enchanter; he held a finger up and a little blue flame danced on its tip as his voice rolled out like oil on water, so that everyone gazed.

"This: young master Airar has said it—the tidings came from the Princess Aurea, and you may put me to the question as well if you get aught from her. Proud, aye, and no more heart than a rotting oak; but she has the iron blood of old King Argimenes, that won a kingdom from the heathen with nothing more than a broken sword he found in the ground, and he a slave then. The cadette knows nothing; if she did we'd have clearer tidings from this young sir, who is her lover. Put these women to the question, you have the round world against you, not Vulk alone, and what of the Twelve Cities he has seduced, but even Dzik. Irredeemable war and a hard, dirty death for all is the end of it, for these are under the protection of the Well. And in the end it is less like that the treason lies with them than with the brother."

"Not he," croaked Pleiander, and now all began to babble, but the moment of Evadne's fierceness had passed, and the end of this stormy council was that Earl Mikalegon would send out the ships to buy provision and to see what was toward—tall ships that could turn in the wind of those northern tides and hold free from the row-galleys they use among the Twelve Cities.

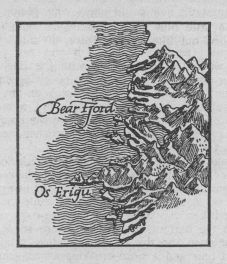

30. Bear Fjord:
The Brand Is Aloft

THE TRUMPET ON THE SHORE-HILL BLEW
double, there was movement and new standards; the
laborers of Briella toiled at the mole to make it wider
than before. Poë said the signal meant that Vulk
himself had come; within Os Erigu, men were now
somewhat less willing to miss labor on the demilune
and Pleiander's great trebuchet, though neither moved
forward at speed, since the best of the Earl's own
people were abroad with the ships and the news of
a treason had leaked down till man looked on man
over shoulder and under brows where dark suspicion reigned.

The Carrhoene captains were somewhat grim with

Airar in those days and even lank Erb had little to say; Trangsted's heir could guess why, seeing the tall man from distance now and again walking with Evadne. Airar found himself much alone but for Poë, with whom (as himself said) it was not so much that he was still out of favor with the Earl as that the latter had fallen on a habit of giving him little notice and found it as hard to break as any custom well-established. Yet this Poë was not a man with much to offer and young Airar found the hours somewhat heavy on his hands till a day when heat made it uneasy to bear armor.

The sun shone; across the blue Northern Sea white-caps danced to the breeze, and a sail showed bright white against the bright blue skyline far away. It was twilight when she laid her anchor beside Os Erigu's mole and her captain under the sea-eagle standard came to the hall of council. All were sober enough there for once and this captain not less, a burly man with red hair and a nose-breaking sword-scar, called Minæé Dark-Thought for his confused speech. So far as one could make out from his sayings, in truth obscure, he had tidings and not small—entrance refused him at Damaria, the same being a port of the Empire, and Earl Mikalegon currently under its ban, so he had sailed north and west. Midway the seas he found a ship of Lectis that said the lords of the Twelve Cities were indeed decided to make alliance with Vulk against the pirate hold that had so often racked them. Yet not all of them, neither; the fleet of the alliance was said to be in no small part manned by people from the Dalarna factories, and Berbixana city would not send her ships at all unless she had the high command, subject to none; the contingent of Xiphon had sailed with the rest but then gone off to Uravedu on the plea they must make a gold-raid to pay their men.

"In fine, Sthenophon leads," interjected Alsander here.

"He leads I do not know; is spadarion and had the heads off a pair of Thaskoi captains; but the Lectis Minima adventurer says he's a small spark

to crawl from his hole and fire so great a flow of
blood. It may be that they have made him scullery-
boy."

Someone laughed; Minæé the captain looked
round puzzle-faced for the cause, which not finding,
he continued with a tale of having borne up to get
more tidings from the fishers of Gentebbi, which is
the world's market of news. But near the islands there
were no proper fishing craft, only a parade of hulls
that shifted "like sands in the sea," gaily painted
and with oars. There was so much wind on the water
that the Erigan craft slipped them, though they came
close enough to throw a crack or two with their bal-
listas; he marked how the sails raised in pursuit bore
the wise wood-rat that is emblem of Permandos.

No other way about it, then; here was Sthenophon
coming, and none could think of a sure resource
against him, though the question was battered till
purple twilight fell beyond the windows. Carrhoene
Pleiander said that from his experience in siege it
was now a matter of patience, they should gather
provision and stand till these new invaders went
hungry home. The southerners must draw food from
the Micton country and would find little, while Os
Erigu's tall ships could vex them on the sea. A good
device; but it was clear enough time would want for
the first step, and the thing would hardly be done
before Vulk the Unreasonable's causeway, with now
two towers on it, came to the walls. Meet them by
sea? The council broke up, all feeling unsatisfied;
another pair of dawns and they learned the answer
to whether this might be done.

Sthenophon and his ships. All eyes were at the sea-
face to watch how under the candid late-summer sun
they hove up out of the south in a line, like bugs
along a floor-joint, and came crawling in. Their sails
were raised; but coming near the castle on its cape,
the Lord of Permandos would vaunt himself; set the
oars out and all ships in order, while flute and drum
sounded the sharp irregular beat that few not born
in the south could follow. The Earl was at the battlement; he ordered a catapult loose and tried a cast,

which fell well short as the ships went past majesti-
cally, their musics louder and more derisive, white
foam curling beneath their toothed ram bows.

As though for show the formation shifted and
changed; sails came down, more oars out, and Airar's
glance followed the line where men pointed, shouting. There was to point at; luck or the lack of it had
brought another of Os Erigu's vessels home, rising beyond the sea-rim to full view. The Permandene
galleys swept round in a long curve whose grace Airar
could not but admire, hate them though he did.
"Go back!" bellowed Earl Mikalegon, as though his
voice would carry. It was a show in the cruel arenas
of Dzik, but distant and soundless. They saw the tall
ship's crown-sails glint as she turned suspicious to
fly, but the galleys were faster in that light air.
They spread to catch her in their net, while on the
castle wall all held as it were breathless.

Earl Mikalegon stamped and chewed handfuls
of his beard; but on the sea the tall ship, their ship,
turned and turned again, then—as her captain saw
escape useless—flung round to charge at the galleys'
midst. Stones flew as specks; a hole and another came
in her sails, she was almost riding down one of the
galleys and may have hurt it badly as the nimble
craft dodged, for it drifted away in a manner that
showed oars smashed, but before this could avantage
Os Erigu, another and another had driven their sharp
rams in her side. The Earl's ship hung, with men
leaping to fight on decks or fall into the sea, she
rolled back and right over, while along the castle wall
went up a cry of fury and despite. There was for
a little time a commotion and gathering round where
the Erigan ship went down; then the navies of the
Twelve Cities put forth their flat sails again, and
again resumed order to come past cape and castle,
slowly, nearer than before, so that laughing and hooting could be heard from them, pointing to their yard-
arms where a few shapes jounced and dangled.

Said a voice: "Master Airar, you have told me you
love; if you do not prove it by saving me from that
man, I shall die."

It was she, and gone before another word. Black evening and black night came down on Os Erigu, succeeded by days of grim. Off the shore there were always two or three of the galleys lying, clear in view by day, showing lights by night, sometimes running in to throw catapult shot toward the three ships that still lay close along the cover of the pier. No other ships came and no tidings; what had happened to the force of Os Erigu on the sea, none knew, and the great Earl behaved like a man half out of his wits, striding gloomily around. The blood seemed gone out of him; it was as though his heart were in the wooden sides of those vessels now invisible. He would stand on the shoreward battlement, gaze sourly at where the Vulkings under mantlets poured down trees and rubble over the scars of the burned causeway to build it anew; take young Visto by the hand and lead him to the Black Tower, from which the air would presently carry some snatch of drunken song. The Vulking towers advanced, nor were restrained even when Pleiander brought a heavy catapult to bear and squashed some of their people like beetles. It was all Pleiander now in the command, with Evadne; the final word on that hint of treachery was that the Princesses should be allowed to speak to none but the one attendant they shared—a one-time dancing girl with a figure now somewhat out of fashion.

Pleiander and Evadne; it was as though she triumphed amid the troubles and was posssesed of a demon. She was everywhere—to the walls in a mail cap to cry "Hearts up!" or exchange bawdy jokes with those at labor balancing the trebuchet; at the council table of an evening to wind her arms around lank Erb's neck and smile on him when he spoke ill of their chance of winning—even to kiss Mikalegon through his black beard, bid him show her the Tower and make him laugh rough and embarrassed, he understanding such play no more than Airar. Her brothers pledged her in cups from a store now dwindling—"Evander!" and Airar was almost persuaded to admire her again till a chance word spoken about the Stassian damsels brought hatred's dark flash to her eye. Yet for all that, Evander-Evadne it was who walked abroad to the pier one night when the wind blew wild enough to toss waves on the stones and the lights of the blocking galleys were gone, they driven from their posts by the gale.

There she found flotsam and brought it to the council hall, supporting it in her arms—Rogai, half-naked and wholly exhausted, gasping that he owed her a life as he drank a dram; he could not have swum much longer. The Earl had gone to rest; Airar also, so he heard the tale when called from sleep; Pleiander was at the battlements, where the enemy had moved so near they had an engine working from one of their towers. By time they were met the Mariolan was somewhat more himself; could talk, sneezing and croaking. He was full of excitements; all north Dalarna (he said) was underly burning, two castellas had been taken in Korosh, and Count Vulk using much of his terciary strength to hold the roads secure—"which, by the Well, he'll not find easy if you but hold here till snow-fly."

Earl Mikalegon grunted: "Not easy that, on our side; I fear you talk to doomèd men. Our provision's small and the blue sea held against us that has always stood our aid. We might run a ship through a chance wreck in such a storm as beats tonight, yet there are three left only, and dare I dare it? so losing our one hope of escape should they break down the door of this rat-hole."

"I had thought you were more of a man of war. Attack these southerners."

"We saw how it fared the once. Their oar-moving ships are too curst agile for our sailors when they're so many in number." (Outside the sea beat up by the storm sounded boom and withdrew again on the rocks; a shivering gust leaked through the shutters and the Earl bit his knuckles.)

"Phlew!" said ebullient Rogai, "You talk like a Scroby knight-at-arms, all courtliness. Do you play a game, or fight for victory? Bah, fah, the woodrat of Permandos runs by day and sleeps sound o'

nights or when storms blow . . . Ha—*chish!* . . .
Strike him in his hole, catch him when he's not
a-swim."

"What do you mean?" asked Mikalegon in a voice
doubtful but somewhat new.

"Why, our friend Alsander . . . *coff* . . . sees it
clear enough." He motioned to where the Carrhoene
captain moistened a right forefinger, touched the
left palm, and slapped the opposite fist therein. "Clear
enough. These row-galleys of the Permandenes are
all but those on duty laid to the shore by night in
Bear Fjord—did you not know? Nay, you're sieged,
cut-off. I joy that I came with this tiding you might
have missed. Well, there they all are, like kernels
on an ear of corn, a stockade built to the land side
since they attend attack from thither by my merry
miners of Korosh or the painted Mictons. But the
sea? They think they rule it and give it never a
thought. What if you ran in on them by night and
storm with a gift of firebands? What if you lost a
ship or two? They'll eat meager in Bear Fjord with
winter upon them."

Said Airar, rapidly: "Lord, this wind tonight is
from the northwest and blows on shore. I do not
know your northern weather, but in Vastmanstad
'twould last all night and the free-fishers I lead can
live in it like otters. Let us make the essay this very
hour."

Somewhat doubtfully, yet as a man waking from
a dream, Earl Mikalegon looked at Alsander. "Old
meat-chopper," said the Carrhoene, "he has right.
Essay! Take the sea before driven by their engines
and power of the causeway."

"I say so, too—" Pleiander. "A siege must go
up or down, and ours has been all down since Sthenophon made alliance with the County Vulk."

"Why, then, let us try it," said Earl Mikalegon
slowly. "But I'll make a proviso—that I am one with
this enterprise as a private volunteer, the sea-eagle
under the master-cat, miaouw. Bag-of-bones, I here
name you my lieutenant and heir if aught go wrong."

"I too," said Rogai, "if his lordship has a half-helm to lend, ha-*chuff!*"

"And I," said Evimenes, generous thrusting forth his sword-hilt for Airar to touch in mastery; but Alsander and Evadne both frowned on this and reminded him that their brotherhood bade them go all or none to peril, whereas Alsander stood now forbidden to go by his new lieutenancy.

At the pier, Airar found that Evimenes (one could count on him for this!) had had firepots made, with sparks streaming to the gale. Erb called the men, who came forth lobster-eyed from first sleep. The tall fisher chuckled as he reckoned them and reminded Airar of his first sailing as a leader, which was the flight from Vagai, "and I call down no curses on a, Master Sharpsight, but who just thought then we free-fishers would follow warlocks so far? Or if my sister Ervilla knew what a's old man did?" Airar answered no word direct; here were a few of Os Erigu's people with the Earl, and he was ordering them.

Under the heaving surf the ship growled and pounded against the quay as they tried to cast off, like to break her seams. Only a rag of sail could be set, and Mariola-Rogai got a fall that was like to break his bones, yet kept gay as a lark, and Airar looked at him with new eyes—unled he might be, and reckless, but there was no more fearless companion when the wild hawk of adventure screamed. They broke free, midwatch of the night, with Airar thinking half on his darling dear and half on this that they must do.

It was a hard claw off the iron-bound coast with the ship's high side catching the storm-wind, and they were not above forty swords, though Airar lost count whenever he tried to reckon them up precisely. The clouds and rain that would follow this wind were not yet come; there were stars, blotted by the outline of the iron mountains of Korosh against the eastern rim. Earl Mikalegon had a battle-axe; he stood on the poop and gripped a stay while the free-fishers shouted round in their dialect of the islands. The Lord of Os Erigu spoke: ". . . a change of ordering," was all Airar caught above the roar of wind and he leaned his face nearer to ask a repetition.

"My father had wrong!" bawled the Earl with the strength of his lungs. "That said men would be faithful to a banner if each followed it from free choice. They need orders—tomorrow's instant punishment or reward. As for those cowardly captains who have deserted me, I will hang them up, for by God, they deserve it."

But Airar was unwilling to give thought to such questions on the rocking poop with battle near; and off the starboard bow the line of foam along the rocks was blacked with the wide entrance to Bear Fjord, the ship swung to a chorus of cries, and her motion became easier as she rode along the waves instead of bucking them. It came to the young man that he had not seen Meliboë the enchanter the night —and for why? A heart-warming thought that perhaps the old man was aiding them by spell, for the tyrant of Permandos against whom they sailed would possess no such immunity to magic as the sons of Vulk. No! That was behind, he had for the moment forgotten, spell led to spell and ever deeper, and now the wind was harrying them along between tall walls of black while up beyond did not the faint false grey of coming dawn a little light the sky?

The fjord turned and broadened; along the farther bay could now be seen a few points of light where the sons of the wood-rat did keep their camp. "Now look-a to weapons, young Master," said Erb, who had been shipmaster, and Rogai tried to stifle another sneeze. Airar as chief had ordered that the few of Os Erigu with certain of the fishers should earliest prance ashore, fire tents and booths and lead the fighting there; the rest, under Erb, run one of the galleys free for escape (since no sailed ship could work out of that gut against such weather), then fire the rest with the ship that brought them. Himself held a trumpet to blow signals, one blast for the onset, two to recall. Forty against a thousand—or more; how many would return?

"Ready all," cried Airar, "The torches, ho!" The

ship turned again under Erb's skilled hand and drove toward where the galleys lay dim along the shore, right in, right in among them with sails aloft and a splintering crash of wood as some spar jarred loose among the breaking hulls. Airar blew one blast and leaped to the side-runway of a galley. A startled head came out clearly from under the forecastle cabin into the light of torches borne behind. Os Erigu leaped past, roaring; Airar saw him drive his battle-axe down on the head which burst as a torch-man pushed past the falling body to fire the forepart of the vessel—all this caught in the flash of glance before Alvar's son ran across the deck to leap down on wet shingle. "This way!" he shouted; Nene of Busk's voice gave a wildcat-yell behind him.

A dozen yards ahead was a booth with a man emerging to cry something, Airar's memory later told him it was to know what passed; but into him now the lad of Trangsted plunged his sword through the middle and looked for, fenced with, and dropped another before remembering he was a leader. He turned as a torch was flung past his hand into the thatch of the booth, catching at once as sparks streamed down the gust—and there another booth blazed up.

The camp was beginning to rouse and run and shout, but in the flamelight all the running was clearly to leftward, away from where Earl Mikalegon's battle-cry sounded heartily. We are well in that quarter; Airar turned rightward toward the upper end of the beach, where Erb would be trying to get a galley free, and ran past tall shadowy ram-beaks shining with bronze. No men; he stumbled over something and, the trumpet in his hand hampering, fell prone. A reached hand caught him up; he footed it once more, and round the corner of the galley-prows men moved, while in the distance a flame ran up and flared against the sky from the shaking masts of the tall ship.

One leaped against him, crying, "Here's one!" as a sword was heaved aloft, but he knew it in time for a fisher-voice and dodged, shouting "Dalarna!"

"My sorrow, Master," said the man who would

have struck. Erb's voice said "Heave!" and under the galley-edge men moved in unified effort.

"What's here? How goes it?" demanded Airar.

Tall Erb turned a puckered face. "Cannot get a loose. A was brought up with winches, and to stir we need more hands."

Airar thought quickly—sound the trumpet for recall and bring Mikalegon and his men, who might bear the foemen with them in on the group before the ship was loose. Yet there the tall ship flared against the sky, casting brands afar, and 'twas no part of the plan that she should burn so soon. He lifted the trumpet, but it was struck from his hand by Sewald, face aglow in the red shine—"A will all come!" his voice high.

"Let them," said Airar. As Sewald snatched, he swept his own blade round furiously to send the fellow down with a great grisly wound, thinking only that there fell a bad man as he blew twice. An arrow from somewhere shot past his head and stuck in the prow of the galley, and Erb pointed; three of the fisher-spearmen doubled down and ran in the direction whence it had come, their faces hard. A form scuttled across a firelit gap, and a thrown fisher-spear seemed to go right through the man, but he ran till another caught him in the legs and down he went with a shriek. Shout and shout; a wild pennon of flame was leaping from thatch to thatch. "Get more beams for heaving!" cried Erb, then turned to Airar and, touching his hand, said urgently: "Master, if we die here, know I bear no malice for that the woman I wish to lie with, lies with you," after which say he turned to shoot a twist-spear at a hurrying Permandene form.

For there was panic in the ranks of those enemies, with some crying "Help, help!" and "Alas!" as they ran toward burning ships and booths, most not knowing what was toward, the boldest stricken down and none leading. Many of the galleys had now been summer-long on the beach, where heat oozed the pitch from their joints; they burst into flame like shooting stars as some of the Earl's people began to fall in toward the rest, Airar blowing again, most of them so quivering-excited that Erb could hardly get them to give a heave.

Yet he did; heave, heave, and she moved, and someone cried, "Go now!" but Airar struck him down with the hilt, crying that never should Dalarna abandon friends. He lifted the trumpet and blew once more, terribly; then not knowing whether they had all come, stood ankle-deep with sword out, but few were the enemies that dared follow against the spears of Vagai, with camp and ships behind them burning. "Come!" cried Erb; a hand dragged him over the side, bumping his belly on the bulwark. Every man must take an oar, even Mikalegon laughing and whooping; but there was no pursuit as they forged down the fjord with all the flames combining in one great fire behind.

Mikalegon rested on his oar a moment: "Young Master, this is verily a deed of arms; old Bag-of-bones is nothing with his capture of Poliolis. Yourself did it—you may tell your grandchildren—and by sounding the recall so precisely. I had no other thought than to have gone on breaking skulls at the moment and would have left my bones to be burned with those rat-eaters. Oh, aye, a feat of arms, for wars are won by wits, and I have met my better; take my allegiance."

"Row!" cried tall Erb, and they pushed out into the stormy sea where clouds of dawn were now blowing in, heavy with a promise of rain.

31. Farewell to Os Erigu

SAID MELIBOË THE ENCHANTER: "YOU HAVE
to learn, young master, this—there is no joy in any
doing, save that of having done to one's own joy. Do
you labor to hear words of praise from men? Find that
drunken harper and give him an aura. For myself,
I'd rather you had borne defeat from which you barely
escaped, yet borne it well."

She said her life hung on it—and now no word."

"Gratitude is the virtue of a good dog. You were
better with Evadne of Carrhoene; no gratitudes given
or asked in that one, only strong impulses that would
keep you ever alight. You, young master, are one
that may turn to a turnip without some such."

Airar laughed outright. "You have taken a divination on't? It was otherwise that time when you said
I must be pushing but advised young Visto to marry.

Now I see myself growing in the ground, with green hair."

Meliboë smiled with red lips between his beard. "Unhappy it is that without divinations none will believe the inevitable till it has happened. But do you laugh, joy, and be scornful exactly in this fashion; since you'll not use advice and must wait on luck, why, let luck have her play." He rose. "So now your time is elapsed, as you said, before you go to the battlement and see what Master Pleiander makes with his instrument. This is a notable and vigilant captain, now so emulous of your feat at the fjord that his heart's engaged—wherefore we may expect miracles."

Outside, the first few flakes of early snow ran past from blue clouds, and melted where they fell. Airar had to put on his armor and duck low along the battlements through shards of splintered stone, for engines were now working from both Vulking towers, and the walls of Os Erigu had taken on a worn appearance. His helmet must have shown some flash or reflection; a steel bolt shot past him and against the wall. But on the broad space of the upper platform Pleiander had set heavy mantlets, all now bruised and battered, with the tall leg of the trebuchet standing through its frame like the sweep of one of those pump-wells they have in Hestinga.

He had never seen such a machine before, and knew they were not easy to build aright. It was near to use, with the ropes tense, but they were still putting fragments of rock into the throwing basket as he came. Pleiander turned as a mantlet quivered to the shock of a crashing ball.

"Have you come to see how war is made, young master?" asked the Carrhoene, cheerfully, patting one of the supports like a lover. "These toys are kittle as women, but if they march, naught stands before them."

"Good luck to this one, then," said Airar.

"Aye—needed." Pleiander wagged his head like a teetotum, mood changing in a flash. "Here's the key of the siege, Master Airar, for all your ramping

around the waters. Never have I seen men who so
labored in the face of all setbacks as these Vulkings;
they are demons, and will have battering-rams
against the wall-foot in another moon, when good-
bye castle."

"Is there no counter to such rams? I had thought—"

"A dozen, if there be enough people for the devices. But what shall we do here with our handful
against two full tercias and the marooned of Permandos?"

A Carrhoene sergeant plucked at his captain's arm.
"Sir, all's in readiness."

Pleiander turned and raised a hand. "Cut, in God's
name!" he shouted. An axe flashed, the huge counter-
weight came down with a deliberation that turned
to flying speed, arm and sling flung up, there was a
crack that seemed to rack the castle as it collided
with the check—and Airar ran to peer with Pleiander
through a gap in the mantlet, as the withy basket
of stones flew in a long parabola, spilling part of its
contents, past the northernmost of the twin towers,
to shatter among the rocks below. An utter miss;
Airar turned again, but could have spared compas-
sion, for Pleiander was dancing with joy, shaking a
fist as he shouted: "Pollute! Pollute! I'll pollute your
bathless arses, frog-spawn of Lacia!"

"Was it not well from the true line leftward?"

"Bah! A facile adjustment. Diades! The throwing
axis a foot to the right; I expect it to be done before another dawn. The question was the carry of
that big jointed throwing-beam—for look! it cannot be lengthened without rebuilding all, and where's
the time? But now all's well and we have gained,
the siege will surely be broke."

"By this one tool? How?"

Out there opinion chimed with the Carrhoene.
Shouts were faintly borne and more catapult balls
discharged where they stood beside the tall engine,
as in a passion. An expression of intense foxiness
came into Pleiander's face, he placed one finger beside his nose: "Nay, Master Sharpsight, Eyebright,
there's been too much of sayings that end with those

Vulkings' having a full tale. I would not tell my own lover so much; why should I tell you for yours?"

Hot retort hovered behind young Airar's lips, but he withheld and went to seek Poë, who said, when the question was put, that he was a free companion, not much of a man for sieges formal, but saw nothing in this to make a mystery. The trebuchet was of all war engines the most frightful and could break down mountains—

"I have heard so much from Pleiander himself," said Airar somewhat dryly.

"Well, then, their towers are of wood, not built to stand such bruises as Pleiander's pebble-tosser can give them. Let him break the front of one, through those hides with which it's hung; the next cast with fire, and though it miss once or twice, not forever, and they'll roast rarely. Hah! There'll be drink poured in the council hall tonight."

It was in Airar's mind to ask with what reason, since the victory was still unwon; nor did it seem to him that those hard sons of Briella would give all up even were their towers burned a second time. Yet, not wishing to be spoil-sport, he said nothing then nor when Poë was borne out by a revel louder than for the triumph in Bear Fjord, perhaps because then they came home weary and wounded after a sleepless night, perhaps because Carrhoene felt a necessity to make itself great beside him. Even Evadne was in a sear, though Meliboë the enchanter, no. Almost the last drink in Os Erigu came to the board, for though the sea-blockade was now broke in pieces, it had not seemed good to spare men on a voyage to seek provision till the land siege were relaxed. Airar marked, not specially marking, that the Earl had a new cupbearer, no languishing lad; and for that matter neither was Alsander on this night, though a man usually judgmatical. When the roast was slit, the cup poured, and the dancers on the floor within the tables, he called one to him and began stuffing gold aurar of the Empire down between her breasts, a torture she bore with right good humor.

All the talk turned loud and loose and Airar of Trangsted hardly knew which way to look, as words ran on the last great feasting, when the cup of war was drunk. It was shouted at him publicly, whether he had lain with the Stassian wench yet?

"And is she as hot as her mother?" cried Mikalegon, madly. "When she was the Knight of Bremmery's daughter in my youthful years, no wellborn lad was counted pubertous till he had split her legs apart. I went down to Bremmery villa in Gentebbi islands to prove my manhood and so gain my father's inheritance, but the Emperor that was then Prince Auraris devanced me, and liked the sport so thoroughly, he must even wed her at the Well."

Airar rose furious and might have thrown his mug or otherwise made stories, but before it could be done the door at the base of the hall burst open and one rushed in with a high shout: "Lord, Lord, the castle burns!"

Not a man but followed Airar to his feet, there was a rush for doors and out, with Alsander spilling his dancing-girl to the floor. In very fact a blaze was leaping from where the Black Tower stood against the sea-wall, and through every window of it, long tongues of flame licking, the roof had already gone in, and along the south wall booths that had held the free companions were caught, their tops going like wildfire under press of a strong wind from the sea.

"Have down some of those buildings! Fetch water! Blow the trumpet!" bawled Mikalegon, running, his face all twisted in the flamelight, and men were hurrying to his shout, the leaders not less than the rest, though Airar felt a structure round his heart, less thought than feeling, that this was a blaze not to be put out. Then Evimenes pointed with a cry, and they could see how two-three brands were already on the roof of the council-hall itself. Pleiander's eye seemed to start from his head; only Alsander kept his head to cry: "We can never do it. They will attack for sure as we fight fire. Brothers, collect the men and to the ships. Carrhoene, this way!"

At another time Airar might have found counsel to stay this flight, but now his mind beat like a wild bird in a cage against the thought that between burning booths and hall-roof already alight lay the house that housed Argyra. Erb? Not visible. He flung to Gynnbrad or another: "He has right. Bring all our people to the pier," and ran across the courtyard. There was no light at window; he shouldered the door and went pitching across the small outer room when it was not locked; pulled up and burst through the inner door, crying: "Up and out!"

He might have spared himself the trouble. All were up and in a tableau hard to resolve by the dim light of a chrysma—the servant crouched on her haunches, Argyra in a cloak hastily wrapped round, with one enchanting shoulder bare and her head buried in the golden sister's arms, who looked across stonily to the other wall, where leaned Evadne of Carrhoene, lips drawn, palms outspread backward for support. There was blood on her blue gown; before he stood Erb the Lank, with a shortsword point levelled at her heaving breast, who turned to Airar:

"Now here's the judge to judge," said he. "Master Airar, this dame has just tried to slay the little princess of the Empire, Argyra. Shall I run a through? The which I might ha' done out of hand but for fear of witch-guilt."

"Strike!" said Aurea, angrily; Evadne's mouth worked, and "Aye, strike," she said, hard and quick. "I do not care what else I lose now. Strike, whoreson bastard."

"No—" almost gasped Argyra, lifting her face: "There's no harm; naught to avenge."

"What's this tale?" said Airar. "Madam, will you truly do black murder?"

"Fa! There are those would say I sought to save lives and cause from treason. These have communion with the Vulkings and have now raised this blaze; but I have failed. Strike, and make an end of one who's but served you."

A little wrinkle leaped between Argyra's brows, and her face tensed suddenly to concentration. "I do not believe it," she said in a voice clear as a song. "I do not believe you have so much as thought it. You found us bed-lying, sleeping sound, and would know then if never that nor my sister nor I would set a fire and lie down in its path. Now you shall tell me why you seek my life, or I will indeed add my voice to the rest that urge strike, and I think my friend Airar will hear."

She reached a hand to take his in a thrilling pressure, and through the opened doors a gust carried a wisp of smoke that made them both cough with the reminder they stood in deadly peril, but Evadne of Carrhoene did not mark. Her hands came away from the wall, she bowed her distorted face in them, then flung them back aside:

"Because I love him . . . my frog . . . I'd cut your throat and a thousand more to keep him from you. . . . I'd share him with you—but no, you Stassian fireside cat, you'd be one that let her man no leman. You do not know what love may be, the passion that shakes, and will be satisfied at any cost. Mew, purr, laugh! You will win him now, and I have failed. Strike, Captain Urd, Erb, or whatever your name is. Make an end." Her voice sank so low Airar could hardly hear. "Curse you, Lord Airar, my love and hate, you have right in the long. Go on to your house-cat; marry her, all fenced round with priests' blessings; I could never stand it. I'd love you fierce and free, no bonds but those in which I hold myself—and they're the ones that bind, for I have been faithful to you alone, though you will doubt it. No, you have right and we wrong; we of Carrhoene are too turbulent, know no laws but those we make, and love loves to live by another's law. All's lost— ah, strike!"

Her body writhed toward the sword-point, but Argyra said: "Lady, you must seek toward the Well of the Unicorn, which can give peace from every despair," and Erb lowered his blade before it touched, saying anxiously: "Master Airar, see how smoke thickens and thatch above us cracks. We must make haste." Two big tears stood on his cheek and another pair had run down his thin jaw.

On that Airar woke as from dream. "Put up your blade," saying to Erb, and to Argyra, "Come!" as he haled her toward the door.

"My robes," said Princess Aurea.

"Burn with them or come," flung Airar, and Erb half carrying the Carrhoene, they were out into a court tormented by the roar and glare of fire, the council-hall roof burning as Sthenophon's ships had burned, and a tongue of flame licking at the lowest shot-window of the baillie. Argyra stumbled, Airar lifted her lightly over an obstacle, there was a confused peening sound from behind and rightward, and they were on the quay, where the two tall ships already moved on sweeps and the row-galley had men in confusion, beginning to shove free.

"Miaouw!" shouted Airar at the top of his voice, and the catcall was enough heard to bring free-fishers to attention, the galley's bow bore in. He swung the girl up daintily to reaching hands. "Where's Mikalegon? Where's the Earl?"

"Not aboard here." "The tall ship *Dragg*." "I saw him—"

"Ho!" came a voice across the widening water. "Have you his lordship?" and faint answer, "Nay; with you."

Airar turned with: "Attend till I come."

"Hold, young master, nay—" called Nene of Busk's voice from the galley deck, but the lad of Trangsted was already pelting up the quay and never caught the end of that word, nor marked feet thudding on the pave behind him as one or two jumped down to follow.

Ahead shapes moved and flew obscurely against the background of flame and falling things. Cinder and brand drifted past; it was not easy to breathe. His guess was the angle where hall did not quite meet with baillie. The Earl kept a cabinet building there, in which he slept when not at the Black Tower. It was a good guess; as Airar ran up to it, shaking a burning flake from his shoulder, one of the vague flitting forms resolved itself to Mikalegon. He had his battle-axe in his two hands; his shoulders heaved as he drove it hard into splintering wood at the door-pillars, then turned to show a face from which all wit had fled.

"Good," he said. "One's faithful. Get an axe. If we have this one down it will not leap to the keep nor the inner battlements take. Come, hurry, in Hell's name!"

"Lord and friend," said Airar, "come; it is too late."

For all reply, the big man grimaced fiercely and would have struck the next axe-blow at Airar, had not the young man stepped nimbly aside. The Earl swivelled round for another stroke at the rending pillar. Nothing to do; Airar whipped the dag of Naaros from its hang, and reversing, tapped the pommel hard behind the Earl's left ear as he leaned forward at the base of his blow. The big man sagged, but Airar trying to catch him was pulled down too, he was like a huge limp side of butcher's beef. A voice said: "Young master, you take the feet and we the head," and behold! Here were the witless Poë and Tholkeil of Mariola that had followed him back, so there was gratitude in the world, after all.

Stumbling, staggering, with the limp Earl between, they made their way down to the quay as the scorch blew round, and were hoisted aboard, Earl and all. Erb was at the steersman's oar, head-gear off and an eye not less than wild. "Row! Row!" he cried, but Airar sought forward to the forecastle cabin where Argyra might be. At its door they had just laid Os Erigu's Earl on the deck, with a vacant eye upraised to the sky; and now one leaped from a rowing-bench where his oar-companion cursed him, to fling down prone, kissing Mikalegon's feet amid tears. It was the cupbearer of girlish form.

"Oh, my lord, my love," he babbled, "forgive! forgive! I did not mean to destroy all, only the Black Tower, where you took that other. I could not bear to see it again. I did not—"

"Poë, bending over his captain, snarled, clipped

the lad to the planks, then pointing to the castle with every window alight, spoke to Airar. "Hard it is," he said, "that all this and the heritage of freemen for generations should go down because of one nasty little traitor."

It was the voice of Meliboë the enchanter that answered: "There is always a nasty little traitor. Only the heritage can live that is strong enough to bear the shock of all that such can do."

"You, forward," boomed Erb's voice, "take oars there and just row."

They rowed then, out into the dawn along a stormy, rocking sea. It came through oar-ports and over bulwarks to set them shivering at the benches; and now all fell on to wonder that the Vulkings had made no attack when the castle burned and occasion seemed so well to serve.

32. Hrakra Mouth: Great Tidings

THAT STHENOPHON HAD RIGHT IN KEEPING his ships from voyaging among the storms of autumn was soon clear; the row-galley took water heavily and by noon was almost awash below, so dangerous that Erb put her poop to the wind, which brought the prow slanting in toward the coast of Norby. The gust held steadily from north-northwest, allowing them to hang out squaresails and give some rest to those at the oars. The Carrhoenes, who use such craft by habit, might have done better with this one, but of the hundred and seven men aboard there was only one Carrhoene, and he a sergeant's servant—the rest all Dalecarles of Airar's following or free companions,

305

with some eight women, including Evadne, the shield-girl, the Star-Captain.

She looked glum as could be in the morning light, with a line or two round her mouth that had not been there before, but Airar marvelled at how boldly she bore herself, and at the cheer of the greeting she shouted across the heaving water to those brothers, when they bore up their tall ships to inquire anxiously. His own heart turned and burned for converse with Argyra. But the first time he sought her, she was in a sleep he forbore to interrupt, and at the second, here was Aurea, the golden sister, all full of chattering—would he not, as leader, exact hard pains from the rash youth that set the fire? Did he not think it strange how one so bold as the Carrhoene maid should speak of love only at the sword's point? Did he believe she truly meant it, or was it said on a moment's spur to hide some other thought?—with a variety of other fantasies as tedious and little important as this, so that Airar had no chance for a word with his love, and at last in desperation cried: "But Carrhoene is part of the Empire!" and strode away, leaving her to think what that might mean, while he sought Mikalegon.

The Earl sat on a winch at the bulwark, with his knuckles in his beard, staring. "What?" said Airar. "Will you despair? I have lost a father's heritage myself, as have all these Carrhoenes, and none of us are dead of heartbreak yet—or as Doctor Meliboë says, hearts do not break."

The big man only grunted without turning head; but as he saw this did not make Airar go away, said slowly: "Aye, I have heard that tale. But what you lost was a piss-poor Vastmanstad farm, like another, where there on Erigu's cape the light and beacon of a naughty world went down—because I was not man enough to keep it high. Where's now that sanctuary for men who'd be free of the sleepy Empire, or of the Twelve Cities that will not let a man rise about his mother's bedroom, or of the Vulking rule where even lords are slaves? Aye, I had even a few from Dzik among my merry companions, who could not bear that a man should be forbid to eat mutton of a Tuesday. . . . All gone; dead, down and drownded, the heritage lost."

"Do you think as much?" asked Airar, earnestly. "Lord, there is Doctor Meliboë, who can discuss these things very aptly, and better than I, but this much I know he would say, even though saying it be to stand with those Carrhoene: that your heritage and mine both are not in acres or stones but in birth and heart that we have from our fathers. How? Must you lead the free companions from Erigu's cape alone?"

"Nay . . . nor from the Bue Sea, neither, where the ships that might have saved all are fled . . . They're lost, and the heritage. . . . Free companions no more. Men will not act together but in fear of punishments. . . . The sea-eagle's chicks are geese, and I'm an old man. Leave me now; you had done better to do as much last night."

Airar did leave him then, seeing how little was to be made of such a mood, for he had sense enough to know that the most of Earl Mikalegon's gloom was not true. It was only a game of words they played together, and he'd no wish to see it carried from words to worse, as it had been on that evening in the forest when Luronne the deserion died. More —there were thoughts of his own to ponder, to wit: how was it that the rule of Os Erigu should fall? To him, watching waves slide from the galley's breast, it seemed not less than true as true what the enchanter had said—that every world coughs up its own traitors, the Baron of Deidei to Salmonessa's Duke; and to Dalarna, such as Britgalt, and aye, his own uncle Tholo, who drank Leonce Fabrizius' wine. Even these free companions that had run away, treasonable against themselves and their own freedom. But had the Vulkings no traitors in their ranks? Not any; their hard rule passed treasons by. No, had they after all the right of it? His mind repelled, and repelling, slid off to ask himself if he were traitor, too—in love, to Gython's memory. "Love is but once and forever," his mother had said before she died, but here was he, twice in the double cycle of the

sun saying, "Now and always." . . . Ah—but now
the thought slid back again to her in person, and
naught else was dear but Argyra, and he would not
go back from her for any people or demons or towns
of towers. So thinking, he was roused by Erb's loud-
shout as the galley rounded in at an inlet of Norby
province, where they dropped sail and anchor.

It was toward twilight and the wind falling as the
tall ships came up to cast anchor beside them, with
pine-clad hills running up steep from the small fjord.
Men began to bail the galley by pot and can; there
was a shout with cupped hands across the wave
and the Carrhoene captains would come aboard to
seek their sister. Hunger woke; a search of lockers
aboard showed none had thought to provision the
galley since she was Permandene, so there was no
bread, only some black murca-flavored olives of the
south, with a little wine of the same. Airar's first care
was to send a couple of Mariolan wood-hunters to
the shore to seek what they might find. The fishers
set out a net or two.

The captains met on the afterdeck. Mikalegon said
not a word but to confirm the allegiance he had given
to Airar's leadership the night of the galley-burning,
which left the latter with by far the most important
band, but he played at modesty, seeking advice on
what's now to do. Pleiander was for seeking some
small city of the north, best Lectis Maxima, the old
town which is across the river from the new city
Minima. There were near three hundred blades all
told, and a quick onslaught, with some help from the
Iron Ring inside, should not find the place beyond
being taken. There they could bid defiance to another
siege, for he had heard the old town was a mighty
strong place, builded on an outcrop of mountain—
"and there'll be help from the new Lectis across the
stream, or your Dalecarles are less for liberty than
they seem to be." Evimenes laughed him down,
saying sieges had not turned out so well for them
that they should seek more. Meliboë would give no
counsel on the ground they were now wandering ad-

venturers to whom all counsels were alike thrown dice—he would take a divination.

"Nay," said Alsander. "I recall a divination of Os Erigu in flames, made for us on the journey thither. These prophecies fall too pat, bring on their own fulfillment. We cannot now lose more than we have lost here in Dalarna. My tale is to make straight for Permandos city, while Sthenophon's adrift in this cold north, and raise the Party of the Guilds against him."

That would have been too desperate for Airar, with two ships only that could make the voyage. Not Rogai, though; he applauded, offering the amendment that their journey be broke at the ports or halfports of Skogalang. "The Iron Ring has power there, and the Vulking strength has been drawn northward. Not to mention that Sir Ludomir Ludomirson's among the forest-masters, who is a councillor of the Empire and the House itself; a stirring man."

The meeting was breaking up on this note when one of the Mariolan hunters returned. Instead of meat, he brought with him a man of Norby, who had been fishing farther up the fjord, not a very clever carle, but had replied correctly to the song of *"Geme, plange—."* His tale was of Norby ready to rise against Vulking rule, and even of some of that kindred themselves discontented by Marshal Bordvin's wildness and hardness of heart, who would lead a wing of terciaries up to conquer in the Micton country in the wintertime, a thing unheard of. Such merchants of the two cities Lectis as were of the Iron Ring had said patience, attending the issue of the siege of Os Erigu. They answered the Count's numerous requisitions with tales of non-possession. There were few ships from oversea, and all commercials much in irritation. If one raised a standard with force beneath it, the cities Lectis might shut their gates against the red triangle.

The council of commanders sent the man back to his fish-traps and sat close on the benches to think new of their case, Rogai now turning to Pleiander's plan of a landing in Norby to raise a war there, and link up with the Korosh bands among the mountains, while one of the cities Lectis should hold the Vulking strength before it. Evimenes called this a silly thought; Alsander, too. The latter furnished sound reason as was his habit, namely that the city merchant-guilds were nowhere stout for the revolt, and these would be turned cold as Moon Mountain peak when they heard of Os Erigu's fall. "Where's our force to raise a standard? Three hundred men? Go to!"

"Better than three hundred against Permandos, hatchet-nose. I wonder you do not tell the real reason why you wish to go back there," said Pleiander, somewhat tartly, "which is that you can have no joy from these Dalarna girls without paying for it."

"While you'd liefer stay here and play the trick of bump-boy-behind without pay," snarled Alsander, and they launched into a long, dirty argument, the first Airar had seen those Carrhoene brethren have, with Evadne sitting silent, eyes darting from one to another, and lips scornful. Rogai yawned openly; Airar said at last:

"Friends and sirs, this leads us where fox leads dog, that is, round and round the tree to nothing. Now it seems to me—if you have my word—that we lack swords to raise a full war in any part. Nor are we like to gain them in Lectis now, where these turncoat merchant-guilds will find them a fondness for Vulking rule, now that Os Erigu's down—"

"It was the Mariupol merchant-guilds waged these!" flashed Rogai, flinging his hand toward the Star-Captains, but Airar: "No unfaming meant; and you shall let me have my say. Our evident need is people. It can be we shall gain some immediate in Skogalang, but more than that, we shall have Sir Ludomir Ludomirson, who is so great a grandee, and can make the ban of the Empire to be removed from us through those he knows in Stassia, the more since we hold the children of the Empire as hostage. . . . More, winter's on us, and the Vulking marchers will be locked by now in these northern lands, since they have no ships, while we snug safe in the Skogalang woods. Yet even to reach so far we need provision, and my say is that you of Carrhoene shall take this galley openly to Lectis Minima with your people, wearing the standard as though it were still Sthenophon's and obtaining our needful as an ally of Count Vulk."

There was a little chatter to and fro on this, Alsander calming to finger his chin thoughtfully and say it was a genial plan. With Bordvin in the north (Rogai added, changing advice like a weathervane) they might obtain more ships and men too, from Naaros, the Isles of Gentebbi, or the Mariolan shore —"where they know now that Vulk's a scorpion, and ban or no, will join us." Evadne still said no word; it was therefore held a thing decided.

It had come on to snow in big wet flakes as they counselled; in the shallop during the exchange of ships, Aurea the princess would know where Airar was taking them, and with what intention. "Is it fair to treat us so, like dogs or dancing girls?" and: "Can you not let us free to be your embassy before Lord Vulk, who is a man reasonable that cannot love these strivings?" Some in the boat laughed to hear Vulk the Unreasonable called the opposite, but her voice held so strong a compulsion, almost like an enchantment, that Airar found it hard to reply or deny.

Argyra said at last: "Sister, you have some authority upon me as senior and by our father's will that I should attend you on this voyage, but there is one thing which is good for you to know, and that is I will wander vagabond across the world before following you to the court of this Count, while Sthenophon the tyrant sits his friend. It may be I am too much heiress to choose who shall wive me; but by the Well! I will say who shall not, or I will seek a convent and be the bride of God."

"It might be better if you did," flung Aurea, but there the conversation fell, for they were close aboard the *Dragg,* and Airar must see to such detail as who should have the watches and the cabin space. Erb was shipmaster, morose of air as he sent a man to climb the major mast and fix there Airar's cat-skull standard. Earl Mikalegon's eagle caught snow in its dejected folds from the other tall ship, for there was little air. The frowning weather and lack of gale were well enough for the galley, but made the other hard to move; night found the armada still un-far from the inlet, anchoring cold and without as much food as hunger desired. Airar shared his share with the Stassian sisters, of whom Argyra sat wrapped in an old ship's blanket, since she had let Aurea take the only cloak between the two. She, Mistress Gold-locks, whined of this and that—Airar thought how little her formal beauty was beside the gayer young sister's mood, speaking of things like snow-time in Scroby, and not at all of war or politic or the burning castle and terrible night.

It was as though they had a treaty in avoidance. But this also Aurea spoiled in the end by asking whether the Carrhoene girl had gone with her brothers or come aboard this ship, then ticked on before Airar could answer: "You are not to be so much censured in his matter of Sthenophon, sister-puss. The Sons of the Well bid us look on all Imperial races as one, but those of the Twelve Cities do often rouse me to shudder. Can one forget Coralis of Steliae, the baron's daughter, and that Phyladean hus-band of hers that kept her locked up in his old mouse-castle till she turned all pale and stupid? Though it was partly her blame, flaunting with the black-haired page-boy from—"

No doubt, thought Airar, she sought to be for the moment gracious. He stood, murmuring good wishes and a good-night; Argyra reached him her hand from under the blanket. A-deck the weather had turned again, cold and still after snow, and spots of star be-ginning to show through tears in the cloud—there-fore a night for thoughts and slow, grave converse with a friend. But he had neither the friend nor the converse, feeling as though all emotion were burned dry out of him in the castle fire, so his mind would only run over and over things already gone, like a blind horse in a mill. He sought rest in a shut-bed forward, but this not to much purpose, there being little sleep for him before the tramp of feet above told waking day, and all night long monstrous vision-figures of Evadne, Mikalegon, Aurea, and others marched past his eyelids through flashing lights, no one he loved.

The morn was clear and mighty sharp, but with enough breeze off the land to drive the big ships somewhat. They made a good passage, the fishers wondering no little at the strange seamanship of these Carrhoenes with their galley, who'd run her well out to seaward with the wind behind, then unship oars and row back toward the coast again, so she progressed in slants, like a crab. At each approach could be seen the tall slopes of Norby standing up, covered with black-green fir upon which the unmelted snow shone in the cold light; but toward evening the heights began to tumble down, there were grey and brown ploughed fields that had not held the fall except along hedges, and houses to see. One of the free companions said this change in the country meant early arrival at the mouth of Hrakra, on which the cities Lectis stand. The galley rowed before them under the lee of the vaster ship, and the Star-Captains said they would rather chance another day than this dark for their enterprise, so it was another night of short commons.

For relief of idleness of mind Airar went over to the galley. Mikalegon was there, a little recovered of his tone, laughing and all admiration for the manner in which the Carrhoene captains had blacked the white streaks in their hair to make them seem other than they were. Evadne looked the completest man of the lot; she had even broidered a wood-rat badge for her cap. The weather was on all thoughts, Mikalegon voicing fear that the wind would turn into one of the north gales out of a clear sky for which this region is famous. It was agreed that the two tall ships should seek shelter in the mouth of Hrakra and stand there anchored, but ready with some sails in handling and war-engines cast loose to beat off pursuit, if pursuit there were. At the last minute and on his own thought, the decision was to take Rogai to the city with the rest; if the ruse failed it was he could seek all needful from the Iron Ring.

There was wind with the morning sun as the weather-prophets had said; the galley labored, running down to the river-mouth, where they wished her godspeed. The falcons from which Hrakra takes its name ogled them, screaming overhead; so did seagulls. Airar's own ship he had anchored near the north bank, and threw an outpost forward along the shore, watching; then himself stood by the rail to watch the river's rolling flood.

"It is not so blue nor so great as the Naar of Vastmanstad," he said to nobody, and was surprised to draw a reply from a Shalland man: "Nor so noble and friendly as our Vällingsveden," the which he had thought a very dirty stream.

Near time to go shut-eye, the galley came back, no doubt in anyone's mind of her success, for torches waved from her poop and men capered there while someone played a whang-whang instrument with strings. Rogai of Mariola shouted from her with joyous excitement:

"All Dalarna's up; the Vulkings fail!" As they munched bread and meat Alsander said he would not give quite so much.

"His face when he saw your hair," said Rogai. "Ho-ho-ho!"

"What was his damned name—Rodvald?" quoth Pleiander.

"And the old devil's dead, never forget," said Rogai again.

"You are my instructors," said Alvar, and Evimenes: "Brothers, will you permit me tell this tale?" then launched into it without more:

"We rowed in; there was snow on the wharf and the welcome somewhat less than mere silence. Diades, that has the most southerly accent of our company, asks for the syndic of the provisioners' guild. A couple of carles with heads so white you could not tell whether they were that color from birth, or grim with old age, thumbed us the way, turning to spit as we passed. Did we take offense? Not we; we wore the wood-rat, and when the beast falls, the otter rises. Live Carrhoene!" He stood, slightly swaying, to drink, and all touched lips to cup.

"The way was thumbed to us; we went. It was a big man receiving us in his hall—oh, very corpulent, gold chain across his belly, and fur trimmings, not the simplicity of our syndics of the south. Looked on us not unfriendly, the old fart. 'Lord—' begins Alsander; 'Lard,' says he. 'When a man lords me these days, I'm being larded for a roast.'

" 'We are your lordship's allies,' says brother Alsander, 'that have nor lards nor roasts to fill our bellies as we siege down these pirates that vex you; and will accept more courtesy.'

" 'Hear a strange thing,' says cushion-ribs. 'I had thought it was victual you desired more than sweet words,' he says, and begins twisting his fingers in his belly-chain. 'Well, where's your authority?'

"Alsander says we were soldiers of the realm and the Well, come far to serve under authority of Marshal Bordvin, and needing no authority beyond that.

" 'Marshal Bordvin, ha!' says our man, and looks very sidelong out of his eyes, sniffing. 'Then you will have his signet or the seal of it,' he says, 'for he knows I cannot give you the Count's good bread without.' This was warrant enough—"

Said Alsander: "Warrant enough for me to seek more time and knowledge. Clearly there was a tort somewhere to this syndic's vitals. I played him like a fish to learn the reason, watching his dewlaps flutter as we argued. There was a writer or two in the background, eyeing our process loathingly. He finally admits that he can give a sheep or two and maybe a dozen sacks of meal, when I begin to murmur about fighting men hungry and how they take what they might need; but of wine had he none. Seemed curious for his curiosity. In the midst of all this appears Master Rogai—"

Rogai: "With two archers of the Vulking guard as footmen."

Evimenes: "Footmen! It was headsmen they wished

to be; could feel in my own gorge wither on the way they looked so longingly at yours."

"The tale," said Airar.

"Sir pudge, the syndic, turns pink and blue. 'What's here?' says he. 'Traitor taken in the article,' say the archers. 'The deserion says you're to judge him in office of senior syndic, since the Baron Barrilis was called away on business of the realm by a messenger that came yestereven.'

" 'Where's the matter evidential?' says the syndic. 'Evidential!' says one of these archer-people. "You do not need more; you have the deserion's word. Would you call him to a common court like a Dalecarle?'

" 'I have not the deserion's word,' says this Rodvald. 'I have the word of a pair of snotty archers.'

"They lower on him and say a thing or two more, and it is almost swords. He looks glum, but sticks to his way, protesting it is high order—and all the while Master Rogai stands there, unconcerned as a cat, humming a music to himself."

Said Rogai: "Because I could see what you could not; that our pot-bellied friend was a friend truly, with a small ring of plain iron on the seal-chain he kept twisting between his fingers. So the music I hummed was '*Geme, plange, moesto mori.*' I doubt it was the first time he'd been called on to do, rather than promise, for the cause; he quivered like a jelly."

"Alsander saw the ring," said Evimenes. "Was it not he who said as soon as the archers left to seek their more authority: 'Lord, if you have no wine, may I at least crave water?' and going with one of the young writers to fetch it, returned with the stain washed from his hair, so the star of our birth stood visible?

" 'Carrhoene!' says our fat friend, looking at him, with teeth knocking together like those bones the Dzik dancing-girls use; then looks from one to the other of us, taking a count. 'Lord, your joy to see us is well dissembled,' says Alsander.

" 'As would yours be in my place,' says he. 'Dear Heaven, witness! I that am senior Syndic of Lectis Minima would give up fortune to be made junior 'prentice, for we in this town are like to have, not Vulking Allies, but Vulking tercias, in a mood full wild, before the moon has changed her form. And now with you here—with you here—'

"He began to bubble and shake, no sense out of him, the which Alsander quieted a trifle by assurance that all we desired was food and leave to depart, but his manner smelled of tidings, which we sought. A true carle, this Rodvald, for all the fears that made him gnaw his knuckles. He helped us well with food, and great his tidings were, to wit: when Os Erigu burned, all that camp on the shore opposite was racked and overrun by a monstrous outburst of trolls, hobgoblins, and other uneasy things that had been laid away among its stones and beams by old Earl Mikal, that builded the place, who was lover to some witchwife queen that I forget the name on. The laboring carles in their camp ran away, in spite of the sword; all was confusion. Some say Bordvin Wildfang the Marshal was eat up of trolls as he tried to stay the rout by spells, some that he was slain by the Count Vulk himself when that one went mad with fear—or by Sthenophon the Permandene. The only thing sure is that the great Marshal's dead as last year's stockfish, the barons of the northern cities are all called in with their terciaries, the rocks shake as they wrangle with each other to the fall of all. Live Dalarna! Live Carrhoene!"

33. The Coast of Skogalang:
Fourth Tale of the Well

THEY ALL BECAME A LITTLE DRUNKEN AF-
ter that, but dawn and cold reflection brought not
only another ship, a cog down from Lectis, the old
city, to join them, but also the thought that the
Vulkings had feuded before and their realm not died
of it, whenas a certain way to make these enemies
put by their mutual quarrels was to present them
with a trouble from without against which their fac-
tions might unite. The plan was still to winter in
Skogalang; all the next day was spent in loading
provisions to the greater ships from the galley and
burning the latter. The vessel of Lectis had brought
some reinforcement and Airar knew their leader for
that golden-haired junior who had sat with him at

318

the table of The Old Sword in Naaros long ago; his name was Oddel, Kevilson.

On the day beyond they sailed—down toward the coast of Shalland. Behind fell the rough capes of Norby where they jut to the sea, and each night the argosy hauled in toward shore, but without winning more tidings. The low shores of Shalland were left behind, they passed Vällingsveden's muddy run on a day when it blew storm. A wearisome journey; as might be expected, Alvar's son sought oftenest the company of Meliboë or of the Stassian sisters, but the latter were not easy to separate from their brother, who on the ship seemed to come forth like a butterfly under sun, all airs as though he were commander. Nor was the enchanter of much avail; answered kindly enough when spoken to, but deep in some concern of his own. If Airar stayed waking late, there would not seldom be seen through the wizard's doorcrack the streaks of parti-colored light, or heard the sharp susurrus which told that spells were made. Once and again, as they lay over in the evening, the older man appeared in the last light and bent a tiny bow with a string made from his own garment against some bird that sought harborage in the rigging. Airar knew of the enchantment; would make the bird a gossip and familiar. Yet none came more than once to the ship, and he could only guess that there might be magics at work against Meliboë's own—as they voyaged down to where the dark wintry rims of Skogalang rose from the shore eastward.

Now as Skogalang comes rolling to the sea under its fur of forest, the coast-towns are these: Diupaa; Bramsos, that is called by the Vulkings, Vervilla, since they have a watch castle on the cape that stands forth there; Smarnaravida; and The Heyr. None are great and only the second has walls, for the men of Skogalang love no cities. Yet it was considered—Rogai protesting that it made them outlaws in their own land—unwise to run in on any but the first and the last. The Carrhoenes kept close aboard at Diupaa; Rogai went in to find some of the Iron Ring and send word through the woods to Sir Ludomir Ludomirson that he should rendezvous with them at The Heyr.

The knight was punctual to that rendezvous, coming to the ships on a grey day when bits of ice tinkled among the ropes, and the wind blew cold. Inshore the dark forest came down in waves to the water's edge, pine and black branches mingled; of the town round its wide bay there was nothing visible but a few houses whose builders had desired a sea view, it being the custom of Skogalang that trees grow into the very streets. Out westerly a line of foam broke on the harbor bar, and Sir Ludomir came over the rail hugging fur about him. His greeting was a hand-touch only before he stepped toward the bowels of the ship, where mulled wine and a fire on the round-stone waited. At this moment who should come forth from the forward cabin but mincing Aurareus with one of his bully-boys. (The other Airar had not seen since the fire; suspected Pleiander of having knifed him in that tumult, but had forborne to ask.) The knight looked; fell on one knee, doffed cap, and took the hand to kiss which Aurareus loftily extended.

"My Prince and very gracious lord."

"You have our favor."

Now as they sat before the roundstone Meliboë came in. Sir Ludomir took to his feet: "What's here?" said he. "Sirs, do you admit to your secret councils the dastard of Well and Empire, who touches the unbearable thing? Small wonder your proceedings have fared but ill."

Meliboë sat down without a word, but Alsander spoke for all. "Ill you may call our doings, sir, but there are some of us, and I one, who would say that mauger the castle's loss, the whole mad Vulking rule racks toward ruin after this siege."

"Would you have us throw off those who stood with us when hope was dead?" chimed Rogai, and this was so much Airar's own thought that he could add nothing to it.

"I do not know on that. But of one thing I am very sure—that you will never be able to accomplish high purpose with the help of demons and devils, for these things the Vulkings do use, and we are against them. How shall magics maintain their mastery if they labor one against another? Nay, there's one end to all gramary, and that is to increase the profit of the men of Briella."

Said Meliboë: "Sir, I know you will not hear me, but for these others I do declare that it is the nature of all things beyond the world never to agree; and hold it no crime nor sin to increase their contentions, the more since all this rule against which we toil is centered in witchery. What!—it was very witchery that brought down Bordvin Wildfang, the great warrior and wizard."

It seemed to Airar that he could recall a day when this magician had left Briella because they would not let him practice the philosophies he now condemned; but he said nothing, for Sir Ludomir had extended a long delicate hand:

"Sir Meliboë, you are a very good sophister; oh, you will make black white. Yet the laws of the Well forbid the practice of your art save in protection, which you will never consent to do as a limit; and the stay of all these lands is the House, and of the House, the Well."

"The Well!" Airar could not restrain himself from exclaiming, who had come to doubt of that great wonder from Argyra's saying; and it must be that he put his doubts into his tone, for Sir Ludomir turned on him like the pivot of a catapult.

"Young sir, I am told that you are become a notable and cunning warrior since last we met, when you were no more than this traitor magician's message-bearer; and great may be your luck. But that luck will decay, I say, unless you have respect to the Well and the rule of the Well that is the world's mainstay, for even the savage beasts pay heed to it.

"Hark you, young sir: my hair is mostly grey, but till it snows and the snow melts, I shall not forget the day when I went thither with our Emperor that is, His Majesty Auraris, for the drinking of his bridal with the Knight of Bremmery's daughter that should sweep away all sins and pasts from them both. He was not a young man then; we must wait by the way in a beechen wood, and it was spring. A she-wolf came out of a thicket to snarl at us. It was marked that she had a bobbed tail and a crop ear and two cubs behind her as we presently saw, but when our lord would have had her taken, his bride said; 'Sweet prince, by whom I shall soon lie in wedded affection, let one woman plead for another, and give me her life.'

"Therefore His Majesty Auraris did no less; he, an Emperor from the golden throne of Stassia, spared the life of the she-wolf. We continued our path; the wolf followed, I do not know whether for curiosity or her own love of our lord, with her cubs trotting behind. Since it was the order to spare, there were those of the train who left for her a bone or a scrap of meat. At the gate of the Well all paused but His Majesty and His Majesty's lady, but we saw the she-wolf scramble among the rocky slopes to follow round, as though she would not be parted from them. When His Majesty came forth later with his bride, their eyes no less than shining for peace and joy, she told us of a wonder; how as they pledged each other in the marvellous cup, the she-wolf had slipped past to the well edge and lapped from the spring, then lifted her muzzle to cry before those lovers Imperial as in salute.

"Sirs, I do assure you that same wolf was later seen by hunters near the region of the Well, who knew her by signs indisputable, to wit: the bob tail, the crop ear, and the twin cubs. Sirs, it was a moon or more later that same spring; they saw this wolf run a deer, and the venison caught by its horns in a thicket. But when she reached the deer it turned its head, and that wild wolf, in spite of being thin with hunger and the young cubs beside her, did give a cry as remembering the peace put upon her by the Well, so slunk away and let the hunters take her meekly. Yet you, young sir, who could have to our aid against the Vulkings the wonders of this wonder that can so work on the savage beasts, you would reject this all to consort with this common herb-brewer."

"Sir—" began Airar, hardly knowing what would come after the one word, and from the side of his eye seeing Meliboë's lip twist to laughter amid his straggle-beard. But before more:

"By God!" said the lord of Os Erigu and his fist banged down as he stood up. "By God! Men keep close from tidings in Skogalang. Reverence for your principles, sir councillor, but for your knowledge, none. Did you not know, indeed, that it is precisely against this rotten House we war, that sells its daughters to Briella's bed and sends its androgyne rat of an heir to be a Vulking spy?"

Sir Ludomir looked like a man who had been struck across the face. "Sir Earl, I am your guest and my knightly duty forbids me to challenge you here, but if you will come to land I may say words that will not be wiped out but in blood; to wit, I would say that you lie."

Said Airar to tall Erb: "My honor to the Princess Argyra, and will she join us here for a little space? You must say that Sir Ludomir Ludomirson is here."

For a brief moment there was no word in the cabin, as Sir Ludomir shivered and pulled at his fur. A light step and she came; the old knight knelt. "Rise," said she, "and sit. I am glad to see my father's councillor. Does all march well with you?"

"Well enough, since I have met your eye. But they do tell me of Stassia things incredible."

She smiled. "They are probably good truth. Was it that my sister was affianced to Count Vulk, and that I would have been taken by Sthenophon of Permandos, but for Lord Mikalegon and the sword of Master Airar?"

He caught breath. "Most gracious lady, I do not question you, but I am of the Council and this touches me nearly. Whose thought could that marriage bond be?"

She shrugged. "The Council's, at Vulk's own suit; the Scroby barons and Sons of the Well. My father— my father—"

"His Majesty is reverend with years and should have good advising from those he has maintained so long."

"There was an embassy with a hard-faced, red-haired man, Vanné, Vanness—"

"Vanette-Millepigue, the Red Baron of Naaros," said Rogai and said it with a snarl.

"I thank you. That would be it. I do not know all the ins and outs, Sir Ludomir, but only that my sister was so affianced, and Aurareus and I to accompany her."

The knight bowed, face working like that of a man who hears the thunders of a tilting world. "My duty, Madame. Lord Mikalegon, I offer you my touch and half of an apology. But upon this matter of the Prince of the House, I make none apology. It is the office we must serve, and should the man be mean, the more our high chivalric duty bids us uphold the place."

"May I withdraw?" said Argyra.

"Gracious lady, withdraw or stay as you will. Nothing in the counsels of its subjects is secret from the members of the House." But when she had gone, he turned a face of death: "A grave and terrible thing has been done here, and I cannot see to the bottom of it. Oh, for the wings of a hippogriff to fly beyond the sea and summon these false councillors who counsel to an Empire's fall."

Said Meliboë the enchanter: "Sir Ludomir, you will not believe my good will, but believe my information. When last I was called to Briella, this thing was already moot—the Count Vulk's plan, since it had reached his ear that the Imperial succession might fall into a female line from such an heir. The Marshal opposed, and not a few of the Vulking Council; you know the old custom of these folk, that they will never have honors hereditary. I know that the Baron Vanette-Millepigue was to be trained in the spells of asisdras and sobrathim that he might draw the Imperial council to his will, while for those who were Sons of the Well and immune to such magics, there was another enchantment, to wit: that of gold.

Such was the plan when last I learned it, but all would have been put aside for a time by the revolt of Mariupol and the war of Salmonessa."

"Why, this is treason most damnable," said Sir Ludomir, "though no more than was to be expected from Vulkings. Small wonder I was not summoned to Stassia when these things were in debate." He pulled a lip. "But I do marvel that the council delegates of the Twelve Cities sent us no warning. They were ever friendly to the Dalecarle kindred. Would they be taken in this baron's wizardous snares?"

Evadne barked a laugh: "Dog-smellers!" said she, and Evimenes: "Old sir, save for the Phyladeans who hate us and Dalarna, too, the Dodekapolis marches no longer in the council of the Empire. They are under this People's Party, that will own duties to the Well, but none to the House."

"Ha, is it so? The mists clear a little, but only toward the past. What's to do? You leave me terraced to the ground, in a world unknown."

"Sir," said Alsander, "it was our thought to winter here in Skogalang, while you and Master Rogai through your Iron Ring seek tidings of how passes the feud of the Vulkings in the north. We plan for no longer, since we are somewhat disagreed, and all hangs by the circumstances of our foes. But we brothers are still persuaded that we shall do down these men of the Mountain till we beat them in a battle, and for that, there's no hope but in our armored riders of the Twelve Cities. We brethren say then—raise what force we can here, but not to fight here. Come to Carrhoene; many from the Dalecarle factory there will join, set us free from dog-smeller rule, and we're your own men for this great campaign in the north."

"A fair offer," said Sir Ludomir, "but what's the price? Who pays your riders?"

"I did not mention price. This is alliance," said Alsander, but he colored under his dark skin, and the knight turned to Rogai:

"Your word also?"

"By no means, now. Rouse the forest-masters of

Skogalang. We shall have the castellas of the whole province before they're ware the wolf is running. Slip northeastward, rouse the Whiteriverdales, cut all the passes southward, draw in force from Vastmanstad, and make our own war in the woods as King Argimenes did in the silver years."

"Being not unhelped by soldiery from the Lacias. We do not fight rash heathen now; without troops regular it will be less than easy to counter these hard Vulkings that make a life of war," said Sir Ludomir. "I do find these plans infect with day-dream. Has any a sounder thought?—But halt here; I perceive these are the bones of schemes already picked clean, and so far nothing's lost. Is it still your fixed determination to plot for the ears of this magic-man that has already betrayed two former masters?"

Silence. Then Airar said: "For my part, it is."

"I will stand with the young master," growled Mikalegon, and Rogai: "And I."

"Then someone must yield, and for concord, 'twill be myself, though I fear this will end ill." He made the sign of religion and shivered lightly as though the chill gust from without had stirred his bones.

Now Meliboë lifted his head, who had sat looking down, modest as a milkmaid since his first speech. "You do no wrong, sir knight," said he. "For I know the thought that is at the back of your own mind without hearing a word about it, so that to exclude me would have gained you nothing but the ill will of many. It is that all here do but peck and tickle round the heart of the whole matter, the said heart being the tie that would bind the House to Vulk, make it an Empire of Vulk. Ah, if that succeeds, all's sped with you; he would maybe poison the very Well, as he has already poisoned lives by closing the lyceums, taxing out the free farmers of Vastmanstad, setting slaves to curb the wool-staple of Mariupol. You have right, sir knight: whatever else is done, you must go to Stassia instanter, seek a full council, put down those bewitched and bribed, cancel the contract of this iniquitous marriage. But you have also wrong: if the war-spirit of these young

Dalecarle masters be broke, all's lost. It will then be no distant day when the armies of the red triangle march in the High House of the Empire. For your war-plan you must look to Master Airar; I have taken his divination and you will surely never find another so lucky in all he does by the sword."

Sir Ludomir hawk-shadowed his eyes: "Hand clips marvellous close to hand, it seems—but have you a war-plan then, young sir?"

"Nay, sir," said Airar, flushing, "nor can have. Do we not know too little for true planning? But this I know: that after we burned the Permandenes at Bear Fjord, our enemies could not move by sea. We could make a new Os Erigu in the Isles of Gentebbi, from whence move south to Carrhoene, west to Stassia, north to Dalarna, as occasion serves."

All now approved this plan after little more discussion, save that when Erb said Marshal Bordvin would have sadly eaten out those islands, the vote was still for Skogalang till spring. One ship should take Sir Ludomir across the Blue Sea; and so they rose, with Meliboë touching Airar's arm for a word as they left. "Hark, young master," said he, when occasion came; "I know better than you that your plan's no plan—a lip-answer to keep clap-jaw quiet till time's womb gives birth. It was well done; but fear Gentebbi."

Of this saying Airar could make nothing, nor Argyra neither, when he told her of it as they sat by a fire drinking cider amid the smell of roasting chestnuts in one of the forest houses of Skogalang. Aurea had gone forth that day with Alsander of Carrhoene who, under pretext of being her warder, had made himself in some sort her squire—in this winter weather, where there was so little to do but run the red deer and wait for news from the north. Said the silver princess:

"Lucky Master Airar, to be for your own self a befriended man. At the High House, when they will still speak friendship, we learn to look at what's desired."

"It may be the case here also, though what have I to give? But little."

"Oh, nay, not little. You are more than you think on; a strong head in council, says Sir Ludomir, and a good blade in the field, as I have cause to thank you for against Sthenophon. It may be earlier than you know that you will have to give what this wizard would most desire. But before that you will learn, as we do at the court, that friendship ever clashes with friendship, desire with desire, and to give one is to refuse another."

"And love? Is that a gift?" said he.

"We were not to speak of that for now."

"What else shall I speak of when I am with you?"

"There's no need you be with me. Go, speak to your enchanter friend that can make divinations, protect you against the unseen powers, master the laughing fear. He may even tell you what the doom is that lies on Gentebbi."

She was in a bad mood for the moment, he told himself. It would pass—or had she caught some hint of his dealings with Gython among the isles?

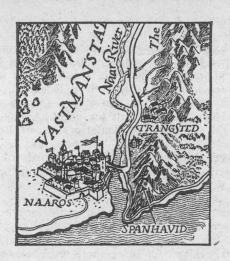

34. Return from Sea

So THIS WINTER SLID PAST IN THE ATTENT
for tidings. From the north, they were sparse; only
of a great force of Vulkings come to quarter in the
larger Lectis, with brawlings on the question—who's
to be Marshal now? The Korosh miners were hungry,
all the towns from which they drew their victual being in Vulking hands, and it was said many of
them ate beastly things among the Mictons. Black
Gallil of Vastmanstad sent through that the Baron
Vanette-Millepigue had marched north along the
great road of the Naar with six deese of his tercia
about the Moon of the Stork, which would be close to
the day when their flotilla reached The Heyr. It could
be believed that he stood competitor for the vacant
marshalate.

The Skogalang folk were kind; they live well concealed in their woodlands, trusting for their diet to

fruits, nuts, and the famous fat pigs that feed on the latter, and this being not the kind of country from which a Vulking can draw much profit, these people had been less oppressed than most of Dalarna. Yet they were of the true kindred, and a cheek would blench or a hand clench at Rogai's tale of the doings in Mariupol, so that not a few came down to The Heyr, as they said, for guesting, but truly to follow the standard of Dalarna's war. Woodsmen all, who could shoot with the bow and never miss the target; there were four full shiploads of fighting men together when spring turned so warm that snow-runners would no longer run.

No word from Sir Ludomir Ludomirson at this hour, and the ship he sailed with unreturned, so there were not four ships to carry the four shiploads of men, and many must use the small fishing vessels of The Heyr. Of these there were few, since the people of Skogalang depended chiefly on Gentebbi for their sea-meat; but what they had, they gave willingly. It was a somewhat strange armada for war, since there must be space for women, the bright princess and the dark, and Aurareus that was half a woman, with attendants for the first two. Certain Skogalang damsels were with them; a fever of wiving had run through Airar's band the winter, and even Carrhoene sergeants had fallen on affections with the woods-girls and would never leave them; while, of the dancers that had served Os Erigu's pleasure, many sought permission to rest in Skogalang. Aurea the princess said it was an example of how unlike is drawn to unlike; but Meliboë, that this drawing was only that of life without labors familiar, and the two-thirds of these alliances would melt beneath the summer's sun—at which Aurea grew much angered, and would not speak with the philosopher for a pair of days.

They sailed, then, with the break of spring, a fine day, when old pine-needles looked worn and there were little white clouds in a blue sky as they rounded Shäta Cape, with its nipple of rock at the tip. Toward evening the clouds increased in weight, a sea-

wind came up, and the ships began to labor. It
had been ill to work against it, but they were now
past the broad promontories that guard outer Skogalang, and could give themselves to run before this
rising gust. Yet as it held, a very damned trouble
arose, namely that all their flotilla was being swept
eastward toward Naarmouth, and could by no means
point into the ever more southering wind to gain
Gentebbi. Lank Erb's face grew long; they swung
in toward the other tall ship and held brief converse
by shouts under the falling light of evening, but the
best counsel that could be taken for the night was
to let down all sail on the larger craft, so they might
drift backward, with their high poops to catch the
wind like weathervanes, and the small fishing craft
lashed in line out beyond, as it were to make a long
rudder, at the same time gaining some protection for
themselves. The said task was much laborious; one
of the shipmen asked Meliboë if he did not possess
a spell to make the weather abate, to which the enchanter replied that if he could do that, he would
not be magician but a god.

A night of little pleasure and less sleep, in which
no peace from wind, nor did the dawning day bring
cheer. Off leftward, the other ship reared and rocked
with her string of fishing vessels trailing. One of
the latter had lost its mast, there was a hole in its
bulwarks, and they seemed to have distresses aboard.
Off rightward and a little astern the lead-grey water
was being thrown up again in clouds of spray, with
a booming sound. Airar clung to the rail to watch
it; one of the free-fishers laughed grimly:

"Good luck, young master, we did not just turn
on this wind more southerly. The embrace of they
white maidens be death; a are the Naarmouth skerries."

Fortune's favor indeed to save them from such
shipwreck; but they could have done with more
kindness of the sort, for all that day the ships and
shallops drifted and the waves battering them. *Dragg*'s
seams began to give; all who could stand upright were
set to pump or with buckets to bail. Out on one of

the fishing craft they saw a man washed over and swept down the tossing waves with a thin cry, nor could any aid him, and the flung rope fell short.

Airar had by now seen peril enough to be peril's familiar, yet he found himself resentful of this danger as unreasonable, not brought on by desire or honest exposure to hazard, but by merest chance. Through most of a second night without rest his anger rose till it came on him that here was a question for Doctor Meliboë, but that one was lying crippled with the unease of the sea, so the succeeding thought rose in him, why should the enchanter do more than himself to resolve his difficulty? But no time now for thought, with the cold seas sliding down the waist of the ship, the men to encourage at bails and pumps under fitful lantern-light, the wind flying past.

Toward day, everyone hollow-eyed and hungry (for it had not been possible to keep fire on the roundstone against such motion), the ship began to heave less easily than ever. Airar voiced trouble to a haggard Erb, but the tall man said no; the sign was in fact good, it meant that they stood in the cross-chop brought about by the outflowing of the river Naar and might find shelter within his western cape, though that were indifferently long. Daydawn made him a good prophet, a whiter dawn than the two before, with clouds more torn and wind less frantic. Soon, far on the northern rim and dwarfed blue with distance, could be seen the unmistakable shape of Spanhävid mountain. It would seem the wind had seen it too, and would abandon them as beyond its power, for with that sight it spun round still more to the south of west and fell sharply in force. Within the hour Erb said they should try getting up a piece of sail, the which done, *Dragg*—answering her helm somewhat sluggishly because of the tow of fisherboats—became a ship again, moving round out of danger of drifting leeward onto the rocks that lie at the foot of Spanhävid peak. Earl Mikalegon on the other ship was a good seaman; had been trying even earlier to hang out canvas, though with trouble because of a broken mast. Now it was done and the twain craft drew near enough together for more talking. To all questions there was but one answer: they must sail straight up Naar River and take their chances at contact with the Vulking guards of Naaros city, for the wind had come dead foul for Gentebbi, and with *Dragg* leaking, the fisher-craft so battered, it was madness to attempt the passage.

Ho for up river, then. The Skogalang boats cast loose and put up their own little sails so soon as the outrush of Naar quieted a little the heave of the sea. At this time one could make out clearly Naaros citadel on its rock; the two princesses came a-deck, Argyra to praise all for having overcome the danger of the voyage, but Aurea asking might she have somewhat warm to eat. She feared a flux of the bowels from the intake of cold food.

They made decent progress, the current being truly not so much against as across their path, for Naar turns his race westerly at the outlet to avoid the front of the mountain; but now the question of what advice to take became troublesome indeed. The Spanhävid flank of Naarmouth is rocky and fierce, the opposite shore holds few beaches short of Naaros city. Words passed from poop to poop; they made for the quieter water by the shore, took down sails behind a screen of trees there, and were making a decision when all doubts were solved from outside by the appearance of a guard-boat, crawling like a waterbug down Naarmouth, with a red triangle aloft at her stern.

On the tall ships the catapults had been badly handled by the storm, and where they had not, the cords were wetted and useless, but this did not apply to the bow-shooters of Skogalang, who keep their tools in cases and care for them not much more than a mother for her child. These made ready under cover of the bulwarks; everyone else was ordered down out of sight to leave an impression of peaceful visitors.

All this hastily done, quick agreement among the leaders in few words as the Vulking waterbug came in from mere visibility to close sight. Had their leader been a man of thought and thoughts, he had wondered to see two tall ships in association with so many fisher-boats, but there were not above twenty Vulkings in the guard-ship, and under the tight rule of Briella a leader of twenty thinks little. On they came, unsuspecting, till Mikalegon leaped up and roared the word; they tried to turn or raise shields, but the arrow-storm caught them all but a few and these fell into as evil a case when the free-fishers leaped up and ran aboard them with spear and short-sword to slay mercilessly all that were left.

Thus the leaders had a victory behind them when they met on the poop of *Dragg* to counsel again, with a torn red evening sky falling away west into promise of better clime tomorrow. Few were the words spoken at first, and those mostly by shipmen —Mikalegon, Erb, the masters of the Skogalang smacks. All said the same thing—voyage to Gentebbi flat impossible, even if the wind would serve. New masts were needed, careening to fix the one ship's leaks, the fishing craft—

"In fine, you'd say we must go up to Vulking-held Naaros and give up our bodies to save our lives," cried hot Pleiander, when these had spoken. "I smell a stink of cowardice!"

Mikalegon growled and reached for a blade, but up stood Airar, straight as a spear. "Call it what name you will and I'll not quarrel—in union's name, for when we want quarrels with you, Master Star-Captain, we'll have heavier debates than this one word. Call it coward; the Earl has merely said we cannot sail. Can we not diddle them as we did those at Lectis Minima, if we are brisk enough?"

Pleiander: "Brisk indeed that must needs be. How of their missing guard-ship? By the Well, I marvel how you northerners have yet to learn that war is death, bloodshed, destruction. What did we swear at old piebald-beard's drinking?"

"It was something about the High House of Car-rhoene, but how does that matter here?" said Rogai. "Do you propose sailing thither still? You have called me rash, but here's rashness redoubled, when you cannot sail to Gentebbi, to propose the longer journey."

"Master Rogai," said Airar, "may I say a word? I give you grace, Master Pleiander—have you another plan than for us to go to Naaros in some cozening manner, as for assistance?"

"That I have, and one a thousand times better. The night falls; they'll not want their guard-ship back till late. Let us all go by road and shore; attack the town, take it by storm. Our ship has a broken mast; we'll batter in the gates."

Earl Mikalegon pulled his beard and muttered. "It is true; cozening's a woman's remedy." Said Alsander thoughtfully: "We slew a deese when we were barely sixty; there cannot be more than four deese in this town, and we're above four hundred."

Rogai's expression changed; Evimenes snapped his fingers. "Surprise by night our aid."

Said Airar: "Why, then, good friends, good gentles, are we not nearly all of one mind that this is an acceptable hour of daring, since nothing else will serve?"

"By God, yes," said Mikalegon.

Airar: "Master Pleiander, confess this is not the word of cowardice."

The Carrhoene shook his head, but touched hands, and the lines round his mouth twitched. They rose; the need was now for haste, and in spite of the fatigue of the storm few were found that felt any weariness, as the word was spread. Men snatched a piece of cold meat, looked to their weapons, and hurriedly came to the shore. There was competition to avoid staying with the ships, and Airar must name a captain of the rear-guard. He told off Erb, who took this ill.

They landed across the rocks of the inlet that held them and with trouble lugged the broken mast through the screen of trees that hid the shore road running from Naaros out into Skogalang. The wind on the water had been accompanied by rain on the land and there was mud, not easy going. The order of the march was that the mast went in the center with torches, the Skogalang men carrying it; bows were no good at night. Airar's fisher-spearmen mingled with the heavy-armed Carrhoenes, who walked like walking lobsters in their mail. Tramp, tramp in the dark, and Airar with the advance, it seemed to him that enthusiasm burned down somewhat and weariness rose on that long, clumsy journey. But all flared up once more when they came round a turn of grove into bowshot space before the city walls, with the citadel on its rock at one side and the southeast city gate before. There were lights in the citadel; wall and gate were dark, but they did not forever stay so as the black tide of men flowed across the road toward the city's inlet, for someone at the wall's foot raised a cry and someone atop it a shout of "What's here?"

Bordvin's ghost come for the Red Baron!" yelled Rogai, the attackers raised a shout, and the men with the mast rushed forward. There was a light grillade at the outer portal. Down it went with a clang and they stormed into the gate-passage in a tumult of sound, a high voice above crying for torches, the watch, spears and bows. Black as a pocket inside, but there were shot-windows among the flanks, where Airar stationed spearmen to jab in should light show behind or any attempt be made to use those fenestrations.

The men with the mast crowded panting past. "Heave!" shouted Pleiander and it struck the gate, thump. "Heave!"

In the dark the timber was withdrawn and again thrown forward, shivering to splinters at the butt, but though the great doors groaned they held, and a man or two went down from the shock. Behind now were confused cries, the Vulking war-shout "A pax!" rising somewhere and the thud of a thrown stone from above.

"Together—put your shoulders to it!" Pleiander screamed, his voice echoing in the passage. "Were you suckled by rabbits? *Heave!*" The mast came forward again, crash, and though this time doors and bars still held, the hinges did not; tore out with a shriek of rent wood, the gate hung dangling, all the Dalecarles and free companions and Carrhoenes tumbled and stumbled through into an inner darkness of space and sky from the passage darkness of surroundings tone.

Airar was one of the earliest, but before he could get his sword free a bold man attacked him from the right with an underhanded thrust. He tried to spin and took a light cut on the leg; it was no deeper because Mikalegon of Os Erigu rose behind him with a great battle-axe that dropped on the arm of the foeman, shearing it off quick as a wink to let a stream of blood gush forth. "Look not so on it," said the Earl; "it is off, right enough." Airar saw the fellow fall down as he went past, crying the Ullu!" of Dalarna in battle.

At their left there were stairs to the wall-head; it would be Pleiander who thought of them and led his armored sergeants to gain the gate-towers. The more part of the in-takers followed Airar and Rogai and Mikalegon and Oddel into the streets, and now there was one brief clash of arms, and another, for the Vulking archer-watch gathered toward the tumult. But they were too few and too unready to deal with full-armed men, down they went like pegs before pigs, and the banners of cat and otter and sea-eagle were borne forward along streets where shutters banged open and people shouted "Ullu!" for "Ullu!"

"To the central square!" said Rogai, and "Where do you think I go?" Airar. There stands the statue of King Argimenes with the old sword lifted from under the plough. At this place lights and people began to flow in, half unbelieving that Dalecarle revolters were in the town, curious that this might be some trick of the red triangle. A fire was lighted; when men saw by the banners that trick there was none, they began to come out in earnest, some with hidden, forbidden weapons, to caper round the blaze, handshaking with strangers, singing warsongs almost forgot:

Marching along, we are singing this song,
With the wolf of Dalarna we're marching along;
Our God is our leader, the heathen have wrong,
As they learn when the Dalecarles come marching
    along!

Strong and strange things were done that night in
Naaros: doors beaten in, Vulking Allies pulled from
bed and their goods strewn in the street, themselves
whipped or worse; and Airar had much to do, since
Mikalegon and Rogai were like a pair of wild men,
and the Carrhoene captains not much better. Pleiander calmed enough to think of the citadel yet un-
taken on its peak of hill; gathered a group of sober
sergeants with some people of the town to stand at
the stockade which shut citadel from city in the normal days, but now city from the Vulking hold. A
messenger went to seek Black Gallil; another to bring
the ships with the women to the quays, strictly warning that none of them should yet land. In the morning's first gleam Airar of Trangsted found himself
sitting in judgment at the foot of King Argimenes'
statue, certain burghers of the Ring as his aids. It
had been so appointed when he said "Nay!" and
called his men to back him, when angry cits would
have hanged a man from the bronze figure's very
form, as being a Vulking-bought traitor.

Against the cold and weariness a dram of schnub-
liquor had been thrust in his hand. "The next," he'd
say.

"Here's Lavén Long-tongue, Havaldson, a Vulking
Ally at the causeway battle when Salmoness' was
overthrown."

"Who calls him Ally?"

"I."

A burgher touched Airar's shoulder "It is his wife's
brother who speaks, and this Lavén's an ill-wed
man."

"I judge that Lavén shall be held for two days to
be judged in a court regular before witnesses."

"I'll bear witness here and now," cried the ac-
cuser.

Airar: "And by what token? Were you, too, with the Allies in that field?" Then there would be a hoot from the onlookers, Lavén led away and another thrust forward, a very Vulking by his black look, who squealed in his own case that he had Vulking blood, but was Morarday, a simple wool merchant of Mariupol, come on lawful business.

"No wool merchant at all, but a spy," cried one. "But he has bought at a fair price," another, and the matter seemed insoluble, but that Rogai peered at him in the flickering light.

"Ha, ha, I have seen you before, my friend," he said. "You were captain and deserion to the Viscount Isclé; were at the murders of Mariupol and later in the house of Madame Slitgullet there, which you left without doublet or badges, which still I have." He drank. "A toast to your neck, which you will not have long. Master Airar, this is a Vulking of the war service, a palpable spy. I bear witness."

"Head him, then," said Airar shortly, as the man began to shriek that he had but acted under orders and not of his own free will, screaming for a priest to give him the consolation of heaven.

Rogai said something through a laughing lip; Airar thought he might have caught a glimpse of one of the sons of Viclid in the press and wondered what that old neighbor who would think to see him sitting there, but no time now, two men more were being driven forward with a prodding of points. But when he turned to them the childe of Trangsted caught breath and the weight of three nights of sleepless struggle fell on him; for through the mist of eyes he looked on Alvar Airarson of Trangsted, his own father that had given him birth and upbringing, with Tholo, of the same parentage.

Airar stood; it would be the schnub-liquor that made him sway, the wound in his leg was stiff, and he saw in the waxing light how he was all one draggle of mud and blood.

"Now will I judge no more today," said he, "for these are kinsmen of mine, and no man judges kinsmen well. Is there a bed in Naaros?"

35. Naaros: "I Am Free"

"I HAVE TRIED TO BE A GOOD FATHER TO you, Airar," said the old man. "It would be a grave sorrow to your mother to see you like this."

His aspect was woe-begone, beard scraggy, a smaller and more whitened man than Airar's memory-picture; now with torn clothes. Yet the manner of speaking unchanged; a minute and Airar realized half-angrily that the thrill running through him was a shiver of fear for a clout beside the ear. He ground out:

"I do not see that my case is so very evil. Had it been otherwise, your own were not so good but now."

Alvar Airarson laid out a wizened hand, where bones and high veins fought to make a mountain system. "My son, my son, you are still too young to

340

see. You thought it unwise of me to give up the stead; yet now look where the clinging to it has brought you—to be an outlaw and a wolf's head, in open battle with our good Count, and under the Empire's ban I do not know that even Leonce Fabrizius, who has so much influence in Briella, can have you pardoned."

"I'll take no pardon from him or any other. We are to throw down Fabrizius and all his kind—aye, and your good Count that lets murder children in his name."

The old man sighed, as one given a burden too heavy to be borne. "Airar, believe me, you should seek a priest, or, it might be, take the peace of a house of religion for a space. Do you not know that all these tales of murderings are lies spread by the evil men with whom you have fallen in—those who would break the peace of the Well, as the companions of Os Erigu, who are but thieves with sword in hand; and the rebel Carrhoenes, that would restore in their own cities the old bad ways of life where a few had all power and benefits, no security against their exactions?"

Airar could but sniff. "Sir," said he, "it does not seem to me that under Vulk all are exactly as free as might be."

"Those are free who do not resist the wave that will heal all our tomorrows. Others are traitors still, to race and fellow man. O Airar, my son, let me persuade you. I have fallen out with friends and have lost much to the edge of death; but it has been for you—to make you a place in the new world where Vulking and Dalecarle are one. Fail me not now; my hope has been set on you since you were so young."

On Airar's thought fell black despair. Briella! And there was much to do. He looked around the little stone-floored room. "Sir, you are my father, ever dear to me as to my mother. I'll call on you again. A guard stands by the door to keep you safe."

"And hold me within," said the old man, spreading his hands.

No more of that for now; Black Gallil was come, looking glum, and the leaders must meet, of whom Pleiander in high humor, since his leadership in the taking of Naaros was a thing to ring through the world beside the famous ambush of Poliolis, that had given the five Star-Captains much of their renown. Alsander was more questioning, careful; when Gallil said their feat exposed the town to certain danger, he nodded his head.

"Aye; but here's hot war and we shall freeze to death with mere precautions. Let us have no regrets, but speak on what we are to do."

"By my word," said Pleiander, never hesitant, "you shall call up all the local levies and bid the world defiance. We have the sea and the monies of a commercial town. With their aid—"

"Touching which," said Evimenes, "we brothers have been good companions without pressing a word of the agreement that brought us to these northern lands. But now you Dalecarles will have a full treasury from the confiscation of your disagreers, and I say fair and forward that it's time to talk of pay."

Eyes swung to Alsander, who averted his own but did not deny. Said Rogai: "I say nay—not to your claim of payment, Master Evimenes, for I helped make that treaty myself and will see it honored, never fear. But there's more urgent matter now, the detail of our war; and I say nay to standing any attack here. We'd be borne down in the long. I say rouse the Iron Ring—all Skogalang, Hestinga, the Whiteriverdales. It must be done some day, and we will have no fairer hour than when the main strength of our enemies is pinned in the north. We'll be helped by Sir Ludomir as well from oversea."

Lank Erb coughed for attention: "Masters, I be no deep war-thinker, but I just say we go to Gentebbi, like a said foretime. Where's force for us, in town or field, against all they tercias?"

Dark Gallil: "Sir, whose name I do not know, you have said most truly. We are not many; might make a fight of it among the woods of Skogalang or the heights of the Hogsback, but what of this brave city?

I fear me heads will rot on spikes at Naaros gate before we're free of what your rashness has brought upon us."

To this point Airar had listened, saying never a word. Now he would have spoken against this despairing counsel, but Os Erigu's lord burst forth: "Bah! Gabble-babble, chip-chop, and no counsel, as with you Dalecarles ever. Seldom have I seen men make less of their benefits. You have captured a great city, with many a heart and hand to help you keep it. Why, Os Erigu maintained a hundred years with less!" He blew his nose on two fingers. "And for why? Because my great-grandfather called a pest on councils and was chief in the castle, saving only the right of all free companions to withdraw. You need a duke, a leader, to give you the word of command; and I'm not the man my fathers were, so you can do no better than choose young Master Airar here, who may bring you something of Imperial aid, since he hangs sheep-eyed round that Princess what's-her-name."

"Oh, nay," began Airar for decency's sake, but Evadne of Carrhoene cut across this with: "In our country we have no single dukes, lest they make themselves tyrants, like Sthenophon. It is a wise rule that gives us all a voice in what concerns all, save when we yield to deeper knowledge, as to Pleiander in matters of siege."

"Aye, wise for Carrhoenes!" cried Rogai, sharply, and Airar marked him as of Mikalegon's advisement, but the Earl with a tale to tell forbore such quarrelsome manners. "Hark," he said, "I'll be quick and straight. A few minutes since, there was question of reward for Carrhoene blades in the service of Dalarna, and well enough; it was their treaty. But it seems to me that when hireling says how master shall do, then he makes himself tyrant, many heads or one. Is that not fairly so, old Bag-of-bones?"

Alsander nodded, somewhat poutingly. "You have right in certain ways, but—" and checked as Gallil held forth his hand for urgent speech.

"All you have said is stamped with right, and I

doubt not that Master Airar has made himself a high captain. Grant him sound purpose, grant his skill; but there's a nasty spot that will not disappear—to wit; that his father's a Vulking Ally. The Iron Ring will never have him. I give you instead Master Rogai."

Meliboë was sitting with them; Airar saw his eyes narrow to speech, but Rogai was quicker: "Nay, the Iron Ring will not have me, neither, for I'll be no duke. Airar's the luckiest of us all, the best leader, least caught in all contentions, and a clerk moreover. Now hear me: I do pledge my word to follow Airar Alvarson while this war shall last and as much longer as need be—for myself and the Ring of Mariola, saving Mariupol city, which is not in my delegation. Who follows?"

He laid his hands in Airar's, who felt his heart swell. "I'll pledge the same for Norby," said Oddel, and: "I for Gentebbi Isles, as far as can be," Erb. Gallil pledged, darting restless glances right and left, and Airar realized he was either jealous or feared a vengeance for that threat of torture long ago.

"I, that know little, must have a main deputy," he said, "for such matters as judgments and governments in the city and Vastmanstad, and therefore if you have me to be your leader, the first thing I will do is name Gallil for that." The man's face relaxed somewhat, and after all he was a good captain. Mugs and meads were sent for and they drank to the Ring and the pledge, while Airar explained what he could make of war-plan, bespeaking advice from all.

He was (he said) of Mikalegon's thought regarding Naaros city, that to give it up would throw all doubters to the Vulking side. "But siege? Sirs, we war to make Dalarna live, but to stand here is her death, for the town will be beat to pieces and many people hurt that are not hurt in battle. I'll have none warring but those who do it uncompelled."

"Well said," said Alsander, "to which I will add one thing more, that it is in the field of battle Briella's great, and there we must make her less. Master Airar?"

"As to that," says Airar, "I do not know today,

but when we come to the pinch, there is one thing I have marked ever since we went with Duke Roger to the causeway before Marskhaun, and that is how they set their battles in order, so that light-armed move with light-armed and heavy with heavy, all being Vulkings without other distinction. But we oppositious still march by provinces. If I'm to be leader, I'll have done with that, the more since we have good captains among us for every wing. So do I now name Rogai master of the bowmen, who shall be captain of all archers and light spearmen whatsoever, be they of Skogalang or Mariola, Gentebbi or Korsor. Evimenes shall lead the lancers, for I have seen him do it before; and your Carrhoene sergeants shall captain the companies under him. But as for you, my lord Earl, I count on you to conduct what heavy-armed foot we may raise, as spearmen and axemen."

"What of our brother Pleiander?" said Evimenes.

"Ah! There is a thought on that. Have you not marked how these Vulkings in the field, when they are menaced of riders, draw into tight knots like a fortress? I had thought we might loosen 'em out with bowshot, but do you not think, Sir Pleiander, that engines like those on walls could be builded, yet light enough to take the field and batter these fortresses of flesh?"

All now began to talk this way and that, wondering how So-and-So of Shalland, who was an axeman, would find it to be under Earl Mikalegon, the former enemy of his land, but mostly saying Airar had done well, till Gallil returned to his glooms with: "Very fine is this, and I can see Vulk the Unreasonable almost hanging from his own palace gate, but for one thing—where's this great host to come from that you lead so lightly to the wars?"

That checked them for a little and they began to reckon. Four hundred and more had come with the ships. Gallil thought they did not know too well the use of weapons. Vastmanstad province might get as many as four times such a number of first-class fighting men in Naaros city with the revolt pro-

claimed, and some more who did not know too well
the use of weapons. Vastmanstad province could furnish few, thanks to the strong farmers having been
taxed out; Mariola had been so raided by Iselé that
though the Iron Ring lived there it was in evil case.
Skogalang is little populous, but its forest-masters
live so much by weapons and hunting that every
man of them was worth double; the people of that
part said as many as thirteen hundreds could be had
with speed and more to come behind when the torch
was raised. Of Gentebbi none knew; their fisher-
craft had not visited Naaros at all the winter.

Agreed: that the tale of resources of people was
enough to deal surely with one tercia, perhaps with
two if their baron commanding were a fool on whom
some vantage of time or place could be secured. The
leaders looked at one another; finally Airar drew
from his mind the thought of taking what force they
could gather up the great north road into the Whiteriverdales. Ravines and narrow passages would make
it easier for the fewer there. That province must hear
the trumpet as well; would furnish a good few of
heavy-armed till they need no longer fear a second
tercia.

"What if they march on Naaros by the roundabout
through Marskhaun, Mariupol, and the southern coast
road?" asked someone.

"Hestinga will warn us."

"Nay," said Airar, and held them for a moment
while he sought to fix the thought that moiled in the
back of his head. "Hestinga must rise also, hazard
life and fortune with the rest. Alsander has right—
we must think always on battle, and I do not see
how we are ever to overcome these people without
a strong force horsed, for in heavy-armed afoot we
shall not be so many nor so well skilled as those
who spend their lives at it."

At this point Gallil said dryly that he had heard
most of this discussion before—at the Inn of The
Old Sword in this very city, a long time gone, when
this same thought of rousing the middle provinces

was rejected and for good reason—"a mistake then, no doubt."

Said Meliboë the enchanter dreamily, but loud enough to be heard: "You have hit it there, master, though meaning only bone-biting. When we make an error, the same problem's repeat, in this world or another, till solved correctly; and this is why so many events are like those that have passed. For God or the gods wish nations and men to reach their own high level, where all is rightly done. So now you of the Dalecarle cities must change the decision that led to the battle of the Red Hills, long ago, when merchant would not stand by peasant; and so the later error of not all rising when beckoned from Mariupol must be expiate. So do I, a Stassian, travail for having thought Vulk's rule meant forward. But as to who these gods be, I cannot tell you, nor—" and his voice trailed off in mumblings.

Through Airar's mind flashed the thought of Gython and Argyra. Rogai was saying no need now for hot haste in moving to the Dales, since it would take Vulk at Lectis Minima a good month to learn the tale of the fall of Naaros—"and cannot we make somewhat of this? I mean with those in Naaros citadel; build them a bridge of smiles, let them go free in a vessel to that Count with the word that we're but a band of quick freebooters, so he will come on us fast and with less force than he might, or per chance send us a little baron to be eat up?"

Meliboë doubted whether the Viscount that would be in command of the castle would be so gulled, but Airar thought the plan worth trying, nevertheless. They rose, the junior leaders to recruit, muster levies, count up arms, but Airar to wait on the Princess Argyra, whom he had not seen since leaving the ship.

Alsander was before him, talking to Aurea; she chat-chattering on how uncouth a man was Erb, till Airar moved in his place and wondered how any could hear such converse without discomfort. The dark-haired sister caught his unease and drew him from the fireside where the others were to a casement window overlooking a bright green tree with pink flowers; Naaros had lodged the two with dignity befitting the Imperial name. She was as eager to hear his tale as he glad to tell it, backward foremost, that he was now leader against Vulk and Sthenophon the spadarion, and he was clever enough not to fail mentioning the last. But as the story went on she grew more quiet, and at the last sat with both hands in her lap, sighing against the bright spring.

"Have I done wrong?" he asked.

"How can I tell? I only lingered a moment on the thought of the man you had the head from in the square, and there was no son to save him, though what had he done that your father did not do?"

"Would you have me send my kinsman to the block?"

He made to rise. She stopped him with a hand. "Nay, surely, you know I would not have it so. But it is a hard law that bears on one and not another; a Carrhoene law."

"I was brought up to know that under all law we owe a first duty to those that bore us," he said; and she: "Oh, aye, and where there's love, no laws are needed, for laws are made to hold men from deeds in which love has no part. Yet still I feel that it is somehow hard to end the life of a man who did but do his duty to his Count and State, as Alvar Airarson to his son."

"Why, as to that, my kinsman saw no penalty, but this Vulking knew well the chance of death that rode with what you call his duty," began Airar, and then stopped. "Argyra! I am free."

"I joy to hear it. From what and for what?"

"Briella! It will never be Briella; I can see it now and why my father has not right. You have put me on the track. Count and State—and what's their Count but a figure of the State? Oh, well to serve the general will of all, as the deserion said, but when Count and State sit, there's a third hand in the pot, and State is not a servant but a master; for its laws do say that none will uncompelled show love to his neighbor or be generous."

She lifted her hands to her face. "If I understand what you say, it may be you have right. The Well of the Unicorn is somewhat so, that was so great a joy and benefit to all when found, but is now become a thing worshipped for itself, without anyone thinking why it is desirable to have such a resource. Speak to my sister, she has more politic than I."

It was a command; he checked the words that rose to carry the question further and instead began to talk of a Vastmanstad spring and the dance around the hale-fires that lasted till dawn on the night of the sun's turning—"though it has been long since I saw them, since the priest of our ort was a Vulking, who held such festivities to be tinged with the heathenism of Dzik."

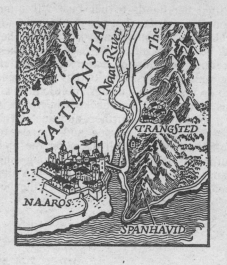

36. Naaros: Duty

IT WAS AS DOCTOR MELIBOË FORETOLD:
the Viscount in the citadel was so far from willing
to evacuate that he even tried spear-casts at their
trumpet of parley. It was also as Gallil had promised:
Naaros city hot for the contest as soon as the rising
general was proclaimed, from 'prentices with bats
who would have to be taught all weapon-handling,
to stout commercials that had fought to save their
goods in the wild lands to the south, and could balance their blades as deftly as Evimenes. There were
not too many of weapons; every forge in town burned
late, and in the ropewalks bowstrings were twisted,
with cords for Pleiander's new engines, which he
would prove by shooting at the citadel.

With the war-plan all marched. The messengers
coming down the north road told no tales of Vulking

350

movement, and every day men of Skogalang came in with bows and quivers slung over their backs, steel caps, and little silver whistles on which they made a martial music, tramping through the gates. Vast-manstad sent up its people, mostly older, in twos and threes—stouthearts who had held out against the pressures to leave their steads, even a few among them grey, and with memories of the day of the Red Hills; full-armed. Mariolans came as word went round Spanhävid, somewhat ragged and hard of aspect for the more part, lacking in good arms, who'd've stormed the citadel and spent life for life gladly, for they had borne much. Airar placed them with Mikalegon to bear the hardest brunt of the fighting, and they liked his rough ways. In the third week a ship sent to Gentebbi came back to say all was confusion there, half Vagai town burned down and ships sunk in the harbor, no sign of Rudr the master-fisher. The ship brought a few men, who embraced those of Airar's early band and told tales of fierce Marshal Bordvin's doings that brought a tear here and there. The first contingent of Hestinga arrived, thirty men from the southern march of the province with their mettlesome steeds. On them Evimenes at first frowned, but later, saying they would make better gentours than the gentours, took them to his heart. Taverns were filled up and houses; and in four days the world turned end for end.

The first was when Airar stood with the other leaders by a table in the old house of the city. Sand had been strewn on the table, a trick of the Carrhoenes; a Whiteriverdalesman traced with his finger the run of the great north road and the best places along it for an ambush—"See here, by Torgsted—" when one entered to say that here was a deputation of the Naaros syndics that would speak to Airar and him alone. Had he been harder in politic, he had said they must speak to all, but it was a young man still. He made excuse and saw them.

They were three; most of the speaking done by a tall, thin man with lips that curled back and up at the corners in a forever-failing effort to have a smile of geniality; richly dressed and purse-proud. The childe of Trangsted had not become so great a man that respect for such had left him; he had the three seated and wine of Uravedu brought in. They discussed the spring weather and how the town was noisy with the coming and going of so many armed men. Said Purse-proud finally (Airar had at once forgot his name), when all easy subjects were exhausted:

"Aye, Duke Airar, a many of armed men; hard for the community to bear; profitless. They make nothing but babble, and though they buy goods, drive them to so high a price with one bidding against another that money's self loses value. The more part of their purchase in any manner profits little; they came here without an aina and but take Naaros silver to return it to Naaros again."

"That is believable," said Airar, wondering where in the name of seventeen green devils the fellow was driving.

"It is ever so with war," said Purse-proud, lugubriously, and drank. "No gain but to those like the mercenaries from the Dodekapolis, as causes at law are profitable only to advocates."

"Ha, ha," said the other two mechanically. Said Airar, forcing the matter: "Even for mercenaries it is not always easy; these Carrhoenes have lost a brother, no light loss."

"Ah, it's that very matter we'd discuss with you." Purse-proud leaned over to tap with a finger Airar's knee, face writhing in the rictus that made him look forth like a river-dragon. "I am master-syndic of the wool guild; these gentles are of stockfish and leather respective. Now even though their trades are so much less important than wool, ha-ha, they are concurred with us that we men who are leaders in Naaros' prosperous trade have a duty to the city and to all Dalarna—to keep trade flowing, a fowl in the pot, and men earning their daily needful for their children. We'll admit that the Count's rule has been sometimes exactious, with his wall-tax and slave factories—" he held out a hand to stay Airar from speech

—"very exactious. We are glad you have come to overthrow it. Yet it must be said that the County offered us peace and good order instead of tumult; and every bargainer knows when his point's won. It is as bargainers, men of commerce and not sword-swingers, that we come to advise you, Duke Airar. You have driven a good bargain the now, Duke Airar; our word on it is that you should close it and win advantage."

"In what way?" said Airar, his bowels boiling.

"Why, put an end to all these man-slayings and levyings of goods that are of profit only to the up-roarious. Peace is what the general need; sweet peace, that a man may sit happy by his fireside and make a competence to leave to his sons. The means to which are so simply at hand that I wonder you have not thought on them for yourself—or it could be, indeed, you have so thought and only wait to know the public temper before beginning. For look, now you are duke of one party, but your kinsman, Tholo Airarson, is very well thought on, very well thought on, by the other. . . . A pity to have lost Master Fabrizius in these tumults; he was a sound man . . . Ah, well, Count Vulk is named Unreasonable, but only in jest. We know his dealings. He'll hear sound advice and give us all we really need by treaty if spoken fair."

Bells rang in Airar's head. For a space he fingered the alternate thoughts of strike the men there or drive them all from the room in hot fury; but before choice made, the memory flashed of how Rogai and Mikal-egon would have him leader because least trapped in contentions. "It is a plan I had not thought on," said he, "and one so grave I'd find it hard to enter without concurrence from the other captains. Yet, where's our gain? What would Vulk give us?"

Purse-proud had caught his eye-flash and moving lip. "Nay, let us advise," he said. "Do not consult, consult, with those who make disturbances for up-roar's sake; they'll never have the peace and order the Count stands for. You are the duke; be dukely. Use your power for the good of all, of whom most will fail to see where the good path lies. As to the detail, we can almost surely have from the Count a remission of the wall-tax, but very surely a decree against the holding of many serfs in ranch or factory. He's of the old Vulking tradition that holds the proper excellent concern of his people lies in war and conquest, therefore he has had many griefs against the Lord Chancellor Lannoy and the magnates. Mark how this simplifies our problem, that he's already of your party, willing to concede. A word whispered here, a hand clasped there, he faces his council and you your captains with a thing done, which they cannot deny, since all honest men of both sides will bless you for saving their lives from a futile war. As for the armaments, they can be used to save some of the Twelve Cities from People's Party government."

Airar looked on the man, of whom no question but that he meant it true. "Yet I am a leader for battle," said he, "therefore unsure. Nay, I must speak this out with Doctor Meliboë, who is a philosopher and will surely find a sound road."

One of the others—the fat one—spoke for the first time in a voice that squeaked like a boy's: "But he's the Empire's outlaw!"

"So am I," said Airar, and pleased with himself for having made this little score, rose to signify there'd be no more.

Yet it was to Meliboë he went straightaway, somewhat troubled in spirit. "How is it they can relish the rule of Briella? Or is it possible they but ask this to trap me?"

The enchanter had been toiling with pieces of philosophic apparatus, as alembics. He seated himself and tilted his head into one hand. "No trap, if you have told me clearly all that passed. Young sir, you'd merely say that you are young—half-hatched. Do not lose that quality; it ensures you adherence from all who think themselves clever. Your syndics? They do not wish Briella's rule, nor yours neither, but their own, in all things of moment to them. They think to have it by playing one against the other, with always more talk and treating, since in their world by talk and barter all is done, with a long-robed judge to yield the prize to the best speaker, and a law that none shall bear blades."

"So they will truly have Briella—the scoundrels, traitors. Is this Dalarna? I had hoped . . ."

"Spare me your musings. You had hoped, I doubt not, that once Count Vulk were down, the world were paradise. Not so; you that think to war and die for some high purpose will fall for less than nothing, since other Vulks with other names will always rise. For that, how dare you name these men rascals? The Dalarna you desire may be as desperate to them as theirs to you."

"We'd have every man free."

"From what and for what? That syndic is not behind you there. He spoke, if you have said correctly, of no wall-tax, an end to serfdoms. Your kinsmen, who are Vulking Allies, would have you free of strifes between blood and blood. Would you have men free like the tall Earl, to lift others' goods that have done them no harm? Nay, nay, young sir, raise your banners, blow trumpets, beat down cities—but not for others' good till they say what good they'd have. You do it for your joy, as I pursue the philosophies." To this point, his voice would have cut iron; now suddenly he smiled. "Hark! I make myself no Vulking advocate; intolerable. Down with him, say I, and am whole-hearted with you in this. . . . Touching which, there's a graver matter here than all your childish scruple. Have you told the main commanders of this plan for a Vulking peace—to wit: the Carrhoenes, Gallil, above all Rogai, who'd suspect his mother of stealing milk from her own breast?"

"Not I. They'd think on death and torture; I would not see the syndics' nor my kinsmen's fingernails plucked out."

"I feared so much." Where the enchanter's nose and forehead met, the overturned pyramid of lines stood close-drawn. "Be sure that your fair friend the syndic will have let them know all the negotiation by this hour—that you heard him complacently, did not denounce or call for penalties, since your family are involved."

"So are the syndics."

"Ah, nay, fair young sir and duke. Accusers are never involved. These gentry have but one thought, which is to reduce all to talk, where they are so skillful. Come, you have been deadly in battle, Vulk the Fourteenth likewise. Suppose the man of the best sword wins, where are these guildsmen? They'd pull you both down, sit council against council with gold aurar shining like stars in the distance, and that is the kind of world they wish."

Airar thought he had not thought that men could be so low, but what he said was: "Then how avoid their snares?"

"Ah!" Meliboë the enchanter placed a finger beside his nose. "You may think, young sir, that I but make a tale to mine own benefit. It is not so; you have in time past seen what a poor doctor of the philosophies can do. I'll meet the matter for you in sound magic. But since the Count issued his decree against mine art, burned down my cot, and let slay my dwarf Cobbo, there is to me a lack of certain equipment. Will you not order that such apparatus as there be in Naaros be brought before me?"

"I would not have this met by magic," said Airar. "Here's something to be solved by what we have, or no solution permanent. Yet if it pleasures you, I will give the order for such instruments as you need."

He said farewell then and stepped forth to find men looking for him, a ship having been sighted coming into Naarmouth with Imperial standards at her head. Airar went dockward; it was true, and she the ship required, bearing Sir Ludomir Ludomirson, who had been to The Heyr and there learned of the taking of Naaros. He was radiant; success. A full council of the Empire had been called in the High House of Stassia, he said, where he taxed the Sons of the Well with taking Vulking gold.

—Ah, no, no, cried they all, whereupon he exposed the griefs of Dalarna under the Count's rule, and the tale of the Mariupol murders, as well as what would come of it, if the marriage of Aurea were allowed to go forward. Thereupon the contract for this wedding was broke, since none durst defend it on the suspicion of bribery. The Scroby lords were out of their enchantments, somewhat bitter at having been dizzled; they spoke of revenges on Vanette-Millepigue. The ban of the Empire was removed from Dalarna's rising, though not that of the Well, whose sons and priests still hate all wars. Sir Ludomir heard the news counter, of Airar's choice to lead the armies, and was for the moment grave. Come evening, he sought private audience and asked that there should be no admissions.

They were afoot as the attendant left, who had placed seats and brought forth cups of bright sweet mead. The old knight set his vessel down, and whether Airar would or no, dropped to one knee and kissed his hand. "Take my allegiance."

"Oh, rise," said Trangsted's heir, in much embarrass, and would not seat himself till Sir Ludomir had done so.

"My grace. That was gently done, sir duke—" his face changed—"if duke you be, for I do not know how a dignity elective will stand before the lawmen of Stassia."

"No duke I," said Airar, "nor claim to title make; only a battle-leader because they could find no other who had not a quarrel to resolve. I'll lay down this phantom dukeship tomorrow."

The knight sipped, looking across his cup. "My lord," said he, "this is most precisely the thing I feared to hear you say. You may not, cannot, never, never, never, lay down this leadership, no more than our sovereign prince, the Emperor Auraris, though he must rule through regents and take all their advice."

"I'll rule none—nor have desire to do it," said Airar.

"My lord, you shall hear me out, though you send me to exile after, for having gone beyond authority. I say you must not think to lay down the office to which God has called you by ways inscrutable. All now hangs on that you possess it, not another—for Rogai's too impudent, Gallil and I too old, Oddel is wed, the Skogalangs not known. All hangs on it: Dalarna's salvation, and it may be that of the Empire itself, from these overweening conquerors of Briella Mountain."

In spite of the old knight's solemn air, Airar could not restrain himself from smile. "This is a great weight to put on one pair of shoulders. Is age such a drawback, then, for leadership?"

"Your lordship is pleased to jest a little, the sign of a sound mind. Believe it when I say this is a high matter, that the leadership must be young now, and unattached by bonds of marriage. I gave to all a tale this morning, but it was a tale partial, of which the whole could not be told where there were so many ears with mouths between them, that might whisper a word heard as far as Lacia, and so distemper all our projects. The case is that there's a flaw in this council Imperial, removal of the ban and cancellation of the Vulking marriage."

"How would that be?" asked Airar, somewhat taken aback to see the knight's good news gone glimmering.

Sir Ludomir shrugged. "How would such things ever be? Not a full council, no more than that iniquitous one last—no delegates from the Lacias, Bregonde, or Acquilème, though these are of the Empire; none from Permandos, Berbixana, or Carrhoene; not all from Scroby. To foot it so was perhaps a dastard and unknightly thing for me to do, and I must make my religious duty to pay for it. But here's the chief concern—that all is as easily tumbled as it was set up, and like to be so wrecked unless it's fixed beyond cavil that you have an Imperial connection."

"How is this point to be won, then?" asked Airar (but his heart began to beat with speed).

"Thus—when I showed forth the woes attendant on this Vulking match with our gracious lady the Princess Aurea, his Majesty did pray me, the council consenting, to accept the guardianship of the Imperial children as their regent."' He fumbled in his pouch for a parchment of proof, but Airar waved a hand. "Well then, my lord duke, I do propose to fix our future by uniting you in marriage with a princess of the House of Argimenes. Hence, it is a young man needed, who'll be duke forever."

"Not Aurea!" a cry from Airar's lips, but Sir Ludomir only smiled. "I have heard somewhat that made me think your choice might fall on the other, lord. Is it a thing done, then?"

"Oh, aye—if she will have me." Then his brows linked. "There's all the war-might of the Vulkings."

"And you will bear against them the sword of the House—touching which, lord, you will pardon an old man that has seen much, but there's one thorn behind the rose of your candidacy, elsewhere so perfect in its bud."

"What would that be, sir?"

"My lord, you need call me sir no longer. But it is commerce with those who serve Briella, in thought and deed."

Airar of Trangsted rose slow to his feet. "You mean my father? You would have me condemn my father?"

Sir Ludomir also stood; for all the younger man's inches, the knight was half an inch the taller. "My lord duke, who spoke of condemnations? Not I. Yet to those we ask for faith, we must give no cause to doubt our faith with them. There are such places where he could be held secure—the Isles of Gentebbi, certain armed steads of Skogalang—"

"My father!"

"Think on it well, my lord. A new day often brings sound counsel."

He bowed and left Airar with pictures of his own dear love and of a glorious future flashing behind his eyes—and must he give it all up for a Vulking Ally? Would Dalarna fall if he did? "All hangs on it," Sir Ludomir had said, a man that knew much. Must he give all up?—yet where was faith if he himself kept not the old faith? . . . "This way, son"

—the glad shout with which a weasel of the mountains was brought home to make for a small boy a cap—his mother's laughter and how they sang together, stave and stave. The first lesson in magic—the stars over Vastmanstad on a winter night—"There rides the club-armed horseman, and see, son, how the unicorn will lift his horn to a point of light."

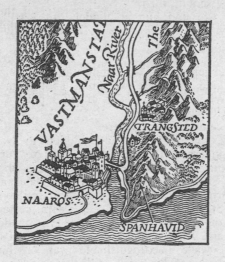

37. Naaros: Wedding Day

YET THE NIGHT'S EXCITEMENT WAS RIDDEN
down by the events of another day when, as Airar
lay late, less asleep than in a daze of wonder how
he might square the circle of his life, there came a
shout without and he went abroad to find a new ship
coming up the stream. By form she was of the Twelve
Cities, but commercial rather than warlike, with high
sides. She bore a standard no one knew, of a green
bush burning, and it was a herald that stepped
ashore, with a tabard and a trumpeter, crying that
he would be taken before the Baron of Naaros.

"Then you must put about and sail for Lectis
Minima," quoth Rogai-of-the-mountains, who had
brought some of his archers to the pier for a guard,
"for that is where he was bound when last heard
on."

"His Viscount, then."

"You will find him at citadel, but I will not accompany you there, since it is unfriendly to this town."

It was a little man, with a peering expression of face, who jerked his head quick and suspicious from side to side, his nose wrinkling as though to sniff truth. "Where's your leader, then? I bear a message from the Twelve Cities."

Airar came forward. "Here."

"Blow, music! . . . I am bidden to Naaros by their highnesses, the six spadarions of Permandos, to announce to your baron and leader, whoever he may be, that the Count Vulk of Dalarna having given harborage and aid to that most foul tyrant and traitor, Sthenophon of no title, with certain other leaders of the People's Party of Permandos, Carrhoene, and Xiphon, these cities do bid him defiance, and will wage inextinguishable war on him, with the blockade of his ports, till the said Sthenophon be returned to us for just punishment; and you, I do defy." He paled in attent of a blow, but bravely enough jerked the iron glove from his girdle and would have cast it down. But before this could be done, he was surrounded and almost smothered with loud shouts and huzzas till Evimenes hacked clear a space around him and snatched off his own headgear.

"Do you know me?" he cried.

"Aye." The herald smiled a toothless smile. "That is, lord, I know your family, but which one you be, no."

Drink was brought for all and the herald taken to the house of the town, where he and the master mariner that brought him told their tale: that, Sthenophon returning not, there had been at Permandos words against his rude rule. Words changed to blows; the sole spadarion's people had the worst of that bout, and were overrun, and the party of the Guilds set in office. Tidings of this spreading fast to Carrhoene, she too had risen against her People's Party, upon whom lay many heavy complaints, as crushing taxes,

and that while excluded from the Empire by absence
of delegates, her people might not trade in Stassian
cities, nor go to the perfect peace of the Unicorn's
Well. The profitable wool ships came not from Dalarna, which was taken to mean turbulence in that
northern land where Sthenophon was; and not un-
likely he was worsted in some broil. When a word
was whispered that Vulk was out of the Empire's
protection, it was war; a defiance to Vulk.

When the tale was all told, Evimenes took up the
word most joyously: "Master Airar, this is all that
was to be looked for of the best. Permandos and
Carrhoene! Now we can bring to you not less than
twelve hundreds of heavy-armed riders—more, have
we the time to summon them, but these at once.
Will you but say the word?"

Airar felt a surge, as on that night when he had
made the sudden plan for the ambush of the deese
near Crow's Tower, and in that rush of pleasure
knew that he had feared the outcome of battle against
the invincible terciaries, but now no longer—not with
the heavy horsemen of the Twelve Cities. The plan!
—in a moment, but all complete: reverse against
the Vulkings the order of battle they knew. Yet while
word was no more than a sound before word, Sir
Ludomir Ludomirson spoke: "At what price?"

The dark Star-Captain pouted: "What would you?
We are allies, and will not haggle, but the men must
be paid. For each moon, a golden aura for each
rider, half for those who follow afoot, and for us
leaders half as much as the others together, with
plunder-rights in field and camp and city. A lordship in the Isles of Gentebbi, which we will restore
and hold of you."

"It is a great sum," said black Gallil, lowering on
them darkly. "More than was asked of Mariola,"
Rogai said.

Evimenes curled a lip and answered only the last
speaker. "In Mariupol's service we were outlaws,
vagabonds, with little to give beyond leadership, but
now we are captains that can bring you what you most
need. Pah! Do you think your bastardly Dalecarle

peasants will stand before these men of war without a seasoning of trained soldier? Your duke Airar knows better, if no other; I have seen him frowning at the exercises. Nor is it so great a price as we asked at Poliolis, nor to the King of Gesebus in Uravedu for setting him on his throne again."

Dead silence for a moment. Gallil persisted: "A great price; would leave us a half-ruined land. The syndics will have it never; you'll drive them to Vulk."

Rogai slapped the table. "The price of freedom and victory is high forever; but there is one thing in this treaty I cannot stomach. How are we to stand for freedom from foreign lordships and yet make a new one? Will you not abate this condition?"

"Nay," said Evimenes. "We have been wanderers too long; need a secure refuge against other turnovers among our cities. For money we might make conditions; on this, never."

Airar could see faces fall, and his own, too, for he was one with Rogai, that Gentebbi should not fall away from Dalarna; but Sir Ludomir said: "Gentle sirs of Carrhoene, what if instead of Gentebbi I offer you a lordship fairer than any you have dreamed upon, in quit-claim for all your aid? One that will make Dalarna and Carrhoene friends forever."

"Name it," said Evimenes.

"Sirs, I will do no less." He drew forth the parchment he would have shown to Airar and tossed it crackling on the table. "I am herein named regent and guardian for the children of the Empire, now in this city, and it seems to me good to gather the new swords of Carrhoene round the old sword of Argimenes. What say you to an alliance Imperial in marriage? The Princess Aurea, her graciousness."

Pleiander wetted lips and looked at his brothers. Said Alsander simply, but with force: "Not for a dozen coronets; she talks too much." It might be Mikalegon who laughed; Evimenes was silent a long moment, and then: "Not her, but if the younger sister—" whereat Airar cried sharply. "No!"

"Your grace, lord," said Sir Ludomir. "Sirs, the Princess Argyra weds our lord and leader, Duke

Airar, master of the soldiers of Dalarna, and this may not be altered. Is it then your last word, that our most generous offer's refused? I warn you fairly we are Dalecarles and sons of the Empire, who at the last breach will make cause with even Vulk if need be, to keep foreign lordships from our land."

"Make it, then," said Evimenes, looked past him, and turned to the other three of Carrhoene. "Brothers, let us by no means continue this profitless discussion, but go aboard that ship of Permandos at the quay and return to our own land."

Alsander and Pleiander half rose with him, faces hot, but—"Brothers," said Evadne of Carrhoene, "you have wrong."

They checked.

"You have wrong. There's an hour when you drive too high a bargain and the merchandise rots. What! Have you forgotten in your heat our brother Alcides, for whom we owe a vengeance? What! Shall we wander forever and win battles to no other end than payments spent on a tavern trot? Nay, brothers, if you love your marriage freedoms so much, I'll sell mine for all. Sir knight and regent, do you have in your regency the marriage of the prince as well?"

Sir Ludomir frowned and reached his parchment. "The children Imperial, madame, which I take to mean aye to your asking."

"Then 1 say here before you all that I sue for the hand of Prince Aurareus of the Empire; and the dowry I bring alone, without my brothers, is that of a spadarion of Carrhoene; but I think that they will be with me in this, and give a quit-claim for all aids to the utmost power of our city; saving plunder-rights only, which we will not lay down."

The Star-Captains all three goggled, but first Alsander and then the others nodded. Mikalegon the Earl brought his fist down with a boom. "Half a man and a woman and a half! It should make a brave match!" Then there was long chatter, and a writer to draw papers, with a messenger to dispatch the ship back to Carrhoene instanter, under the Star-Captains' authority for troops; but as they left the place some little later, Evadne worked her way to Airar to say:

"Lord and love lost, this is my reparation for injury and my last service to you ward. Be happy; think well of me."

He would have kissed her, but she slipped his grasp like smoke, with tears shining under eyelids, and then he would have gone to Argyra, but Sir Ludomir said nay. Time pressed a hasty wedding for the very tomorrow, and in Dalarna as in Dzik it is the custom that a groom shall not see his bride on the day before their union. There were small matters to handle and a bent man from the tailors' guild came in, with two assistants, one slew-eyed, the other drooling, to measure Trangsted's son for wedding garments. While they did so, here was a messenger from the north to say that all word from Stavorna was cut, so the Count Vulk would be moving at last. Airar fidgeted; the bent tailor skipped about the room, while in the street below a disorderly tramp of hooves told that a new contingent of Hestinga horsemen was come. "What shall we do with the band of Mariolan exiles that came with Vardo? They will not serve under Carrhoene, holding it the Star-Captains' fault for the failure at Marskhaun causeway, yet they are good men with horse and lance."

The climax of a bad nervous day came after evening meat, and the beginning of it was that Airar flat refused an offer of Oddel and Rogai to be merry with them through the last night of his bachelorhood; saw their faces fall, and heard a murmur of something on those who overreach their origins. Now, as he mused on how little of his own life glory seemed to leave him, here was another delegation of syndics —the same negotiator as before, but with new companions. They would know whether Airar had thought on their previous visitation, and the result?

In a gust of anger and weariness beyond assoil, he answered that aye, he had thought; but to make peace now would be treason to those who had chose him their leader for war—and to the Empire, whose standard he would bear. Had they not (he asked) told through the town that he was ready to sell all to the friends of Vulk?

The wool-syndic slipped the accusation and asked whether peace were so dreadful a thing, then? which he held most men to desire, the Well for witness. "As to the Imperial standard, trust not in it for long. The old Emperor is doddering and will follow tomorrow the advice he gets tomorrow. Look how our Count was his daughter's expectant but now."

In the midst of this chess-game without issue, in came Sir Ludomir, who made snap-eyes at the syndic-men till they left, saying they'd speak on the matter further.

Airar: "No sir, you will not; not to me."

The negociant smiled his glabrous smile. As soon as he had gone the old knight once more gave cold warning that such things could not be, Airar must say at no late date where lay his loyalty, and hold to that, outward and in. "Intrigue, my lord, is a leader's privilege and play, but he must play it through the hands of his servants."

Now there was another clash of wills, to no real end, like the former, but with the adviser of princes at last departing on the note that he would charge himself with proof that Airar meant no treason to the cause in holding by his relatives. The groom prospective, unhappy over his pre-wedding day, lay down to wait for the crack of dawn, tingling through every muscle, and full expecting it to be a night sleepless but for jerks; so swung his thought to the loveliness and graciousness of Argyra, whom even to imagine possessing was delight. But as soon as his head touched pillow, he slipped into another world, and knew it would be one of those nights of dream that always seemed to presage some change in his condition.

Wild riders were in that dream and a golden crown to gain; the cold winter stars, with the constellation of the unicorn rising. He sought to reach it, but that hideous worm he had seen long since in the cot of the magician Meliboë gnawed at his wings, so he fell tumbling down a long slant till there were calms and white arms around him—"Is this death?"—then all in his dream and knowing he was dreaming, made to himself a song:

Into the night I go, when the moon fades,
To watch the north lights shiver up, like ghosts
Of flames in cities sacked by shades,
And see beyond, the powerless burning hosts—

but was still trying to reconcile the rhyme when Poë the Witless touched him behind the ear to waken without sound, a rushlight in his hand. The air beyond the window was steel-blue with coming day.

"What tidings, friend?" asked Airar.

"I fear that all's not well. In the night, stampings and mewings, with cries and blue lights from where you set the guard over the two old Vulking Allies, your kinsmen."

Airar was on his feet at once. "We will go."

The streets were silent all, so that a nocturnal cat with her tail aloft was a spectacle and a man drunk in a doorway was a landmark. Poë's voice whispered; the man by the door-pillars of the little stone house at the jewel market clutched his spear with white knuckles. By gods and gryphons he swore that none or nothing had gone in this only door; but an hour since, he and his mate heard the sound of heavy tramping above, with witch-lights and cries. The floor at the ground had been used by a shop and was now vacant; Airar went up the stairs at once, but the door at the top was barred within. He would have hurled his shoulder on it when none answered his knock, but Poë said: "My lord duke, this is very stout oak; but permit me"—and, drawing a short-sword, began hacking at the panel with skillful strokes that left long curling chips on the flag-stone floor. The noise woke an inquisitive head in the building across the way, then others, who talked till someone decided to bawl for the watch.

The man who had been door-guard went below to quiet them, and was known for the sea-eagle badge on his half-helm as a free companion of Os Erigu.

The gathering people began to chatter and howl that some had come to lay the traitors by the heels and hang them up, so Airar heard cries of "Rope, rope!" and "Build a fire!" The hole was as yet but a couple of inches, and a dreadful sense of urgency ran through him, but now he must halt the hacking, go to the lower door, doff cap and be cheered for himself, while Witless Poë was sent for an archer-guard and axes. Someone heard him say the order and, before Poë could return, here was an axe and a heavy man to wield it, who heaved a few times till the door-panel splintered and one could get an arm in to throw down the bar.

The door half-opened, half-fell. As soon as Airar stumbled into the apartment, with a press of the curious behind him, he was ware of Meliboë the wizard's work: not only an odor of death in the place, but another so ghastly that the strong, stupid door-chopper turned round and vomited down the frame, with the feel of magic crowding heavy enough to make the eyes start from the head.

"Stand back!" said Airar. "More than your lives are on it." And dared not himself go deeper in till he had asked and received a pouch of corn with which to draw a pentacle and raise from within it the weightiest dismissal spell he knew. The dole-shiver came upon him, and the faces crowding round the head of the stair relaxed into more human semblance, then vanished as Poë and his archers arrived, too late.

Beyond the little outer room was another, the swing-window to which stood a trifle ajar. Over its sill and across the stone floor lay a long trail of green, evil-smelling slime, dirty hook-marks along either side, leading toward the bed-chamber, and Airar knew why he had dreamed of the green-worm yammering in its cage. It was as fear told him: inside the bed-chamber lay the father that had generated him and been his friend, beard toward the ceiling, still, shrunken, bloodless as though carved in ivory, with beyond him Uncle Tholo, face down and the back of his neck torn out by a wound that was all pale flesh and no red whatever.

Airar gave a cry and flung himself down; was still there, he did not know how long later, when bells in streets and churches began to ring, and men came to say it was his wedding day, it was time to be dressed. Staggering, he was supported down the stairs into a street that babbled and took off caps, its clamor for hanging now forgot in the presence of death and true sorrow. Farther along the way, where the news had not yet spread, the tone changed, headgear was being tossed up, with shouts for Dalarna's leader and champion and a happy bridal.

Sir Ludomir was waiting, with Rogai and Mikalegon, who were to stand his guardians of the occasion. "My father's dead!" cried Airar; between dolor and the weakness-backlash of his heavy spell, the knees went from under him, he was down on a tapestried rest-bench, with sobs so it was hard to catch breath. Sir Ludomir, the old knight, touched on his shoulder with kind, courtly words of comfort, but they did not ease the smart, nor did the thought that whirled fantastically past, that there was only one whose words could have been of use, and that one was Meliboë the enchanter, Meliboë the philosopher, who had done this all. He felt as though there were knots in his brain-pan, but this at last relieved him of the passion of his weeping.

Sir Ludomir, well-pleased that his ministrations had been successful, said: "Now I must go, for there is much to do, with the colloquy of the bride to be held, since I as regent stand for her father."

Said Earl Mikalegon: "What, lad, will you outlive your ancestors?" and handed him a dram of firewine. The hunchback tailor came in with garments, and a priest to instruct him in the ritual, while outside there were shouts and Skogalang whistles blowing beneath the chiming bells, as the town's mood of gayety grew, with wine-cups poured and one encouraging another to joy. Since Aurareus was an heir Imperial, his marriage must of course precede the other. There was a long wait. Airar could eat noth-

ing; time dragged, the priest's words seemed senseless, and a whit of irritation came to the good man's
eyes as again and again Airar forgot the responses.

At last a youth, all radiant, with a new cat-head
badge to his sleeve, came dancing up the stairs to
cry that all was prepared, and Airar roused himself
enough to inquire where was Meliboë?—to which
the answer was that none had seen him the day,
he'd kept close to his coop since receiving the philosophical devices ordered to him from the resource of
the town. Trumpets began to blow in the street;
though feeling still as though the skin were stretched
to a drumhead across his face, Airar found that the
air, the musics, the excitement of the occasion con-
spired to rouse him. Mikalegon helped him up the
wedding-car with a clap on shoulder, and: "Bravely
done as at Bear Fjord, young master; I knew then
you were one that would not down."

At the cathedral there was no bishop, only a common priest, for the lord spiritual of Naaros was a
Vulking and had been let go as he desired. From
his one side-glance at Argyra as they knelt, Airar saw
she was ware of somewhat amiss in him; but after
all, he missed only one of the responses, that where
he was to say he'd take his bride with no dower but
the blood of King Argimenes, and this was not from
the usual service in any case, but for the Empire's
daughter. "I have grief for you," she whispered (the
first words as his wife!) as the pipes, strings, and
shouts of the leaping marriage-dancers led them from
altar down the aisle to the cathedral door.

As the Prince's dignity was the greater, the house
of the city had of course been taken for his marriage dinner with Evadne, so that for Airar's bridal
it was the hall of the leather-guild, not unsplendid,
but with a drift of tanning odors in the air, through
the high, embrasured windows. People came and
went from one feast to the other, who must be greeted
and told farewell; Mikalegon drank like a whirlpool,
nested like a rude buffoon, and it was past torchlight
when they rose, with the singing of the marriage song.
"—so now we leave you," its last words rang on

the stairs beyond the door as Duke Airar, in a passion of weariness and desire turned to take in his arms the bride he had vowed to win. But she returned his embrace with one gentle, then let her arms hang loose, and to his seeking lips turned a cheek as cold as Gython's or as the ultimate mountains of the pole. He released and stood back, his voice barely whispering:

"No love, then? Oh, Argyra, my love—"

In the street someone blew a horn discordantly; there was a choir of banging on metal and freefisher voices crying the obscene wedding greetings of that folk. Argyra the princess faced him steadily:

"Lord Airar, I am given to you as your wedded wife. You may unbind my girdle, do with me as you will. But love? I told you once, between us stand the Seven Powers. I am a daughter of the Well, yet you come to me this night that a woman must hold most dear, all smelling of dirty, deadly magic. I cannot give but what is in me."

For so brief a time there passed through his thought the plan of seizing her masterfully. His eye ran to the ready bed, but the whip fo Meliboë's spells and his own had left tears standing behind his eyes and his whole frame as impotent as that of an old gelding. The raucous shout rose from the street again, and out of a pit of despair, he cried:

"An end! I'll have an end!" and snatching up his sword ran down the stair.

38. The Whiteriverdales: Wedding Night

"Young master," said Meliboë, "There are many would say instead that I had rid you of your worst enemy. I do not know why it is that the accident of birth so sets its bonds on men that they'll not choose for themselves what friends to hold by. Your future lies in this; aye, and not yours alone, but of many more. No hope of bringing the old man to our side. On this point we were concurred, myself and the old knight-councillor, who in other matters is somewhat a scoundrel."

Startled from the line of his speech, Alvar said: "Scoundrel? Sir Ludomir?"

"Aye, Sir Ludomir Ludomirson. Oh, all filled with golden phrases and high purpose, I will give that,

373

having seen many of the same sort before. Vulk the Unreasonable's another; purpose of uniting the two peoples, so high he holds that the means are meaningless, like a man who would not sorrow his children drowned if he taught them to swim."

It fell away. Airar said: "I do not know for that, though it would seem to me that you yourself have just now looked on end rather than means, besides which you are playing in the game of choosing other people's destiny, which once you told me no man should ever do. But this I know, that you have cost me my father and my love at a blow; and now it can be no more countenanced that you stay in free Dalarna than if you were some biting monster."

Meliboë: "You have lost nothing you had not lost before, and on the points philosophical you are of course wrong; for I have no high purpose beyond that of watching how the world passes, and there's no need to me to do as I advise others. But as you will; I'm no stranger to banishments, have heard that the land of Dzik is fair and its people none so squeamish. Will your lordship be pleased to allow me a ship for the going?"

So ended that meeting, too, in a tale of breaking, and in the morning came the first clear tidings from the north, by a messenger who had ridden fast. Vulk was moving slowly southward with much enginery, intent on breaking Naaros, but with three tercias only, his trouble being to find food for more, only his vanguard at Stavorna. Of the gentour people, he had few with him, and these chiefly employed far in the north along the roads from the Lacias, which the Korosh miners and the Korsor mountaineers were raiding so fiercely that even along the main highways it was hard to bring down provision from Briella—yet brought it must be, for Norby was all eaten bare by the winter's war, and nothing came from oversea.

"Who told Korsor to rise?" No matter; with Vulk at Stavorna, Airar the duke of war was now concerned to get forward to grip this nettle of Briella among the Whiteriverdales as firmly as he might. That very night he rode forth fiercely with the horsemen of

Hestinga and the Carrhoene lancers around him.
Rogai and the light-armed foot to follow fast; Mikalegon as fast as might be. Pleiander and Evimenes
remained at Naaros to forward what aids came from
the Twelve Cities with the remainder of the levy.
Runners went to warn the rest of Hestinga to join
across the Dragon's Spine by the pass of the Count's
Pillow, making no secret of their march. If they
came early, well; if they came late, Count Vulk must
at least wear down his force to throw out guards to
eastward, and have more loose enemies to vex his
convoys. Argyra kissed him farewell as he was
horsed; he had not told her of the enchanter's banish-
ment (scorning to take such means of winning), and
her lips were unmoving as they touched his.

The spring trees were out in full leaf as Airar rode
north along that road where he had once walked
southward by the side of the decent Vulking archer
—what was his name? he could not recall—but trees
were blackened along the track that led to the magician's cot, which brought him sharper memories
than passing Trangsted itself. For Meliboë's cot was
clean destroyed, had the bitter air of ruin; but at
Trangsted, which they passed early the second day
of march, all remained, but nothing destroyed or
familiar. Only the honest fences that had been kept
with the sons of Viclid on the south, Sumarbo on
the north, were broke down to make one single wide
slave-worked latifundia, the house painted different,
no sign of life.

They camped that night on the slopes of Vastmanstad toward the Whiteriverdales. A house had
been found for Airar to sleep in as leader, but he
refused it, though there were spatters of rain. The
next night when they lay at the hamlet of Kobbing
and all slept on floors or at worst in barns, there
was a Salmonessan wench brought in for him, with
her laces cut, but he'd have none of that either,
and let Alsander have her, who was not so nice.
Beyond Kobbing one is in plain dales, even if the
country be still called Vastmanstad. The Hogsback
eastward has broken, then risen sharply into the

craggy reaches of the lower Dragon's Spine, while to the west gentler but nearly as lofty slopes go up to the Shield Boss Hill that shut off Skogalang and Shalland.

The north road winds somewhat in this region, though the Vulkings that built it love no windings; on each turn they had set a castella, but all these were now vacant, some merely abandoned, but a few burned with fire, which Whiteriverdalesmen had done when the war-word went round. The Dalesmen in ones and twos kept falling in on their band, but few of these go a-horseback to war; therefore Airar gave word for them to assemble at the nearest castellas and wait Mikalegon's coming, since himself must travel fast. It would be Airar also who thought to tell the womenfolk of the Dales to take refuge, since there might be fighting in this region; but Carrhoene Alsander who had advised, before they went, that all possible provision should be brought to the same castellas for the host that followed. The Hestingerna pushed out ahead, to east, to west, in little groups, searching for tidings. Those they brought back were of moderate good omen—namely, Count Vulk still clearly detained in Stavorna, collecting waggons and victual. It was said that Vanette-Millepigue, the bloody red baron of Naaros, was named his marshal.

On a spring morning of mist and drizzle they came to Torgsted, the town that is the heart of the Dales and so called; nothing great, but with some forty houses of sturdy stone, the rest being wooden, lately built. The Vulkings had planted one of their Salmonessan colonies nearby, but these shiftless ones lacked even the wit to flee when the growl of coming war rose round them. Airar had only to order that they be taken from the houses where Dalecarles had been dispossessed, and kept under close survey, for it was needful to his plan that the sons of Briella have no clear warning of how he was to meet them.

The great road splits Torgsted midway; the Naar swings in so close that the outermost houses of the town peer over its bank, and there is a stone bridge across, with a road not much better than a track running away through the Shield Boss to Skogalang. The river, unfordable, Airar designed to use as a ditch before the left flank of his battle-line; its western bank had at this time strong tree-cover with thickets. Along the other side the Vulkings had, as usual, cut back all growth to give their road free lawns, but there had been since the date of the cutting some pushing forth of boccage, which formed a screen close by the east bank of the stream. Where it was thickest Airar put all the artisans that could be found to building four bridges, not of great strength, but only for this battle.

Among the more northerly houses of the town there ran down to the Naar a ditch, now dried and near filled with rubbish, which had been the front of a stockade in the old days of the heathen wars. The Salmonessans were set to clear this ditch, with promise of reward, and when Rogai came with the Skogalang men, who are of all Dalecarles the most adroit in woodwork, they went to rebuild the old furniture as strongly as they possibly could; for here Airar designed to place Earl Mikalegon and the heavy-armed to hold the onrush of the enemy, and he was troubled lest they be too few in number for all those terciary soldiers. The road itself he bade the Skogalang men bar, but with a barricade movable held, this would be the way of egress for the sergeants of Carrhoene to counterstroke. A tall stone building overlooked the ditch just where the road crossed it. This should be a fortress; where the upper story overhung, Airar had the floor bored through, with a quantity of weapons and kettles of pitch to be heated at the fire sent aloft there.

The eastern flank was more troublesome. Here the lawns are not made, but natural, sweeping up in a long, slow slope for some hundreds of paces before they meet trees at the base of a cliff-like climb. The fathers that founded Torgsted in the old days had clean avoided their problem on that side by bringing back ditch and stockade, and carrying them south round the town. This would never do for Airar, since the Vulkings would be sure to come down round the

place there, crowd past and throw his force back into
the unfordable Naar, then push right on. He doubted
that time would stay long enough to make a new
ditch there, and Alsander agreed; but they did what
they could by carrying from the angle of the old ditch
forward a maze of trees cut down with their branches
interwoven, sharpened, and pointing outward, ending
only where the trees and bushes below the steep
began.

Behind this screen all the spear-armed Dalecarles
should take their place, whether those like the fishers,
who cast, or the Whiteriverdalesmen and Mariolans
with long spears that thrust. All the archery should
lie behind the Naar on the opposite wing, where it
would not be easy for the foemen to come at them,
shooting at the right side of the advancing enemies,
where they have no shields. Thus matters were ordered so the Vulkings must come down the center
through a double alley of weapon-fire, toward where
Mikalegon waited them with his axemen behind the
stockade. Behind him, among the houses, the tagoi
of Carrhoene, armored horsemen (if only more of
them came in time!), would stand, ready to jact forth
when the Vulkings showed any sign of waver, or,
if it were needed, to cover a retreat. In front of all,
concealing all, the light riders of Hestinga, who might
escape from the main attack through the town and
by the new bridges across the Naar.

Alsander said it was planned as well as could be;
all little Torgsted town filled with the eager hope of
coming battle as men came in by the dozen and score.
Airar's days brimmed with joyous activity, as naming an under-captain here for a band newly made
up, or seeing to the manufacture of more arrows;
but his nights miserable, his heart burning and ach-
ing for Argyra, of whom no word this fortnight. He
began to wonder how long he might hold this host
together, for food was running down in spite of that
Evimenes kept up a flow of carts from Naaros;
thought also how everything would be confounded if
Vulk took the route south by Shalland and the
Skogalang coast. Alsander said as to the last there'd

be no trouble, which proved to be no less than true, for on a day of sunshine from a blue sky a man of Norby came in, who had been picked up by the Hestinga horsemen.

He had been with the Vulking Allies and was equipped as one of them, but showed by proofs indubitable that the Iron Ring of his own province had sent him into their ranks for a spy. Vulk was provisioned at last, he said, and moving down the great north road, with all three tercias and some force of gentours. The gossip of his camp was that south Dalarna had risen generally and mustered in the dales; the Count meant to crush this revolt in a battle before it should spread. His siege engines and the clumsy waggons that drew them, he had left behind; could take Naaros at his leisure when the fight was done. So many of the gentours as could be were drawn in from their road-guarding to gain more force for combat; a half-tercia had gone down into Shalland to hold that province secure, and another would move, as soon as forage could be found, through Korsor and the northern turn of the Dragon's Spine to burn out all the steads of Hestinga. There was talk also of the standard of the Empire up against the Vulkings, and great anger on that account among them. The Count had sent out proclaimers in every direction to say it was not true, he stood still the Emperor's deputy; but it was notable that two barons with a very gilded suite had set out from Stavorna toward the cities Lectis, which would mean they were sailing for Stassia.

Battle early, then. Sure enough, it would not be another three days before a band of Hestingerne came riding in with three of their number bound on led horses and pale with loss of blood. They had been in a clash with gentours not long up the road. Always ingenious Alsander had them taken through the camp to seek leechery, so that all might look on the hurt men and be encouraged to fury of battle thereby; but Airar was now troubled till he wished he were no leader. Evimenes and the aids from Carrhoene were not yet come, and his whole hope of a high victory rested on breaking this heart of the Vulking rule utterly; if merely beaten back before his barricade, they'd rally and come again.

He might have spared the pain. Another day, and there was a tale of battle from the light horse, who had driven in a wing of gentours, but then been held by a tercia, not two days' march distant. But as the war-leader of Dalarna sat sleepless that evening, there were shouts along the street and torches waved, and here was faithful Evimenes, with three full tagoi of Carrhoene, fifteen hundred lances, thundering and dusty, crowding all the houses and alleys of the little town. A Carrhoene fleet stood in Naaros harbor, said they; more of these same lancers followed in another. Of Argyra, she had some tort with Sir Ludomir Ludomirson; the old knight had suddenly taken ship for Stassia after a public farewell at which she would barely address him. Aurareus was holding court in great state in the city; but most people preferred to take judgments from Gallil or even his wife. Airar in turn explained his battle-plan; Evimenes thought it prime; half-drew and slammed back his sword in its scabbard at the thought of leading the chiefest charge, eyes winking. "The bastards! We'll ram our toothpickers up their arses!"

Again a day and scouts said the Vulkings had come down to pitch camp soon after noon, which was against their custom, but they had surrounded it with a rapid stockade as usual. They clearly knew where Dalarna's forces lay and meant to fight right through. A force of gentours had with much difficulty been ferried westward across to the left bank of the Naar, and through the twilight began to filter among trees there, down toward Dalarna's archerflank. Airar turned the Hestinga horsemen thither to hold them, though it meant losing part of his surprise at the center and uncovering the Skogalang men to attack by the bridges. He had not thought the Vulkings meant to find a way round, but Alsander made light of it all. "In war the captain against is always sure to find something one's forgot. Why, down in Uravedu—"

The Master of Dalarna did not hear the rest. Battle-even again, up or down, live or die, and more on the issue of this contest than anything of himself, yet in it all he could feel but little engaged, as though it were an old tale told at a fireside about people long dead, in which his only interest was to know the end. Argyra, he thought, and thought of how he might have held and cherished her with better manners, yet could not find himself at fault for having raised that dismissal spell to penetrate to the room where his father lay dead. Where had lain his fault, then?—that his father had given him a clerk's instruction when he was a lad?—that he had taken the companionship of Meliboë the enchanter, when his own fortune and that of Dalarna lay at their lowest ebb, that night in the marshes? Perhaps there, and perhaps then; it would seem to have cost him the love that was only the shadow of a love and now this great one that filled his life, so that it had become no difference whether the battle tomorrow were won or lost. But how? Must he suffer forever for one fault? Too deep for his thinking, he thought, and so thinking, shook off all thoughts, ducked into his helm and went below to walk the order of his battle and see that all was arranged, for if the Vulkings had camped betimes yesterday, they were the more likely to attack early in the morn.

Without, the street was full of smoky cooking-fires, with men around them, here and there a bottle passed and floating converse. They saluted him jubilantly at the door when he was seen; from the lower end of the street, where the road bent to enter the town, came shouts, and down there Airar thought he saw something that moved like marchers, and heard sounds not the ordinary ruffle of camp. He paused; the march moved nearer in the fading light, and it was indeed a march of armed men, with three on horseback and a banner at their head, hanging so limp in the still evening air that its style could not be made out. The men behind were all in order; they halted clanging at a word of command and the three came forward to where Airar stood at the door.

One young, with a surcoat bearing a red rose, leaped nimbly down.

"Gentles," he said, and swept off a hat from which a pheasant-feather dangled, "I seek the most worshipful Airar of Trangsted, leader of Dalarna's war."

"I am he."

The big man behind had dismounted more slowly. Pheasant-feather turned: "This is the Baron Ioventinian, of Scroby and the Empire."

The baron accepted the touch of hand and jerked forward a sword-hilt in obeisance. "I am commanded by the Council and Regents of the Empire," said he, "to lead aforce in war against the false traitor and magician, Count Vulk of Briella—to wit, four hundred men-at-arms of Scroby. Provided only that no magic, witchcraft, or gramary be employed in this service, for such is clearly counter to the ordinance of the Well, as established by His Majesty of glorious memory, the Emperor Aureolus."

"No magics," said Airar, heartily taking the Baron's hand in his. "And you come very appropriately. We fight Count Vulk in person on this ground tomorrow and it is exactly in men-at-arms we are most lacking. Will you greet Mikalegon, sometime Earl of Os Erigu, but now of our free Dalarna?"

Ioventinian hesitated, throwing back his head a little, for the sound of that name had no sweet ring to Imperial ears; but he touched hands. "Will you have meat?" said Mikalegon. "You have had a long and hard travel to come so fast with men afoot and armor; for it was but a day since the Carrhoenes came, and they expertly horsed."

The Baron let himself be drawn to talk. "Not so very hard, neither. We came through Naaros port, where we found the Spadarion Pleiander, whose sister is wed to our gracious prince, and he said that though he had engines of war to speed hither, we were of more need, therefore rode us all finely in a great collection of carts he had made. . . . Touching which," he turned to Airar, "our gracious princess and lady, the Princess Argyra, waits your attendance in one of the same carts, Lord Airar. I sought to—"

Lines of Scroby men in their tall spiky helmets and flaring shoulder-plates stared as he ran like a wild man past them. It was true. Though her smile was kind he dared not quite take her in his arms as he helped her from the cart, and could only speak of the coming battle and her peril in riding up to it, whereat as he led her to the house of his quartering a certain constraint came on them both. There were many things for him to do—places in the camp to find for this unexpected increment of Scroby; where they should stand in the line of battle (the more part with Mikalegon, but one strong body to the right, where the spearmen were); food for all. It was already late, the campfires dying and only the night guards still abroad with their watchwords, when Airar could assuage his impatience to go to his wife.

"Why have you come then?"

"Do you not wish me, my lord? I have come to share your fate, whatever it may be, knowing the chances of battle. I will not have Sthenophon; and, my lord, take mine apology. I wronged you. I have it from his own lips that it was Sir Ludomir, in the face of his oath as a councillor, that set the magician working his arts on your father."

He felt face-muscles working. "Sir Ludomir, whom I had thought a high man! . . But had you thought me so base? It was true, then, when you said that you—you said—you do not—and I am still a clerk."

Argyra: "Will you make me confess? I have thought on it all alone there in Naaros. I cannot change you, nor would. Be a clerk if you will, but let me say that I love, and am like to lose you in fighting against these very mighty men tomorrow."

Facing him, she undid her own girdle and shamelessly slipped down her gown.

39. The Whiteriverdales: No End

AFTER THEY HAD SATISFIED THEMSELVES
and lay, lip to lip, he said: "Tell me, you who know
so much of people—why did I hold to him, the old
enchanter?"

"Oh, that is a light matter, my lord. Because he
gave you something new, day to day. Even at the
ultimate you did not let slay him because his answers
still were new. I am new to you now, but the day
will come when you will weary of me, Lord Airar."

"Not ever; never," said he, and buried her words
with kisses. "I have you; naught else lives. But then
I have banished the man that was best to me, my
other father, but for whom you and I had never
met."

She curled and purred against him. "Not so. It
is at every turn evil, his magic. All fails by it. Had

384

your enchanter never been, you were still of the revolt against Vulk and his Sthenophons, and you had
found your way to Os Erigu somehow, where I was.
There's a magic in love that is better than all your
spells."

But as to this, which he doubted, Airar lying happy
replied only by a sound of comfort and the next they
both knew the door was being beaten, with word
that the Vulking troops were stirring.

Outside, Airar Alvarson learned at the first taste
of air why he had before lacked interest in what
would pass, for now it was blood and death and
everything, with his sweetheart back among the buildings. He set a guard over her of Hestingerne,
who should see her safe if there were disaster. A
hasty cup and sup and he was riding down the lines,
full armed but with his helmet in hand—"for this
mightily encourages men at the edge of battle, to see
a leader"—and Nene of Busk bearing his cat-head
before. Not much time for this; Airar had barely
reached the rightmost point of the line when shouts
and a metal clang from across the valley leftward
told that the gentours were already falling on along
the opposite side, among the trees across the Naar.
He hoped Rogai would have skill enough to use
some of his archers against the mounted men, and
said as much to Alsander, whereat the latter:

"No one will ever do a thing as well as one's self,
which is why we hope in Heaven instead of making
our own paradise here with others' help; yet Master
Rogai will do as well as another. Ha!"

He pointed; beyond the rise of the road a low
film of dust arose, and it was the Vulking array, in
order, spread wide from side to side of the lawns
to drive straight through Torgsted, shield on shoulder, flutes piping, red triangles high. Airar wheeled
his mount, hoping to reach the opposite flank before
rash Rogai should let his arrows go too soon; but he
was late for that. He had barely reached the town
when Skogalang whistles began to blow, the archers
behind the Naar rose to their feet, and loosed, wholly
together. Down went Vulkings by the half-dozen and

score under that level storm from their unshielded wing, which nailed the helmet to the head, the armor to the arm, and the arm to the ribs, so that the leading ranks of terciaries were driven to their own left, toward the twist-spear men among the tangled trees.

There were good captains in those Vulking bands. When they saw how it fared with the first tercia, the second did not press straight on, but wheeled toward the source of the arrow-hail, opened ranks, and, shield in front, charged toward it. Many went down; the rest came right on, and when the broad stream checked them, bunched toward the light bridges Airar had let build for the convenience of his own, to force a passage. Now the remains of the first ranks, and no few of them, were into the barrier of trees under the cliff, hacking and pulling, disregarding the thrown spears, chopping off the heads of the thrusters, and as this action closed on both wings, the third Vulking line of battle trotted right on down to break through at the village. Airar heard an enemy trumpet sound signal; from his left wing a desperate messenger to say: "They break through at the second bridge, and we lack force." Half a tagoi of Carrhoene must be sent to make a rescue and fight, sword in hand.

No time to see what happened there, or even himself to go; for all along the line the battle closed dark and heavy, Vulkings in against the stockade, their short swords stabbing at the axemen of Mikalegon's band. Skogalang arrows still came from the wing, lightlier now, they were so close engaged in hand-strokes at the bridges; yet enough so the tide of Vulking battle veered more and more toward the other wing. Many died among the tangles there, but they died cutting through; presently there was a small band within the barrier, then a larger, and a whole line, against whom the spears of Mariola could not hold, and it was seen as often that by itself devotion wins few victories. The Vulking shout rose lustier; Airar saw one or two of his own people false

enough to drop weapons and go running faint-heart
from the fray.

"Where's Ioventinian?" he cried, and the Baron
being found (who was fortunately man of war enough
not to handle weapons himself till urgency required):
"My lord, we're lost unless we halt these on our
right. Disengage what you can, and come." He swung
in the saddle. "Bid Evimenes charge by the road as
soon as ever he can. It is not time, but we may no
longer stay."

Airar had his banner borne with Ioventinian and
the Scrobies. Many of them were weary and few had
faced the skillful Vulking weapon-handlers before
this day; but they were full armed in proof, the short
spears of the Vulkings tinkled and fell from their
breast-plates like rain from a turtle's back, and when
it came to handstrokes, their heavy swords at cut
beat down both shield and thrusting arm alike.
Airar of Trangsted's horse went down somehow, he
found himself afoot, but from the corner of his eye
as he fenced he caught always a glimpse of the same
green bush and knew the advance was stayed, the
decision of the battle turned elsewhere.

That elsewhere would be at the center, along the
road. The stockade was pierced in two-three places,
when the Carrhoenes laid lance in rest and charged.
They caught Briella at the loose, fighting in little
hand-to-hand groups, bore all before them, treading
some down, transfixing others with their spears. Airar
in his whirlwind of fighting heard Vulking battle-
cries turn to pain; the man he was engaged with
dropped sword and raised shield in surrender, and
he looked forth in time to see the iron mass of Carrhoene pour out across the lawns, taking all in the
rear to the uttermost limits of the Vulking bands. He
was astounded to see the sun already westering.

By night there were prisoners, feasting and joy
among the dead and wounded, while the wild Carrhoenes were wrangling with Hestinga and Skogalang
for the plunder of the Vulking camp, and austere
Scroby men-at-arms stood guard where Airar sat
with his lady. She touched a laming wound he had

not noted till the battle was done; he had kept her from seeing it when Earl Mikalegon brought in the head of Count Vulk the Fourteenth with a fine air of achievement; or from knowing it that Mariola-Rogai had lopped off Baron Vanette-Millepigue's fingers before he slew him, the Marshal being prisoner at the time.

So now it was victory and Dalarna free, Evides the Carrhoene released from durance, and glory everlasting, and one might think the tale ended there. Not so; it ends some time farther on, with the red leaves of autumn blowing and a messenger in the house of the city of Naaros, where the Master of Dalarna drinks sweet wine.

"Lord Airar, there is a great invasion of heathen ships from Dzik into the Gentebbi Isles, with magics that make our men afraid, and the heathen swear that you not having the peace of the Well, they are not in treaty with you."

Argyra: "My dear lord and love, will you not drink of the Well with me and them and put all this down?"

Said Airar: "We will summon the levy of Mariola and Vastmanstad. There is no peace but that interior in us"—and wondered why she wept.